A NOVEL

Noel Michaels

Library of Congress Control Number:		2007907976
ISBN:	Hardcover	978-1-4257-7565-0
	Softcover	978-1-4257-7561-2

To order additional copies of this book, contact:
Xlibris Corporation
1-888-795-4274
www.Xlibris.com
Orders@Xlibris.com
41585

ACKNOWLEDGEMENTS

Special thanks to the following people for their help along the way: Thanks to the Nassau (N.Y.) Regional Off-Track Betting Corporation for their continued support of my endeavors. Thanks to Chris Donofry for his excellent graphic design of the book cover. Thanks to the real Matt and Mad Dog, Matt Hegarty and Madeline Hopkins, for offering their valuable advice. Thank you Joe McGinniss for your inspiration. Thanks to Charles Hayward of the New York Racing Association for your support. And last but not least, thanks to all the degenerates in the racing industry who were responsible for all of the real life scandals, mishaps, and "misunderstandings" that are parodied in this book, you know who you are.

Most of all, thanks to my wife, Venice, for her love and devotion.

This book is dedicated to Velda and Norman Garfinkel.

PROLOGUE

May 2003. Plaza Hotel, New York. Room 2742. Wednesday afternoon. Amateur photographer Larry Lipwinkle. First-time model Lacey Bragg.

"Oh, Larry, come on. Hurry up and fix the video camera and come to bed. The sooner we do it, the sooner I can get paid and get out of here."

"Relax, baby. I splurged for the Plaza Hotel. What's the rush? Besides, I just want to make sure I snap enough photos before we get started with the video. You want to be famous, don't you? Now give me another one with you on your back and your legs up in the air. Smile for the camera!"

CLICK, CLICK, CLICK. "Yeah, just like that, baby!" *CLICK, CLICK, CLICK.*

"Are you sure this is how Carmen Electra got discovered? She's my personal idol and role model, you know."

"Are you kidding? Of course, this is how Carmen Electra was discovered! Christina Aguilera and Madonna, too! Now, forget about them. I need you to get on all fours and look into the camera." *CLICK, CLICK, CLICK.*

"Can't we just get to the sex already? My knees are starting to hurt. I'm cramping up."

"Just a few more photos. You see, the streaming video of the sex will be what people see when they go to your Web site. That's big. Huge! But we still need the photos because they're important, too. I'm sending them in to all the big monthlies like *Glamour, Allure, Hustler,* and *Mademoiselle.* Even *Playboy.* Me and Hef go way back."

"*Playboy*! Really? Carmen Electra did *Playboy,* you know."

"I know. Not just once, but four times! Carmen's gonna be small potatoes next to you, though. Now push your chest out farther. Don't lose focus." *CLICK, CLICK, CLICK.*

"I just know you're gonna make me famous, Larry. I trust you. But I still can't help but be a little distracted. I can't stop thinking about what my dad's gonna say about all this."

"Forget about your old man, baby. Who needs him? From now on, you can call me daddy."

"I wish it were that easy, but my dad's so strict. He's a police detective. He'd never understand any of this if he ever found out."

Larry clicked off a few more shots as he began fiddling with the video camera tripod. "Find out? I can't imagine how he'd ever find out. Can you?"

"Well, he *is* a detective after all. He has a way of knowing stuff. He works in the fraud division. I know it doesn't sound like much, but he's a real hard-ass. He'd kill me if he ever found out about this. And you? I don't even want to know what he'd do to you."

"Don't worry, Lacey honey. I'm not scared of your big bad dad. All I care about is making this video, taking these pictures, and then making as many people see them as possible. Just a few more, okay? Big smile, okay, kiddo? Yes! That's it!" *CLICK, CLICK, CLICK.*

"I'm sorry if I'm bringing you down, Larry. I just can't help feeling guilty, that's all."

"Bringing me down? You're not bringing me down. As a matter of fact, things were just beginning to look up," Larry remarked with a sly chuckle as he gazed downward toward his zipper. "Besides, I like a little danger. I have some experience with the cops. I once got arrested and did some time, ya know."

"You did some time? Really, baby? Now you're turning me on."

"Yeah, that cop who busted me, I hated him so much all I could think about was getting him back. I waited a whole year, but thankfully, it's been worth the wait."

"What'd you do to get back at the cops?"

"I didn't want to get back at the *cops*, I wanted to get back at the *cop*. I must admit, my plan was pretty demented. What I did was, I went out and found the cop's daughter and got involved with her. I made promises, lied to her. It looks like I'm really screwing her!"

"Get out! No way!"

"Yes way! Well, enough about me. The video camera is ready, and it looks like we finally have enough photos. So, baby, what was I just saying about Carmen Electra?"

"Ohhh yeah, baby. Tell me again how I'm gonna be famous. It gets me in the mood! Roll that tape and get over here. Yippie!"

"Oh I'm coming, baby. And don't worry, you're gonna be famous. By this time tomorrow, the whole world is gonna know who you are. You can count on it."

1

Austin Jackman watched intently as a field of Thoroughbreds sped around the oval racetrack in a blur of bright colors. Pounding hoofbeats echoed off the track as the horses made their final turn into the homestretch. The field thundered into the last furlong, racing down the straightaway in front of the grandstand. The track announcer's voice boomed excitedly over the PA system as he called the race: "It's Dizzy's Dream in front, now Garage Band by a nose. They're dueling down the stretch. It's going to be a close one . . . " The leaders approached the finish line. The boisterous bettors came to their feet, and a frenzied chorus of cheers and jeers followed the horses to the wire.

The horses crossed the finish, and the crowd sorted out into winners and losers. Austin again was one of the losers. He was not the world's worst horseplayer, but today, he certainly wasn't the luckiest. He would have to wait for yet another race or another day to finally make his fortune. Until then, he would have to go on trying to scratch out whatever living he could by betting on horses.

Austin's life at the track wasn't always about losing. He won occasionally, and when he did, the winning days were usually enough to wipe out the losing ones and provide enough money for him to keep coming back for more. Unfortunately, the wins came in spurts and could not be depended on for a steady source of income; so when he lost, Austin still had to scramble for ways to pay the rent.

Austin's game was picking winners, and he made a business out of it as best as he could and fared better than most. He bet enough money at the track every month to earn himself a seat in the elite clubhouse of the racetrack, the Turf Club, at the tracks on the New York circuit. Modern conveniences such as off-track betting, telephone betting, and computer betting made attending the racetrack in person unnecessary, but Austin went to the track anyway in order to be as close to the action as possible. The racetrack was his place of business, and being there gave Austin the advantages of seeing the horses in the flesh and being able to rub elbows with horse owners, trainers, track executives, and a handful of other serious bettors in the line at the Turf Club lunch buffet.

Austin was in his early thirties but had one of those ageless faces that could appear to be either older or younger, depending on the clothes he wore on his sleek six-foot frame. He had short dark brown hair that outlined strong features like a prominent nose, chin, and cheekbones, and he had the ability to flash a hustler's smile and use it as a weapon to get what he wanted—except, of course, for that one winning bet that would finally put him over the top.

Austin had looks and plenty of charm, but unfortunately for him, those things never came in handy for making him any money at the track. Thankfully, however, he was able to put them to good use for something nearly as important. Austin had landed a girlfriend—one that anyone in his right mind would have said was too good for him. Her name was Alana, and the fact he'd met her went a long way to explaining why Austin's heart was no longer into living the life of a full-time professional horse bettor.

Austin did his winter betting at Aqueduct Racetrack, in Queens, which was one of three tracks open seasonally on the New York circuit along with Belmont Park in Long Island, and Saratoga located upstate near Albany. The days at Aqueduct were short and gray and monotonous, and Austin felt he was finally ready to move on to the next phase of his life. It was the phase that was going to revolve around Alana instead of the racetrack. The only problem was Austin had no idea how he was going to get his life from Point A to Point B.

That, perhaps, was the reason Austin was so pleased to hear from an old college friend named Jimmy Holliday, who called him out of the blue and suggested the two lapsed friends renew their acquaintance with a day at the races.

Austin accepted the invitation and joined Jimmy at the track for a day of the three Bs—betting, beers, and buffet.

The old buddies sat at Austin's private Turf Club table, which was quietly tucked away in the corner of the oak-paneled room and surrounded by television monitors.

"You hit anything in that race?" Jimmy asked while finishing his lunch at the completion of the day's third race.

"Nope, nothing but losers. How about you?"

"The damn six horse split me out of the exacta," Jimmy said as he tore up his bets. He had bet the four and seven horses to finish in first and second place, but a last-minute surge by the six horse had made the order of finish four, six, seven. It had also made his bet worthless.

"Welcome to my life. All you can do is turn the page and go on to the next race. Who do you like in the fourth?" Austin asked as he flipped the pages of his *Daily Racing Form*, perusing the listings of how the entrants had performed in previous races.

"Austin, before we look at the next race, I've gotta tell you why I asked you here today."

"What? I thought *this* was the reason—you know, betting and catching up with each other."

"Yes, but it's more than that, too. There's something I want to talk to you about. It's a plan I was trying to work out. Some might call it a scam. I thought maybe you could help."

"We've been here two hours, and all of a sudden, you've had enough of the small talk and want to get down to business? All right, out with it. What's the real reason you asked me to the track today?"

"Austin, in college we were like brothers. I loved you, but let's face it, you always kinda thought I was a hustler, and we both knew it. Since college, neither of us have ever worked a legitimate day in our lives. Whether you want to admit it or not, that makes us the same, doesn't it? We have more in common than you'd like to admit."

"What exactly are we talking about here? You know I'm no criminal, Jimmy. I just like to place the occasional wager."

"Austin, you and I go way back. We might not see each other much anymore, but I trust you the way I trust only a handful of people in this world. I've got money problems, so I'm coming to you. Is that so wrong?"

"Jimmy, I hear what you're saying, but I think you've got the wrong guy. You're looking for the Austin of a few years ago. You're not looking for me. It's like I told you on the phone—I met a girl, and I'm trying to change my life around. I've grown up, and I'm a different person than the guy you used to know. I can't take this gambling lifestyle anymore. I want to settle down. My girlfriend wants to get out of town and start fresh somewhere else, and I decided that's what I really want, too."

"What's this other shit you were talking about on the phone? I think you mentioned Mexico." Jimmy was fishing for information. He polished off his fourth Heineken of the afternoon. "It sounded like you were serious about it."

"Jimmy, you may not believe it, but I really want to change my life. I have different priorities now. Everyone has dreams, and mine happens to involve moving to Mexico with my girlfriend."

"I have dreams too, but mine are mostly about money. You think I'm getting rich doing this penny-ante shit?" Jimmy admitted as he leaned forward across the table. "Sometimes I struggle, but do you think that stops me from dreaming? Like I said before, we're not as different as you think. I don't want to do my work anymore, and by the sounds of you and all your Mexico bullshit, it sounds like you're trying to get away from your work, too."

Jimmy was right. Austin figured he had maybe another year in him as a gambler before burnout and stress finally took their toll. The problem was his girlfriend. She had a commitment from Austin, but she wouldn't wait a year. She was ready to leave New York, and said she'd be going pretty soon with or without him.

"Look, Jimmy, this is the way it is—Alana, my girlfriend, she's like this big yoga and exercise instructor. She's been doing it forever. Anyway, we've taken a few vacations down to Cabo together—that's Cabo San Lucas, Mexico. Turns out we found this place down there we both love. It's a small town near the tip of the Baja Peninsula called Todos Santos. There's this empty place there we want to buy and turn into a yoga studio and hotel, right near the beach. We've already done all the research. The hotel part's my idea."

"Tacos Santos? Yoga? Listen to yourself, Austin. You live in Brooklyn. Do you even know what the hell you're talking about?"

"I live in Brooklyn, Jimmy, but I'm not *from* Brooklyn, and I don't belong there anymore. I do belong with Alana though. And if she's going, then I'm going, and I have to make it happen right now. For both of us."

"Yeah, but I don't understand what this Tacos Santos has to do with anything."

"Not Tacos Santos, *Todos* Santos. And the thing about it is that it's still undiscovered. A blank canvas. Just like me. It's close to all that Cabo tourism, but totally different. Todos Santos is still the real Mexico, but it won't be like that forever, so we want to get in on the ground floor. Right now, there are only two things the town is known for—surfers and the Hotel California. After we get down there, someday it'll be known for us, too."

"Wait a minute. Do you mean the Hotel California, like in the Eagles tune?"

"'On a dark desert highway, cool wind in my hair . . . ' Legend has it that the Hotel California the Eagles were singing about was a little place in Baja California, called Todos Santos. That dark desert highway is Mexican Federal Highway 1. You pick it up in Tijuana and drive down the Baja coast and just keep on going until there's more cactus than people. Highway 1 turns off onto Highway 19, and that takes you right into Todos Santos. Near all the people down in Cabo, but still far enough away. Pretty close to the end of the world, dude."

"Sounds like a nice dream," Jimmy had to admit. "But dreams like that cost money. Are you telling me you're so flush with cash that you can make that happen?"

Jimmy was right again. Austin didn't have the kind of scratch necessary to make the move he was talking about. Austin knew he needed money, but he hadn't had a real job in so long that he no longer had any idea what he would do in New York if he did rejoin the legitimate workforce. That's why he kept plugging away at the racetrack, waiting for the day his big score would come.

After ten years, Austin was still waiting. He did have some cash, but what he had, he used as his betting stake. He had no real savings or nest egg to show for his work.

"What exactly are we talking about here, Jimmy?"

"It's real simple. I need money, and lots of it. Quickly. No loans, either. I'm talking about making some serious money."

"Where do I come in? You have connections. You probably have your hands in a lot of pies. Why me?"

"The question is not, why you? The question is, do you want to make some real money? I'm talking about enough money to get you to Mexico and even a whole lot farther if you want. Listen, I'm not gonna lie—I'm in a little bit of a slump these days. I could stand to make a score. Hell, so could you if you'd only admit it. All I'm saying is just hear me out. Work with me. I have some ideas. I already made some calls. I want to get Larry and Tony in on this, too."

"You called Larry and Tony? What are you talking about? Get them in on what? The last I heard, Larry was in jail, and Tony had settled down."

"Well it seems you're a little behind on your information. Larry is out of jail, and Tony got married, but he's far from settled down."

"I still don't know what you want, Jimmy."

"What I'm thinking is me and you, and them, too. We can pull off something big. All of us together, just like in college. See, I know a lot about a lot of illegal shit. I also know that you know everything there is to know about betting and the racetrack, and I figured we could use that. Use it for a—uh—a creative business endeavor I thought of. Larry and Tony, they've also got things we can use."

"Jimmy, I've never been into anything illegal in my life. That's your bag."

"Relax, Austin old buddy, old pal. What I have cooked up is foolproof. It's gonna make us a ton of money. And nobody gets hurt. It's barely different from hitting a big payoff at the track. Just trust me, and I promise I'll get you and your little girlfriend down to Tacos Santos before you can say Pick 6."

2

Austin, Jimmy, Larry, and Tony were as close as brothers all through their college years at Central New Jersey State University. They weren't fraternity brothers or anything official like that, but they still all considered themselves brothers, nonetheless.

There are many great colleges and universities in the Northeast, but Central New Jersey State University has never been considered one of them. Within the hierarchy of universities in the state of New Jersey, CNJSU never quite attained the reputation or enrollment of other, better educational options like Rutgers University, Monmouth College, or even those much lower on the totem pole, like Trenton State. The fine students of the Garden State who were not accepted into any higher-profile institution, but still wanted to avoid community college, usually filtered down to CNJSU. From there, they eventually entered the world at large with rotted livers, one or more venereal diseases, and diplomas that look sharp hanging on the wall of an auto repair shop, beauty parlor, or prison cell.

CNJSU was not a place for promising young minds, nor was it a place for out-of-state students. Higher, less-economical out-of-state tuition costs made it impractical for residents of neighboring states such as Pennsylvania, New York, and Delaware to attend the New Jersey school. A cut-rate education for New Jersey residents at CNJSU was not as much of a bargain for others, who could easily attend an equivalent college in their own state, save a ton on tuition, and not sacrifice anything in terms of the quality (or lack thereof) of their education.

For four years in the early '90s, Central New Jersey State University was home to a combined total of four out-of-state students. They were Austin Jackman and Jimmy Holliday, and their best friends, Larry Lipwinkle and Tony Martini. As members of such a small minority, the tiny band of out-of-staters formed a strong bond and ended up living together all throughout their college years at CNJSU.

Central New Jersey State University was not a big school. As a result, CNJSU students had only three on-campus housing options to choose from. The remainder of the student body lived in an assortment of

14

fraternity and sorority houses. The three dormitories varied in size, and each was named for a famous New Jerseyite. The largest dorm, Aaron Burr Hall, was named in honor of the third vice president of the United States. Born in Newark, Burr had a long political career before becoming famous for being the man who mortally wounded Alexander Hamilton—of ten-dollar-bill fame—in a pistol duel. Burr Hall was home to mostly underclassmen majoring in everything from poli-sci to phys ed, but was much better known for high noise levels than high GPAs.

The second dormitory option was smaller and quieter and housed most of CNJSU's business, information technology, and computer programming majors. The building, formerly called William Henry Vanderbilt Hall, in honor of the famous financier from New Brunswick, had just been renamed General Norman Schwarzkopf Hall for the victorious Gulf War commanding officer who originally hailed from Trenton. After the name change, the rather drab-looking two-story structure was nicknamed "the Barracks."

The Barracks was known as the New Jersey epicenter of date rape and alcohol poisoning. It was a great place for opportunistic guys of all ages to go to pick up assorted girlfriends, acquaintances, and other freshman dates for typical evenings of pizza, movies, underage drinking, and the illegal administration of Rohypnol.

The third and final dormitory at CNJSU was the one reserved specifically for out-of-state students. The dorm was small and little known around campus and was basically nothing more than a typical-looking brick duplex with the university's seal nailed to the front door.

The building had originally been known as Aldrin Hall in honor of moon astronaut Edwin "Buzz" Aldrin, but recently had been renamed Piscopo Hall after comedian and *Saturday Night Live* alum Joe Piscopo. A native of Passaic, Piscopo donated a large sum of money to the university in return for having a building named in his honor. In doing so, he had assumed the name Piscopo Hall would be proudly hung over a glorious math or science center and not an eyesore that could be easily confused as low-income housing. Luckily, but not surprisingly, he never paid a visit to make sure.

Austin, Jimmy, Larry, and Tony lived together in Piscopo Hall for their entire college careers. Austin and Jimmy were occasionally approached by fraternities, but neither ever joined. They both figured they were much more compatible with each other and Larry and Tony than they ever would be with the frat boys from New Jersey. Instead of joining a fraternity, the gang of four decided to form their own brotherhood. The fraternity of sorts was nothing formal, but it did serve as an excuse for the guys to all call each other brothers like the guys in real fraternities did.

The most outgoing, and therefore least popular, resident of Piscopo Hall in the early '90s was named Tony Martini, a fast-talking overweight business major with dreams of becoming either a Wall Street tycoon or a porn star. Martini became well-known around campus for handing out business cards to coeds at parties that read Tony Martini, Professional Stunt Cock. Unfortunately for him, Martini never became a professional stunt cock. Instead, because of his weight problem and Italian heritage, Tony earned the nickname Tony Bologna around campus. With that humiliation hanging over him, Martini decided to concentrate on business pursuits. He started carrying a *Wall Street Journal* with him wherever he went. He never actually read it, but he liked it because he felt carrying the newspaper gave him that certain "serious businessman look" he was aiming for. This might have been true if it wasn't always the same badly outdated copy of the paper.

Martini was originally from Wilmington, Delaware, but chose CNJSU as his college because he believed it was important for him to attend a university close to downtown Manhattan. Tony was no geography major, but he knew New Jersey was closer to Wall Street than Wilmington.

The Piscopo Hall resident annually voted by his peers as the most likely to succeed (in a 3-0 vote) was Laurence "Larry" Lipwinkle, a computer enthusiast from nearby Bristol, in Bucks County, Pennsylvania. Every bit of knowledge crammed inside Larry's brain had something to do with either computers or *Star Trek*, and as a result, Larry had developed the interpersonal skills of a pencil.

While the rest of CNJSU's student body regarded Larry as a computer geek, the other members of Piscopo Hall knew him as the zit-faced kid at the end of the hall who was able to hack into the university's mainframe and turn their D grades into Bs without being detected. Larry never attended class and didn't even officially finish high school, but he figured he needed a college degree to be successful in the job market. He chose to attend CNJSU because it was the college whose database was the easiest for him to break into. He hacked into CNJSU's records, gave himself an SAT of 1390 and a high school GPA of 3.85, and was instantly accepted to CNJSU with no questions asked.

The third CNJSU out-of-state student of the early 1990s was Jimmy Holliday, an accounting major from Ronkonkoma, Long Island. Jimmy was a numbers man, and he probably could have made something great of himself if he had focused his skills on something besides his two favorite hobbies—betting on sports and betting on horses. He was the resident sports bookie at Ronkonkoma High, a trade he also plied at CNJSU each fall, during football season. Jimmy had plenty of local college choices open to him in New York but chose to attend college in New Jersey so he could avoid being constantly referred to as a Ronkonka-moron—the localized Long Island nickname for all people from Ronkonkoma.

The kid credited with turning the residents of Piscopo Hall into a brotherhood and keeping them together for their entire four years at CNJSU was Austin Jackman, a fresh-faced hospitality science, hotel/ restaurant management major from Reseda, California.

Austin came from a broken home. In the midst of a divorce and a midlife crisis, Austin's dad quit his job as a produce specialist at an organic foods market in California and moved to New Jersey to fulfill his dream of becoming a rock-band roadie for Bon Jovi. Austin's mom remained in Reseda where, after her divorce, she developed a successful start-up dominatrix business out of the family's small two-bedroom apartment. Both parents wanted Austin to stay with them, but the choice to remain with his dad was an easy one due to his mother's newfound profession. Austin moved away from Southern California and chose the first college in New Jersey that would take him.

The turnover rate at CNJSU's dorms was similar to most other American schools. Students typically arrived in the dorms as freshmen and spent between one and two years in the same rooms before joining a fraternity or sorority, moving off campus, or dropping out. It was rare for students to live in a dormitory for their entire college lives. Rare, that is, except for the residents of Piscopo Hall between September 1989 and June 1993, who all stayed put for the duration of their college careers.

The group of four students became constant companions. They named their fraternal order the Dude-Men Brotherhood—or the Dude-Men for short—because they usually referred to each other as either Dude or Man.

The typical Piscopo Hall conversation usually went something like this:

"Dude, whatcha doin'?"

"Nothin, man. What's up, dude?"

"Dude, check this out. I'm failing Spanish, man. Can you fuckin' believe it, dude?"

"No shit, dude. That sucks, man."

"Yeah, man. That's some seriously messed-up shit, dude."

As the years passed at CNJSU, Austin began to lose interest in hospitality management. He scheduled all his classes in the mornings so he could drive over to nearby Freehold Raceway each afternoon to bet all of his money on the harness races.

Freehold Raceway, known as "America's Fastest Half-Mile Oval" or "the Afternoon Delight," was the place that Austin directly blamed for his lengthy losing streaks and his constant state of empty-pocket syndrome. He claimed you had to be an insider to win money at a place like the track, and he vowed that someday he'd end up on the inside, instead of being one of those guys who was always on the outside looking in. As Austin's grades continued to drop, his love of the racetrack and determination to win began to rise, and soon, he was at the track more than he was at school.

By the time graduation came in May of 1993, Austin was ready to enter the outside world with the skills necessary to become a full-time horseplayer. After spending nearly every day together for four years, Austin, Jimmy, Larry, and Tony left CNJSU, and all went their separate ways. Their lives were all different, but they retained a tight bond as brothers that they all swore would never be broken.

3

Austin was going on twelve years at the track since graduation from CNJSU, and it was a tough way to make a living. The best part of every day was when he came home to Alana. The couple lived in a small one-bedroom apartment over a dry cleaner in Brooklyn. They moved in seven months ago on a six-month lease and were paying rent month to month until they figured out what they were doing with the rest of their lives.

Alana Moore was in her late twenties but street-smart enough to know what she was getting into with a guy like Austin. She was petite—not short or compact like a girl jockey—but petite in a feminine way, with a well-defined figure to show from her years spent in yoga studios. She had long straight dark brown hair that shone with brassy reddish highlights when she spent too much time in the sun. Her skin was fair, and she liked to wear makeup despite the fact she didn't need any. Perhaps her most distinctive feature was her light blue eyes, which were as clear and translucent as the waters of the Sea of Cortez on a sunny day.

Austin met Alana nearly two years earlier at a bar outside Yankee Stadium. Austin had plans to meet a friend there for opening day, but the game was canceled due to a freak early April snowstorm in the Bronx. Not wanting to waste the day, Austin and his friend still decided to meet and get some beers outside the stadium. It turned out Alana was doing the same with some of her friends. Austin and Alana instantly clicked. Austin thought it was love at first sight. Their friends went home. Austin and Alana not only spent the rest of the afternoon together, but they also went on to spend the next thirty-six hours straight with each other and had been together ever since.

Alana had been a Spanish major in school but never pursued a nine-to-five job. She liked yoga, and although she was never going to get rich as a fitness instructor, she did make a living by teaching several classes a week at various studios in Brooklyn and Manhattan. She developed a good and loyal following of students through the years. The Brooklyn gigs were convenient and close to home. The Manhattan yoga classes were the ones that paid her bills, which really only consisted of subway fares, a couple of credit cards, and the rent.

Soon after meeting Austin, Alana was clued in on his profession, or lack of one, but she didn't immediately scram like most girls, who would think twice before getting involved with such a man. Alana admired Austin's independent spirit and his "me against the world" attitude. It was the same attitude that she'd had growing up with her father in a single-parent household. Besides, Alana's late father had loved the racetrack all his life, and although he was never rich, she knew him to be a hardworking man and good dad.

Alana learned all about the racetrack and gambling from her father, and while she never shared her dad's interest in the ponies, she learned that taking a chance on a guy like Austin Jackman may not be the world's worst bet. She eventually got rid of her own apartment and moved in with Austin in the Brooklyn neighborhood known as Down Under the Manhattan Bridge Overpass, or DUMBO for short.

As for Austin, he was the lucky one in the relationship, and he knew it. He loved everything about Alana, especially the fact that she didn't mind that he made his meager living at the racetrack and couldn't even be depended on for a steady paycheck. She was independent, and she let him do what he wanted, trusting him enough to go along with his crazy ideas.

Alana had no love for the track, but the couple did share a lot of other things, including, foremost, a hatred of winters in the Northeast. They were the kind of winters that crept into spring, just like the day they met at Yankee Stadium. Neither had family ties in New York, and both Austin and Alana had goals of picking up and moving somewhere warm. Austin's mother still lived in Southern California, so that was always a possibility, but Los Angeles's traffic jams and high cost of living were not considered strong selling points by either one of them.

On a vacation to Cabo last year, Austin and Alana had both fallen in love with the small southern Baja California town of Todos Santos. The town was situated on the coast on the rough and largely deserted Pacific side of the southwestern Baja peninsula. The townsfolk were very bohemian—mainly Mexican artisans, American expats, and wayward surfers searching the area's rough waters for the next big wave. Unlike the developed tourist areas down in Los Cabos, oceanfront property in Todos Santos was still readily available and affordable, but it was starting to go fast and wasn't going to be out there forever.

Austin and Alana had few ties to New York and always planned to pick up one day and drive down to Mexico, where they could build a business and start a new and unconventional life together south of the border. On their most recent trip to Todos Santos, the couple stumbled upon a property consisting of four quaint cottages set around a grass courtyard, just off the beach. The property had been vacant for a few years and, therefore, was bargain-priced and ripe for the picking for someone with the money who came up with the right idea. The lightbulb went on for Austin and Alana simultaneously. They could live in the biggest of the four cottages and rent out the other three to surfers and the occasional tourist. Alana would hold sunrise and sunset yoga classes for locals and visitors in the ocean-view courtyard, and Austin could manage the rentals. It wasn't too far of a stretch to think the idea could work in a growing town full of artisans and surfers, with no yoga instructors currently in residence.

Home from another day at the track, Austin grabbed a beer from the fridge and sat down with Alana at the kitchen table to tell her about his day. "I met my friend Jimmy at the track today. He's the guy I told you about from college. We had an interesting conversation. I told him about our plans for Mexico, and he said he had a business proposal for me."

"Business proposal? Didn't you just get done telling me the other day that he's a crook?"

"Not a crook—well, maybe just a small-time crook."

"Right, a small-time crook. So what gives, Austin?"

"I don't know. I feel bad for him, I guess. I think maybe I could help him out. We used to be great friends."

"Austin, I know you're trying to do the right thing, and I know your heart's in the right place, but I don't know if I like the sound of this. From what you've told me so far, I'm pretty sure when a guy like that mentions a business proposal, what he's talking about isn't going to be legal."

"Yeah, but Jimmy's talking about getting our gang back together from college. That's really the thing I'm interested in. It's not like I'm gonna give him money or anything like that. I just want to listen to what he has to say and see if there's anything in it for us. We could use some extra money, after all. What I'm saying is that if my friends and I can pull something off together—something big—then I might want to be a part of it. I just want to give it a chance."

"I trust you, Austin. I just don't know if I can trust this Jimmy guy. By the sound of him, I doubt he knows what he's doing, and I'm not even talking about your other friends. I *know* they're incompetent idiots."

"They might be idiots separately—we all might be—but together, the whole is bigger than our parts. It was always like that in college. And I don't know, maybe Jimmy has a point. Maybe it can be like that again. I wouldn't consider this otherwise. I know these guys inside and out. I spent every day for four years with them. I think we can do anything we set our minds to."

4

Larry Lipwinkle stood behind a yellow line in an orange jumpsuit. A corrections officer situated behind a large cage near the front gates of the Yaphank Minimum Security Prison in Long Island read down a list of items being returned to Larry's possession.

"One pair of men's trousers, size 28 waist, 36 inseam. Plaid. Check.

"One men's short-sleeved, button-down shirt, white, size 14 collar. Check.

"One white undershirt with silk-screened lettering. Says Captain James T. Kirk for President. Stained. Check.

"One shirt pocket protector—plastic—containing three ballpoint pens and a solar calculator. Check.

"One baseball cap. Chicago Cubs. Check."

"Can't we just get on with this already?" asked Larry, who was anxious to get outside and meet his ride.

The officer was reaching the end of his checklist. "One canvas wallet, Velcro, contains driver's license—expired; a library card—expired; two Trojan brand prophylactics—no doubt expired; a lifetime warranty card on an Apple Macintosh home computer system; and forty-three dollars in cash."

"Step forward and sign here for your belongings, Mr. Lipwinkle. You've officially paid your debt to the state of New York."

Larry signed for his stuff and vowed that his first day out of jail would be the first day of the rest of his life as he collected his personal effects and was led out the front gate of the prison with an officer walking on each side of him.

"Good luck, Mr. Lipwinkle," said the officer on the right as he unlocked the final gate, officially making Larry a free man for the first time in ninety days.

Larry walked out into the parking lot where he immediately noticed the hot car du jour—a brand-new Audi TT roadster convertible, with fifteen-inch alloy wheels, rear spoiler, premium sound, and vanity plates reading Big Tent.

Tony Martini was at the wheel of the Audi, which was double-parked in a blue handicapped zone. He was wearing dark sunglasses, and his head was bobbing to Judas Priest on his stereo. "I'm your turbo lover . . ."

Tony laid on the horn. "Yo! Over here, scumbag."

Larry rushed into the Audi's passenger seat. He was happy to see a friendly face after his second trip to the slammer in the span of four years. He and Tony had been through a lot as friends, but things weren't always as bad as they had been lately, and Larry knew that no one identified with that better than Tony.

Tony Martini and Larry Lipwinkle both had their share of ups and downs after college, but at least Tony never did any hard time.

Tony graduated CNJSU with a degree in business administration and took advantage of a great early '90s job market to land a low-level Wall Street job on the floor of the New York Stock Exchange. Tony was put in charge of sitting at a bank of phones and relaying trade information from the floor to and from his firm's home office. He wasn't actually trading and certainly was not in charge of anyone's stock portfolio, but he managed to carve out a rather nice living working the phones. His salary and bonus were easily enough to buy him a modest townhouse in Staten Island, complete with two bedrooms, one bath, and a postage-stamp-sized front yard.

Tony eventually caught the eye of a few corporate higher-ups, who noticed he never went anywhere without a crumpled copy of the *Wall Street Journal* under his arm. He became known as the enterprising young go-getter on the floor of the exchange who never missed a day of work and who could work the phones like lightning. The attention Tony received from the suits eventually earned him a raise, and then another, and another until Tony had so much disposable income that he didn't know what to do with it all.

With all that cash around and no real hobbies to turn to, Tony discovered the things he most liked to spend his money on were alcohol, drugs, gambling, and strippers.

Tony and the other guys at the Exchange were making a lot of money and were all single, young, and reckless. The money Tony made all started going into a costly cocaine habit. Whatever was left over, he'd blow on lap dances at the high-class downtown nudie bar called Beavers Showclub. Tony's money was disappearing faster than dancers' bikini thongs in Beavers's one-hundred-dollar-minimum Platinum Lounge, and he knew it was time to make a change in his life.

Tony quit snorting cocaine and focused his energy squarely on gambling and strippers.

At the strip clubs, Tony fashioned himself as a high-rolling powerful big spender. Someone along the lines of Al Pacino's Tony Montana from the movie *Scarface*.

Instead of Tony Montana, however, and much to his dismay, Tony became known around the gentlemen's clubs in lower Manhattan as "Tony the Tent," a nickname he got in reference to the shape of his pants every time he exited Beavers. The nickname wasn't as bad as his college moniker, Tony Bologna, but it was close. Instead of a big shot, Tony was a laughingstock, and unfortunately, it was the laughing-at-you kind of laughing, not the laughing-with-you kind.

Larry also started off well, following college. After hacking himself straight As and graduating magna cum laude from CNJSU with a degree in information technology, Larry was presented with numerous opportunities to ply his trade at various high-paying corporations. Instead, Larry opted for the offer he coveted most—a job at Star Trek Enterprises, the worldwide headquarters for all things *Star Trek*, including product licensing, book publishing, Star Trek convention and fan club management, and the home of the burgeoning Star Trek Web site.

After a couple of years on the job, Larry had completely revolutionized Star Trek Enterprises's computerized record keeping, data collection, and information recall capabilities. For instance, before Lipwinkle's tenure at Star Trek Enterprises, if a Trekie had wanted to know the date and site of the convention where Leonard Nimoy gave his infamous "Reasons to Suspect Spock Was Gay" keynote speech, you would have had to elbow past ten other geeks wearing pointy ears on the way through the official Star Trek Home Office Library and Archive where you could cross-reference piles of dusty records. Thanks to Lipwinkle, however, the information was now easily searchable and instantly retrievable via Star Trek Enterprises's Web site.

When the Internet started becoming a major medium for information and commerce in the mid-1990s, Lipwinkle was one step ahead of the learning curve. He designed Star Trek Enterprises's commerce Web site and always kept them on the cutting edge technologically. For this, Star Trek Enterprises paid a handsome premium to retain Lipwinkle and made him a rising star within the organization in the process.

On the way to Tony's house to spend the night and get back on his feet, Larry thought about how the good old days seemed like so long ago, ever since things started to unravel for both Tony and him in the late '90s. Larry contemplated his uncertain future and thought about what went wrong at Star Trek Enterprises as Tony revved his Audi's engine and burned rubber out of the prison parking lot toward the westbound lanes of the Long Island Expressway.

The trouble all started when Tony finally settled down and when Larry finally got laid during a vacation to Las Vegas to see the Star Trek: The Experience at the Las Vegas Hilton. On that trip, Larry met a young Lieutenant Uhura look-alike named Bianca Smalls while visiting the Experience's signature Klingon Encounter exhibit. Later, at the second-floor lounge of the Warp Speed Bar and Grill, Larry fell in love with Bianca over a romantic lunch consisting of two orders of cheese fries, a plate of buffalo wings, and two large drafts.

That night, in his *Star Trek*-themed hotel suite, at the age of twenty-seven, Larry Lipwinkle boldly went where he had never gone before. He fulfilled his longtime dream of having Uhura work his Com, twice, in a bedroom decked out to look like the bridge of the starship *Enterprise*.

Larry and Bianca spent every night together for the rest of the week. Larry would role-play as James T. Kirk, the sex-starved star captain with a fetish for African American women in positions of power. He couldn't get enough of Bianca's skimpy red uniform, and even got her to put her hair in an Uhura-like beehive for him on one particularly hot night back at her room.

At the end of the week, Larry was head over heels in love while Bianca was on her way back to her real life, her husband, and her small child in Philadelphia.

Subsequent phone calls from Larry to Bianca went unanswered, except one time when Bianca accidentally answered her phone without first checking the caller ID. She told Larry that she had a great time in Las Vegas, but "What happens in Vegas, stays in Vegas. Sorry, baby."

Larry became obsessed, and that obsession made it harder and harder for him to concentrate at work. He was slowly turning from an ordinary, run-of-the-mill stalker into a new brand of superstalker. He called Bianca's cell phone at all hours of the day and night, searched her personal information on the Internet, and drove to Philadelphia unannounced so he could secretly follow her around town as she went to the market, got her hair done, and pumped gas. His usual routine also involved seeking out Bianca at Star Trek conventions, begging her to leave her husband, and then being rejected in a horribly emasculating, neck-shaking, finger-waving public tirade.

Larry continually got into the habit of making ugly scenes at Star Trek conventions all over the East Coast. This eventually led to what became known in Star Trek circles as the "Hartford Incident," which involved Larry coming on a little too strong to sixty-five-year-old actress Nichelle Nichols, who played Lieutenant Uhura on the original *Star Trek* television series at a convention. The "Hartford Incident" led to Larry's first stint behind bars. After Larry finally needed to be restrained by Uhura's security staff, they handcuffed the hapless stalker, escorted him from the building, and then took him straight to jail. The judge in that case ordered Larry to stay five hundred feet away from Nichols at all times for the stalking charge and then tacked on an additional thirty days in jail for disturbing the peace.

Counting that first conviction and the jail time he just completed for credit card fraud, Larry now had two strikes against him. He had gotten caught after creating and maxing out phony credit cards in roughly a hundred different aliases. Larry wished he hadn't had to resort to the credit card scam in the first place, but the truth was he had no choice after he lost his job at Star Trek Enterprises when the shit there finally hit the fan on January 2, 2000.

Larry had been put in change of Star Trek Enterprises Y2K preparation program during 1999 but was so preoccupied with the loss of Bianca that he never got around to working on the project. Thousands of lines of information in Star Trek Enterprises's database that Larry Lipwinkle was supposed to change from 99 to 1999 throughout the course of the year were never changed.

On January 1, 2000, every computerized system in Star Trek Enterprises's mainframe clicked to 00 and crashed into flames faster than a speeding Federation starship piloted by a piss-drunk Mr. Sulu.

On January 2, 2000, when his boss returned to work to find Star Trek Enterprises in shambles, Larry Lipwinkle was fired from the only job he had ever wanted, or indeed had.

Tony looked across his car's front seat over at Larry as he pushed eighty in the carpool lane of the Long Island Expressway. *What am I going to do with this guy?* Tony mused before turning his thoughts to his own problems. *He's my friend. Maybe I could help him if I wasn't married. Maybe he could stay with me long enough to get back on his feet. Too bad Julia won't let him stay. What the hell was I thinking when I got married to her? I'd be a lot happier if I was one of the guys again.*

Tony had spent years trying to shed his Tony the Tent image. That was when he finally met a girl he could take home to his mom while riding home late one evening on the Staten Island Ferry. Julia Esposito had just started riding the ferry after getting her first hairstyling job in New York City. She instantly fell victim to Tony's many charms, which were indistinguishable from the many zeros at the end of his bank account.

Julia considered Tony quite a catch. He had lots of money and a nice little home, and he seemed perfectly ready to settle down in a life of domestic bliss.

Tony loved Julia because he thought she had great big cans, a nice curvy backside, and always wore the latest trendy hairstyles—a rarity among the girls in Staten Island.

The couple soon became engaged, despite the fact that Tony still loved his strippers and had no intention of giving up his wild after-work life. He was still Tony the Tent, and probably always would be.

With full knowledge that his decision to settle down may have been a bit hasty, Tony officially left the single life behind when he made Julia the new Mrs. Tony Martini on June 3, 2000, at a lavish ceremony in front of two hundred family and friends. Standing up for Tony at the wedding were four husky Italian Wall Street brokers from Staten Island and one pale, skinny, recently unemployed computer specialist turned superstalker, who had begun to behave erratically from the symptoms of manic depression.

Jail time did not change Larry. He was still an obsessive-compulsive. However, instead of being obsessed with Lieutenant Uhura, his new obsession was getting revenge on the cop responsible for busting him for the credit card fraud. Detective Bragg. If he couldn't get to him, then he'd get to his family. He'd get that guy back if it was the last thing he ever did. Larry was comforted by those thoughts as he looked out Tony's window and watched Long Island whiz by all around him.

The convertible top was down, and the wind whipped through the Audi. Larry felt his freedom. Tony wanted to *feel* free too—that's why he liked driving with the top down and the sun shining on his burgeoning bald spot. In reality, he couldn't feel free. He was a gambler and a swinger tied down in a marriage he no longer wanted.

Tony sped Larry toward his home in Staten Island. Larry would spend one night, then Tony would return to his married life, and Larry would be out on his own. Just him, his computer, and his revenge.

5

Jimmy Holliday set up a reunion of the Dude-Men at an Irish pub in downtown Manhattan. The gang walked past a long brass-and-wood bar to a booth with red cushions at the back of a dimly lit pub dining room. Green fixtures hung from the ceiling, and there were only a couple of other tables occupied inside the narrow room.

The Dude-Men ordered a round of Guinness and sat at a quiet back table on a midweek afternoon. The drinks flowed freely as the group caught up with each other, all together in the same place for one of the first times in over a decade.

Austin knocked back a shot of Jose Cuervo while telling Tony and Larry about Alana and his plans to move to Mexico.

Tony flashed his wedding ring, which he called "the ball and chain," and advised strongly against Austin getting tied down with a woman—unless, of course, she was a stripper.

Larry hadn't seen Austin and Jimmy for a while. He informed them of his criminal record but said it had been a couple of years since Tony had come to pick him up from his last stint at Yaphank. Larry said work had been difficult to come by since losing his job at Star Trek Enterprises. His convictions for disturbing the peace and then credit card fraud were generally a turnoff to potential employers. As a result, Larry continued to be unable to hold down a legitimate job.

"So how was the slammer, man?" Jimmy asked. "Was it all gangs and gays like everyone says?"

"No, dude. I didn't mind jail so much. It was one of those country club places," Larry said. "It gave me some time to get my head back on straight. Still, I had a lot of time on my hands. I needed a project, so I spent some time using the department of corrections computer system for access into some law enforcement databases in order to pursue my main goal at the time. I was able to track down the public records of the smart-ass cop who busted me. It was some prick detective named John Bragg. He abused me real bad when he busted me."

"My god, Larry, that's terrible," Austin said.

Larry's face brightened. "Yeah, but it's all good. I had plenty of time to come up with a revenge plan, and boy did I nail that guy good." Larry drained his beer. "He's probably still looking for me to this day, hoping to kick my ass. But I'm telling you guys, it was worth it! Ha!"

"What did you do?" asked Austin incredulously.

Larry grinned with pride as his glasses began to fog up. "I tricked his eighteen-year-old daughter into sleeping with me, then I posted it on the Internet!"

Jimmy was taking a drink of Guinness from his pint glass as Larry's comment reached his ears. The swig of beer in his mouth sprayed mistily into the air. "You did what?"

"You heard me," Larry said. "When I got out of jail, I used the information I had on Bragg and hacked his records on the Internet. The reports I got gave me the cop's address, phone number, and a bunch of other personal information such as the names and ages of his siblings and children. The first thing I noticed was the guy had an eighteen-year-old daughter. I then was able to track her down. The first thing I noticed was that his daughter was a hot little biscuit. So you know, I kinda did what any guy would have done. I followed her around for a couple days. I spied on her at the gym, the coffee shop. I listened to her conversations and was able to surmise two things. One, she was a ditz, and two, she was obsessed with being discovered and becoming the next Carmen Electra.

"That's where I stepped in and decided for once to use my computer skills to get laid. I told this girl I was a Hollywood agent and could make her famous. The whole thing worked—she slept with me. I videotaped it and posted the whole thing on the Internet. She signed a waiver. I told her she'd be the next Carmen Electra. It was a mutually beneficial relationship—especially for me. Anyway, in the end, I took a bunch of naked pictures of her, signed them, and sent them to her daddy the cop. Oh, I wish I could have seen his face. It must have been priceless! Ha!"

"You're one sick fuck," Austin said. He was not sure if he meant it as a compliment.

Jimmy finally raised his voice and refocused the group on the task at hand. "As much as we'd all love to hear more about what a pervert Larry is, we do still have some business to discuss. Let's get started, shall we?"

Jimmy was of average height and build, but he had a commanding presence, nonetheless. He was tan and had dark wavy hair that had started to turn salt-and-pepper at the temples, making him good-looking in a certain Benicio Del Toro, sexy-ugly way. He usually wore jeans and favored untucked button-down shirts with the sleeves rolled up to the elbows.

After graduating CNJSU with a degree in accounting, Jimmy the math whiz passed his CPA exam at about the exact same time he realized he had no desire to spend the rest of his life studying spreadsheets. Through some old New York connections, Jimmy knew a group of shady dealers who ran a network of betting shops out of the backs of certain clubs and bars in Queens and Long Island. With his knowledge of sports and an uncanny ability to figure the house percentage of any bet, he was a natural at the bookmaking business and soon rose through the ranks in the area's illegal underworld of sports betting.

Jimmy made a comfortable living for a few years until the world of backroom bookmaking began getting smaller and smaller in the late '90s, thanks to the advent of offshore Internet sports books. The offshore books offered everything Jimmy's people offered but were more glitzy, more convenient, and—most importantly—more legal than Jimmy's operation. Jimmy's business consisted of aging non-computer-literate gamblers, who were slowly dying off and not being replaced.

Jimmy needed a new stream of income, and fast.

Jimmy was too busy handicapping sports and running the numbers to have time on the side for much of a personal life. He worked long hours and dealt primarily with men, which made meeting women and maintaining relationships difficult. The people he knew were criminals and other assorted untrustworthy low-life sleazebags. After sorting out the deadbeats and losers, Jimmy was left with a few solid connections who owed him a long list of favors for things he'd done down through the years. Before he started to call in his markers, however, Jimmy decided to take one last chance at organizing a syndicate on his own. He only trusted a few people, and most of them were sitting right there with him at the Irish pub.

Jimmy sat back in his chair and lifted his Guinness to his lips repeatedly until he had the group's full attention. "Okay, everyone, here's the deal: I've talked to each of you separately, and now I want to pull this all together. Everyone here has something unique to offer, and the way I see it, all of us can band together and make a lot of money. I don't know why I didn't come up with this earlier."

Jimmy caught Tony watching the rear end of a waitress who was walking past the booth on her way to another table.

"Hey, hey, hey! Yo, Tent Boy, I'm talking now! Would ya please pay attention?"

"Sorry, Jimmy, I got a little distracted there. Don't worry, I'm still listening," Tony apologized.

"Good," Jimmy said. "Because we're going need you, buddy. We need you to be our money man, the guy who can put up the capital we're going to need to get us started."

Jimmy looked over to Austin. "What I have in mind is a betting scam at the track, and that's where Austin comes in. He knows everything that goes on there, and he knows the ins and outs of what we'll be dealing with and what we'll be up against."

Austin nodded in acknowledgement.

"And then there's Larry, the pervert and convicted felon over there who also happens to be the key to the whole operation. His virtuoso computer hacking skills are the linchpin that's going to pull this off for us."

Larry blushed, then saluted his friends across the table. "At your service."

"Here's the deal," Jimmy continued. "I asked Austin to tell me about the tote company that operates the odds for the New York tracks. You see, when you make a bet on a horse race, the bet goes through the tote system, which then calculates the horses' odds and figures the payoffs of the winners."

"It's all done through a computer system," Austin interjected.

"And we all know there's not a computer system that's been invented that Larry over here can't hack into and fuck with," Jimmy said, with his hand on Larry's shoulder.

"Once we're into the system, we can manipulate just about anything," Austin said. "I spoke to Larry about it, and he says we can print out our own counterfeit betting tickets or, on a bigger scale, even go into the system and punch in actual bets on horses after the races have already been run. That's something like what I'm envisioning us starting with."

"I know I can get into any computer system. That's the easy part," Larry said. "The main thing will be whether or not we're detected. If we're not detected the first time, then we can go back in and rip them off once more before they even know what hit them."

"That's why we've gotta start small," cautioned Jimmy. "I got an idea to get in there once and get some bar codes and serial numbers off some old winning tickets that are still in the computer system. Tony's money can buy us some state-of-the-art code-breaking software, then Larry can run the bar codes through the software, add the serial numbers, and voila! We're cashing in on our own winning tickets on bets we didn't even make. It's like printing money!"

"Yeah, and if that works out, then we go for the kill on some much bigger game on our second go-round. I'm talking about the Pick 6. The

Pick 6 on a day when the track is offering a big jackpot!" The excitement in Austin's voice was apparent.

"Oh, yes, the Pick 6. The Holy Grail, dude," Jimmy said.

Tony, who loved to gamble but did not know a lot about horseracing, asked, "Tell me more about this Pick 6. What is it?"

"The Pick 6 is the mother of all horseracing bets," Austin said. "It's the hardest bet to hit, but it also pays the highest payoffs. We're talking hundreds of thousands of dollars sometimes. Sometimes picking just one winner is tough enough, but what you have to do in the Pick 6 is successfully pick the winners of six straight races on one day, one racing card. The wager must be made in advance on a single bet, but you're allowed to include multiple horses per race on the same ticket as long as you can afford it. The unique feature about the Pick 6 is that it's so hard to win, it can go days before somebody finally hits the jackpot. When nobody wins, most of the money that was bet that day carries over to the next day and then to the next day and so on until somebody wins. That's called a carryover because the money carries over to the next day. If it goes three or four days with no winners, the jackpot can reach a million dollars or more. That's why all the big horse bettors start pouring money into the Pick 6 when there's a big jackpot. I'm thinking that's when we should make our move, on a day when there's a big jackpot."

"Right, but first things first. We still need to know we can hack into the tote company's computer and come out with reliable results," Jimmy said. "That's why we need a test run, and printing counterfeit betting tickets with information we get from the tote company's computer system is the best test run I can think of."

"If I can get into their computer system undetected this one time, I know we'll be able to go back again safely at least once more," Larry said.

"And when we go back in later, that's when we target the Pick 6 payday. It'll be something we can do once and make enough money so we don't have to risk doing it again," Jimmy said. "For me, it's all about risk and reward. After we've been into their computer system twice, there's too much risk. Before then, though, it's nothing but reward, dudes."

"The thing that's great about this entire plan is that this tote company's whole system has been in place since the dark ages. It's antiquated," Austin said. "The company is called National Tote, and from what I hear, they're just coasting along on the status quo. They maintain a computer system that millions of dollars of bets flow through every day, yet security isn't too high up on their priority list, from what I've heard. Their manpower is going into just keeping their whole ancient system up and running."

"Doesn't matter," Larry said. "No matter how much they update their security, they still can't stay ahead of us hackers even if they tried. This sounds like a piece of cake."

"So then what are we still sitting around here for?" Jimmy demanded. "Let's get on top of this ASAP."

Tony shifted in his chair. "Hey, Jimmy, I definitely like what I hear, but I don't really understand what's in this for me. I mean, I've got lots of money *already*. I see that you need Larry for the computer stuff, and it's obvious that Austin can help you with his racetrack knowledge. But where do I come in? You just need me for my money, right?"

But Jimmy was a pro. He had come prepared to handle any doubts Tony might have. He took it in stride and reassured him by playing on his weaknesses. He knew Tony was miserable at home and was always the type of guy who was desperate to be included in anything that had to do with his buddies, just for the sake of not being left out.

"Tony man, we don't need your money, we need *you*. If we didn't get the dough from you, we'd get it someplace else. The main thing is you're one of us. You're one of the guys. We want you in on this because we like you, man. Besides, we all know how that wife of yours drives you crazy. This is your chance to get out of the house every so often. As far as the money goes, we know you've got money, but that doesn't mean you'd want to pass up an investment opportunity like this, does it?"

"I guess you're right, Jimmy. I really do thank you all for including me on this," Tony said, cracking a small smile on the outside but absolutely glowing on the inside from Jimmy's words. "You'll get all the start-up cash you need. You guys can count on me. But listen—for now, what's the rush? We all have the afternoon off, I'm here with my old buddies, and the Beavers Showclub is just down the street. Whataya say? Anyone have time for a pit stop?"

6

Four men walked through the Aqueduct Racetrack grandstand turnstiles early on a Saturday afternoon. Had it been a Quentin Tarantino movie, the quartet would have been walking in slow motion, and each stride would have been punctuated by jazzy background musical accompaniment. Since it was real life, however, the men walked into the racetrack at normal speed, and the near-empty grandstand was so quiet that you could almost hear a pin drop.

Regardless of the number of people on hand, the four men tried desperately to blend into the sparse crowd. They wanted to become one with the masses. Just four faces in the crowd. Four needles in a haystack. They had counterfeit tickets to cash, and they didn't want to be noticed or make themselves stand out in any way, shape, or form.

Saturday was usually the busiest day at the racetrack, but that wasn't saying much since only a few thousand fans showed up in person at Aqueduct even when it was busy. That was because the majority of bettors made their bets at OTBs, through phone or computer accounts, or from other racetracks around the country. The patrons who were at Aqueduct rattled around inside the cavernous structure that was built for bigger crowds from an earlier age.

Racetracks like Aqueduct are very utilitarian places. Unlike certain grandiose tracks that draw eclectic crowds, like historic Saratoga Race Course, Churchill Downs, or beautiful Del Mar where the turf meets the surf north of San Diego, Aqueduct is essentially designed to be a betting factory. The track provides patrons a betting product and a place to make their wagers. Then they do little more than open the doors and let the fun begin. There are few amenities offered to patrons other than those designed to make one's wagers easier and more convenient to place.

The insides of most such racetracks contain all the atmosphere of an airplane hangar, and that is certainly true of Aqueduct. As Austin, Jimmy, Larry, and Tony passed through the building, they mainly saw a lot of television monitors and rows and rows of people standing in lines at windows that looked like teller's windows at a bank. Some were manned by actual people while others were simply occupied by SAMs, or Self-Automated Machines, which are the racetrack's version of ATMs.

The idea was for Austin, Jimmy, Larry, and Tony to blend into the Aqueduct crowd as soon as possible and then split up in order to cash counterfeit bets at SAM machines in different parts of the racetrack. Before they could split up, however, they wanted to get into a position where all four men would be equidistant from their target SAM. In order to get into position, the Dude-Men had to pass by a colorful assortment of racetrack characters as they weaved their way through the Aqueduct grandstand.

Horseracing is often called the Sport of Kings, but that term refers to the brand of horseracing practiced at showplaces like Saratoga, Del Mar, Churchill Downs, and a few others, like Arlington Park in Chicago, Gulfstream Park in Florida, stately Belmont Park in Long Island, and Santa Anita in the suburbs of Los Angeles. Outside of those places, and particularly at winter racetracks like Aqueduct, however, grandstands are primarily blue-collar havens filled with retirees and assorted lost souls, hoping that today is finally their lucky day. The so-called kings in the sport of horseracing—blue-blooded families like the Whitneys and Vanderbilts—were unlikely to show up at Aqueduct in the middle of winter.

Nevertheless, there is still a hierarchical class system at work at tracks like Aqueduct that usually depends on how high up you are in the building, or how close you are to the finish line. Higher up and closer to the finish line equals more classy. Lower down and farther away from the finish line equals no classy. Bigger bettors and simulcast players tend to gravitate to the high floors of the track or the slightly more expensive clubhouse where they can sit in dining rooms close to the finish line and remain in a relatively clean environment.

The lowest level of the racetrack hierarchy is always the ground floor of the grandstand. This level is regarded as a home to the two-dollar bettors, novice newcomers, and assorted racetrack lifers. This area of any urban racetrack usually houses enough weirdos to make the insane people look normal while at the same time making the normal people look like weirdos. Actually, at the track, even more so than other places, the line between normal and weirdo is extremely thin or maybe not even existent. In any case, the ground floor is a place where people lose their shirt, trash often does not find its way into the proper receptacles, and the prevailing smell is not always that of roses, Black-eyed Susans, and white carnations.

The four Dude-Men made their way up the escalator to the second floor of the grandstand where they instantly noticed a difference in the demographic. The second floor was quieter and offered a lot more seating than the first floor. The additional seating makes it a draw for the racetrack's core group of older patrons. In addition to some lunatics who'd straggled upstairs from the ground floor, the gang noticed a lot of retirement-age men milling around on floor number 2. The majority of the men seemed to be there as much to socialize with their peers as they were to bet. Socializing in their case usually meant arguing, but it was still socializing, nonetheless.

Besides old men, the next-most-represented group in the second floor of the grandstand was the track's large Jamaican contingent. Like the old men, they were also arguing with each other, but nobody around them even seemed to notice. This was either because everyone was already used to hearing the Jamaicans argue, or because nobody else could understand the Jamaicans' form of English, which was clear only to them. Besides the arguing, the most memorable thing about the Jamaicans at Aqueduct was they reeked of ganja. This was good because if you wanted to sit by them and could put up with their bickering long enough, you would usually be rewarded with a bitchin' contact high. With munchies a constant concern for the Jamaicans, it was no surprise they usually hung around close to the track's makeshift food court, which consisted of a Sbarro pizza franchise, a Nathan's hot dogs, and a generic coffee/soda/beer stand. The Dude-Men passed by the Jamaicans and arrived at their mission's preplanned staging point at the back of the food court.

"Where are all the women at in this place?" Tony said, feeling like a fish out of water.

"It's the Aqueduct winter-spring meet, dumb-ass. The only women here are over seventy," quipped Austin, who meant it as a joke but spoke the truth nonetheless.

"Okay listen, guys," Jimmy said, redirecting the conversation back to a more relevant topic. "We're going to go our separate ways, just like we talked about. Everyone put on your gloves and check to make sure you've got your phony betting tickets with you. Remember, no fingerprints."

Austin opened his wallet, Tony fished in his pockets, and Larry removed his right shoe and reached inside. All three pulled out and held up their own unique small white square of paper the size of a Post-it note. Each paper was blank except for some serial numbers and an intricate bar coding at the bottom consisting of five lines of alternating blank spaces and dashes.

Provided by Tony with the best code-breaking software money could buy, Larry had hacked into National Tote's mainframe and run his software against every bar code encrypted in National Tote's files. He then ran a master list of every uncashed winning ticket in National Tote's archives. Larry not only looked for big payouts, but he was also looking for the older outstanding tickets.

Winning tickets are good for one year, and not all winning tickets get cashed immediately. The older an uncashed ticket gets, however, the greater the probability that the ticket is actually lost and not still sitting in the pocket of some random procrastinating horseplayer.

The whole operation took Larry less than a week. When he was finished, he not only had found four valuable lost tickets, but he also knew the corresponding bar code that identified each ticket. On his home computer, he printed the bar codes onto four small squares of paper the same exact size and shape of real pari-mutuel tickets. For one day, they had the ability to turn worthless pieces of paper into real money.

Austin, Jimmy, Tony, and Larry were unaware of the history of the winning bets they were about to cash. The real tickets were all lost, and to them, the story behind each ticket was irrelevant. However, each ticket had a unique story.

Austin examined his betting slip. "How does someone lose a winning ticket?" Austin asked as he held a square white piece of paper in his hands. He'd never know that, in a former incarnation, his ticket had been a $200 win bet on a horse called Midnight Run originally made by a racetrack regular named Sal Bernstein, a retired podiatrist from Brighton Beach, Brooklyn.

When Midnight Run won, he paid $19.80 for every two-dollar bet, making Mr. Bernstein's $200 win ticket worth $1,980. Unfortunately, Bernstein never got to cash his winning ticket. Regrettably for him, it fell out of his pocket and accidentally dropped onto the men's room floor as he rummaged around his Dockers for some spare change to give the attendant. The attendant accepted his crisp one-dollar tip from out of Mr. Bernstein's pocket but swept up and threw away the even crisper $1,980 winning ticket lost from Bernstein's pocket, making his tip $1,979 less than it could have been if he were a little bit sharper. Bernstein looked all over the track but could never relocate his lucky windfall—a windfall that was now resurrected in the hands of Austin Jackman as a square crisp, clean, dry white piece of paper worth exactly $1,980.

Tony Martini stood and silently scrutinized the small square of counterfeit paper in his meaty paws. He didn't understand exactly how this paper was going to be worth so much money, but he had been told the bar code imprinted upon it was the precise match of a lucky $20 exacta bet that had won some four months ago and paid $1,800. The straight exacta bet made on Mirobolant and Napoli Express became a winner when the two horses finished first and second in a grass race at New York's Belmont Park the prior fall. The $2 exacta payoff was $182, meaning that a $20 wager on that same exacta was worth $1,820.

The real winning ticket was briefly the property of Ronny Gullo, a cement contractor from Long Island with a quick temper. Ronny didn't cash his winning exacta right away. Instead, he chose to show the ticket around to a few friends and wait until after the next race to cash. In the next race, however, Ronny's horse got beaten by a nose at the wire, which sent him into an obscenity-riddled fit of rage. In the heat of the moment, Ronny mistook his winning ticket from the race before for the one that had just lost, ripped it into a thousand tiny pieces, and scattered it all over Belmont's grandstand. Upon realizing his mistake, Ronny tried to demand his money anyway despite having no winning ticket. When the mutuel clerk finally stopped laughing, he had Ronny forcibly escorted from the building by five very big and very unsympathetic security guards. Ronny learned a valuable lesson about being more careful before ripping up his tickets, but that particular $1,820 ticket was gone, and there was no way he was ever going to get it back. Now, months later, that unclaimed $1,820 was about to become the property of Tony Martini.

Jimmy squinted as he examined the intricately printed bar code of the counterfeit ticket he held in his own right hand. The bar coding and serial number corresponded exactly to a successful $100 win-place-show wager originally placed by "Big" Bill Burkmeier of the Klien, McMillen, and Burkmeier law firm at his company's annual "Day at the Races" office field trip.

Big Bill had been making large wagers all day with the hopes of impressing Mona, the hot new paralegal Bill had just hired right out of college. In the next-to-last race of the day, Big Bill plunked down $300 ($100 to win, place, and show) on one particular across-the-board play on a horse named Let It Ride who sat at 15-1 odds on the tote board, with approximately twelve minutes remaining until post time. For Big Bill's ticket to be worth anything, Let It Ride had to finish first, second, or third in the race. If the horse won, Big Bill would get the money for all three positions; but if it finished third, he would only get the show money.

Let It Ride won easily twelve minutes later, but Big Bill never saw the race. At the time the horses were crossing the finish line, Big Bill sat blissfully unaware of the results in the back of the company motorcoach as Mona prepared to give him one of the world-class hum-dingers she was renowned for throughout her hometown of Bay Ridge, Brooklyn.

Big Bill closed his eyes and recalled that during the job interview process, Mona stressed that she was quite skilled at taking dictation, pronouncing it "dick-tation." Big Bill never did know exactly what she meant until that very moment.

While Big Bill concentrated on his attention from Mona, two thoughts repeatedly crossed Mona's mind. First, "how long do I have to wait before I ask for a promotion?" and second, "why the hell do they call this guy 'Big' Bill?"

Big Bill forgot all about his across-the-board wager and never realized that he'd won a bet paying a grand total of $2,510. Mona sued for sexual harassment the following week and eventually settled out of court for $200,000, officially making Big Bill's back-of-the-bus blow job the most expensive two minutes of his entire life.

The fourth and final bogus bet slip was the one that Larry decided to keep for himself, and it was a doozy. The ticket's bar code corresponded to a lost $20 straight trifecta that had hit for $5,850.

The original holder of that winning ticket was Chip Majors, a junior at nearby Hofstra University in Long Island. Chip had consumed twenty-one Miller Lites in a five-hour period at the racetrack's "Party in the Park" area, with a group of his college buddies over the summer. Chip already had dropped his fall semester book money on the day's first seven races and realized he was in deep shit when only $20 of the $400 he started with remained in his wallet. He was left with no alternative but to put his last $20 on a desperate 1-2-3 trifecta in order to try to win back his book money and still be able to afford to go out for beers and pizza later that night.

Once the race was finished and Chip realized that the numbers 1, 2, and 3 finished first, second, and third in that precise order, the postrace celebration that followed was earth-shattering. Chip was doused with a dozen beers from every direction and lifted onto the shoulders of his cheering buddies, who chanted "Chip! Chip! Chip!" Eventually, the well-intentioned drunk mob lowered their lucky but increasingly light-headed friend to the ground and then jammed the business end of a beer bong into his mouth and down his gullet. Chip tried to scream but nearly choked as an entire six-pack drained through the top of the beer bong into his open mouth all at once.

As Chip struggled in the dirt, none of the elated revelers had noticed a stiff wind had begun to pick up, carrying with it Chip's $5,850 trifecta ticket. Chip clawed at the air as he felt the ticket slip from his fingers, but his buddies mistook the hand motion as a request for more beer. As the second dose of beer streamed down the tube of the bong and muffled his screams, Chip watched from the ground as a wind gust picked up next semester's book money. The betting slip took flight, sailed through the air, and finally landed far out of reach in the middle of the track's infield lake.

As Austin, Jimmy, and Tony each surveyed their phony betting slips, Larry launched into a melodramatic pep talk he had prepared earlier that morning. "The four of us each holds in our hands the shattered hopes and dreams of a different broken-down horseplayer whom we'll never know—"

Jimmy cut him off immediately. "All right, enough of that bullshit, Larry, we've got things to do. Okay, everyone listen up. You guys all know the drill. We each go to a different part of the track and run our tickets through one of the track's automated betting machines. The machines won't be able to tell the difference between our tickets and the real ones, which means they should recognize them as actual winning tickets. The machines can't give you cash, but they will print you a cash voucher, which is the next best thing. Your ticket is fake, but the voucher the machine will print you is real. That's the whole idea. After you put your ticket in the machine, the touch-screen display should show a credit balance equal to the winning amount of the actual winning ticket. All you have to do is touch the Return Balance button on the screen, and the machine will print you out a new legitimate betting voucher that can be cashed by simply returning it to any pari-mutuel teller in the building. Just hand in the voucher, and they'll give you the cash. You get your money and get out of there. We'll all meet back at my car in the parking lot. The whole thing shouldn't take more than ten minutes. Anybody got anything to add before we do this?"

"Yeah," Austin spoke up. "You don't want to be remembered, so when you go to a mutuel teller to cash out, try to find one that looks ultraindifferent. Don't worry. It shouldn't be too difficult around here."

Jimmy added, "By the time they open up those automated machines and see those fake tickets, we'll be long gone."

"That's *if* they find the fake tickets in the machines. There's no guarantee they even ever look at the spent tickets they take out of the machines before they trash them," Austin said.

"All right then," Jimmy said. "Let's do it!"

7

Suite 3104 at the Carlyle Hotel had been home to corporate CEOs, foreign dignitaries, Hollywood actors, rock stars, and the occasional royal family member throughout its illustrious history near the top of one of Midtown Manhattan's choicest hotels. This particular morning, however, it was home to four hustlers, a professional yoga instructor, one dial-a-date, and two skank shift strippers from the Beavers Showclub downtown.

The gang had done some serious celebrating after walking out of the racetrack with more than twelve thousand dollars the day before. Austin, Jimmy, Tony, and Larry started by driving to Jimmy's pad. From there, they embarked on an unparalleled night of drinking and money spending in a rented limousine in Manhattan.

In need of some female companionship, Austin called Alana and told her that he and the gang had a huge day at the track and invited her along. Jimmy went through his black book—which was really more like a pamphlet than a book—and called up a girl named Deb, a full-time Manhattan dog walker, who had been his "friend with benefits" for years.

The strippers were invited by Tony as dates for Larry and him. Tony scoffed at inviting his wife, Julia, and instead opted for a phone call to Beavers. "They're changing shifts down at Beavers right now. They know me there. I'm a regular! I oughtta be able to land me and Larry some hot dates!" Tony had boastfully said.

Tony called up Julia and told her it was going to be another late night. With that business behind him, he rang Beavers Showclub to see which of the dancers there was about to get off work. The Beavers afternoon shift, known to patrons as the skank shift, worked for eight hours from opening time at eleven in the morning until the Beavers A-team took to the stages at seven.

Tony contacted Carmine, one of the club's bouncers. Carmine put the phone under his chin and relayed Tony's request for company to the skank shifters before they headed out toward the exit.

"Yo, ladies, I got Tony the Tent on the phone here, and he's looking for a couple of dates tonight. Any interest? Anybody?"

The room erupted in a loud chorus of moans and groans. Some girls started cursing loudly. A rolled fishnet stocking hit Carmine in the face before landing in a heap of static cling on his chest. Candy, the club's resident candy striper/nurse-themed dancer threatened to kick Tony right in his tent the next time she saw him. Cinnamon, a Puerto Rican mother of two from the Bronx with huge breast implant scars proclaimed she wouldn't do Tony the Tent if he was "the last *pendejo* left on earth."

Carmine's gaze shifted over to Mandy and Sandy, the club's Swedish bikini twins, who once had been A-listers but now were pushing thirty.

"No way. He's too greasy," said Mandy.

"Yaaaaaa. Too greasy," Sandy agreed.

Two more chances left, thought Carmine, as he nonchalantly strolled up to Corvette and Mercedes, the last two girls remaining in the dressing room.

"Listen, girls. Will you help me out? Please? Tony the Tent needs a couple of dates tonight. He's giving me $500 to find him two girls, and there's $500 in it for both of you two if you're up for it. It's a no-sex type deal, just a night on the town. Any rough stuff, you give me a call. What do you guys say?"

The party of eight revelers, which included strippers Corvette and Mercedes, hit the streets of Manhattan later that evening. The Dude-Men were still flying high from their successful scam. It had given them hope for their future Pick 6 plan as well as a whole lot of money to burn that night.

The gang was hungry, so Austin instructed the limo driver to make his first stop of the night at the Palm steakhouse up on Second Avenue. Austin gave the maitre d' a crisp $100 handshake. "Table for eight, please. No reservations."

The group was seated at the best (and only) available table for eight, right in between smiling caricatures of former New York mayor Rudolph Giuliani and Jets quarterback Joe Namath, who was depicted throwing a football and wearing a fur coat over his green-and-white uniform.

The table ordered multiple bottles of Dom Perignon and munched entree-sized appetizers of Florida stone crabs. Austin then switched to a dry California merlot just in time for the prime porterhouse steaks to arrive sizzling hot at the table. The group polished off the meal with key lime pies and Irish coffees before hopping back into the limo and heading to their next stop.

Half of the limo's passengers wanted to hear some low-key live music. The others wanted to relax over martinis. Austin directed them over to the Café Carlyle at the Carlyle Hotel where they caught the end of a cabaret performance.

The Carlyle's cabaret room had been made famous by legendary Carlyle house performer Bobby Short, who was known as the world's greatest saloon singer until his death earlier that year at age eighty. With Short gone, Austin had to pay eight sixty-five-dollar cover charges to sit at the bar in the back of the room and hear the second half of singer/actress Betty Buckley's live set, which consisted mainly of show tunes. They sat at the bar in the back. Austin and the guys ordered martinis. Straight up. Olives. The girls ordered cosmopolitans, and plenty of them.

After the show, it was back to the limo for the next stop, the Club Macanudo on East Sixty-third Street. Since the city's strict smoking laws were passed in 2003, the smoking club, bar, and restaurant was one of only a handful of places left in Manhattan where New Yorkers could still light up without being considered polluters, criminals, or even worse, not health conscious.

Alana and Deb engaged in the art of girl talk with Corvette and Mercedes at a small table covered with a collection of colorful cocktails. The Dude-Men sat at an adjacent table and bonded through a cloud of gray cigar smoke. Austin had opted for a spicy Montecristo No. 2 figurado, which he paired nicely with a snifter of Hennessy Special Reserve cognac. Even drunk, Austin still took pride in being able to select the perfect alcoholic beverage for any situation.

Corvette and Mercedes eventually had enough of sitting around, informing the group they'd much rather be shaking their asses than sitting on them. The visual in Tony and Larry's heads was enough to get them drooling and nodding in agreement. Austin chose the new nightspot Bloodpressure on the Upper East Side because of its selection of three bars, two swank dance floors, and a prime sunk-in lounge complete with plush sofas, movie screens, and billiards. Everyone danced and hung out until the evening's sum total of alcohol consumption started to take its toll, just past two.

The limo filled up one more time and made its last stop back at the Carlyle, where the blurry-eyed octet secured an oversized suite for the night. Austin paid the driver and transported the party's emergency liquor supply (consisting of a case of beer and a fifth of Jack Daniel's) up to the Carlyle Signature Suite on the thirty-first floor.

By sunup, the booze was polished off, and the last of the revelers had passed out in the sprawling corner suite with a view of Central Park.

*   *   *

Six that morning, a telephone rang at the Dover, Delaware, home of Bill Hanrahan, the general manager of National Tote, Inc.

"Sir, sorry to bother you, it's Peabody in operations over at the betting hub . . . Yes, I know what time it is . . . Yes, sir, I know it's Sunday . . . Yes, I'll try to make it snappy. We thought you should be informed that the integrity of the tote system was breached yesterday. I just got word from the boys down in security. They're checking it out now, sir."

"Does it look like an inside job?" asked Hanrahan.

"No, sir, it looks like it was an outside hacker," replied Peabody. "We're looking into what steps to take."

"What did the bastards get?"

"Looks like they just got some bar codes from some moldy uncashed winning tickets. Looks like we're dealing with some really sharp and sophisticated criminals here. It may even be organized crime. We're contacting the authorities in the appropriate jurisdiction. It looks like it will be the New York State Racing and Wagering Board since the tickets were Aqueduct tickets, sir."

"Good job, Peabody," said Hanrahan. "Keep me informed, and for god's sake, keep this story hush-hush. The last thing we want is the whole world knowing how easy it is to hack our tote system!"

"Will do, sir."

*   *   *

Across town as the first streaks of sunlight began to paint the eastern sky, another phone rang. It awakened the lone occupant of a rent-controlled one-bedroom apartment on the Upper West Side. A groggy voice answered, "Yeah, Bragg here."

"Detective Bragg. It's Putnam here, sir. Listen, I just got a call from the guys over at Racing and Wagering. Seems there were some irregularities over at Aqueduct Racetrack yesterday. Looks like someone found a way to cash some counterfeit mutuel tickets. They need a man from fraud division down there this morning, if possible."

"The New York State Racing and Wagering Board, huh? I don't suppose they care it's 7 friggin' a.m. on a Sunday morning?"

Silence, followed by "No, sir. They think they've stumbled onto something big over there at the racetrack. Could be some big crime ring. It looks like whoever did this was extremely smart."

Bragg smelled a big fish. "Tell them I'll be right there."

*   *   *

The normally sedate Carlyle Signature Suite surroundings were turned upside down on this particular morning. The contents of the minibar were strewn across the floor, where they lay alongside beer bottles, cigarette butts, discarded clothing, and the bodies of passed-out partiers.

Since there weren't enough beds in the sweet suite to afford everyone a good night's sleep, Tony, Larry, Corvette, and Mercedes had had to improvise.

Tony slept in his boxers and took the suite's antique oak couch with white and yellow handwoven upholstery. The couch began the prior evening in pristine condition, but later ended up on a van to a garage sale in Queens after the housekeeping staff came in and discovered it stinking and soaked through with Tony's ample perspiration.

Corvette and Mercedes slept on the floor under a bedsheet, using their padded bras as pillows.

Larry spent the night sleeping atop the grand piano that sat next to suite 3104's picture window with a grand view of Central Park. During the night, Larry found that the top of the piano was too cold and hard to sleep comfortably on. He soon fixed the problem, however, by ripping down the gold and violet velvet curtains from the picture window and rolling them into a makeshift sleeping bag.

Unfortunately for the rest of the group, Larry's use of the curtains left the windows bare and allowed increasing sunlight to creep into the room all morning. As a result, everyone was awakened by noon and feeling the ill effects of a night of too much drinking and not enough sleep. The best solution to this problem, the group decided, was a little hair of the dog down at the Carlyle's Sunday Champagne Brunch. Austin, Alana, Jimmy, Deb, Tony, Larry, Corvette, and Mercedes combed their hair, threw on some clothes, and headed downstairs for some much-needed grub.

An hour and a half and five hundred bucks later, the men and the women decided it was time to go their separate ways for the remainder of the afternoon. The guys had some serious plans to make for the Pick 6.

Jimmy and Deb kissed and said good-bye. He promised he'd call her later that week. Deb wasn't holding her breath but smiled and waved anyway as the door of her taxi closed, and she headed off up Madison Avenue.

Tony and Larry each dug five hundred dollars out of their wallets and thanked Corvette and Mercedes for their dates.

"See you later, dolls," Tony said.

Corvette and Mercedes stuck the wads of bills into their bras and answered in unison, "Anytime, Tony the Tent!"

Austin walked Alana out of the hotel toward her subway stop around the corner. He was anxious to join the other Dude-Men back up in the suite since he still couldn't tell Alana what was going on. Austin knew he'd have to tell Alana about the Pick 6 plan eventually, but he wanted to wait until the moment was right. He told her he was heading back to the room to help clean up the place.

"I told you getting together with my old friends would be a good idea, didn't I?"

"I don't know, Austin. You said Jimmy got in touch with you because he had some kind of plan in mind, but then you never mentioned it again. Is there something you're not telling me? Did you really just have a good day at the track, or is there something else going on?"

Austin reassured her that the gang had merely had a good day at the track before kissing her good-bye.

When the Dude-Men met back at the suite, the first order of business was assessing the financial damage they'd done the night before. Of the original $12,160 stake, only $5,830 remained. That meant that last night's party cost $6,330—an amount that included dinner, drinks, tips, cover charges, cigars, brunch, the limo, the hotel suite, and, last but not least, female companionship.

"Being rich sure ain't gonna suck, I'll tell you that," Larry said as he reclined in a chair by the window with his feet up and his hands clasped behind his head.

"And I'll tell you something else," Tony said, strutting across the room toward Larry. "That five hundred we both paid was the best money we ever spent. Ha!"

High fives. "You said it," Larry said.

"Are you guys talking about what I think you're talking about?" asked Austin.

"Ohhh yeah," Tony said.

"No way!" Austin said. "I thought you'd have no shot with Corvette and Mercedes. I saw them pass out at around four, and I never remember them leaving my sight before then. So what did I miss before four?"

"Whoa, who said anything about *before* four?" Tony asked with a wink.

"Yeah, but I distinctly remember them passing out at four sharp . . . Wait a minute! What are you saying? . . . Whoa, hold on! . . . Don't even tell me! . . . You two guys did it *after* they passed out? . . . You sick fucks!" Austin said in disbelief, not really knowing if he meant it as a compliment.

"Haaaa!" Tony and Larry attempted another high five, but this time Larry missed Tony's hand, lost his balance, and tumbled off his chair to the floor.

As usual, Jimmy, unfazed, stepped in and calmed down the rest of the group. "All right, all right, settle down, you perverts. Enough of that. We need to start to start thinking about getting down to business."

8

Detective John Bragg had spent his entire Sunday morning at Aqueduct Racetrack investigating Saturday's phony betting ticket scam that took the track for twelve thousand dollars and change. It was not glamorous police work. Instead, most of his day had been spent filling out reports, interviewing witnesses, and searching for and collecting evidence.

This kind of work was a long way from Bragg's heyday with the police force. In earlier years, he had worked his way up through the ranks from beat cop to detective, dealing only with the most dangerous and violent homicides and drug cases. Bragg's approach to the job could best be described as merciless, and if there were such a thing as good cops and bad cops, he would certainly have been classified as the latter.

Bragg took the term "beat cop" literally, doling out a heavy-handed brand of street justice that made him respected among his peers and feared on the streets. He took that tough attitude with him up the ladder until he finally stepped over the line, arresting and savagely beating what turned out to be an innocent bystander in a case of mistaken identity during a drug raid on the wrong address in the Bronx in the late 1990s.

The subsequent internal affairs investigation turned up so many claims of police brutality on Bragg's record that they could no longer be ignored. Down through the years, it appeared that Bragg had left scores of thugs complaining of broken limbs and broken faces in his wake. That was in addition to the dozens of Bragg's detainees who'd charged they'd left his interrogations with fewer teeth than when they'd arrived. Reports of false arrests swirled, and a disturbing pattern of violence began to emerge that told a story of a cop on or past the edge.

Internal affairs had no choice but to take Bragg off active duty and stick him behind a desk for a year until they figured out what to do with him. Their eventual solution was a month of rage-management training and a reassignment in the quieter and less violent fraud division. There, Bragg would be dealing with greedy corporate shit-eaters who siphoned money from their clients and zit-faced geeks who stole credit card numbers off the Internet while living in their parents' basements. In the fraud division, there'd be no hardened street criminals whom he couldn't help himself from hurting.

So now, this was Bragg's life. Being awakened at seven on a Sunday morning to work alone in a dark back room at a racetrack in Queens, sifting through printouts that were supposed to prove how some white-collar guys duped some other white-collar guys out of approximately twelve grand. Back in the day, he never had to wake up at seven on a Sunday. Say what you want about drug dealers, but at least, they had the good sense to sleep in late on weekends. No self-respecting drug dealer ever got up earlier than noon on a Sunday, and if someone did, it was because they had to go to church.

Bragg had accomplished precious little on this wasted Sunday until late in the day when he unsuspectingly struck gold while completing his review of a pile of surveillance tapes from the security cameras that hung above the automated betting machines and mutuel tellers involved in the scam. His best-case scenario with the surveillance tapes was to match up the video footage with the exact time that the makeshift betting tickets were placed through the machines in order to come up with a look at the face of the person or people who pulled off the crime.

What he found on the tapes was something far, far better than what he'd hoped for.

Bragg watched the grainy black-and-white video until something, or rather someone, caught his eye on film at the exact time that one of the counterfeit tickets was being exchanged at the racetrack the day before. He had to do a double take, rubbing his eyes and shaking his head to make sure he was really seeing what he thought he was seeing, or if he was just imagining it. On the video monitor, Bragg could clearly make out a tall skinny man with curly hair and glasses making a transaction at one of the betting machines in question. Bragg recognized the skinny man on the videotape. It was the one man he never wanted to see on videotape again.

The man in question was none other than Larry Lipwinkle.

Bragg had arrested Lipwinkle and put him in jail for credit card fraud a few years back, and still dreamed of the day he'd again cross paths with Lipwinkle and lock him up for good. And now, here he was, gift-wrapped and dropped off in a ribbon and bow on Bragg's doorstep. He almost couldn't believe his good fortune.

Bragg had spent every spare hour of the last two years looking for Lipwinkle, waiting for the day he'd once again come across the man who'd defiled his daughter before an Internet audience of millions. Many a morning he'd wake up in a cold sweat after yet another nightmare featuring the video playing over and over inside his head. That damned video. Explicit enough to make Paris Hilton's sex tape look like it belonged in the Blockbuster Video family aisle between the Teletubbies and SpongeBob SquarePants.

"That low-life filthy little prick!" Bragg exclaimed as he watched the video of Lipwinkle, his nemesis, walking up to the mutuel teller, turning in his ill-gotten voucher for cash, putting it in his pocket, turning, and exiting to the left, out of the camera's eye.

"No one makes a fool of me, you little shit," said Bragg as he sat alone watching the tape. "You're gonna regret the day you ever met me. Your skinny little ass is mine, loser."

Bragg hit the Eject button and grabbed the tape out of the player as he headed out of the security office to inform track officials and New York State Racing and Wagering Board investigators what he'd found.

Lester Farley from Aqueduct's mutuel department and Frank Sanders from the NYSRWB and a few other cops from fraud were sitting around a table in a back room, eating Krispy Kreme doughnuts and drinking coffee. Their jocular chatter ground to a halt when Bragg swung the door open and came into the room wearing a sinister grin. It was not a happy look. Instead, it looked more like the smile that Jack Nicholson wore when he burst through the door in *The Shining* and announced, "Here's Johnny!"

Bragg was waving the videotape. "I got something off the surveillance cameras. It's a positive ID on one of our perpetrators. I recognize him from a case I worked a few years back. Credit card fraud. His name's Larry Lipwinkle. He's a real sicko scumbag."

"That's great news," said Sanders. "If you can positively ID this guy, then why don't you have your guys find him and pick him up? Case closed."

"Whoa. Just a minute there, Colonel, it's going to be a little harder than just sending a squad car out and picking him up," Bragg said in response to Sanders. In addition to his many other charming personality traits, Bragg loved to push people's buttons. He figured that addressing Sanders as "colonel" ought to do the trick.

Bragg watched Sanders getting hot under the collar but continued anyway. "I'm telling you, this guy's one slippery sonofabitch. I've been trying to find this guy for a year with no luck."

Sanders was staring at Bragg. "First of all, jackass, don't call me Colonel. Second of all, excuse me if I don't understand, but would you mind telling me why you've been looking for this guy for a year and why the hell he's going to be so hard to track down?"

"We have a history together, this Lipwinkle guy and me," Bragg said. "It's personal. He knows I'm looking for him, and he knows I'm gonna kill him with my bare hands if I ever find him. He took me for a ride and got the best of me once. But I can tell you one thing—payback's going to be a bitch."

"But I don't understand, Bragg. Why the hell can't you find him?"

"He's a computer specialist or something. I don't even know what he does. Anyway, as soon as he figured out I'd come looking for him, he went into the public records and changed a bunch of stuff. Made new aliases. Created about a hundred different false Larry Lipwinkles in the DMV system. Can you imagine that—a strange name like Lipwinkle, and now there's a hundred of 'em in the computer. We don't even know which of 'em, if any, is actually him. He's got a real sick sense of humor, this guy."

Sanders's face was beginning to turn red. "So what you're telling me is we got this guy red-handed and we know who he is and there's not a goddamn thing we can do about it? Is that what you're telling me?"

"Not exactly, Colonel," said Bragg, making Sanders's face turn from red to purple. "We won't be able to come to him, but we can let him come to us. These guys think they just got away with twelve grand. My gut feeling is that they'll be back for more."

"That's $12,160 to be exact," corrected Farley, representing the racetrack. "So what's our next move?"

"You guys keep your dicks in your pants. I'll make the call to National Tote and tell 'em we've got a lead. I'll tell them to keep on the lookout for anything suspicious in the next week or so, but also tell them not to do anything to warn these guys that we're onto them. We'll set the trap, and let these bozos walk right into it," Bragg said. "Me and Sanders's boys at the Racing and Wagering Board will do what we can on our end. As for this Lipwinkle character, you leave him to me. He's all mine."

9

Larry's apartment was a studio walk-up on Manhattan's gritty Lower East Side, located just off Delancy Street. A hop, skip, and jump away from the Williamsburg Bridge. The building resembled a tenement, probably because it had been one once and was not far from being one again.

Larry lived in squalor in the sparsely decorated single-room apartment. Larry's place was, however, where the all-important computer equipment was located. Therefore, it was the perfect place for the Dude-Men to meet and plan.

Larry's apartment was dominated by a vast network of computer monitors and hard drives. There were wires slithering all over the floor, connecting one piece of machinery to another. The clutter left just enough room in the apartment for Larry to fit the only other pieces of furniture he owned—an entertainment center with television and stereo, a kitchen table and chairs, and a futon where he slept. The apartment had only one small closet, which was full of junk. As a result, Larry's clothes and personal effects were strewn haphazardly all over the place in true bachelor-pad style. In other words, it was a comfortable place for Larry but an inhospitable place for visitors.

Regardless of the ambience, the Dude-Men gathered at Larry's on Thursday to talk about the Pick 6. The group focused on the simulcast races from Santa Anita in Southern California because that track has the most Pick 6 action. The track's jackpot had been hit on Sunday, and then after no racing on Monday and Tuesday, the Pick 6 went unhit on Wednesday, resulting in a small carryover of sixty-five thousand going into Thursday.

Austin, Jimmy, Tony, and Larry sat around the kitchen table, holding bottles of Bud Light. "I just wanted to get everyone together so we can be prepared to make our next move when the opportunity presents itself," Austin said. "Nobody hit the Pick 6 today, and while that itself isn't big news, it could be our chance if nobody hits it by the end of the week."

"Way to keep on top of things, Austin, that's why I wanted you to be part of this," Jimmy said. "We should get a plan started now so we have exactly what we need in place exactly when we need it. Larry, what can you tell us?"

"I went back into the National Tote computer and fished around a little the last couple days. I think I figured out the key to making a phony Pick 6 ticket."

"That's awesome. How can we do it?" Jimmy asked.

"The first thing we're going to need to do is set up a betting account with National Tote. We're not going to be able to just go to the track and buy a Pick 6 ticket there because that will give us an actual paper ticket, and a paper ticket can't be changed. Instead, we're going to need to place our bet over the computer straight into National Tote's system. That way there's no paper trail."

"Good. I like what I'm hearing so far," Jimmy enthused. "What happens after we make the bet? We all know we're not really going to be able to have all six winners."

"Right, but what we actually bet doesn't even matter. We just need to have some kind of a bet logged into the computer system. It can be anything. We just need to make it look legitimate. Then as the races are being run, we'll go into the computer system, access our bet, and change the numbers so they correspond with the winning horses."

"It's called past-posting," Austin said with wide eyes. "It's when you find a way to bet on a horse after the race has already been run. I can't believe this is gonna be as simple as past-posting!"

"Once I'm into the computer system, it really will be as simple as that," Larry said. "The only thing I ask is that when you make the original bet, try to make it stand out in some way so I can locate it in the computer files."

"How can we make it stand out?" asked Austin.

"What I mean is our bet has to look different from all the other bets in the computer so I can easily find it when I break into National Tote's system on the day of the scam. Let me explain. Once we've made the bet, the computer's record of the wager is going to be located in the system along with the thousands of other Pick 6 bets made that day. I'm going to have to sort through all the bets in order to find which one's ours. That's the tough part. Once I've found our bet, then changing it is easy. I'd say the best way to make our bet stand out is by making it some unusual denomination, or by cooking up some strange combination of horses. That way, I can create what we hackers call a sniffer program that will enable me to sniff out our bet in the system and distinguish it from all the other bets."

"That sounds easy enough," Jimmy said.

"Pick 6 bets are traditionally made in two-dollar denominations," Larry said. "Since we need to make our ticket stand out in the crowd,

we can make our bets for ten dollars each. Then we have to think about
how we're going to structure our tickets. I'm thinking we use just one
single horse in each of the first four races. That'll keep the cost of the
ticket low. After each of the first four races, I'll go in and change the
number on our ticket to the number of the winning horse. Then, to
save us all some aggravation, we can circle every horse in the last two
races of the Pick 6 to ensure that no matter what happens, we win."

Jimmy added it up. "Okay, so let's say that, on average, there's about
ten horses per race. If we cover every horse in both of the last two
races of the Pick 6, that's ten times ten or exactly a hundred possible
combinations we need to bet in order to have every combination covered
in those final two races. The bet's denomination will be for ten dollars,
so a hundred combinations at ten dollars each comes to a thousand
bucks. That's not too bad."

"Also remember that there's only about twenty-five minutes between
every race, so we're going to need to be pretty fast. As soon as the
race ends, we need to find our bet in the computer, change our horse
number to the winning number, and then sit back and hope for a big
jackpot," Austin said.

"We've got this covered," Jimmy continued. "The first thing we need
to do is set up this account with National Tote. Tony, you're the money
man here. You have no criminal record, and you've never set up any
kind of horse-betting account before. You'd be the perfect one to open
our account in your name."

"Whoa, wait a minute, Jimmy. Why is it my name we hafta use? That's
bullshit, man. It's your plan, and it's his computer," Tony said, pointing
over at Larry.

Jimmy shifted into damage-control mode. "Tony, easy man. I thought
you wanted to be a part of this. I thought you wanted to be one of the
guys."

"Yeah, I do, Jimmy, but—"

"No *buts*, man. Listen, we're cutting you in for a quarter. We've each
gotta pull our own weight."

"Why can't Larry just make up a false name?"

Jimmy and Austin looked at each other and thought about it for a
minute. "Yeah," Jimmy said to Larry. "Why don't you just make a false
name?"

In reality, there was no good reason for Larry not to cook up a phony
name for the account. It was pure laziness. A false name would require a
lot more work for Larry. He'd need to set up an address, a social security
number. The whole works. Larry could do it, but it would take a lot of
time and effort. Larry just figured he'd save himself some work by using

Tony's name. Besides, he had complete confidence he'd be able to erase everything once the scam was done and the money changed hands.

Larry spoke up, "Listen guys, you're just gonna have to leave the technical stuff to me. I'm telling you, we need the account to be a real person or else it's not gonna work."

"But what if we get caught? I'll be fucked!"

"Don't worry about it, man," Larry said to Tony. "After we collect our money, I'll just go back in and erase your name. We won't get caught, and even if we did, there won't be any trace back to you."

"I want to help you guys, I really do. I'll let you use my name, but I'm telling you ahead of time, I'm doing it under protest."

"Duly noted," agreed Jimmy.

"Where should I go to open up my betting account?" Tony asked.

"As I said before, the key to this is being able to go into the National Tote computer and not be detected," Larry said. "I poked through National Tote's network of off-track betting affiliates looking for the ones with the oldest technology. I found a perfect one in upstate New York called Adirondack OTB."

"I've heard about that place," Austin said. "It's supposed to be a pretty sloppy operation. Some would even say sleazy."

"If they're running a sloppy operation up there, it can only help us. But the biggest reason that they'll be perfect for our needs is because their computer system doesn't use any transaction history files. They have no backups."

"What does that mean, no transaction history files?" asked Jimmy.

"A transaction history file is just what it sounds like. It makes a record of every betting transaction made at any particular location," Larry said. "It means that the changes we make to our Pick 6 ticket won't be recorded onto a disk at that Adirondack OTB location. In order to catch us, they'd have to catch us live and red-handed because once we log off, there will be no proof we were ever in there. We won't even have to cover our tracks, except to erase Tony's name."

"The only way they can catch us red-handed is if they know about us in advance," Jimmy said. "Larry, you're sure we weren't detected the other day?"

"As far as I know, we pulled it off cleanly. No trace. My gut feeling is that if they knew they got ripped off, they would have made some security changes in their computer system. As of now, I haven't noticed any changes. They must be playing with themselves over there or something."

"Do you guys realize what we're talking about here?" Jimmy said as he stood up, suddenly not feeling small-time anymore. "We're guaranteeing ourselves a Pick 6! The only thing we can't guarantee is the size of the actual payoff. We've gotta get lucky in that department, but if we can catch a big jackpot, we could be talking about something like a million-dollar ticket! Even split four ways, that's still a quarter-million each! I don't have any figures in front of me, but I think we're talking about pulling off the biggest betting scam in the history of American sports! And the best part is we don't even have to fix a single race. We're just fixing the bet, not the race. And we can do it right over the computer. We don't even need to leave Larry's living room. Not too bad for a bunch of misfits from CNJSU, huh?"

10

Bill Hanrahan's busy Thursday afternoon routine of reading the sports section and munching on beef jerky was interrupted by a phone call to his office at the National Tote headquarters in Delaware. "Bill Hanrahan, general manager here," he said as he sat behind his desk and hurriedly fumbled to zip up his pants. "How can I help you?"

Hanrahan's father, Paddy Hanrahan, founded National Tote thirty years ago and built it from the ground up as a viable alternative to other older and larger tote companies that had been serving the pari-mutuel betting industry for the better part of the twentieth century. Paddy Hanrahan ran the company with a strong work ethic and, over the years, was able to build up an impressive client list by offering personalized service at competitive prices.

When Paddy's health began to fail in the late 1990s, however, he was forced to bring in his son Bill to take over the reins of the company. Bill Hanrahan had been a failure in the business world and was very grateful for the opportunity his dad gave him to bypass the middle management level and join the National Tote corporate hierarchy right at the top of the bureaucratic trash heap. Paddy, who clearly was a better businessman than a judge of character, trusted Bill and personally groomed him to take over the company when the time eventually came for Paddy's retirement in 2001. In the four years since, Paddy recuperated from prostate cancer down in Palm Beach by joining a country club, playing a ton of golf, and otherwise taking it easy in the Sunshine State. Bill, meanwhile, like so many others in history whose fathers came before them, promptly ran his family's company into the ground. Bill accomplished this by spending all his time sitting at his desk, reading the sports section and playing with himself.

"Mr. Hanrahan, this is Detective John Bragg calling. I'm the officer in charge of the investigation going on over at Aqueduct."

"Aqueduct?"

"Yes, sir, Aqueduct. You know, it's the racetrack in New York."

"Oh, yes, yes. Aqueduct. Right. Tell me, Detective, have you made any progress yet on last weekend's improprieties?"

"That's why I'm calling, sir. In addition to wanting to introduce myself as the man in charge of the investigation and the man you'll be working closely with, I just wanted to give you an update as to where we are at the present time."

"Okay. Where are we?"

"Well, Mr. Hanrahan, it turns out we have a strong lead on the person that hacked into your computer system last weekend. We have a strong suspicion that he's going to try something else in the near future."

"That's great news! Sounds open-and-shut to me. If you know who the guy is and what he's up to, you should be able to catch him before he strikes again, right?" Hanrahan queried, anxious to break open the seal on another Slim Jim.

"Unfortunately, it's not going to be quite that easy. That's the other reason I'm calling. I want to ask for your full cooperation in our investigation."

"Of course we're cooperating. What did you have in mind?"

"We don't have enough to go on to enable us to find these guys before they strike again, but we're reasonably sure they're up to something else. That's the profile. What I'm saying is that we think we can catch them in the act if we're prepared next time."

"Next time? Next time! I didn't think there was going to be any next time. That's what I thought you guys were there for. What the hell are doing over there, sitting around on your dicks eating doughnuts?" Hanrahan demanded as he downed another Slim Jim.

"Sir, we need your full cooperation on this. We need you to get a team of your best men to closely monitor all computer activities and transactions on your network in the coming days and weeks. You need to resist the temptation to change or upgrade your security. That way, they'll be tempted to commit another crime. We'll be setting a trap for these dimwits to walk right into. When your men spot anything suspicious, I need you to contact me immediately."

Hanrahan took a moment to carefully assess the situation. He'd never even considered spending the money necessary to upgrade National Tote's security. That could cost millions and piss off the shareholders. Now, the cops were on the phone telling him not to upgrade security, which gave him a built-in way to save his own ass if the company got ripped off again. News of National Tote's security breach had not yet reached the media; therefore, there was still no outside pressure on Hanrahan or anyone else at National Tote to take any measures in regard to anything. The only thing Hanrahan really needed to do was lie to Bragg and tell him he had a "team of best men" ready to spring into action and get cracking on this problem immediately.

"We had planned a major restructuring of our security system," Hanrahan lied. "But if you insist, I would be willing to hold off in order to accommodate you—based on your recommendation, of course. I can also assure you that we'll have our best men monitoring the computer system for break-ins day and night."

"Sounds good. I'll send you my contact information, so all you have to do is let me know the next time your security's been breached. We'll take it from there," Bragg said. "Thank you, Mr. Hanrahan. We'll be in touch."

Hanrahan hung up with Bragg and immediately dialed Dick Peabody, his director of operations.

"Peabody, it's Hanrahan. I just got off the phone with the police investigating last week's break-in. They say we need a team of our best men monitoring our computer system. They think whoever pulled off last week's scam will soon strike again."

"Best men, sir? We don't have a team of best men."

"Well then hire some, godammit. Or better yet, call that shut-in, Smithers. He doesn't do anything else around here. Tell him he's going to be pulling eighteen-hour shifts until this whole thing blows over."

11

Midday on Friday afternoon, and the sequence of six races involved in the Pick 6 had just begun at Santa Anita. After the Pick 6 had gone unhit again on Thursday, building the carryover up to a juicier $180,000, Tony took off work early on Friday so he could watch the day's Pick 6 unfold at Larry's apartment. In New York, simulcast horse races are televised live to a million homes on two channels of basic cable, making it possible to both watch and wager from home. With nowhere better to be on a workday, the others were already at Larry's, sitting in front of the television when Tony arrived.

On days when the Pick 6 jackpot reaches a two-day carryover, betting money from big horse bettors from all over the country starts pouring in. This influx increases the likelihood that one or more people will end up winning a share of the jackpot, but also can make the amount of the next day's carryover increase exponentially if nobody is still able to collect the pot.

Austin, Jimmy, and Tony sat around Larry's place, trying to have a serious conversation while at the same time trying to avoid touching any of Larry's belongings as if they were toxic waste. The subject, as always, was the Pick 6.

"Right now we have a decent two-day carryover of $180,000," Austin began. "Generally speaking, Pick 6 carryovers at this stage usually multiply by three or four times a day. That means, counting the carryover plus what gets bet today, there could be a total of about $600,000 in the pot. Technically, we could go for it today."

"That's great," Tony said.

"Wait a minute," Jimmy said, sensing that Austin had more to say. "Austin, do you think we should go for it today?"

"Well, a $600,000 jackpot is good, but if there're several winners—which there could be—then the pot will get split up several different ways. We could come out with only like $100,000, and we'd have to split that four ways."

"Let me remind you guys that I'm only risking one shot at this," Larry said. "When we go for it, we have to make it count."

"We'll be taking a risk," Austin decided. "But I say we wait it out one more day and see if nobody hits the Pick 6 today. If we get lucky and it carries over again to tomorrow, we should be looking at a jackpot up over two million dollars. That would be the ideal situation for us."

"Well then, unless anyone has any objections, it's settled," Jimmy said. "Let's cross our fingers today and hope nobody picks six."

The gang settled in at Larry's, still trying not to touch anything while watching the day's races. They all decided they were rooting against favorites. When favorites—or horses with the lowest betting odds—win races, it increases the chance that more and more players will stay alive in the sequence and eventually win the Pick 6 because these horses tend to have the lowest odds, as they are the most likely to win, given their past performances, breeding, etc. When longshots—or horses with very long odds not thought by the betting public to have much of a chance at victory—win, it tends to knock out most players and reduce the possibility that the jackpot will be hit.

Austin and the Dude-Men were ready to remain glued to the television all afternoon, hoping that a series of longshots winning throughout the day would thwart all of Friday's Pick 6 bettors until no more live tickets remained. If someone won today, they would have to start waiting for a big jackpot all over again.

The first leg of the Pick 6 came and went with the third favorite winning the race. That turned up the pressure for a longshot to win in the second race of the six-race bet. The Dude-Men got their wish when a 14-1 shot won the race at the longest odds on the board. *That one surely weeded out a good percentage of Friday's hopefuls*, Austin thought, *but it wouldn't be enough to eliminate everyone*. More longshots were needed if the betting pool was going to carry over.

In the third leg of Friday's Pick 6, it was crucial that the big odds-on favorite, One Tough Guy, lose the race, since Austin figured that a lot of bettors had him as their single live horse in that particular race, and he fervently hoped the horse would just refuse to run. It's common for bettors to bet several different horses on their Pick 6 ticket, particularly if none of the horses are a standout. But One Tough Guy looked like a sure thing, and Austin felt certain a lot of bettors had bet only him to win this race to try to keep the overall cost of their tickets down. Austin's wish came true when One Tough Guy stumbled at the start and never completely recovered before going on to finish third behind a winner who paid 6-1 odds.

The Pick 6 was halfway home, and the gang still needed at least one more longshot, and probably two, in order for the jackpot to carry over to Saturday. The pressure was starting to get to Austin, who got up from Larry's computer console and headed toward Larry's cushioned futon. He cleared a space for himself in between a half-empty bag of sour cream and onion Doritos and a pile Larry's unwashed clothes that Austin recognized from the day before, and plopped himself down on the sofa like a rag doll. Austin tried to relax but couldn't while sitting next to Larry's dirty laundry, which may as well have been a radioactive pile of rat shit from his point of view. The thought hit Austin that maybe Larry could benefit from going out and finding himself a girlfriend.

"Hey, Larry, you know what I was thinking? This place could really use a woman's touch. You ever think of getting yourself a girl?" Austin asked as he felt something scurrying past his feet under the futon.

"Oh, a girlfriend, huh? Well let's see. Tony's married and cheats on his wife with strippers, and you have a girlfriend who's dragging you off to some godforsaken place in Mexico. No thanks, dude. I'd say I'm the one who's doing okay, and you guys are the ones who're messed up."

"He's got a point there," Jimmy said.

"First of all," responded Austin, "she's not dragging me to Mexico. I want to go. Secondly, if you don't want a girlfriend, at least you could clean up in here yourself. If not for your benefit, then at least for the benefit of your guests."

"Fine, but I don't want no girlfriend though. Nuh-uh."

"What about those strippers from the other night, Corvette and Mercedes? It looked like they liked you just fine," Austin suggested.

"Well, that didn't count."

"Why not?"

"Because they only liked me when they were unconscious."

"You're one sick fuck, Lipwinkle," Austin said, pretty sure this time he didn't mean it as a compliment.

"Hey!" Jimmy said. "They're getting ready to run the next race at Santa Anita."

The gang gathered around the television for the fourth leg of the day's Pick 6. Austin figured they needed a horse to win at around 10-1 odds to knock a bunch more people out of the running for Friday's jackpot. Turning for home, the race came down to a stretch duel between the favored number 2 horse and the number eight, who had gone off at 11-1. Austin yelled at the television, "Come on eight, come on eight!" Jimmy rose to his feet and started whipping his thigh with a rolled up copy of the *Daily Racing Form*. Larry and Tony were cheering "Go, go, go!" in unison as the two horses came down to the wire with the number eight horse surging to a slight advantage.

The number eight crossed the line a neck in front of the favorite, and Larry's studio apartment reverberated with the sounds of cheering and high fives as the Dude-Men all celebrated.

There was suddenly a loud knocking on the wall from Larry's next-door neighbor. A voice came through the wall, "Shut the hell up in there, you freakin' punks!"

"Thin walls." Larry blushed. "Don't mind him. That's just my old neighbor, Mr. Himler. He's harmless."

"All right," Austin said. "We've got to settle down, anyway. We're not quite there yet. We probably need one more longshot in the next two races, and even then, we'll have to sweat out the Pick 6 results and pray somebody doesn't have a freakishly difficult combination."

Leg five of the Pick 6 came and went with the second favorite winning the race and paying 3-1 odds. This meant that whether or not the gang would try for a Fix Six attempt on Saturday was going to come down to the final race of the six-race sequence.

Austin looked over the ten-horse field and found four horses in the odds range that could help the gang's cause. "We're going to need one of the four horses in the race who are in 15- to 20-1 range to win in order to knock out the rest of today's remaining live tickets. And even then, it won't be a sure thing that nobody wins. Pray for a miracle, dudes."

"What the heck, some chance is better than none," Jimmy said.

Post time for the sixth and final leg of the Pick 6 finally came, and the ten-horse field began to load into the starting gate one by one. Tension was everywhere in Larry's apartment. Austin leaned up against the TV as Jimmy nervously paced back and forth in the back of the room, Larry twisted his hair into knots, and Tony sweated profusely.

One of the four longshots in the race showed early speed while battling for the lead with two of the favorites. The pace was fast. On the turn, things started to look bad as the horses on the lead began to fade and none of the other three longshots trailing him in the race appeared to be making a move from off the pace. As the field entered the homestretch, the door was wide open for a horse to win the race with a strong late rally from behind.

"Where are we, Austin? Where are we?" Jimmy yelled as two horses sprinted into the picture from the back of the pack.

"There!" screamed Austin. "The two-horse on the far outside! He's 20-1, and he's charging like a freight train!"

The pair of late runners, one a 20-1 longshot named Choices and one a low-odds favorite named Shattuck, zipped past the leaders and were neck and neck approaching the wire.

"We need that longshot! Go, Choices, go! Go, Choices, go!" yelled Austin.

Larry increased the volume on the remote. The track announcer excitedly raised his voice as the horses alternated for the lead as the race reached the final strides.

"It's Choices, now Shattuck! Choices, now Shattuck! Choices, Shattuck! On the wire . . . It's too close to call!" screamed the announcer.

"It's a photo finish! Nobody move," Austin ordered as he put his hand over his eyes, too afraid to look.

It all came down to the photo finish. If 20-1 shot Choices won, there would surely be no winners of Friday's Pick 6, and Austin and the gang would be able to proceed with their Fix Six plan the next day. If Shattuck won, someone would be holding a winning Pick 6 ticket, and there would be no jackpot carryover to Saturday.

Austin, Jimmy, Larry, and Tony collectively held their breath as a tension-filled minute passed. Then another minute, and then another. Dark circles of perspiration started forming on Tony's shirt under his arms. Larry pulled his own hair out, Jimmy continued to pace, and Austin resorted to chewing on his *Racing Form.*

Finally, the announcer's voice returned. "The results of the photo finish are now official. The winner of the race was number two, Choices!"

Larry's apartment exploded with yelling, screaming, and cheering as four grown men jumped up and down. Hugs, handshakes, and loud celebrating continued until Mr. Himler's voice came booming through the wall once again.

The announcer came back on over the loudspeaker and made it official. "There were no winners of today's Pick 6. There will be a carryover of $605,602 going into Saturday's races!"

"Yes! We made it, guys. We made it! The jackpot we've been waiting for is actually going to happen! It's on, gentlemen. Our Fix Six is on for tomorrow!"

12

Tony's wife, Julia Esposito Martini, was not an unattractive woman, and she'd had plenty of suitors down through the years before ever meeting Tony that night on the Staten Island Ferry. Julia's main problem, in the romance department, had always been that she was too good looking. The guys from her community in Staten Island were all over her like mustard on a pretzel all through high school, and as a result, Julia had already exhausted all her local dating possibilities at a young age without ever finding Mr. Right. By the time she was twenty-two, everyone around town that she hadn't already dated had either left for college, gone off to work, or gotten married to someone else.

Julia's working class parents didn't have the money to send her away to college, so she stayed home and attended junior college instead. She eventually earned an associate's degree before moving on to beauty school where she studied the delicate arts of haircuts, makeup applications, and manicures. It was in beauty school where Julia finally found her true calling. She graduated as the top hairstylist in her class and immediately got a job at a mall in Staten Island where she quickly became a star stylist for the local big-haired, gossipy, gum-chewing set. This job was good for her career but bad for her social life, since it again prevented her from expanding her boundaries beyond Staten Island's ever-evaporating dating pool.

That all changed when Julia finally got her big break and landed a job in SoHo at a hot new hair salon called Hair Box. The Hair Box's motto was "Cutting-edge hair with flair," and Julia's unorthodox, outer-borough work was all the rage at the avant-garde salon in Manhattan's trendiest neighborhood. In SoHo, Julia's eyes were opened to a brand-new world of updated clothes and hairstyles and a whole new breed of successful single men who mainly worked downtown on Wall Street.

In the city, most of Julia's boyfriends were older men. She liked older men because they would usually take her out a few times and buy her a few things before trying to get her into bed. One of those men was Tony Martini, who was a little on the young side for Julia, but still old enough to treat her right.

Tony eyeballed Julia on the ferry for months before finally getting the courage to ask her out. Tony was so surprised when she said yes that he responded by taking her out to the fanciest dinner she'd ever eaten. Tony would ask her out again and again, and when Julia kept saying yes, Tony would always respond with another expensive dinner or a truckload of lavish gifts. It wasn't hard for Julia to fall for Tony. She had been in a dating slump and thought she'd hit the jackpot with the richest and most generous single man remaining in the five boroughs.

Tony showed Julia an all-new cosmopolitan world that she'd never experienced in Staten Island, and best of all, he had money. All she had to do was train herself to accept Tony's weight problem and accept his hobbies of craps and strip clubs, and that's what she did. For her trouble, Julia was rewarded with a big rock on her finger and a nice little house on Staten Island.

Tony's late-night gallivanting continued to eat at Julia, but Tony's time at the illicit gambling dens and strip joints became less and less when he was constantly on his toes courting her. Julia figured Tony would outgrow his love for strippers. She was wrong.

After the wedding, Tony's interest in Julia began to wane. He stopped lavishing her with attention and started going back out to the clubs and bars, especially Beavers Showclub. Julia was not thrilled about this habit, but still accepted it as long as Tony never crossed the line. Julia wasn't the cheating kind, and she sure wouldn't tolerate being with a man who was. Tony always claimed Beavers was just good clean fun, and Julia was forced to believe him. Besides, like most wives in her situation, she tended to believe what she wanted to believe. She decided she could deal with Tony's strippers as long as he kept bringing home the bacon and frying it up in a pan.

One unfortunate side effect of Tony's penchant for gambling and strippers, however, was that it left Julia in a constant state of suspicion. The possibility Tony was messing around was never out of her mind. As a result, she kept feverishly working away at the Hair Box, building a large client base and socking away enough money to hire a good lawyer in case she ever caught Tony with another woman. She'd been working so hard for so long that before she knew it, she could afford O.J.'s defense team if she wanted to take Tony for all he was worth.

One day Julia was working her normal afternoon shift at the Hair Box, finishing up a routine haircut and blow-dry when she was interrupted by a rare phone call from Tony's office on Wall Street. It was Tony's supervisor, trying to track him down.

"Tony was AWOL from work this afternoon, and we're just trying to figure out if this is something we should worry about," Tony's supervisor told her. "You see, normally this wouldn't be a problem, Mrs. Martini, but he's missed a lot of time lately, and it's beginning to affect his job performance. We called his home number and his cell phone, but there was no answer. We were hoping you would know another way for us to contact him."

This was the phone call Julia had been dreading during all her years of marriage, and she was quick to jump to conclusions. All her fears were being realized all at once. Tony had never mentioned anything about missing work. The fact that he was hiding something like this from her led Julia to believe the worst. This could only mean one thing. Tony was sneaking around in the afternoons.

"The fat fuck is cheating on me! That fucking bastard!" Julia said through clenched teeth.

"Julia, what's wrong? You look like you're ready to kill somebody," said Julia's boss, Patty, the owner of the Hair Box Salon.

"I'll tell you what's wrong. It's Tony—he's cheating on me. I just know it. He's sneaking around. He must be having an affair. A little afternoon delight as the case may be. It's these old friends he's been hanging out with. They're a bad influence. Just wait until I get home tonight. I'm gonna cut his freakin' balls off and feed them to him if I find out he's cheating on me!" Julia ranted as she snipped the scissors in front of Patty's nose.

Julia's head was flooded with thoughts of Tony with another woman. She clutched her scissors in her hand as a look of rage came over her face. She wanted to kill Tony and reveled in thinking of all the ways she could do it. After one look in her eyes, Julia's four-thirty appointment scampered out the door without her haircut, screaming something about leaving her oven on as she ran out the door of the salon.

Julia cooled down enough to make it home back to Staten Island later that night. Still clutching the pair of shears she'd brought from the Hair Box, she waited for Tony to come home. When he arrived, she gave him an earful that he, or any of the neighbors within earshot, would not soon forget. Julia accused Tony of cheating and threatened castration. Tony kept his eyes on Julia's scissors, covered his groin with both hands, and claimed he was only out of the office in order to work on a business deal with his friends.

Tony begged for forgiveness. Julia spared his family jewels but banished him to a long night on the sofa. If he wanted back in bed, he was going to have to make a choice: his friends or his wife.

13

The nervous Dude-Men awoke to a sunny day on Saturday morning. Tony's ears were still ringing from getting chewed out by his wife, and his back was aching from sleeping on the couch. Larry had been up for much of the night, making adjustments and fine-tuning his computer equipment. Jimmy called Austin and told him he was too stressed to sleep. It was still early, and the Dude-Men needed to find a way to pass the time until first post at Santa Anita, which wasn't scheduled until four o'clock. After that, it would be another hour or so until the Pick 6 began with the fourth race on the card.

Sensing Austin was tense about something and not knowing why, but assuming it had something to do with his friends, Alana suggested that he and the guys attend her Saturday morning yoga class in Brooklyn. It would pass some time before the group planned to meet at Larry's place just before one and could also serve as a good stress reliever for the Dude-Men, who were all pretty wound up about planning a major felony later that afternoon.

Alana said her Saturday morning class was an entry-level class, which meant it was the easiest level and suitable for beginners. Austin and Jimmy considered this a good idea and had no trouble convincing Tony, who couldn't wait to get out of his house and maybe even do something to help his backache in the process. Larry said he'd done all he could to prepare his computer system for the Fix Six scam and had no problem trying something new. Even yoga.

Alana was suspicious. She promised she'd go easy on the four rather inflexible newcomers. She lied.

The small storefront yoga studio was half-filled, but the Dude-Men still stuck out like sore thumbs in a room filled mainly with thin in-shape vegetarian women. The gang took off their shoes and socks and grabbed four mats in the back. All wore T-shirts and sweatpants, except for Larry, who wore shorts which revealed way too much of his pasty white skin that clearly had not seen the light of day for quite some time. Austin and Jimmy tried to stretch and limber themselves up, while all the while pretending not to notice Tony's gnarled curly yellow toenails.

Soothing music started to fill the room as Alana asked all in attendance to be seated in a comfortable cross-legged seated position for the beginning of the hour-long session. She asked the class to clear their minds of any thoughts or concerns and let go of their stress through a series of deep breaths. "Take a deep breath and exhale out all of your thoughts, emotions, and troubles. Just try to be present in the moment, concentrating only on your breath."

While the rest of the class assumed a peaceful meditative state, the Dude-Men each tried desperately to clear their minds as they sat in the back, tightly clinching their chakras in very un-Zen-like ways. They didn't know what to be more nervous about—the enormous crime they were about to commit or the humiliation they were bound to be subject to for the next sixty minutes.

The class started with some light chanting and moved on to warm-up stretching to loosen up the neck, shoulders, and spine. Larry's neck creaked and cracked as he rotated his head around and around atop his shoulders. As the class was instructed to enter into a seated twist position, they each placed one hand on the mat in front of them and one hand on the mat behind them and twisted to the back of the room in order to, as Alana instructed, "Wring out your spine."

Suddenly Austin heard a popping noise emanating from the general direction of Larry's vertebrae. When he looked up, he noticed that Larry had not yet released the seated twisting pose along with the rest of the class.

"Austin," Larry whispered, "I think I'm stuck. I can't move. What do I do?"

"Just stay there. You're in the back corner of the room, maybe nobody will notice," Austin advised.

"Time for some sun breaths," Alana said as the class rose to its feet, with the exception of Larry.

Alana went on to lead the class through a series of bendy, twisty, stretchy postures, which were all relatively foreign concepts to Tony's overweight and out-of-shape body. Finally, on the class's eighth downward-facing dog maneuver, Tony collapsed to the mat, clutching his heart. Tony's classmates either didn't notice or didn't care as they continued to work through a series of assorted yoga poses, or *asanas*.

"Maybe your body is trying to tell you to lay off the Italian sausages?" Jimmy suggested to Tony while in the midst of a forward bend.

Tony responded by giving Jimmy the finger, losing any good karma he might have been building up for himself.

Austin and Jimmy managed to make it to the end of the class, sweating through what seemed like endless forward bends and warrior poses. They finally assumed Tony's patented flat-on-the-back pose, called *savasana*, at the end of the hour session.

"Larry, is there something wrong?" Alana finally asked. "You're not lying down."

"I can't move. My back gave out, and I've been stuck in this twisted-up position for the last hour."

"Nothing that can't be corrected. I'll come and spot you," Alana said as she walked over to Larry, put her knee into his back, grabbed his neck, and uncorkscrewed him with one swift jerking motion.

Larry's spine made a crunching noise, followed by a ripping noise that he thought sounded like someone tearing a coupon out of a newspaper. Larry fell flat to the floor in a heap and joined his classmates in a peaceful, quiet *savasana*, otherwise known as corpse pose.

*   *   *

After spending the morning rejuvenating their minds, bodies, and spirits, the Dude-Men were as ready as they'd ever be for what promised to be a hectic afternoon of horseracing, felony wire fraud, and conspiracy. They headed back to Larry's apartment to proceed with their plan to conquer the Pick 6.

The gang picked up some lunch and made it back to Larry's place in time for Saturday's first race at Santa Anita, which went off at four o'clock. The Pick 6 was scheduled to consist of races 4 through 9 on the nine-race program.

Larry had set up an online betting account with plenty of money in it in Tony's name at National Tote's Adirondack OTB outlet. Larry's first order of business was getting Tony's account logged on in order to do a small test run on Saturday's daily double. This would confirm Larry's ability to break into the computer system and make the changes necessary to successfully complete a fraudulent transaction, turning a losing bet into a winning one.

"Larry, are you sure it's safe to do a test run?" Jimmy asked. "Aren't we taking a risk by doing anything that could be detected before our real plan is in motion?"

Larry brushed off Jimmy's concern. "Are you kidding? This daily double bet will be so small and insignificant that it couldn't possibly land on anyone's radar," he said with confidence.

When the three-horse won the first race, Larry was able to hack into the National Tote database and run his sniffer program to locate Tony's bet among the thousands of others in the tote system. Once Tony's wager was found, Larry had no trouble changing the bet's losing number to the winning number three, just as Larry had promised he'd be able to do.

Larry wouldn't be able to go into the system fast enough to make a change after the second half of the daily double was completed, so Tony's wager was constructed to include all eight horses entered in Santa Anita's second race. The gang would be automatic winners of a small daily-double bet no matter which horse won the second race. The gang just had to wait for the race to be run so they could see if the money from the winning payoff was actually credited to Tony's account.

When Tony's account balance was updated to include the earnings from the winning daily double, the Dude-Men were reassured their Fix Six plan would go off without a hitch.

*   *   *

Roland Smithers brewed himself a fresh pot of coffee and broke the seal on a brand-new issue of *Penthouse* magazine as he settled in for what would be his third consecutive eighteen-hour shift monitoring for suspicious activity in National Tote's computer security control room.

When Bill Hanrahan sent a memo to Operations Chief Dick Peabody asking him for a team of his best men to monitor the company's vast database, Peabody responded by finding his employee directory and immediately dialing the number of the low man on the totem pole in the security department.

That man was Roland Smithers. And by sheer coincidence, he was one of the best men at National Tote.

Smithers was new on the job and eager to take on any assignment that could boost his stock within the National Tote organization. In the first few hours after his deployment in the control room, however, Smithers quickly realized how difficult a job it was going to be for one man to monitor every database in the system all at once for eighteen hours at a time. Smithers's request for backup was turned down by Peabody, who claimed he couldn't waste any more manpower on the project.

To remedy his hopeless situation, Smithers responded by writing a series of computer programs designed to detect any unauthorized action or access into National Tote's supposedly secure network of servers. He then hooked up his newly created detection program to a collection of flashing lights and buzzers that would loudly alert him to any impropriety as it was happening, even if he happened to be asleep at the time. Once that was taken care of, Smithers was then free to settle into a routine of reading porno mags, drinking Scotch out of a flask, making long-distance phone calls, and sleeping on the job in order to pass the time.

The control room had been dark and quiet night and day for two and a half days until just past four o'clock on Saturday afternoon. Smithers was just starting to get an eyeful of the *Penthouse* Pet of the Month when a series of loud sirens suddenly broke the silence in the room. Caught off guard, Smithers jumped up, spilling coffee all over both his and Miss March's private parts. As he set down the wet magazine, he was dazzled by half a dozen flashing red lights that lit up his control panel and indicated an outside security breach into the National Tote computer's most secure area was in progress.

Smithers was able to determine that the security breach affected the National Tote server that held and stored all incoming wagers. His best guess was that a break-in into this area most likely meant that someone was attempting to past-post their bets. He couldn't tell yet whether or not they were successful.

As instructed, Smithers made the call to Dick Peabody to inform him that the security issue he'd been assigned to was happening at that moment. Peabody, switching into corporate peon survival mode, wanted to take himself out of the line of fire as soon as possible. He immediately called Bill Hanrahan and quickly passed the problem along up the corporate ladder. Hanrahan, in turn, called Detective Bragg, who had been waiting for Lipwinkle and his gang—mainly Lipwinkle—to make the next move so he'd be able to catch them in the act.

Back at Larry's apartment, the winning daily-double payoff had been deposited in Tony's National Tote account, thereby successfully completing the gang's all-important test run.

"The money showed up! It just popped into our account. Everything worked! We should be home free," Larry gloated.

"All systems go," Jimmy said. "Okay, Larry, log back on and bet our Pick 6. This is the moment we've all been waiting for."

At the National Tote hub in Delaware, meanwhile, the scent Smithers had picked up a half hour earlier had gone cold. Smithers did have some news to report, however, as he was able to track down the source of the earlier alarm. He could see that the bet in question had been a past-posted daily double. Unfortunately, because of the small scale of the transaction, Smithers was still unable to ascertain whose account had been responsible for placing the bogus bet.

Smithers bypassed Peabody this time and passed along his information to Hanrahan, who then got on his hotline and relayed the news to Detective Bragg. "It looks like the infiltrators were involved in a very small transaction, and now whoever hacked into our system has already gotten out of there. We don't have the account that's responsible yet, but my team of best men are guaranteeing me they'll be able to get that information. Listen, Detective, I've got hackers busting in and out of my system here. I'm trusting that you're on top of the situation. I hope you don't let me down."

"Don't you see, Hanrahan? This was only some sort of test run. It's just the tip of the iceberg. I suspect they've got something big planned for later today. What could it be? What's happening today in the world of horseracing? Anything out of the ordinary?"

"Well, let me see. I did get a memo on my desk yesterday. I wish I'd actually read the damn thing. You know how it is with memos. Anyway, I think it was something about an expected spike in off-track betting handle for today due to something going on over at Santa Anita. Something having to do with a big Pick 6 or something."

"That's it, Hanrahan! Don't you see? They're gonna go for the Pick 6! I thought I told you to keep me in the loop on these things. What were you doing over there, sleeping?"

Hanrahan didn't know how to respond to Bragg's insult. Come to think of it, he had, in fact, been napping when the memo arrived.

"Anyway, it doesn't matter now," Bragg continued. "What matters is that you get back to me with the name on that account. Once I have that, I'll take it from there and nail this guy's ass to the wall."

The first leg of the Pick 6 had just been run. Larry reentered National Tote's secure betting server and changed the number on Tony's ticket from the number one to the winning number seven. This action once again lit up Smithers's control panel like a Christmas tree, setting off multiple bells, whistles, buzzers, and sirens. Smithers soiled himself and Miss March with spilled coffee for the second time in just over an hour.

After a quick and failed attempt to clean the brown stains off his crotch, Smithers was back on the phone with Hanrahan to inform him that another security breach was now in progress.

"I'll bet my left nut they're going for the Pick 6 today," Hanrahan said, trying to make himself sound smart for Smithers's benefit.

Smithers was not fooled. "A monkey could have figured out they're going for the Pick 6. What do you want me to do?"

"Our first priority is tracking down the identity of the account holder that we're looking for. The cops need it. Second, you're going to need to root around in our system and find the fraudulent Pick 6 ticket these guys have created so you can put a freeze on it. I'll call the detective and tell him where we stand. You get back to work. We don't have any time to waste."

Back at Larry's dive, the Dude-Men were anxiously waiting for the second race in the Pick 6 to be run.

Austin offered a progress report, "We had a carryover in the Pick 6 of just over $600,000. We won't know until the end of the day how much money bettors actually will bet today, but we can expect from history that it will be more than three times the amount of the carryover, or about $2 million."

The favorite had already won the first race of the Pick 6. "Damn, we need some longshots to start winning, and pronto," Austin said.

The second leg of the Pick 6 went off, and for the second time in a row, the winner was the favorite.

"Shit," Austin shouted as Larry hurriedly went back to work to add the winning number to the gang's rapidly shrinking Pick 6 ticket. "This sucks. Don't you guys see that if these favorites keep winning, then there'll be hundreds of guys out there splitting the jackpot with us, and they're not even cheating!"

Back at National Tote's headquarters in Delaware, Roland Smithers was still laboriously cross-checking the amount of that afternoon's past-posted daily-double payoff against every betting account in the system, one by one. Once he had a list of accounts with payoffs matching the bogus daily-double award, he'd need to look into each account individually until he found the one that was time stamped *after* the start of the daily double. Smithers looked up from his computer screen to see more flashing red lights. The hackers were at it again.

Larry completed the change on Tony's ticket to include the number of the winning horse of leg two of the Pick 6. The switch went off without a hitch. Larry was making the changes race by race instead of all at once in order to avoid a time crunch situation at the conclusion of the six-race sequence. The system was working well, but the Dude-Men were still hoping for some cooperation from the horses. They were now two-for-two in the Pick 6, but so was nearly everyone else—literally thousands of people.

Austin tried to keep his composure. "There are still four races left, and at least, everything is going according to plan from Larry's end of things. It's too early to panic. There's still plenty of time for some longshots to come in and knock everyone else out, just like what happened yesterday."

"This is true, Austin, but even as it stands now, those two winning favorites have virtually guaranteed that there will be some other winners today besides us. Every favorite that comes in from here on out is going to cost us tens of thousands of dollars," Jimmy said.

"We're just going to have to wait and see," Austin said. "If we won the whole jackpot, we'd be talking about over two million dollars. Even if we end up splitting this thing twenty different ways with a bunch of other guys, that's still a hundred grand for every two-dollar bet. Remember, we bet ten dollars, which means we still could be looking at something in the neighborhood of half a million at this point. That's not too bad, right?"

"Hey, I don't know about you guys, but like the sound of five hundred grand," Tony said.

"We've only got this one chance," Jimmy reminded everyone. "We have no control now. We're at the mercy of the horses."

"Guys, we'll know more in just a minute," Larry cut in. "They're getting ready to load into the gate for the third Pick 6 race."

The four friends gathered around the television and watched the race unfold. Each of the guys tried to see a horse moving from the back of the pack that would give them hope after the favorite sprung out of the gate in front and attempted to win going wire-to-wire. Enthusiasm slowly started to turn to despair, however, as it became apparent that no one was going to catch the runaway favorite.

"We're getting buried here," Austin mumbled.

Just then, in a basement in Wilmington, Delaware, 140 miles to the south of Larry's tenement, Smithers completed his printout of all accounts that were possibly guilty for the earlier daily-double transgression. He was beginning to check the individual accounts on the list to find the one with the incorrect time stamp when Hanrahan called to check on his progress.

"I haven't identified the account holder yet, but I'm getting close. I'd say it will be another half hour, tops," Smithers told Hanrahan.

"Good job, Smithers. I don't have to remind you how important it is that we find that account. We need to know the identity *before* the Pick 6 is complete so we have time to freeze that account and prevent them from getting away with any money. Then I can call the cops and let them go catch the bastards."

"Like I said, boss, I'm real close. The next time you hear from me, I'll have the name of the guilty party."

The Dude-Men were in the midst of a near-panic situation in Larry's apartment. They needed some luck and weren't afraid to bring out the heavy artillery in order to get fortune back on their side. Larry had fished around some drawers until he came back with a dusty old rabbit's foot. It wasn't dusty because it was old. It was dusty because it had been lying in Larry's drawer. The amputated appendage had supposedly brought him good luck on many other occasions, but if it really was a lucky charm, Austin figured he probably would have been using it a lot more often.

Austin rubbed a penny that he had found heads-up on the ground earlier that day. Tony, considering himself a good Catholic, except for the strippers and cheating and stuff, crossed himself repeatedly and prayed. Jimmy didn't believe in luck, so he did what he usually did and just paced around the room brimming with nervous energy.

Larry had gone into the National Tote system and made the change to Tony's ticket to reflect the correct winner of the third race of the Pick 6. The Fix Six ticket was halfway home but would clearly no longer be worth as much as the gang had hoped it would be.

Things were going badly for the Dude-Men. Unfortunately, they were about to get much worse.

14

Smithers continued to check off his list of potential suspects and turned to the next name on his list, a Mr. Tony Martini of New York, New York. Smithers saw that Martini was a new National Tote member, signing up for the first time with a deposit of a couple thousand dollars. The daily double in question was one of only a couple bets Martini had made so far, along with a big wager of half the money in his account on Saturday's Pick 6 at Santa Anita. Smithers thought this could definitely be the guy he was looking for and began checking for the time stamp on Martini's daily-double bet.

The time on the account read 4:15 p.m.—fifteen minutes after the start of the daily double. "Holy shit, I got him. I got him!" Smithers exclaimed as he rushed over to the phone to deliver the news to Hanrahan.

"Boss, I got it, I got it! I got the name—Tony Martini from New York. Our guess was right—he currently has a ticket alive in Santa Anita's Pick 6."

"Good work, Smithers. Now freeze that account while I call the police back and let them know we have our man."

Detective Bragg was in his office, waiting for the phone to ring and trying to pass the time by throwing some darts. He had fashioned a custom-made dartboard with the likeness of Larry Lipwinkle's face emblazoned on the front. Several darts already launched at the dartboard were lodged all over Larry's mouth, cheeks, and forehead. Bragg still held a number of the razor-sharp projectiles in his hand as he lined up his next shot, this time aiming for Larry's eyeball. "Gotcha! Direct hit! That will teach you to defile my daughter, you shit-eating puss-wad."

Bragg's dedicated hotline to and from the National Tote headquarters finally rang, sending the detective diving across the room for the receiver. Hanrahan read the name of the guilty account holder—Tony Martini.

"Martini? Are you sure it's not Lipwinkle? That's my man, Lipwinkle. You've got nothing on a Lipwinkle?"

"No, Detective Bragg, we're quite sure. It's a Tony Martini. Lists his address in lower Manhattan down on Wall Street. I'm guessing it's a work address."

"This has something to do with Lipwinkle. Mark my words. He's using a phony name again. Or else he's got this Martini character in on it with him. Either way, I'm going to crucify him. Torture him. Real bad."

"I'll leave that to you, Bragg. In the meantime, we're freezing Martini's account. They won't get a dime. The rest will be up to you."

*   *   *

The four Dude-Men sat in stunned silence after the fourth leg of the Pick 6 came and went with another favorite finding its way into the winner's circle. What was supposed to be the horseracing heist of the century was being foiled by a parade of favorites that ensured that the Pick 6 payoff would look much more like a hill of beans than a mountain of money.

The winner of the fourth leg of the Pick 6 ended up being the horse the Dude-Men already had on their ticket, the one-horse. That meant Larry did not need to rush back into the computer system in order to change the number. With four winners down and every single runner covered in the final two legs of the bet, the Dude-Men were now guaranteed to win. They knew, however, that the winnings would barely be enough to cover the amount of their bet.

Larry started doing the math and getting cold feet. He decided that he didn't want to risk even the smallest chance of getting caught. He was officially giving up.

"That's it, guys, I'm pulling the plug," Larry told the others.

"Whoa, whoa. Pulling the plug? We never said anything about pulling the plug. What if some nice horses win the last two races?" Jimmy asked, desperately trying to hold on to any hope.

"The payoff will be too small. It's not worth even the tiniest risk of us getting caught."

"So you're just gonna make the decision for all of us? You're in charge now, Lipwinkle?"

"I don't hear Austin and Tony arguing with me, do you?" Larry said.

Austin and Tony couldn't make eye contact with Jimmy.

"The way I see it," Larry said, "that makes it three against one. I'm pulling the plug."

Jimmy was stunned as Larry hacked back into the computer system. Instead of changing a losing number to a winning one as he'd been doing all along, this time he wanted to change a winning number into a losing number—any losing number. Jimmy's dream of making the big time was done.

Larry logged on to National Tote's secure server and accessed the file for Tony's Pick 6 ticket. This time, however, he found he was unable to delete the bet and redeposit the money into Tony's account as planned.

He tried again. No dice.

"Uh, guys. I think we've got a minor problem here," Larry said at barely above a whisper.

"What's wrong, Larry?" Austin asked.

"I'm logged on to Tony's bet, but something's wrong. I can't seem to be able to delete anything. Now I'm just trying to make some changes and it's not letting me do that, either."

Larry now had everyone's full attention. "What does that mean?" Austin asked worriedly.

"It could mean that the system is just really slow and clogged up with a lot of traffic right now. It could be a technical glitch on their end. Or, more likely, it could also mean there's some kind of a freeze on our account."

"But in order to freeze our account, they'd have to know about us first. I don't understand," Jimmy said.

"They know about us? You're saying they know about us? It's my name on the account. That means they know about *me*," Tony cried as he fell to ground, clutching his chest again just as he had in yoga class a few hours earlier. "Oh, I'm so screwed! This can't be happening! Damn bad karma!"

"Why can't you just hack through the freeze? Why is this different than hacking a secure system in the first place? I understand we'd lose the stake money, but why not delete the account and let's forget the whole thing? With no trace of the account, they'd have nothing on Tony or any of us," Austin suggested.

Larry continued to frantically hit buttons on his keyboard, to no avail. "I don't know what's happening. All I know is I'm not getting anywhere here. I'm jammed. I think we're busted. I'm still blocked from making any changes. We could be in really, really big trouble, dudes. Well, I mean Tony could be in big trouble since it's in his name," Larry amended.

Tony curled up into the fetal position on the floor and began to sob.

"Tony, don't worry, man. We're all in this together. We're not going to leave you high and dry," Jimmy said. "We've got to think. What are we gonna do?"

"Maybe I'm overreacting," Larry said. "We don't really know anything yet. Let's just watch the last two races and see what happens. Our bet's gonna be a winner, so if we see the money get deposited into Tony's account, I think we'll be okay. At this point, I'll just take whatever measly payoff we can get. I'll gladly call it a day and be happy to get away with this without going back to jail."

But the gang's worst fears were realized. At the end of the Pick 6, the Dude-Men were holding a winning ticket, but the winning sum—paltry as it was—was never deposited into Tony's account. It had to mean the account had been discovered, and all the bets and funds within it were frozen.

"Here's the situation, Tony. We got too cocky and messed up when we put your name on that account, and now there's nothing we can do to change it. I'm guessing the cops are going to be looking for you. We can't let you go home," Jimmy said.

"I don't know if I was welcome back at home anyway, but where the hell am I going to go? What are we gonna do?" Tony said, still sobbing.

Austin picked Tony up from the floor and made an attempt to calm him down. They sat on the futon and waited for Jimmy to come up with an idea. Something—anything—that could extricate Tony from the situation. Larry just sat in his chair and stared at his computer screen like zombie, wondering what went wrong.

Jimmy finally broke the silence. "Well I don't know what you guys are gonna do, but I'll tell you what I'm doing. I'm not giving up. I can't come so close and come away with nothing. I'm getting the hell out of here. You guys can call me if you decide you want in," Jimmy said, already reaching for his coat.

"Wait a minute. You're leaving?" Tony protested. "You're just gonna leave me high and dry? Whatever happened to all that we're-all-in-this-together stuff?"

"Tony, you'll be all right. Just lay low for a while. I've got some thinking to do. I'll come up with something. Just promise me you won't go home. Give this thing some time to blow over."

"Blow over? Blow over! These things just don't blow over, Jimmy! I'm fucked! Don't you see—they're never gonna forget about this, no matter how long it takes," Tony whimpered.

"We don't know that, man," Jimmy said. "Listen, the only thing we really know is that they can find your address, so you can't go home. Hey, it's not even like you mind, anyway."

"Please, you guys can't leave me," Tony pleaded. "The only reason I did any of this was to be part of the gang. That's all I cared about. I'm miserable at home. I've got plenty of money, but what I need now more than anything is friends."

Austin was moved by what Tony said. Unlike Tony, Austin did need the money, but when it came right down to it, Austin's primary motivation for getting involved with Jimmy's Fix Six scheme was his friendship.

"You're going to have to find somewhere to go, Tony. That's all I have to say—at least until I get a chance to think and come up with something," Jimmy continued.

"I can't even believe this is happening yet. I thought this whole thing was foolproof! Whatever happened to fucking foolproof?" Tony questioned.

Everyone looked at Larry.

Larry stared off into space, then turned his attention back to the group. "What? Now you're all looking at me? I don't know what the fuck happened. Why do you assume it's my fault?"

"You did use Tony's name, Larry," Austin said. "You guaranteed him it was safe."

"Listen, all I know is I can't go back to jail. I need you guys to get out of here, okay. I've got a lot of work to do. I've got to start deleting stuff from my hard drives. I've got to think about covering my tracks and saving myself."

"Now you're kicking us out? I just got done saying I've got nowhere to go. This isn't my fault. This is all Larry's fault. He screwed up, not me," Tony whined.

"Hey, don't point the finger at me, Tony. Remember, this whole thing was Jimmy's idea in the first place."

"So now it's my fault! Listen, you guys can argue about this all day, but I don't care. What's done is done," Jimmy said angrily. "I'm outta here. You dudes know where to find me."

Austin was watching the Dude-Men disintegrate right in front of his eyes.

Jimmy went to the door and slammed it behind him.

"Listen, guys, I really just want to cover my own ass right now," Larry said again. "Austin, why don't you get Tony out of here and maybe try to think of some way to help him?"

"Help him? I don't know what to do."

"Please, Austin."

"That's fine, Larry. I don't want to be here anymore anyway."

Austin grabbed Tony and led him out of Larry's apartment, down the stairs, and out onto the street. He'd have to be the one guy to stick by Tony.

"Okay, listen, Tony. You heard what they said. It won't take the cops long to connect the dots and find where you live, so you can't go home. I can't bring you home with me because Alana doesn't even know about any of this. That's a whole 'nother story I've gotta deal with. In the meantime, do you have anywhere else to go?"

"I don't know, man. Maybe I should just go home to Julia. If not, there's always Beavers, I guess."

"You can't live in a strip club, Tony. Get a grip."

"No, you don't understand. They've got a basement storage area there that doubles as a place to stay for their regulars who may get too bombed and can't be sent back home to their wives. It's a perk for top customers. If I decide I'm really not going home, I bet they'll let me stay there for a few days."

"Then what?"

"I don't know, man. I need help figuring out that part. I've got money. Lots of money. We can use my money. Just see what you can do. Talk to the other guys. I'll do whatever you say."

"I'll see what I can do. It sounds like I've only got a few days to come up with something. I'll try my best."

15

"God, I am *such* an idiot," Alana said for the hundredth time since Austin arrived home and finally came clean about what he and the boys had been up to all along.

Alana tried her best to remain relatively cool and levelheaded as Austin explained the Dude-Men's plans, from the original idea to the eventual unraveling at Larry's apartment.

"What the hell were you thinking? The racetrack scam of the century, with that bunch of idiots? Ha! Those guys couldn't even figure out which end of a horse shits and which end eats. You should have known it would never work, Austin. You should have known."

Austin felt more horrible than he'd ever felt before in his life. For the first time he could remember, he actually had something really good going, and now he was risking losing Alana because he'd let himself get wrapped up in something he never should have gotten involved with in the first place. He was in way over his head, but he still had an agenda. He still felt an obligation to help Tony.

Austin did have one idea. It was an idea that he thought could not only help Tony but also placate Alana at the same time. His idea was to get Tony out of town. The only person Austin knew out of town was his mother, who lived in Los Angeles. It was the only place he could go. He also figured heading west to California would move him a step or two closer to Mexico. He and Alana could briefly stay at his mother's house, figure out Tony's next move, and then continue onward to Todos Santos once and for all. The whole thing was a little extreme, but getting Tony out of town would buy him some valuable time while also giving Austin and Alana a couple of chances to put some much-needed cash in their pockets, either from Tony or from Austin's mom.

"On top of everything else, now you're telling me to pack up for California to see your mother while you help one of your sleazy loser friends? You're giving me some choice, Austin. It's either stay here and watch you leave without me, or pack up and leave for Mexico with absolutely no money in our pockets. That's great. Just great. I've wanted to go for so long, but not like this."

"Alana, I wish the circumstances were different. I really do. But no one knows I was involved in anything wrong yet, and I don't think the authorities ever have to find out, especially if I get out of town. We wanted to leave New York, anyway, and this is our chance to actually do it. The timing is off, and we need to hurry, but maybe it's not such a bad thing. We can get out of our lease. I have my gambling money to get us started, and you have a few bucks, too. We can take a few things with us and stick the rest of our stuff in storage. We'll be in California for just a little while until I fulfill my commitment to my friend, and then you and me will be off to Mexico. Todos Santos, here we come!"

"Austin, you know I don't want to lose you this way. Maybe I'll go, and maybe I won't. But don't think for a minute that I'm letting you off the hook this easily. If I go, it's because I want to, not because you're telling me to. I figure I've been ready to leave here for a while, and maybe now is as good a time as any."

That was what Austin was hoping Alana would say.

"If I do come with you to California, it's just a stop for me on the way to Mexico. The only decision I have to make at that point is whether or not I want you to come with me."

"Alana, I won't let you down. In the end, it'll work out for us. Besides, look on the bright side—I'm taking you home to meet my mother. Isn't that a major step in every serious relationship?" Austin asked, trying to lighten the mood a bit.

"Austin, your mom is a dominatrix. It's not like she'll be baking cookies for us when we get there."

"It's going to be great. You'll see. I promise, I'm going to make everything up to you. I'll do whatever it takes."

*   *   *

Bragg sat in his office that night and opened the files he'd received pertaining to the National Tote case. He had his suspect—Anthony Vincent Martini, thirty-four years of age, resides at 2233 Veterans Drive in Staten Island, New York. Married to a Julia Esposito Martini, thirty-one, since 2000. No kids. Employed by the Steadfast brokerage firm on Wall Street since 1993. Received promotions in 1995, 1997, and 1999. Graduated from Central New Jersey State University in 1993 with a degree in business administration. C student.

Bragg considered the time of the night and decided that his best course of action at this point would be to wait until early Sunday morning to drive out to Staten Island and apprehend Martini. That would give him time to put together a report and make the appropriate calls over to the Staten Island precinct to get a couple of uniformed badges and squad cars lined up for the bust.

But something about Martini's personal history bothered Bragg. It was something about Central New Jersey State University. He remembered seeing that school on someone else's rap sheet, but he couldn't quite place whose, or when he'd seen it. The question continued to gnaw at Bragg until he reconsidered the possible connection between Martini and the real man he was looking for—Larry Lipwinkle.

Burning the midnight oil, Bragg opened his old case files on Larry Lipwinkle. Bingo! There it was. Lipwinkle had graduated Central New Jersey State University in 1993, the same time as Martini. That had to be the connection.

Reassured now that Martini's arrest could lead him directly to Lipwinkle, Bragg quickly went to work on setting the wheels in motion for what he hoped would be a textbook early morning residential raid on Staten Island.

16

It was a cold winter morning on Staten Island. Most people in Julia Martini's neighborhood were sleeping late, and the traffic on the roads consisted mainly of semis heading off to New Jersey and garbage trucks coming and going from the nearby Fresh Kills landfill.

Bragg had assembled a team of four uniformed cops in two squad cars just around the block and out of sight from the Martini residence. The men stood around, sipping coffee and making their final plans for Tony's arrest.

Bragg put his coffee down on the hood of the car to give the final instructions. You could see his breath in the cold air when he spoke.

"This guy has no past criminal record, and my guess is that he won't be armed, so we go in cold, weapons put away. However, that doesn't mean he's not a flight risk, so I want all exits covered. There's also a wife in the house, so you want to be careful there. If we get any trouble from either Martini or his wife, or if we can't get in, you've got permission to use force. Let's make this as quick and painless as possible."

"What's this Martini guy look like?" asked one of the team members.

"I can't really say. Probably your typical fat-ass. The wife—I'm not sure about her, either. Now this Martini fella should be home, but I want everyone to be on the lookout for another guy. It's a long shot, but I want the place searched nonetheless. This guy's taller, skinny, light curly hair, glasses. A real putz. His name's Lipwinkle. If he happens to be there, it's hands-off for you guys. You leave him to me." Bragg winked. "I'll take care of him."

*　　*　　*

Julia Martini hadn't slept well for the second night in a row. She was lonely since kicking Tony out of bed, not for Tony in particular, but for some kind of male companionship in general. She was already awake and downstairs in the kitchen, cooking herself a comfort breakfast of bacon and eggs. She didn't notice the NYPD pulling up in front of the house.

Julia had just poured the milk over her cornflakes and cracked open her home-delivered copy of the Sunday *New York Post*. Amidst the war in Iraq and global fears of terrorism, the *Post's* front-page headline read *OOPS, Britney Spears does it again!*

Julia had just begun to read up on the pop diva when she heard rustling in her backyard followed by voices and a knock on her front door. She pulled her robe closed and walked to the door, expecting to find Tony holding flowers and begging to be let back in the house. She thought if she played her cards right, she could probably milk this situation for those new diamond earrings she'd been eyeing at the mall.

The expression on Julia's face was one of disappointment more than shock as she looked out the door to see three police officers instead of her groveling husband. She nudged the door open just a hair. "Yes, can I help you?"

Bragg stood on the doorstep with his badge in hand, flanked on either side by a uniformed officer. "Mrs. Martini? I'm Detective Bragg, NYPD. May we come in, ma'am? We have a warrant for the arrest of Tony Martini."

Julia flung the door open. "Police? You have a what? For the who?"

"We have a warrant for Tony Martini's arrest," Bragg reiterated as he and his backups edged past Julia into the living room. "If he's still in bed, I'd suggest you wake him up."

"Whoa, what the hell are you talking about? Tony's not even here. I kicked the lousy cheat out," Julia said, still holding her "Hairdressers do it with style" coffee mug.

"Men, go ahead and search the place for Martini. See if he's upstairs," Bragg ordered as the uniformed cops spread out and went through the house.

"I'm telling you he's not here. What's this all about, anyway?" Julia was protesting, while all along thinking to herself, *Well, well, well, what do we have here . . . this cop is one very attractive older man.*

"We need to bring your husband in for questioning. You say he's not here? Do you know where we can locate him?"

Hubba, hubba, he's not only attractive but very direct. What a hunk! He reminds me of Anderson Cooper!

"No, I don't know where he went. He wouldn't tell me—said it was a big secret," Julia replied.

"Mrs. Martini, your husband is in some trouble. If you don't tell us everything you know, it makes you an accessory to the crime."

"What crime? Listen, I don't know anything except that he called me last night and said he wasn't coming home. He said he's taking off for a while. The fat fucker cheated on me, and evidently, now he's left me, too. What else do you want to know?"

The cops returned to the doorway and confirmed that Martini was nowhere to be found in the house.

"Did he leave a telephone number? Do you have any idea where he may have been heading? Do you know of any family or friends he might want to go and see?"

What is this guy? Forty-five, fifty years old? My, my, my, oh my, is he in good shape.

"I have absolutely no idea where he could be going, and I don't even care right now," Julia said. "He told me he'd call me whenever he got where he was going. I told him to go to hell."

"I'm going to have to ask you to call us the minute you hear from him. We're also going to have to put a tap on your phone. I'm afraid I have to ask—did he happen to say if he was traveling with anyone else?"

The heck with Tony, let's talk about you and me, Officer.

"He didn't mention anything about anybody else."

"What about a guy named Lipwinkle? Larry Lipwinkle. Is this man an associate of your husband's?"

"Larry Lipwinkle? Yeah, we know a Larry Lipwinkle. He was at our wedding. A real loser. Does that four-eyed fuck have something to do with this?"

"We think so. My guess is your husband fell in with the wrong guy. This Lipwinkle is bad news. If you talk to your husband, tell him I might be willing to offer him a deal if he can lead me—I mean us—to Lipwinkle."

"What did Tony do? Why are you looking for him?"

"I'm not at liberty to discuss that, ma'am. It has to do with Lipwinkle. Try to think for a minute. Do you have any other information we may be able to use to track down your husband?"

No, but I'll give you my phone number if you'd like.

"Yeah, I'll tell you one thing's for sure. Wherever Tony goes, he'll find himself a strip club. I guarantee you that. He can't live without his go-go dancers, that horny piece of shit."

"Thanks for the lead, Mrs. Martini. It's not much, but it could help. We'll try to track him down. In the meantime, we're going to post an unmarked car outside of your house, just in case your husband returns."

Why don't you stay and wait for him yourself? I promise I'll make it worth your while.

"Thank you, Detective. Before you leave, maybe you and your men would care to stay for a quick cup of coffee? I make the best in Staten Island," Julia said as she let her robe slip open just a tad.

"Thanks for the offer, Mrs. Martini, but no, we can't stay. That will be all for today. We'll be in touch," Bragg said as he and the other cops left the house.

Julia stood in the doorway, watched Bragg go, and thought, *What a handsome man, and no wedding ring.* She needed to fan herself in order to cool down. *I've been with Tony so long I'd forgotten what a real man looks like.*

Bragg was unaware of Julia's attraction. He got in his car and drove back to Manhattan to try to explain to his boss how the prime suspect had slipped through his hands.

17

Austin was hard at work on making his California plan a reality. He knew Tony would go for any plan that could possibly save him. He also knew that if he actually got into a car and pointed it toward Mexico, there would be little chance that Alana would not be along for the ride. All he still had to do was tell Jimmy and Larry that he was leaving.

Austin tried to pick up the phone but never even got the chance to call Jimmy. Jimmy beat him to it and rang Austin's phone just one day after the collapse of the Fix Six.

Jimmy was back on his feet and already thinking about his next plan. Once he'd sniffed the big time, he could never go back. His wheels were turning.

Austin quickly threw Jimmy for a loop when he told him he'd already decided to leave New York for California.

"Jimmy, my mother lives out in Southern California. I talk to her a lot but haven't seen her in years, and Alana's never met her. Alana and I agree this is the perfect time for us to leave here. I'm gonna help Tony. We're taking him as far as California on our way to Mexico. At least I know someone out there, and it doesn't hurt that she may be able to help both Tony and me, too."

Jimmy had to think on his feet. There was a pause on the phone as Jimmy put his head in his hands and ran his fingers through his hair.

"Los Angeles, huh? All right, all right, let me think here. Your mom is there. That's good. I know I must know someone out there. Think, Jimmy, think."

"Wait a minute, Jimmy, hold it right there. This ain't about you. This is about Alana and me and the obligation I feel to Tony as his friend."

"Now that I think about it, I do know a guy out in LA. He's a good connection—a racetrack hustler type. His name's Tommy Boy. I know he'd be able to get us all set up out there. Maybe he'll even turn us onto something. New York isn't the only place with racetracks. We can run another scam somewhere else. You wouldn't have any objections to doing some business while you're out in LA, would you? Maybe you could earn yourself some traveling money for Mexico?"

Jimmy put a whole new wrinkle in Austin's way of thinking. Maybe he was giving up on the Dude-Men way too soon. If he could make Alana happy and his friends happy at the same time, then it could only be a good thing.

Austin was thinking of ways that having Jimmy in the picture could help him.

"I'll tell you one other thing you could do for me. If we all go out to LA, you could really help me by taking Tony with you in your car. That way Alana and I could make the trip alone together."

"That's no problem, man. Whatever you say, as long as you're in with me on whatever I set up out there."

"I haven't even called Tony and told him about any of this yet," Austin said. "He's holed up in a secret basement at Beavers and waiting for me to contact him. I told him I'd try to help him out of this any way I could. He said he'd go along with anything and that he'd even provide all the money."

Dollar signs were ringing in Jimmy's ears. "Why don't you let me call him and tell him the plan? After yesterday, I think he'd want to hear it from me that I'm not leaving him high and dry."

"Sure, Jimmy, but we're taking off soon. If you can help me pull this off and pull up stakes on short notice, then more power to you. It's no sweat off my back. If you want to come to California and hook us up with something, then sure, I'll certainly have to consider it."

"What's the matter, you think I'm so small-time that I can't operate on both coasts and on short notice? This is small potatoes for me. I'm gonna call Larry. I need to apologize to him for storming out of there yesterday."

"Wait a minute. You're gonna apologize to him? He's the one who screwed up. If you ask me, it's his fault Tony's in this situation in the first place."

"I know, man, but I get the feeling that whatever we end up doing in LA, we may need his computer stuff. If I say I'm sorry and take the blame, I should be able to convince him to come with us. After all, it's not like he has anything better to do. The guy has no job and no life."

Austin was relieved that things were turning out the way they were. He had written off the Dude-Men only the day before. Now it appeared things had definitely taken a turn for the better.

18

Jimmy considered himself a master fast-talker who could talk anybody into anything when he wanted to, but he never needed to put those skills into action when it came to getting Tony and Larry to go along with his agenda of getting the Dude-Men back together and moving them to California.

Larry was happy to hear that Jimmy was taking complete responsibility for the Fix Six debacle and, knowing that he was really the one to blame, was also anxious to take part in anything he could in order to make things right once again between him and his friends. Jimmy offered to help Larry pack up as much of his computer stuff as possible, as long as Larry would make himself available to leave at the earliest possible moment. With Larry having no life, this was not a problem.

Jimmy's next job was getting in touch with Tony down in his Beavers bunker. Jimmy called Carmine, the bouncer, and had his call patched through to where Tony was hiding out. He told Tony that the whole gang would stand by Tony and that they had rallied together with the common goal of helping one of their own. Then he informed Tony that the gang would be taking the fugitive to California for a while. He also informed him that they'd be needing access to as much of Tony's cash as possible in order to make the whole operation doable.

"Tony, if you haven't already, I suggest you get yourself to a bank or ATM as soon as you can in order to get as much cash as you possibly can before the cops start seizing your assets. We're gonna need as much cash as you can carry."

Tony had his money neatly stashed around in a few different accounts. Over the weekend, he was only able to hit a few ATMs for some walking-around money. His plan was to start withdrawing large amounts of cash from bank branches once they opened again on Monday.

Jimmy was satisfied that Tony could get the cash he needed. He instructed Tony to leave Beavers and come straight to his apartment as soon as he could so that he and Larry would be ready to hit the road to Los Angeles with him as soon as possible.

The only thing left he had to do was make a call to Tommy Boy—his man on the scene in Southern California.

* * *

Jimmy never knew Tommy Boy's real name—no one did—but he did know that Tommy Boy wasn't it. The names Tommy Boy and Bahama Boy, as he was sometimes called, were both shortened nicknames for a man originally known as Tommy Bahama Boy—a small-time hustler who Jimmy knew from a few years before in New York.

Tommy Boy got his name because of his affinity for the Tommy Bahama line of casual yet elegant men's clothing. In New York, and in a line of work where men favored finely tailored haberdashery and dark colors, Tommy always stood out in his colorful array of cotton, linen, and silk outfits that were inevitably comfortable, casual, and island-appropriate. Tommy felt the sportswear reflected his laid-back and relaxed attitude, and therefore would never be seen in public when he wasn't decked out in Tommy Bahama gear from head to toe.

Whenever Jimmy's bookmaking dealings took him to the racetrack, which was often, he always considered it a must to stop and see Tommy first for inside knowledge of everything that was going on around the backstretch. If a trainer was drugging his horses, Tommy knew about it. If a jockey was slowing his horses, Tommy knew about it. If a race was fixed, Tommy knew it. Tommy knew who was sleeping with whom, who was getting high, who was gay, and who was cheating on their wives. He then took that information and used it to his advantage through the delicate arts of manipulation and blackmail.

Tommy left New York in the late '90s and moved his base of operations to Florida, where he found the year-round sunshine and laid-back attitudes much more befitting of his pseudo-island lifestyle. It also didn't hurt that the Tommy Bahama label had just opened a flagship boutique store on Las Olas Boulevard in Fort Lauderdale that provided Tommy Boy the ultimate in convenient one-stop Tommy Bahama shopping.

For a couple of winters, Tommy plied his trade at South Florida's Gulfstream Park—running bets, signing IRS tickets with bogus signatures, and occasionally blackmailing jockeys and trainers.

Eventually, Tommy moved again. His first stop after Florida was Las Vegas, where two new Tommy Bahama boutiques had opened on the Strip at the Fashion Show Mall and at the Desert Passage shops at the Aladdin Hotel. Most recently, Tommy settled in Southern California after

Tommy Bahama flagship stores had popped up near every racetrack on the circuit in places like Pasadena, Manhattan Beach, and La Jolla.

Tommy Boy kept in touch with Jimmy through all his moves, and Jimmy knew that it had taken Tommy Boy less than two years to become firmly entrenched in the Southern California racing scene. Tommy now operated at all the big tracks, including Hollywood Park, Del Mar, and Santa Anita, which happened to be running the current race meet through late April. That's where Jimmy reached him on his cell phone late on Sunday afternoon.

19

For the first time since he'd bought his 2002 forest green Ford SUV, Jimmy was glad he'd opted for the SUV over a sports car. Big cars, trucks, and SUVs are a pain in the neck to own in New York due to the fact that they're nearly impossible to park on the city's cramped and overcrowded streets. Small nimble cars are usually preferred over large cars that don't fit into tiny parallel-parking spaces. Leaving town in a hurry, however, Jimmy needed as much cargo room as possible in order to accommodate his things as well as both Larry and Tony and all the possessions they could carry. The roomy but impractical New York-based SUV was finally coming in handy. Even with Austin and Alana driving out to California on their own, there was no doubt that a regular car would have been too crowded for Jimmy, Larry, and big Tony to travel cross-country in with all their stuff.

Jimmy had slept the night in his apartment and awakened at the crack of dawn to begin the chore of tying up all his loose ends in New York. He took as much money as he had and drove downtown to Larry's rathole to collect him and his stuff.

Tony spent the night at Jimmy's place and was ready to go early in the morning after helping pack up the back of Jimmy's SUV.

Tony was concerned about retrieving the money in his bank accounts before the police inevitably froze his assets. He was able to make a couple of cash ATM withdrawals for some traveling money, but what he really needed to do was visit his bank branches in person to remove his funds. He needed to get his hands on the lion's share of his cash assets, which he calculated to be in the neighborhood of $200,000.

Jimmy instructed Tony to avoid using his credit cards because they would be traceable by the police. Tony agreed to an extent but informed Jimmy that he'd still be needing to visit branches of his banks in person at some point along the way to Los Angeles in order to get to as much of his money as possible. He realized the police could possibly track his bank records, but he wasn't willing to just forget about nearly a quarter-million dollars.

Tony and Jimmy compromised. Jimmy said he'd keep an eye out for branches of Tony's banks along the way out to California as long as Tony agreed to never use his ATM card once they made it to Los Angeles.

With Tony feeling a little bit better about his finances, Jimmy, Tony, and Larry were finally ready to hit the road. Jimmy made great time through the lower Manhattan streets in Monday morning traffic. In no time, the three friends emerged from the Holland Tunnel into New Jersey to begin their three-thousand-mile journey west.

In honor of New Jersey, Jimmy cranked up Bruce Springsteen on the CD player. "Baby, we were born to run . . ." The song blared through the speakers as the three college buddies sung along and headed toward the open road for what would be a four-day extravaganza of chips, sodas, mini-mart chili dogs, and roadside motels en route to Los Angeles. The men were twelve years removed from college but still were intent on making the journey into a college road trip.

"We'll be there in four short days," Jimmy said. "I plan on calling my man Tommy Boy again from the road. That way, I'm sure he'll be waiting for us when we get there. Not only that, but if I know him like I think I know him, he'll have a scam ready and waiting for us once we get there."

*   *   *

The scene at Austin and Alana's Brooklyn apartment was very active Monday morning as the couple rushed to pack their things and hit the road. Austin decided he should leave on Monday, and Alana decided that she was coming along with him. She made him no promises, however, just in case she changed her mind. Especially in light of the new information that Jimmy and Larry were also on their way out to Los Angeles in order to meet up with them.

On one hand, Alana was happy that she and Austin could hit the road and make their trip without Tony in the car. That was the good news Austin had given her. The bad news was that, all of a sudden, the trip to California wasn't all about Austin and Alana. It was also about Austin and Jimmy and Larry trying to help Tony and themselves by getting involved with another one of Jimmy's harebrained get-rich-quick schemes.

Alana was wavering in her decision to go with Austin but finally gave in and called the DUMBO landlord and told him they'd be vacating the apartment immediately. She told him to keep the security deposit, which would more than cover anything the couple could have owed due to their hasty departure.

Austin was not very sentimental, even for a guy, which made packing up easy. He had accumulated very few things in the apartment that he considered irreplaceable. Alana was not a pack rat, either, always throwing out everything she didn't need or wasn't sentimentally attached to. The couple packed everything they could fit—mainly clothes and personal belongings—into the back of Austin's black Nissan Maxima and made their final preparations for a week on the road.

Austin and Alana hit the road a couple of hours after the rest of the gang and planned a more leisurely drive out to the coast than what Jimmy had in mind. They weren't planning on making any touristy stops or detours to see the world's largest ball of twine on Route 66 or the world's largest thermometer in the Mohave Desert. However, they did plan to make a stop or two out west on their way across the country.

Austin called his mother and told her he was on his way out to Los Angeles. After all these years, he was finally coming out to visit, and Austin's mom couldn't have been more thrilled. Austin told her he was finally making his move to Mexico with Alana. Austin's mom promised to get the house ready for the couple's arrival as soon as possible.

Austin started up the car and pulled away from DUMBO heading west on the Brooklyn-Queens Expressway. He followed the road toward the Verrazano-Narrows Bridge in the direction of Staten Island, then New Jersey, and beyond. Alana turned around, gazed out the back window of the car, and watched Brooklyn slowly get farther and farther away before finally disappearing over the horizon for the last time.

20

Lieutenant Wayne Washington was Bragg's boss at the NYPD. Bragg and Washington had known each other for quite a few years since both had worked on the violent-crime task force in their younger days before advancing to their current positions. Despite once-parallel careers, however, the two could not have been more different. Washington was ambitious and analytical, which proved to be two qualities that helped him advance to the rank of lieutenant. Bragg's violent temper, meanwhile, only served to hold him back from ever advancing beyond his current rank of detective on the force.

Bragg thought of Washington as a desk jockey and a pushover, even referring to him behind his back as "Rubber Stamp Washington."

Washington regarded Bragg as a loose cannon that he wanted out of his hair.

Fearing career suicide by osmosis, Washington endeavored nothing more than to stay out of Bragg's way as much as possible, and that's what usually he did. Bragg and Washington rarely crossed paths, and that arrangement worked well for both parties involved. Washington had very little control over Bragg anyway, and he knew it. Bragg knew it too and wanted to keep it that way. Therefore, Bragg was still willing to follow the formality of meeting with Washington whenever the men's jobs would intersect on a case. The Martini case was one of those times.

Bragg needed to find out where the NYPD stood on the Tony Martini investigation, so he scheduled a meeting with Washington to get the scoop. The fact Bragg showed interest would serve as his shot over Washington's bow to warn him that he was still involved in the case and was not ready to give it up anytime soon.

Bragg updated Washington on his detective work of the past couple of days. "Lieutenant, the suspect, Tony Martini, has left town and appears to be heading west, based on some bank transactions we've been able to track. I'm monitoring his bank accounts and credit cards and tracing any phone calls he might make back to his wife. So far, the wife's cooperating. She ain't bad looking, either. Anyway, according to my information, Martini has been withdrawing enough cash from his accounts to set himself up comfortably for a very long time. We still have the option of freezing Martini's finances, but I figured we should let him have his fun just as long as his bank transactions keep providing a money trail that we can use to track his progress west."

"Good work, Bragg," Washington said.

"The only other lead we have is that this Martini guy has a big-time stripper fetish. According to his wife, I think he's likely to turn up at one or more of the area strip clubs once he reaches his destination."

"You don't say. The wife told you that, huh?"

"Yes, sir. She also said Martini may be traveling with an accomplice, an ex-con by the name of Larry Lipwinkle."

"This case is out of our jurisdiction now, but we can still do a few things here on this end," Washington said, trying his best to appease Bragg. "Let's wait and see where his money trail ends, and then we'll get in touch with police departments in that area and alert them to look out for Martini. Then we'll send them everything we have—photos, evidence, the works. Then, when we know where he's at, we'll personally get in contact with every gentlemen's club manager in the area and make sure they get a copy of Martini's photo. I want his mug hanging from the door of every topless club in a fifty-mile radius. Wherever he turns up, we'll be able to ask the local police to lean on the area club owners a little bit to make sure they cooperate. He'll turn up eventually."

"What about the FBI? Are they getting involved?" Bragg asked.

"They're not interested yet. Remember, these were New York guys making bets on New York races at an upstate New York betting outlet. The feds need evidence that these guys have turned up in another state, or are committing a crime across state lines before they pick up the case. But it's just a matter of time until they take over. Until then, we'll do whatever we can."

"I'll tell you straightaway that I don't want to drop this case yet, Lieutenant. I want these guys bad. If it's all the same to you, I'm going to stick with this case. I want to make sure that wherever they go, the police over there don't drop the ball."

Wanting to stay out of Bragg's way as much as possible, Washington was all too pleased to allow Bragg to do the legwork on the case. "Fine. You stay with it long enough to make the handoff to the feds when the time comes. Then we're out. You're going to have to give it up and move on after that."

"Yes, sir," Bragg said as he left Washington's office, knowing damn well he wasn't going to let this case go until he knew Larry Lipwinkle was either dead or in jail.

*   *   *

Jimmy, Tony, and Larry made excellent progress in their cross-country trek after leaving New York Monday morning. They'd made it as far as St. Louis on Monday and Albuquerque, New Mexico, late on Tuesday. If they drove straight through, they could reach Los Angeles by Wednesday night.

Tony was able to take out most of his money during stops at bank branches along the way to California. Jimmy found a National Union Bank branch for Tony just outside Columbus, Ohio, on late Monday afternoon, and then stumbled upon a branch of Tony's American Trust Bank during a food stop in Amarillo on Tuesday. Those two banks accounted for the majority of Tony's funds.

Tony's third and final bank account was at Eastern America Bank, which had no branches west of Ohio. Even without his Eastern America Bank funds, however, Tony was still satisfied that he'd recovered enough of his money to last him quite some time. His walking-around money now filled two attaché cases, which were both locked securely away behind the backseat of Jimmy's SUV. Besides, Tony figured that if he needed to access his Eastern America Bank money in a pinch, he still could get to it with his ATM card. He kept the card a secret from Jimmy, who had instructed him never to use an ATM, even in an emergency.

Before setting out from Albuquerque early on Wednesday morning, the group consulted their trusty road map over a breakfast of coffee and French toast. They noticed that Las Vegas was only an hour's drive off Interstate 40.

"Hey, look," Tony said, poking his finger down onto the map. "Vegas!"

Larry awoke from a half-asleep state. "Vegas? How far?"

"It's only like half an inch on the map. Hey, we'd be driving over the Hoover Dam! We gotta stop, Jimmy. Can we go, can we go?" Tony pleaded to Jimmy.

The long drive had gotten old very quickly for the three friends, who'd already endured all the bad motels and greasy diner food they could handle. Jimmy considered Las Vegas for a minute as he sipped his black coffee. A detour to Vegas would be a welcome diversion. He could get a good meal in Vegas, he thought, and a stop at this point in the trip would afford him the opportunity he was looking for to call his Los Angeles contact and set up a meeting.

"Vegas? Yeah, I can go for a stop in Vegas. We can be there by late this afternoon, but we gotta be out of there tomorrow. Everyone cool with that?" Jimmy asked.

"Vey-gaass! Vey-gaaas! Vegas, baby, Vegas!" Tony and Larry answered like panting dogs.

"Vegas it is!" Jimmy said.

Jimmy sped through the four hundred miles between Albuquerque and Kingman, Arizona, on Interstate 40 before he eased the green SUV off the highway toward Route 93 North bound for Las Vegas.

Soon, the car was on Route 93 toward the Hoover Dam, driving down the side of a ravine formed by the Colorado River, which in that area serves as the border between Arizona and Nevada. Jimmy, Tony, and Larry gaped and gawked at the enormous dam, taking pictures like a group of tourists as they crossed the bridge over to the Nevada side of the river. From there, they'd have to drive back up the other side of the ravine, and they'd be in Vegas before they knew it.

Jimmy finally reached the Las Vegas Strip by midafternoon. He drove past Vegas's glistening world-class resorts like Mandalay Bay, Caesars Palace, and the Mirage and continued down Las Vegas Boulevard toward downtown. The green SUV whizzed toward Freemont Street as if it were caught in a tractive beam of neon lights, wedding chapels, Elvis impersonators, and hard-core gambling. Unlike the Strip, Jimmy liked that in downtown Las Vegas, you could park your car in one place and still be within easy walking distance of any number of different casinos, poker rooms, sports books, and strip joints.

Jimmy, Tony, and Larry opened the doors of the SUV, stretched their legs, and instantly scattered in three directions. Larry went in search of single-deck blackjack tables to try out his card-counting theories. Tony found a bank branch where he could withdraw more money, then predictably made a beeline for the world-famous Pink Passage Topless Cabaret, even though he knew that in late afternoon, the skank shift was still likely to be on duty.

Jimmy made a quick check of basketball odds for the NBA playoffs and the Final Four, and then searched for a quiet place where he could go to make a serious call to Tommy Boy.

Tommy Boy answered his cell phone.

"Tommy Boy, it's Jimmy. How ya doin? Whatcha up to, man?"

"Jimmy. Hey, man, it's great to hear from you. How are you doin?"

"Good. Tommy Boy, do you have a minute? I really want to firm up some plans with you."

"Listen, I really want to talk to you, but I'm doing some business right now, and you caught me at sort of a bad time."

"Business?" Jimmy asked.

"Yeah. I'm working on a blackmail job right now. I'm currently outside a barn, staking out a top trainer that I think just solicited a young

Hispanic man dressed in high heels and hot pants. It looks like there's gonna be some real fireworks in a minute. Can this wait?"

"Sounds like you got your hands full there. Yeah, it can wait, but here's the thing. I'm gonna be in town—in LA—tomorrow. I want to set up a meeting with you."

Tommy Boy was gazing through binoculars and preoccupied with the man he was watching.

"These poor foreign guys—they come to work at the racetrack, and the next thing you know, they're putting on dresses and hot pants in order to make ends meet. I tell you, it's weird stuff. Profitable for me, mind you, but weird for them."

"Tommy, did you hear a word I just said? This is important! I'm going to be in LA, and I need to set up a meeting with you ASAP!"

"Great, count me in, dude. I'll let you get here and get settled tomorrow. How about you meet me trackside at Santa Anita on Friday morning, say eight o'clock. Do you know where Clockers' Corner is at Santa Anita, down at the end of the grandstand?"

"Yeah, I know where it is. I'll be there at 8 a.m. sharp on Friday."

21

Austin and Alana were a couple of days behind the rest of the gang en route to Los Angeles. Unlike Jimmy, however, they were in no particular hurry to get there. After spending all Monday on the road, they pulled into Chicago late on Monday night and checked into a hotel in the River North section downtown where they intended to spend a day.

The calendar said the end of March, but it was still snowing in the Windy City. "I guess we haven't made it far enough west yet, huh?" Austin quipped as he and Alana changed plans and pulled out of Chicago in blizzardlike conditions on Tuesday. Austin drove down Interstate 55 until the weather finally cleared up halfway to St. Louis. It turned out to be a nice day there, so Austin allowed for a photo-op pit stop at the famous Gateway Arch on the banks of the Mississippi River. After that, it was back to the car and back on the road again, with the goal of making it as far as Kansas City by nightfall.

Alana was quiet during the ride through Missouri, doing a lot more thinking than talking. She was unsure about her decision to stay with Austin before leaving New York but started to feel better about it when she began to consider the life—or lack of one—she was leaving behind in Brooklyn. Alana had no family, and few friends outside of Austin and a couple of yoga girls she hung out with from time to time. She knew, however, that those girls were the types of casual friends that could be replaced with new ones down in Mexico, or anywhere else she ended up.

All Alana really had was Austin. She knew he wasn't perfect, but he still was better than most of the other single guys who were out there. Alana believed she still had time to mold him into exactly the kind of person she wanted to be with once she was able to take him out of the world of horseracing and betting that had stunted his growth for so long. When she thought about everything, Alana knew her problem had nothing to do with Austin. Rather, it was with his friends—the misfit band of losers that referred to themselves as the Dude-Men. Alana suspected she'd have to get Austin away from the Dude-Men as soon as possible, or else they'd never make it down to Mexico together. She decided to give the whole thing in California only a couple of weeks to run its course.

In the meantime, Alana looked forward to meeting Austin's mother—the dominatrix. Alana never knew her own mother and viewed Austin's mom as something of a curiosity based on her strange occupation. Some mom was better than no mom, so Alana decided she wasn't going to judge a book by its cover. She had always lacked a strong female influence in her life. Who was to say that that woman couldn't be a dominatrix?

Austin was blissfully unaware of Alana's concerns. Setting out from Kansas City on Wednesday morning, Austin's only worry was making it to Albuquerque by the end of the day. This would keep him only a day or two behind Jimmy and the rest of the gang and give him and Alana enough time to make a stop or two out west, if that's what they wanted.

During Wednesday morning's drive, Austin talked to Alana about his mother and the surprises she might have in store upon their arrival in Los Angeles.

"So tell me what your mom is like," Alana asked.

"She's a trip. First of all, like I've told you, I haven't seen her in fifteen years since I left for college in New Jersey with my dad. Things were strained back then, you know, because I chose my dad over her. But as the years went on, we started to talk more and more and became closer again."

"Why didn't you ever go out to California to see her?"

"Her whole sex business has always really freaked me out. She was young when she had me—just twenty-two—so that made her forty when she discovered her dominatrix fetish. She started running the business out of our apartment back then. No one wants to see their mother abusing guys while dressed in leather from head to toe. That's nasty!"

"So that puts her in her midfifties now. I can't believe she's still doing that stuff," Alana said.

"Well that's the thing, she doesn't actually participate anymore. She's more of a manager now. A madam, I guess you'd call it. Anyway, things got better between the two of us once she retired from the whips-and-chains end of the business."

"There can't be much business for an aging dominatrix pimping for other girls, is there?" Alana asked.

"Are you kidding?" Austin retorted. "It's LA! Do you have idea how many freaks there are out there? You'd be surprised. There's a huge market for what she does. Plus, it doesn't hurt that she's quite successful at it. They call her the Melrose Madam. She's got a list of clients you wouldn't even believe—executives, filmmakers, athletes, even police and politicians. She's practically running the city! You couldn't imagine how many guys there are willing to pay good money to get the shit kicked out of them by a woman wearing six-inch heels."

"I guess not. But you're right, it is a little creepy," Alana said. "It's a little too far out there for my tastes."

"Don't worry, my mom's okay. You guys will get along fine. Plus, she's rich as hell. She'll put us up at her mansion in the Hollywood Hills when we get there. She's got herself a huge house with a swimming pool, you know. Not too shabby, right?"

"Austin, I don't understand. If she's so rich, why don't you just ask her for some money? She'd help you out, wouldn't she?"

"I don't know if I can ask her for money now, not after leaving her all those years ago and never coming to visit. She'd probably help me out, but remember, I haven't seen her in fifteen years. I'd rather find out what Jimmy is up to first before I just show up at my mom's and ask her for money."

"I guess I can see where you're coming from. So where does that leave us?"

"For starters, it leaves us with a really nice place to stay in LA. Aside from that, it leaves us back at the same place we've been all along. I'm helping Tony and following Jimmy, and seeing where that takes me. That's all I can do right now."

"Jimmy, Jimmy, Jimmy. That's all you ever think about these days. As far as I'm concerned, having him in the picture is a bad idea. It was bad in New York, and it'll probably be worse in California."

"There's nothing I can do about it now. If they were driving straight through like they said they were doing, then they would almost be there by now. I wonder what those guys are up to."

*   *   *

The sun rose on a new day in Las Vegas. Jimmy had opted for gambling instead of sleep and eventually tracked down Tony and Larry at the Pink Passage Gentlemen's Club, just past five.

Jimmy ran a blockade of bouncers, paid a twenty-dollar cover charge, and headed off down the long pink neon tunnel which fittingly served as the Pink Passage's entryway. Once inside, he was greeted by a pounding bass beat that rocked his tired eardrums. A new mix of Prince's eighties hit "Erotic City" accompanied topless dancers who slid around on poles in various states of undress on three separate stages. Jimmy couldn't see Tony and Larry on his initial scan of the room and figured that, after approximately twelve hours in the club, it was probably a good bet that Tony had made his way back to the VIP room by now.

Jimmy found the VIP room at the back of the lounge. "I'm with Mr. Martini's party," Jimmy told the VIP room bouncer as he handed him a crisp twenty. "Can I go in?"

The bouncer laughed. "Are you kidding? Anything for a friend of Tony the Tent," he said as he pulled the red velvet curtain open and allowed Jimmy to step inside. "The party's just starting to wind down, but have a good time anyway."

Jimmy stepped into the dimly lit room that looked like it had been decorated by Larry Flynt or Howard Stern, or maybe both. Pink sofas shaped like lips were scattered around art deco drink tables in all four corners of the square darkened room. Posters of porn stars and centerfolds hung from the walls, and empty champagne bottles littered the floor. A mirrored disco ball dangled from the ceiling, casting little white dots of light all around as soapy bubbles spewed out into the air from a pink Day-Glo bubble machine that sat in the center of the room.

This was not a room for the faint of heart or the light of wallet. Customers who visited the VIP room needed to spend a load of money, and just in case they ran out, there was an ATM tucked discreetly in the front corner of the room. Against orders from Jimmy, Tony had visited the ATM three times during the night. Tony figured it would be his little secret. Jimmy would never need to find out.

Jimmy looked around and saw young naked girls with rolls of money in their shoes all around, but there were no signs of Tony and Larry anywhere. The only men Jimmy *did* see were a pair of half-passed-out black biker dudes, who were crashed out on a couch on the left side of the room.

Jimmy walked toward a banquette in the back corner of the room where the highest concentration of girls was gathered. He carefully started peeling away one girl after another until he finally revealed Tony and Larry lying at the bottom of the pile of strippers. Larry wore only a pair of Fruit of the Loom tighty-whities and a smile. Tony sat in a trancelike state, wearing a torn open shirt with a chartreuse garter belt wrapped around his neck. A hundred-dollar bill was stuck to his forehead. He looked surprised to see Jimmy.

"Jimmy! Hey, great to see you, man. Where ya been? The girls here were just playing their third game of Grab-the-money-off-Tony's-forehead-with-your-butt-cheeks. You wanna join in?"

"No thanks," Jimmy said. "By the way, I can see now why they call you Tony the Tent."

"Whoa, hey, sorry about that, Jimmy. The thing has a mind of its own."

"Forget about it. Do you know what time it is? It's almost sunrise, Tony. We've gotta get out of here."

"Oh come on, can't I play just one more game?"

"No, man, we've gotta go. Now."

A chorus of naked girls suddenly chimed in from behind Jimmy. "Ohhhhhhh, please, please, please, can't we play another game?"

"Sorry, girls, it's past Tony's bedtime," Jimmy said.

"Ohhhhhhh." A collective sigh from the girls.

"Get dressed, guys. We'll grab some quick grub and then we're off to La-La Land. There'll be plenty of time for strippers and sleeping some other time. We've got an appointment with Tommy Bahama Boy tomorrow morning, and I don't want to blow it."

"Okay, okay, we're leaving, we're leaving. First, I want to say good-bye to my new friends."

"All right, be quick and say good-bye to the girls."

"No, Jimmy, not the girls. I'm talking about those two guys over there—Matt and Mad Dog," Tony said, pointing to the woozy leather-clad African Americans sitting dazed in the opposite corner of the room. "Too bad they couldn't keep up with us."

"You mean those big black guys are with you?" Jimmy couldn't believe it.

"They weren't when we came in here, but they are now."

"We haven't got time for any long good-byes, man," Jimmy said. "Bring them along if you must, but we've gotta get going right now. We can't stick around here another minute."

*   *   *1

Matt and Mad Dog were members of the California Black Knights' Motorcycle Club. They were strong and extremely menacing-looking men, but really were nothing more than big teddy bears underneath all the muscles and leather clothes.

Mad Dog was not a large man, but you could tell he was tough. His head was shaved clean, drawing attention to the six or seven silver hoop earrings hanging from both ears. Tattoos covered both arms from his wrists all the way up to where his bulging biceps disappeared into the sleeves of a black T-shirt.

Matt was by far the bigger of the two men. He stood at least six foot three and weighed in at somewhere between 250 and 300 pounds. In contrast to Mad Dog's baldness, Matt was hairy. He had a dark Brillo-like afro and a fuzzy beard. Just the sight of him would be enough to frighten most people away, but Tony and Larry were not most people.

Matt and Mad Dog regained their wits and left the strip club to join the rest of the group for breakfast at an all-night diner across the street from the Pink Passage. The sign outside read Steak and Eggs Breakfast: $3.99 and Best Dam Cof ee in Las Vegas. *Damn* was misspelled, and the second *f* fell off the sign.

Blurry-eyed early morning diner patrons cowered in their booths as Matt and Mad Dog walked in and joined Jimmy, Tony, and Larry at a table for five. In an attempt to fight off oncoming sleepiness and inevitable hangovers, all five men ordered black coffees and asked the waitress to keep them filled while they perused the menu.

"So you all just met tonight, right there at the Pink Passage, huh?" Jimmy asked, trying to make small talk. "What're your names?"

"I'm Matt, and this here's Mad Dog," said the larger of the two men. Both were dressed in black from head to toe. "We pulled into town on our hogs about a week ago from LA, and we've been hanging out at the Pink Passage every night since. I've gotta say though, last night was the most fun we've had. These guys are madmen!"

Tony stood up from his chair and clasped hands with biker dude Matt, then launched into the series of handshakes, hand slaps, and high fives which comprised the California Black Knights' Motorcycle Club's secret handshake.

"Ha, ha! You see that, Jimmy?" Tony asked. "I had 'em teach me their secret handshake. It's like we're blood brothers now."

"How did you guys start talking to each other?" Jimmy asked. "It wouldn't appear that you would have that much in common with each other."

"Well, I'm a big *Star Trek* fan, and I happened to overhear Larry talking about *Star Trek* to one of the dancers," Mad Dog said. "The rest is history."

"I found another *Star Trek* fan," Larry bragged. "Who'd woulda thought?"

"Oh yeah," Mad Dog said. "It all started about five years ago when I was a security guard at Star Trek conventions back east. That's when I really started to become a fan."

"You worked at Star Trek conventions? Me too!" Larry said.

"Oh yeah, I was at a lot of 'em. Lots of weird shit used to happen at those conventions. For example, I remember this one time in Hartford, I was working security for Nichelle Nichols, you know, Uhura. She's one fine sister. Anyway, there was this skinny white guy making a pass at her, and he just wouldn't quit until I finally had to chase him out. Never did see his face, but I heard they ended up putting him in jail. I'll tell you, man, it was crazy."

"Ahem!" Larry cleared his throat and wiped perspiration from his brow. "Wow, sounds like a real loser. I never heard that story before."

"So, Matt," Jimmy started to ask, "why don't you have one of those cool biker names we're always hearing about. You know, kinda like Mad Dog here?"

"Well, the truth is, I'm new at this. I haven't earned my name yet. However, I think I'm gonna get one pretty soon. I'm sorta partial to the names T-Bone or T-Rex though, so I've been campaigning pretty hard for one of those."

"Oh yeah, I get it. So Matt is just a temporary biker name? Your real name must be Tim or Tom or Trent or Ty. Something like that, right?"

"No, my real name's Matt."

"I don't understand. If your real name's Matt, where does the name T-Rex come from? Wouldn't your name have to begin with a *T* in order to make you a T-Rex?"

Matt and Mad Dog looked at each other and then glared across the table at Jimmy, who began to sink lower into his seat.

"Hey, here's our waitress!" Jimmy called out, trying to loosen the noose he'd tightened around his own neck. "Who's ready to order?"

The five men ordered the $6.99 Hangover Buster of steak and eggs, jalapeño peppers, hash browns, a short stack of buttermilk pancakes, and large orange juice. Their plates were cleaned in minutes.

A half hour later, Jimmy was standing outside the diner, waiting for Larry to say his good-byes to Matt and Mad Dog.

"We're heading to LA to meet back up with our gang in a couple days, man," Mad Dog said. "If there's ever anything we can do for you guys out there, just let us know," Mad Dog offered Larry his California Black Knights business card. "Tony bought us so many lap dances last night that I figure we'll be indebted to him for the rest of our lives. By the way, where is the big man anyway?"

Jimmy and Larry looked at each other, then at the bikers, then back inside the diner where they spotted Tony yelling into a pay phone. "There he is," Jimmy said. "He seems to be in an argument. Looks like he's calling his wife."

22

"Detective Bragg, hello, this is Julia Martini. I'm calling to let you know that I just heard from my husband. You asked me to call you as soon as he contacted me."

"Yes, thank you, Mrs. Martini. What can you tell me?"

"Please, Detective, call me Julia."

"Okay. Julia, what can you tell me of Tony's whereabouts?"

"All I'm saying is, since I'm going to be a single woman again very soon, we may as well be on a first name basis, don't you think? What's your name?"

"It's John. John Bragg. Listen, Mrs. Martini—"

"Julia!"

"Julia, right! Sorry. Listen, Julia, I really think we should keep this conversation focused on Mr. Martini. Do you have any information—anything at all—that might help us locate your husband?"

"Well to tell the truth, he didn't say much, except that they'd almost reached their destination. Did you know that fat fuck cleaned out all our bank accounts? Every cent? What am I supposed to do?"

"Mrs. Martini. Julia. You mentioned 'they,' as in 'they'd almost reached their destination.' Does 'they' refer to Larry Lipwinkle?"

"I guess that's what he meant. I really didn't ask him about Larry."

"Thank you, Julia. You've been very helpful. I'm personally going to be pursuing this case."

"Thank you, Detective Bragg. I hope you catch the little shits. Listen, I don't know when you'll have this case all wrapped up, but in the meantime, what do you say you give me a call sometime?"

"We'll stay in touch, Julia. I still might be able to use your help."

Julia reconsidered. "Or better yet, why wait? Why don't you call me later tonight?"

"Are you asking me out, Mrs. Martini? I mean Julia."

She was asking him out. "We'll see. Just call me back later," she said.

Detective Bragg hung up the phone and sat in front of the television in his favorite brown leather recliner at his Upper West Side digs, trying to relax on a Thursday afternoon after pulling a double shift on the job. The small one-bedroom apartment was neat but sparsely decorated. A place for everything, and everything in its place. Bragg's decorating style focused on military-type organization throughout—picture Jerry Seinfeld meets Detective Andy Sipowicz.

Bragg popped open a beer and flipped up the leg rest on his recliner, but he just couldn't relax, no matter how much he tried. All he could think about was Lipwinkle. Out there. Somewhere. Out on the road, probably having the time of his life while Bragg was sitting on his ass in his living room, doing nothing but feeling miserable about himself.

Being a cop was still rewarding for Bragg, but it was no longer as satisfying as it used to be. He had ascended to the rank of detective and was looking at a pretty sweet pension a few years down the line, but what had all his years of work really gotten him? He lived in a nice apartment, but he didn't own it and could only afford it because it was rent-controlled. He got divorced ten years ago and had been married to his job ever since. Technically, he was already married to his job before the divorce too, which was the reason for the split up in the first place. Bragg didn't mind being alone at this point in his life, but he still felt lonely from time to time.

The only person Bragg really had left in his life was his daughter, Lacey. His beautiful little girl. The apple of his eye. After the whole Lipwinkle episode, however, Bragg had no choice but to do the last thing on earth he wanted to do. He sent her away to college. Not just away, but far away. Far enough to where no one recognized her so she could start over again.

Lacey had recovered from the whole sex debacle with Larry faster and better than her dad had. She was now a senior at the University of Hawaii, studying Polynesian cultures. "Not much use for that degree in New York," Bragg would always say. "She's never coming back to me, no way."

Bragg was happy that his daughter was happy, but the reality was that Lipwinkle hadn't ruined Lacey's life, he'd ruined *Bragg's* life. The whole Internet sex scandal earned Lacey a one-way, all-expenses-paid-by-Daddy ticket to paradise. She was fine, and she would always be fine. It was Bragg, however, who was sentenced to a lonely existence without his daughter around anymore, in a crappy apartment he didn't own.

At least if he were a street cop, Bragg thought, he could feel good about himself again. He missed the feel of a gun in his hand, pointed at some motherfucker who'd just held up a liquor store. He missed the sound a nightstick made as it smacked the back of someone's skull or busted someone's kneecap. He missed action. Real action.

Sure, he could still lock up the bad guys, but he couldn't hurt them anymore, really make them pay. The perfect example of that frustration was Lipwinkle. Sure, he'd nailed him for credit card fraud, but where had that gotten him? Lipwinkle was out in no time, committing other, far worse, crimes. Crimes like taking advantage of a young girl for his own perverted thrills. Where was the justice? Where was the retribution? Even if the police caught Lipwinkle for the racetrack scam, so what? He'd probably serve a few years as a second-time offender, but then he'd be free again. For Bragg, that just wasn't good enough anymore. A sick bastard like Lipwinkle shouldn't be allowed back on the street. A sicko like that shouldn't even be allowed to breathe. Someone had to do away with this guy once and for all, and that someone had to be none other than Detective John Bragg.

Bragg hadn't taken a day off in a long time and figured he must've had a shitload of time off coming to him. Between vacation time, sick days, holidays, personal days, and overtime, Bragg calculated he had built up over a month of comp time at work. More than enough time to go find Martini, and thus Lipwinkle, and do away with him on his own. Outside the law.

Bragg walked to his bedroom and looked at himself in the mirror above his dresser. "What's to keep me from taking a paid leave and hunting down Lipwinkle myself?" Bragg asked his reflection. "I have the same information to go on that the cops out there have, except I can devote more time to it than they can. I know he's traveling with Tony Martini, and Martini is a sure thing to end up at some strip club wherever he goes. If I find Martini, then I find Lipwinkle. What will take the local police months shouldn't take me much more than a couple weeks. Why leave it in someone else's hands when I can do it myself?"

Bragg went to his closet and found his suitcase. He wanted to be ready to roll at a moment's notice once he had information on Tony Martini's final destination. He'd still have to clear some vacation time with Lieutenant Washington before he'd be allowed to leave, but his decision to take off and hunt Lipwinkle down himself was already made. In the meantime, he thought of taking out Julia Martini, even though he was concerned far less about a possible date with Mrs. Martini than he was about his impending date with destiny with Larry Lipwinkle.

23

Tommy Bahama Boy held a cup of coffee in one hand and a stopwatch in the other as he leaned against the railing and watched racehorses go through their morning workouts at the Santa Anita racetrack early Friday. To his right, Santa Anita's stately grandstand stretched a full quarter mile into the distance adjacent to the track's homestretch. To his left was Santa Anita's sprawling stable area, which was as big as a small town, consisting of dirt roads and scores of barns that were home to more than a thousand Thoroughbreds. Horses breezed past Tommy who looked out onto the track and beyond as the Southern California sun shined brightly against the face of the majestic San Gabriel Mountains, forming a stunning and dramatic backdrop to one of the world's prettiest racetracks.

Tommy Boy arrived early that morning, in anticipation of his meeting with his old friend Jimmy Holliday and his two colleagues at eight sharp. The designated meeting place was a horsemen's hangout called Clockers' Corner, which sat at the end of Santa Anita's immense grandstand. Clockers' Corner was where trainers, owners, and handicappers gathered each morning to view their horses' daily training while also socializing and sizing up the competition. For Tommy Boy, it was also the best place to go to learn the latest gossip and gather some inside information that could be used for a betting edge on the public. This was Tommy's world, and he was a fixture in it every morning for the workouts and every afternoon for the races.

Jimmy, Tony, and Larry arrived in the Los Angeles area from Las Vegas on Thursday morning and checked into a motel virtually around the corner from the racetrack, in the town of Arcadia. After a meal, a shower, and twelve hours of sleep, the gang woke up early Friday and was as ready as they'd ever be to meet with Tommy Boy. Jimmy's SUV pulled into the parking lot directly behind Clockers' Corner as Tony and Larry gawked out the passenger-side windows to get their first look at Santa Anita's green and yellow facade.

Jimmy walked up to Clockers' Corner with Tony and Larry trailing close behind. He scanned the outdoor tables and chairs in search of his old friend. In a crowd of casually dressed horsemen who favored jeans and barn clothes, Jimmy figured a typically colorful Tommy Boy outfit would make him visible in the crowd. He was right. Jimmy instantly noticed Tommy standing along the rail despite the fact his back was to him and he hadn't seen him in years.

Tommy Boy turned to reveal the full grandeur of his outfit. He looked as if he'd just stepped off the runway at a Tommy Bahama menswear fashion show. He wore an orange-peel-colored Vintage Viva camp shirt loosely draped over a coconut white South Seas crew neck tee. The T-shirt was tucked into olive green Havana Palms pants from the Tommy Bahama Island Soft collection. Tommy accessorized with a silver Island Heirloom watch, King Fish brown lace sneakers, and a pair of chocolate-colored San Juan sunglasses.

Tommy's sharp clothes were well complemented by sharp looks. He stood six foot with an athletic build. He was Jimmy's age but looked younger, thanks to a dark tan and wavy sandy blond hair. Larry thought he resembled the Marlboro Man—if the Marlboro Man had gone berserk and traded in his cigarettes, blue jeans, and boots for a pair of sunglasses, some freshly pressed green silk slacks, and a pair of loafers with no socks.

Jimmy called out, "Tommy Boy, over here. It's Jimmy. How you doing, man?"

Hugs were exchanged. "It's great to see you! You look great," Tommy said. "Aren't you gonna introduce me to your friends?"

Tommy Boy passed handshakes all around as Jimmy introduced Larry and Tony. Tommy then led the group away from the other people who were hanging around and sat at a square table under an umbrella, out of earshot from a few nosey onlookers who were curious to know who the new faces were.

"We should be able to talk here with no interference. So what brings you to my neck of the woods, Jimmy? Swimming pools, movie stars—"

"The truth is that we got ourselves in some trouble back in New York, and we needed a change of scenery, if you get my drift. My old college buddies and I have recently gone into business together. It's Larry and Tony and me along with our friend Austin, who you'll meet later. Anyway, to make a long story short, we got a good group of guys here, but we haven't grossed one red cent yet. I was hoping that maybe you could turn us onto something out here and let us take it from there. You help us, and we'll help you."

"Well, Jimmy, I'd say you fellas came to the right place. I pretty much do it all here. You want to drug a horse? I'm your man.

"You want to fix a race? Talk to me.

"Bribery? Blackmail? Money laundering? I'll set you up.

"Just tell me what it is you're looking for. It's not just racetrack stuff, either. I deal in everything. Arson, identity theft, you name it. How 'bout women? I've got a few bitches, or as I like to say 'be-yatches,' in my stable. You just say the word. I also sell ecstasy, eight balls, uppers, downers, and little tootseroosky. For you laypeople, tootseroosky, that's cocaine."

"No, no, Tommy, we're talking strictly racetrack stuff here, you know, some kind of a scam."

"I've got dime bags! Who needs a dime bag?"

Tony and Larry shifted uncomfortably in their seats and exchanged looks with Jimmy. Tony leaned over to Jimmy's ear, "This guy is obviously a low-life scumbag, Jimmy. A well-dressed scumbag, but still a scumbag. I say we should bag this whole idea and get out of here, man."

Jimmy held up his open hands to Tony as if to say "whoa, big fella," then turned his attention back to Tommy Boy. "No, man. Look, no dime bags, okay. No arson, no identity theft, none of that. We're here to talk business. The reason we're here is to make some money. Between my friends and me, we have all the tools for a great scam. We need you to turn us onto the right people and get us started in the right direction. If I remember correctly, you like to work alone. And you're never one to take on partners, particularly out of towners. That's why we're prepared to offer you a finder's fee for whatever you help us with. What do you say, man? What can you do for us?"

"Like I said, Jimmy, you came to the right place. I'm prepared to do anything to help out an old friend, but no finder's fee, okay?"

"No fee? But I couldn't do that to you, Tommy Boy. You know I always take care of your interests."

"No, what I meant by no fee was that I want a percentage. Cut me in for 25 percent, guys, and you can count me in. Do we have a deal?"

"There's five of us, including you. You're forgetting my friend Austin. We'll cut you in for one fifth. That's 20 percent. What do you say?"

"I'd say you got yourself Tommy Boy, at your service," Tommy said as he shook hands with the whole group.

"So, Tommy Boy, what do you got in mind for us? Anything good?"

"Just so happens you are in luck. Listen, there's been a lot of trouble around here lately with horses turning up lame. Really suspicious stuff. The investigation has been focused on a few trainers so far, but my sources tell me that the real culprit is a veterinarian named Marcus Bellvue. They say he's a real twisted bastard who decided he'd get back at a few trainers who fired him by harming some of their horses. Anyway, I tailed the guy for a couple days, and sure enough, I got him on film injecting a horse with some illegal shit that later turned up in the horse's positive drug test. I've got this guy dead to rights. I was gonna milk some hush money out of him for a while and then turn him in anyway, but since you're here, why don't we pay him a visit and find out if you guys can work out something better? Maybe we can get the inside scoop on what he's up to. Make some bets. It's worth a shot, right?"

"You've done good, Tommy Boy. Real good," Jimmy said. "Tell you what—you're on. Just give my friend Austin a few days to get here, and we'll go pay this Bellvue guy a visit he won't soon forget."

24

Austin and Alana drove all day Thursday after spending the night in Albuquerque, but they were still in no particular hurry to rendezvous with Jimmy and the rest of the Dude-Men. Instead of taking Jimmy, Tony, and Larry's detour through Las Vegas and continuing west toward Los Angeles, Austin and Alana decided to drive south. Their plan was to whet their appetites for Mexico by visiting the town of Rocky Point, located on the shore of the Sea of Cortez, just south of Arizona, in the Mexican state of Sonora.

They drove south through New Mexico on Interstate 25 and headed for Tucson where they could go out for a dinner of Mexican food and then get a good night's sleep. From Tucson, they could then make the short drive into Mexico as a final pit stop on their way out to the West Coast.

Austin and Alana pulled into Tucson by nightfall on Thursday and dined on chiles rellenos and shredded steak chimichangas at the Mi Nidito Mexican restaurant in South Tucson. They set a timetable to arrive in Los Angeles by late Sunday, which left them enough time to spend the night and the following morning in Tucson before driving to Mexico for forty-eight glorious hours at Rocky Point.

They toyed with the idea of driving across the border on Friday afternoon and not ever looking back, but a quick reassessment of their funds brought them back to reality and reminded them why they were going to California in the first place.

Friday morning, Austin and Alana did some legwork to find out what was required of them in order to bring a car into Mexico. They were pleasantly surprised to find that no formal arrangements were necessary to drive to the Mexican states of Sonora, Baja Norte, and Baja Sur, which were the only states relevant to their upcoming travels, both on this trip and on their future drive to Todos Santos. Those states were all part of the U.S.-Mexico Free Trade Zone, meaning that all Austin and Alana needed to do was secure Mexican auto insurance at the border, and they were set.

With that taken care of, Austin and Alana had time for a casual but leisurely lunch. In Tucson, they drove to a Mexican food stand named

Gorilla, a place best known for selling what's called a Sonoran hot dog. The decadent hot dog *el estilo Sonora* consists of a bacon-wrapped weenie stuffed into a fresh-made *botillo*, or soft bun, and then loaded with beans, salsa, lettuce, tomato, hot peppers, mustard, and mayo. Austin and Alana ordered theirs to go and drove up to the Gates Pass scenic outlook in Tucson Mountain Park. There they enjoyed their sandwiches along with a panoramic view of Tucson in one direction and the Tucson Mountain Range and surrounding Sonoran desert in the other.

After lunch, Austin and Alana said *hasta luego* to Tucson. They drove down a desert back road until they hooked up with Arizona Highway 86 and drove west before crossing the border at Sonoyta, Mexico. It was a desolate drive. There was nothing but mountains and cacti in the distance as far as the eye could see, with only a couple of very small towns along the way. The only things growing there—aside from the cacti—were a few small patches of colorful desert wildflowers, which sporadically straggled along the sides of the road.

From the border town of Sonoyta, it was exactly an hour's drive to Rocky Point—or Puerto Peñasco, as it is officially known—on the south side of the border.

Austin and Alana arrived in Puerto Peñasco late in the afternoon. When they got there, they found it was a small city of about fifty thousand residents, located right on the Sea of Cortez and surrounded in all other directions by barren desert. It was the only place they knew of within driving distance that they could go to be reminded—even remotely—of Todos Santos. Puerto Peñasco was a far cry from Todos Santos, but it was the best Austin and Alana could do at the time, and that was good enough.

For many years, Puerto Peñasco was primarily known as a spring break destination for Arizona college students. Unlike Todos Santos, which had still eluded major American development, however, Puerto Peñasco had not been so lucky in recent years. The rest of America finally started discovering Puerto Peñasco in the 1990s. The gringos quickly bought up the entire coastline and turned the area's pristine public beachfront into private gated communities. As Austin and Alana drove into town, they noticed that less than half of the roads in town were paved. Dusty dirt roads prevailed in every direction except for the areas of the city frequented by Americans.

As Puerto Peñasco grew, so did the hotels along its shoreline. Areas that once had only small quiet casitas were now covered with affordably priced resorts, some reaching as high as ten stories into the sky. Using the tall beachfront hotels as their guide, Austin and Alana headed for the shore where they planned to spend two nights soaking in as much

Mexican flavor as they could. They considered staying at one of the resorts, but Austin and Alana thought they were there for the tourists, not for soon-to-be Mexican residents like them. Therefore, they opted to bypass the big hotels and follow the old local spring break tradition of renting a tent on the beach and staying down by the water where they could look up at the stars and hear the sound of the waves.

*   *   *

Austin and Alana settled in on the sand and enjoyed a stroll on the beach. They walked toward the west and watched as the sun set over the water. After a winter in New York, the hot air and sunshine felt good upon their skin. Late March, temperatures usually reached the mid-eighties in Puerto Peñasco. That was nearly the same temperature year-round in Todos Santos.

Austin and Alana mulled their dining and entertainment options on the walk back to the tent as a cool evening breeze took the place of the heat and day turned into night. The two hadn't eaten a bite since Tucson and were eager to go out that night and see the town. Some fellow visitors recommended a place for dinner and told them not to miss out on a trip to Micky's—a local watering hole that also sold Mexican handcrafts in the heart of downtown.

Micky's was best known for serving legendary tequila punch. Their version was a lethal orange-colored blend of tequila and fruit juices that came in a large clay jar and was often served by Micky himself. The potent, icy concoction was as delicious as it was dangerous, which Austin and Alana quickly found out. The other thing they quickly found out about was Micky's unique brand of hospitality, which becomes funnier and funnier as customers get drunker and drunker. Micky would greet his lady visitors with a kiss on the hand and then serenade them in Spanish in a deep baritone voice whenever they ordered another round. Men received a much less formal hola followed by a punch in the fist and a titty twister. After just one of Micky's tequila punches, however, visitors usually didn't mind how good or bad Micky sang, or where Micky punched or pinched them. After two drinks, they'd never remember it anyway.

Austin and Alana stumbled back to their tent on the beach. The couple lay on their backs for a while, looking up at a sky filled with a million stars. Austin fell asleep, but Alana stayed awake and thought about how much she wanted this to be her life. The sun and the moon and the stars and the beach and the water were what she really wanted. Maybe even more than she wanted Austin. She dreamed all night about

Todos Santos. She couldn't wait to get there. Her goal was still one thousand miles to the south and on the other side of the Sea of Cortez, but Alana had never felt closer to her utopia than she did that night under the stars on the beach in Rocky Point.

The whole night was something of an epiphany for Alana, and suddenly, she knew for sure that Mexico would be her salvation. Maybe it was the melancholy influence of all the drinks, but she also began to at least tentatively and halfheartedly forgive Austin for all the trouble and let him do what he needed to do with Jimmy as long as the end result was and always would be Mexico.

The next day, Austin and Alana enjoyed themselves more than they had in a long time. For a day, it felt good to be a world away from where they came from or where they were going. Austin and Alana drank beer, lounged in the hot sun on the beach for a couple of hours, and then took a break from the heat by ducking into a beachfront bar and eating lunch on a cool covered patio. Austin drank margaritas and polished off his seventh drink of the day. It was only three-thirty.

"Make me a deal," Austin joked, beginning to feel good from the alcohol. "If I die tomorrow, I want you to drive me back to New York and bury me at the top of the homestretch at Belmont Park because that's where most of the horses I bet died."

Alana was laughing but not going along with it. "Come on, Austin, you're not going to die. Besides, I still need you to get us enough money to get started in Todos Santos. After that, maybe I'll consider killing you myself."

Austin and Alana stuck around for a while and then joined the bar's sunset happy hour celebration outside on a large waterside deck. They knew they had to wake up early and drive the next morning, so they turned in early that night. It was important for them to get a good night's sleep. They both knew they'd be meeting Austin's mother the following evening in Los Angeles.

*   *   *

The Dude-Men shifted into tourist mode to pass the time while they waited for Austin to arrive in Los Angeles. During the day, Jimmy, Tony, and Larry saw all the sights in Hollywood, from Grauman's Chinese Theater to the Hollywood Walk of Fame to the Hollywood Bowl. They even spent a day taking the tour at the Universal Studios theme park. At night, Jimmy took Larry out to Hollywood hangouts like the Formosa Café, the Derby, and the Dresden lounge. Jimmy particularly enjoyed the Dresden, where they spent an hour or so each night marveling at the lounge act of Marty and Elayne and drinking the house's specialty—Blood Sand Margaritas—from the comfort of a red banquette. After Marty and Elayne wrapped up their set with a rousing rendition of the Bee Gees' "Stayin' Alive," complete with a five-minute electric organ solo, Jimmy and Larry finally ended their evenings with late-night meals of pancakes, omelets, and coffee at the 101 Café on Franklin Avenue.

Tony was not a part of Jimmy and Larry's Hollywood nightlife tours. He had more important business to attend to. He needed to begin his hard-target search of the local gentlemen's clubs until he finally found the one most to his liking. After sightseeing in Hollywood, Tony surmised that the highest concentration of adult entertainment was located in that area. There were many more-convenient clubs located closer to where he was staying in Arcadia, but Tony decided that if he wanted the best of the best, a bit of a car ride over to Hollywood from Arcadia was a small price to pay.

In Hollywood, Tony looked at big clubs, little clubs, clean clubs, dirty clubs, cheap clubs, expensive clubs, new clubs, and old clubs. He was intent on finding just the right place.

In order to make what he thought was an educated decision, Tony felt he had to sample everything a club had to offer on every visit, including the club's VIP rooms. The problem was that the VIP rooms always turned out to be more expensive than he originally budgeted. Running out of money would always leave Tony with a lot of hairy decisions to make. For instance, he could either leave and go home or he could hit an ATM and buy himself an extra hour or two of fun. Tony knew that he was absolutely forbidden to go near an ATM, but what could the harm be if he took out just a few bucks here and there? Did Jimmy really expect him to get up and leave a strip club when his tent was fully popped? Tony decided that whatever Jimmy didn't know wouldn't hurt him. He narrowed down his search to three establishments, including the Seventh Veil, Cheetahs, and the Love Tunnel and eventually settled on the Love Tunnel, based on its casual ambiance, welcoming atmosphere, and two-for-one table dances. The dozens of girls with huge racks stuffed into dental floss-thin bikini tops didn't hurt, either.

The girls at the Seventh Veil and Cheetahs were nice, but Tony thought the Love Tunnel girls were even better. He liked the rough stuff, and the staff at the Love Tunnel seemed amenable to slapping him around for a few extra bucks and going the extra mile for their customer.

Tony decided he'd keep going to the Seventh Veil and Cheetahs occasionally, but he was sold on the Love Tunnel. He proudly proclaimed it his new home away from home on the West Coast.

25

On Sunday morning, Austin and Alana feasted on huevos rancheros with homemade tortillas and a pitcher of hangover-busting freshly squeezed orange juice. They drove out of Puerto Peñasco and picked up Mexico Highway 2 back at Sonoyta for a drive through the desert on the Mexican side of the border. After two hundred miles of rocky desert vistas filled with saguaro cacti as far as the eye could see, the couple finally reached the Baja Norte capital of Mexicali. There they crossed back over into the United States at Calexico, California, just south of Interstate 8. From there, Austin followed Route 86 to Indio while Alana dozed off in the passenger seat. Austin then picked up Interstate 10, which turned into the San Bernardino Freeway and took him directly into the LA metroplex.

Alana awakened from her nap when Austin exited the San Bernardino Freeway onto the Hollywood Freeway. She stared out the window as Austin went a few miles up the Hollywood Freeway toward the Hollywood Hills.

Austin pulled his Maxima off the Hollywood Freeway at Highland and then turned onto Franklin to drive through Hollywood parallel to the base of the Hollywood Hills. Austin found the street he was looking for—Outlook Drive—and turned right to go up the hill.

Austin wound his way up and up the Hollywood Hills before finally finding his mother's street. Her estate was in a section of older homes in a secluded and affluent area. Austin pulled into his mother's well-lit driveway. He was surprised to see it was already filled with cars.

The driveway snaked up to a split-level art deco-style house surrounded by thick shrubbery. A narrow leafy footpath off to the right led to five stairs and opened into what appeared to be an immense pool and deck. Light from the city down below glowed in the distance.

Austin and Alana got out of the car and stretched their legs. They heard low music coming from out near the pool.

"We finally made it. What a long, strange trip it's been!" Austin said.

"By the looks of this place and the sound of that music, I'd say it's gonna start getting even stranger in a minute. Are you sure your mother's expecting us tonight?" Alana asked as she started up the walk toward the front door.

"I'm sure of it. Maybe she's hosting a party in our honor."

"What if this is no party? Maybe this is just what it's like here every night."

Austin rang the doorbell and tried the knob, only to find it unlocked. He and Alana stepped in the doorway. Austin stuck his neck inside and called out, "Mother, I'm home!"

*　　*　　*

From the outside, Tiffany Jackman's house looked like any other on her block. It was a large two-story home on a dead-end street with a giant pool and a great view of the city down the hill. There were two other houses on the short block. Tiffany's neighbors were a bond trader and his wife and young daughter on one side, and an old Hollywood actor best known for playing one of the members of the Lollypop Guild in *The Wizard of Oz* on the other. Next to Madam Tiffany, however, the Lollypop Guild guy was only the second strangest resident on the block.

Madam Tiffany ran to the front door when she heard Austin's voice and threw her arms around her long-lost son. Austin introduced Alana to Tiffany, who took an instant liking to her. Alana was officially the first girl Austin had ever brought home to mom.

After the welcoming, Madam Tiffany gave Austin and Alana a tour of her spacious house, which served as both her home and place of business. Madam Tiffany's first floor looked just like an average house. A white tile entryway led straight into a large L-shaped living room, which was ordinary looking except for an overabundance of sofas, loveseats, and chairs. When the house was full, Tiffany used this room to host cocktail parties and meet and greet clients upon their arrival. When the house was empty, Tiffany used the living room as a place to put her feet up and watch TV in her jammies. To the left of the living room was a modern kitchen and separate formal dining area. Tiffany used this area to entertain and welcome special guests of hers. To the right, the living room angled around to a pair of large sliding glass doors that opened to a pool deck with an elevated view of the city.

All things considered, the place seemed normal enough once you got used to the handcuffed and shirtless middle-aged men milling around at the behest of beautiful black-haired women in leather bikinis and thigh-high boots.

Upstairs was where things really got weird at Madam Tiffany's. "Now it's time to see what Mommy does for a living," Tiffany said to Austin as she gave him and Alana a look inside some of her bedrooms. With the exception of Madam Tiffany's master bedroom, the other bedrooms had all been converted into bondage chambers, complete with chains, whips, straps, and everything else a dominatrix might need to discipline one of her very, very bad customers. One room came complete with a custom-made spinning leather bondage wheel, while another featured a trapezelike swing hanging from the ceiling. Austin blushed, and Alana tried to hold back laughter at the sight of the room.

Austin and Alana's arrival into town happened to coincide with Madam Tiffany's weekly customer appreciation pool party, hosted by Tiffany and six or seven of her most popular dominatrices every Sunday night. Therefore, mother and son had only a few emotional moments to savor their reunion after fifteen years apart before Tiffany had to return to her guests. She showed Austin and Alana to a bondage room she had cleared out and fashioned into a guest bedroom for them to use for as long as they stayed. It had a window and its own bathroom and was more or less a comfortable place to stay once you learned to ignore the mirrored ceiling and the leather straps that were still attached to all four corners of the bed.

Tiffany wished Austin and Alana good night and invited them to breakfast the next morning where they could all get better acquainted.

26

"Can I bring you a fresh-squeezed juice?" asked a waiter wearing a rhinestone-studded codpiece.

"No thanks, I'm fine," answered Alana.

Austin and Alana slept well on their first night in Los Angeles after a long day of driving and an eye-opening view of some interesting alternative lifestyles during their first night at Madam Tiffany's. When they came down for breakfast the next morning, they were surprised to find Madam Tiffany waiting for them at a formal table presided over by a staff of helpers.

Waiters descended upon them as soon as they took their seats at the dining table. The waiters unfolded neatly pressed napkins and placed them on Austin and Alana's laps.

Alana took a good look around and instantly began to notice the fruits of Madam Tiffany's success were everywhere.

"So you can see that business is doing quite well," Tiffany said as she sipped her favorite rare imported tea from a Limoges teacup of fine bone china.

Alana couldn't help but ask the obvious question as she was served an oven-fresh croissant, personally prepared by Tiffany's live-in chef. "If you don't mind me asking, Ms. Jackman, how are you able to operate something like this right out of your house? Don't the police know about this place?"

"The police? Who do you think most of my best customers are? Half the guys here last night were cops." Madam Tiffany laughed as she broke open a scone and topped it with heavy cream and Duerr's Traditional Strawberry Preserves, shipped in from England. "I guess you can say we have an understanding with the local police. They keep quiet about my operation, and I protect their dirty little secrets. It's quite funny actually. I give them freebies. They think they control me when in reality, I control them. I have more power over the police force than the commissioner, who, by the way, happens to be a great guy and one of my best customers."

Austin finished a plate of eggs Benedict and dabbed some free-range, farm-fed chicken's stray egg yolk from the corner of his mouth with a hand-sewn lace napkin imported from the remote Caribbean island of Saba. A tuxedoed waiter quickly descended to whisk away the empty plate. Austin was startled to notice that the otherwise formally attired gentleman had on a rhinestone-studded codpiece over the crotch of his trousers.

"Madam Tiffany, I mean, Mom, I don't want to lie to you. We're out here in California to meet up with some friends of mine from New York. We got involved in some trouble back home, and it's possible that the cops might be looking for my friend Tony. If they find him, they could eventually come looking for me too."

"What kind of trouble are we talking about here, Austin?" Tiffany asked as the codpiece-wearing waiter offered her a hot towel out of a Lalique French crystal serving tray.

"I really don't want to get into it, if that's okay with you, Mom. Let's just say it's the kind of trouble where nobody got hurt. Anyway, we'll be here for just a few weeks, maybe a month—just until I can sew up some business I need to take care of. While I'm busy with that, Alana was hoping she could spend a lot of time around here relaxing by the pool."

"That would be delightful, darling," Madam Tiffany said to Alana. "I have a lot of time off during the day, so we'll be able to spend some quality time together."

"That's great," Austin said. "I hope we're not asking too much. You're really doing us a favor by letting us stay here. I know you're busy, but I promise we won't get in your way or cause you any trouble."

"Austin honey, it's no trouble. It's my pleasure to have you here. Not only that, I'll even do you one better: If you tell me who your friend Tony is and why the cops are looking for him, I promise to help make the whole thing go away. No questions asked."

"You can do that? Just make it go away, just like that?" Alana asked as her glass of freshly squeezed orange juice was refilled from the Waterford crystal carafe by a waitress wearing a French maid outfit with circles cut out of the front where her bra was supposed to be.

"Well nothing happens just like that, dear. We may need to perform a few more nipple clampings and maybe dole out a few extra spankings for the next few months—you know, stuff like that. Nothing is free, but you can be assured that if I want the cops to forget about something, they'll forget about it."

"I really can't say how much this means to me. Thank you, Mom."

"Don't thank me, dear. I figure that beating the shit out of a few perverts is the least I can do for my beloved son, who I've missed so much all these years. Now, enough of all this shoptalk. Who wants more fresh Kona coffee? It just arrived from Hawaii this morning!"

* * *

Austin contacted Jimmy after breakfast, checking in with the rest of the group for the first time since he'd arrived in Los Angeles. The Dude-Men's meeting with Tommy Boy at Santa Anita racetrack had been three days earlier, and Jimmy was starting to worry that he was never going to see or hear from Austin again. He was relieved that Austin was still part of the gang.

On the telephone, Jimmy told Austin that the other Dude-Men had met with Tommy Boy and already had a plan in the works involving blackmailing a shady veterinarian named Marcus Bellvue. Jimmy told Austin all about Tommy Boy and said he believed Bellvue could be coerced into providing them with valuable information they could use for their next betting scam.

"Now that you're here, we can set up a meeting with Bellvue," Jimmy said. "Then I'll let you decide what is the best way for us to use the information we get so we can turn it around and make a score."

"Just let me know when the meeting is, and I'll be there," Austin said. "Blackmail really isn't my department, but I'm sure I can help you figure out what to do with any inside information you get."

"Good. I'm glad you're coming," Jimmy said. "I must admit I was beginning to worry you weren't gonna join us here in California."

"I wouldn't stiff you guys, Jimmy, and I really appreciate you moving so fast on this new gig. As far as I'm concerned, it's the sooner the better. I just want to get this done fast and get out of here."

"I'm surprised to hear you say that, considering your friend Tony is still in a heap of trouble with the cops back in New York. You remember your friend Tony, don't you? Don't think for a minute the cops can't find him out here, either."

"Jimmy, you've got it all wrong, man. As a matter of fact, it's just the opposite. I think I've found a way to keep the heat off Tony for a while. As long as Tony stays in Los Angeles, I think he'll be okay."

"What do you mean you found a way to keep the heat off of Tony? You mean the cops? What are you talking about?"

"I really can't go into it right now. Just trust me on this; the cops around here aren't going to be bothering Tony. I know this for a fact. Just promise me you'll keep an eye on Tony. I'm taking care of the rest."

"I guess I underestimated you, man. I can't imagine how you're pulling this one off, but I've got to say we owe you one."

"I'll make you a deal. Just make sure we meet with this Bellvue guy as soon as possible, and we'll call it even."

27

Marcus Bellvue, the veterinarian, was a tall rail-thin man with a dark mustache, dark eyebrows, and a dark Charles Manson-like look in his eyes. His black hair was styled into a unique spiral comb-over, which swept around the top of his head in a circle, feebly attempting to cover the bald spot that encompassed 90 percent of his head.

Growing up a shy, gangly young man with good grades and an odd personality, Bellvue always found it difficult to socialize with his school classmates. With no friends to speak of, Bellvue was forced to turn to animals for companionship. When no people would talk to him, Bellvue started keeping himself company by talking to the animals.

Everything was fine until one day, when the animals started talking back.

Bellvue began considering himself a real-life Dr. Doolittle who suffered from pot-induced hallucinations. He pursued what he considered to be his true calling at veterinary school, where he excelled before eventually graduating near the top of his class out of the prestigious program at UC Davis.

Bellvue was always a few bricks short of a load, but he completely lost his marbles a few years out of college.

He joined a veterinary clinic near UCLA in Westwood where he treated small animals. His practice was relatively successful until one spring when, under the influence of some very potent hash, he cut the balls off a prize-winning schnauzer after mixing up the schnauzer's veterinary chart with that of a common shih tzu who'd been brought in to be neutered.

Two hours later, the shih tzu still had a spring in his step while the schnauzer, who had been suffering from an ingrown toenail, hobbled around twice as badly as when he came in.

The owner of the schnauzer understandably sued for malpractice, subsequently causing Bellvue to lose his job—and his mind—while miraculously retaining his license. Meanwhile, Bellvue came to his own defense by claiming the schnauzer told him to cut his balls off, and he was only following orders. The whole incident was settled out of court, but resulted in Bellvue becoming the laughingstock of the entire Southern California veterinary community.

After the schnauzer incident, Bellvue began believing that all animals had turned against him. Instead of wanting to help animals, Bellvue started wanting to harm any animal he could get his hands on.

With a license to practice but no clinics willing to hire him, no references, and no shred of sanity, Bellvue refocused his career energies on large animals and eventually found work at the one place where he'd have no trouble putting his veterinary knowledge to use for evil instead of good—the racetrack.

Bellvue worked harder and earned less money on the backstretch than he had at the veterinary clinic, but he soon found he could easily supplement his income by engaging in all sorts of hanky-panky, including drugging the racehorses. To this end, he had the option of hiring out his services to disreputable trainers or freelancing out on his own in order to stiff horses and cash bets. He ran this illicit operation undetected for several years until Tommy Bahama Boy finally caught him in the act. Now he had to play ball with Tommy Boy if he hoped to get himself out of hot water and back in business.

Tommy Boy threatened to release proof Bellvue had been drugging horses if he didn't cooperate with his demands. Bellvue agreed to a prearranged midnight meeting with Tommy Boy and the Dude-Men in Jimmy's motel suite in Arcadia near Santa Anita. Jimmy, Tony, and Larry sat around the motel, waiting for Bellvue to arrive. Tommy Boy promised the meeting would go as smooth as his silk pants.

Austin arrived for the meeting and was reunited with the rest of the Dude-Men for the first time since the Fix Six caper had gone awry in New York. Austin was finally introduced to Tommy Boy but didn't have enough time to talk with his friends or size up Tommy Boy at all before the gang heard Bellvue's van pulling into the motel parking lot.

Bellvue knocked on the door, and Tommy Boy let him into the motel suite. Tommy was unfazed by Bellvue's creepy appearance, but the rest of the gang was instantly put off by the evil-looking veterinarian who wore dark clothes, a menacing scowl, and clearly was very displeased to find himself in his current predicament.

Rather than concentrating on Bellvue's looks, Tommy couldn't help but focus on his all black outfit. In contrast to Bellvue, Tommy shunned black clothes. Instead, he opted for a lovely ensemble of pressed khaki sands trousers and a Paloma Palms silk camp shirt in moondust blue for the meeting that night. He accessorized with a Silver Palm watch and a two-tone pair of Tommy Bahama Eagle dress shoes in cocoa and camel brown.

"I've informed Dr. Bellvue that I caught one of his recent improprieties on film and sent him a copy to prove it. I have him dead to rights," said Tommy Boy. "Therefore, he has agreed to help us with whatever we might ask of him tonight. Isn't that right, Dr. Bellvue?"

"Let's just get on with this, okay. Tell me what it is you want."

"Well, Bellvue, that's going to be up to you. My friends and I plan on making a lot of bets in the coming days. We figure you might be able to offer us an edge. Isn't that right?"

"Perhaps. Is it just information you want?"

"We want it all, Bellvue. Tell me what you can do for us. Don't hold back, either. Give us your menu of services," Tommy Boy said.

"I can do so many things. You're going to have to be more specific. For starters, I can list for you the horses I've treated lately. I can tell you the ones that I've helped to win, or I can tell you the ones I've helped to lose."

"Go on," Tommy Boy said.

"If you want to be more proactive, I can sneak into almost any barn on the grounds and shoot up a horse with just about anything. The horses will test positive for drugs, but by the time they catch it, the bets you've made will already be paid. Or if you want to go another, slightly more harmless, route I have other ways of getting horses to run a big race—ways that won't show up on any drug test. I can tell you the horses I'll be treating in the next few days. Many of them run for some of the biggest trainers on the grounds.

"Finally, if nothing else works, then I can always go to my secret weapon."

"Secret weapon?" Jimmy asked.

"Oh, you're gonna love this one, Jimmy," Tommy Boy said. "Tell 'em what it is, Doc."

"Well, if you must know," Bellvue gloated. "What I do is I take the colts, and I burn their testicles a little bit. It works like a charm."

"Burn their balls? What do you mean burn their balls?" Austin asked, starting to get angry.

"What I do is mix together a fine powder made from hot chili peppers—jalapeños, habaneros, and the like—and then I take that chili powder and smear it on a horse's testicles right before a race. I've found it can make a horse run faster. The best part is, there's nothing to show up on a drug test. I worked that scam to perfection in Florida with some stiff of a trainer a few years back. He won like 50 percent of his races and the training title, and nobody could catch us."

"Did you just say you smeared hot chilis on horses' nut sacks?" Austin asked with a look of disbelief and distaste on his face.

"You don't believe me? I've done it, and it works. You'd run faster too if you had hot peppers burning your balls off, don't you think? What's the matter, boy, you don't have the stomach for my line of work?"

"No, actually. I don't. This whole thing just turns me off, that's all," Austin said.

"Whoa, whoa, whoa, nobody's gonna be burning any balls here—right, Bellvue?" Tommy Boy interjected.

"With the type of work I deal in, sometimes horses get hurt. If you're lucky, however, it won't be permanent, like with the chili powder. But hey, if you don't want chili powder, then fine, we won't use chili powder."

"What else you got in your bag of tricks, Doc?" Tommy Boy asked.

"If you don't want to deal with drugs or hot peppers, I have one other alternative. I know this guy who imports horses from South America—his name's Levi Cinzano. You see, the horses from South America don't have the identifying lip tattoos that all North American horses have. What this guy does is, he brings up two horses at a time from South America—one good and one lousy—and then he switches their identities. I examine the horses and give them the okay. He and I are the only two people who know the truth. He pays me and then he bets on the ringer, who, of course, looks like a rat and then runs like a champion."

"Kinky! I like that one, Doc," Tommy Boy said, "but we haven't got that much time. These guys want to make a quick hit and get out of here."

"Well then it's up to you. I've told you what I can offer," Bellvue said.

"How about you just do whatever you were going to do anyway and then let us in on the information. That's all. Just tell us who will win and who will lose. We don't want to be involved in it any more than that," Jimmy said.

Bellvue reached into his black doctor's bag and pulled out the largest needle anyone in the room had ever seen. Bellvue began to smile and giggle under his breath as he stuck the needle into a vial and pulled back the plunger to fill the syringe with clear liquid. His eyes brightened as he held the needle up to the light and released a small squirt of poison into the air for dramatic effect. "Good. I have some work to do in the next couple days. It's work I quite enjoy, actually. Why don't you just let me do my work? I'll inform you of what I've done so you can make whatever silly little bets you want to make. Once you've cashed in, you'll hand over your photos to me along with the negatives, and our business partnership will be complete. How does that sound, Mr. Bahama?"

Tommy Boy looked around the room and got nods of acknowledgment from all except Austin.

"This guy is clearly a psychopath," Austin said. "I can't believe you're all going for this crap. Why don't we just turn this scumbag in and find another way to do this?"

Jimmy pulled Austin aside for a talking-to. He whispered, "Austin, you've gotta understand that we're not having this guy do anything that he wouldn't be doing anyway. We're just using the information. That's all. Once we have what we want, we're turning this guy in no matter what. I promise you that. We're gonna fry this fucker and make sure he never touches another horse. Tell me you're with us."

"All right," whispered Austin, "but this guy is seriously disturbed. I'm going to personally see that he gets nailed for everything he does."

"You got it, dude. Let's just make our money first," Jimmy said as he turned around and gave the thumbs-up sign to Tommy Boy.

"You've got yourself a deal, Bellvue," Tommy Boy said. "You do whatever voodoo that you do. You tell us who to bet. When we have our money, you'll get your negatives. We'll forget this whole meeting ever happened."

Bellvue put his needle back in his bag and moved toward the door. "You'll be hearing from me later in the week."

*   *   *

The nameplate on Lieutenant Washington's office door read Lieutenant Wayne "Action" Washington. Detective Bragg chuckled as he entered Washington's office. He had a whole new joie de vivre about his demeanor.

"What's gotten into you, Bragg? Is that a smile I detect on your face?" Washington asked.

"Yes, sir, it is. I met a woman, and not only did I have a hot date last night—my third in three nights—but then I came into the station this morning and saw that the information I've been waiting for about Tony Martini finally came across my desk. It says he made a large bank card transaction at an establishment in Las Vegas called the Pink Passage, then a bunch more cash transactions this week at several strip joints in Hollywood, California."

"Hey, that's good news, Bragg. It looks like the boys from the LAPD should have a few good leads to go on. I'd say we might be able to catch this guy after all. It's a real shame you won't be around to work on the case anymore, huh, Bragg? Just when it was starting to get interesting, too."

"What do mean, Washington? I thought you said I could stay on this case!"

"You can stay on the case if you still want to, Bragg. It's just that I received some more good news for you earlier this morning. Your request for a month-long leave of absence has been approved! You can leave for vacation on Friday. Congratulations! I hope you enjoy your time off," said Washington, who was genuinely relieved to be getting Bragg out of his hair for a month.

Bragg was incredibly relieved to hear the good news. He couldn't wait to get cracking on his search for Larry Lipwinkle.

"I just hope you're right about the LAPD tracking down those leads," Bragg said. "I need to tell you, though, that I don't trust them. I called a few detectives out there this morning and mentioned Martini's name to them. I ended up getting bounced around to a few different phone extensions, and then I kept getting transferred to the same guy over and over again. He was named Chief Brown. He told me that the force out there was not able to pursue the Martini case at this particular time. I asked him why, and he said it was top secret."

"Wait a minute, are you telling me your leads dried up before you even knew about them? That's awfully strange. I wonder what happened? My guess is the LAPD must have known about this guy already."

Bragg was totally perplexed. He was thinking to himself that he couldn't wait to get out to Los Angeles to check things out personally.

"Well, in any case, all of this is none of your concern anymore, Bragg. You're going on vacation, and I'm sure this will all be wrapped up in a month, when you get back from your trip."

"I'm sure it will be, Lieutenant."

"By the way, you didn't tell me where you're going to be spending your vacation?"

"California, Lieutenant. I'm going to California."

28

Austin and Alana occupied most of their downtime together in sunny California by sitting around the swimming pool, getting tan at Austin's mother's house. Despite the couple's presence, it was business as usual around Madam Tiffany's, with clients continuing to come and go at all hours of the day and night.

Madam Tiffany came out to her pool to offer Austin and Alana some cool drinks. She wore six-inch stiletto heels and a leather Catwoman mask.

"How are you kids enjoying yourselves out here? Can I fix you a drink? A lemonade or an iced tea, or maybe a couple beers?"

Austin looked up and down his mother's outfit. "Mom, are you sure you're just the madam in this place? It looks an awful lot like you're working to me."

"What? Oh, this silly costume? Don't worry, it's nothing. As a matter of fact, this is part of the special package we're offering Police Chief Brown. You do still want him off your backs, right?"

"Yes, Mom, but I only want him off our backs if it doesn't involve you getting on *your* back!"

"Like I told you, I've got young girls around here for that kind of thing. Listen, Chief Brown just has a fetish where he sometimes likes to be blindfolded, tied up, and locked in a room for a while. I got called into action on that one. It's part of his bonus plan. I role-play the bad guy, the disciplinarian. Anyway, when he finally starts yelling and screaming for someone to release him, that's when I send in one of the young girls. We'll dress her up like some kind of twenty-year-old bondage commando on a mission to rescue him. It's all pretty standard stuff around here."

Austin and Alana looked at each other and burst out laughing.

"What's so funny?" asked Madam Tiffany.

"Nothing, Mom. You make it sound like this is normal stuff. Other moms bake cookies to pass the time. My mom keeps the police chief locked in her bedroom."

"That's not fair, Austin. I do too bake cookies. Damn good ones!"

"You know what? Come to think of it, a couple of lemonades would be great right now. Thanks, Mom."

Madam Tiffany disappeared inside to fix the drinks.

"I don't know how you can stand it around here, Alana. I've seen fewer crazy people at an insane asylum, or the racetrack. Same difference," Austin said.

"The only reason I can take it is because of this pool and the beautiful weather," Alana said. "Also, your mom has been so nice and hospitable. She keeps me company, and she's trying to teach me about the finer things. We're actually getting along quite well."

"Hey, maybe you'll learn some tips around here. Perhaps eventually you can take over the family business!"

Alana hit Austin in the face with a rolled-up towel. "Very funny, Austin. But seriously, you have no idea the kind of stuff I've seen around here the last couple days. Yesterday, there was this one guy. He came in, they put a dog collar on him, and then took him for a walk. They kept giving him commands like 'sit,' 'stay.' Every time he obeyed an order, they gave him a biscuit. A half hour later, he put his pants back on, paid, and drove away, looking like a perfectly normal guy again. I heard he's the district attorney or something."

"That's freaky stuff, Alana, but I'll tell you something, this guy I met last night—this veterinarian—he was much creepier than any of the guys I've seen around here so far. This guy seemed like a real honest-to-goodness psycho to me. First of all, he shows up wearing all black from head to toe. Black! Whoever heard of a veterinarian who wears all black? Then he pulls out the biggest needle you ever saw in your life and starts waving it around like a freaking sword. I'll tell you, he really scared me."

"This is the vet you guys are supposed to go into business with now? The one Jimmy's friend set you up with?"

"Yep, that's him. I'll tell you what, Alana. I'm really starting to get cold feet about this whole thing. At the beginning, I was thinking about how good it was to be in on something with my old friends again and what a great gang we were going to make. Now I'm having second thoughts and starting to think that maybe I'm making a big mistake. Maybe they really are just a bunch of losers like you said."

Madam Tiffany reemerged from the sliding glass doors out to the poolside deck, carrying a sterling silver tray with a pitcher of lemonade, two glasses, a bucket of ice, and a cordless telephone. She set the tray down, picked up the phone, and handed it to Austin. "Phone call for you, sweetheart. It's your friend Jimmy. I'll leave you two alone to enjoy your drinks."

Austin waited for his mom to go back inside and tend to the police chief before seeing what Jimmy wanted.

"Austin, it's Jimmy. We've got trouble. Can you talk?"

"Yeah, I'm here at the pool with Alana. What's going on?"

"It's Bellvue, man. He just got busted for something. It looks like our whole deal is off."

"He got busted? Oh shit, we aren't involved in it, are we? Please tell me no, man."

"No, Austin. Nothing to do with us. It was something else from before. The racetrack officials got Bellvue for the same thing Tommy was holding over his head all this time. Some serious shit went down. From what I heard, one of the horses Bellvue treated broke down during a race yesterday. Broke his leg. They had to euthanize him right there on the track. Terrible stuff. Anyway, they take the horse off the track, and get this—the horse disappears before anybody gets to inspect what happened to him."

"What? He disappeared?"

"Well, after that, the story goes that the track officials got a tip that someone on the backstretch spotted Bellvue with the missing horse's body in an empty barn. The racetrack sent a couple of its Pinkerton security guards to check out where the tipster told them to go. Sure enough, they catch Bellvue—the sick bastard—in the act of sawing off the horse's leg. Literally caught him red-handed!"

"Wait. Back up a minute! Did you say they caught Bellvue sawing the horse's leg off?"

"Yeah, I'm talking about the missing dead horse. I guess he was probably trying to get rid of some evidence or something. Anyway, that's when the security guys rushed in. There was a big struggle between Bellvue and the guards, with Bellvue ranting something about how the dead horse told him to cut his leg off. Then the guards finally wrestled the leg away from Bellvue. Once they got it, they started waving it around and inspecting it like a bunch of umpires at a baseball game looking inside Sammy Sosa's corked bat. Meanwhile, in all the commotion with the leg, the guards forgot all about Bellvue. He slipped out the back and got away! He's still on the loose, but he'll never be allowed back at the racetrack ever again. His practice is over. He's absolutely losing his license now. He's finished!"

"That means our plan is finished too," Austin said.

"No so fast, Austinie," Jimmy said. "That just means that *that* plan is finished. You're right about that. However, Tommy Boy told me he's already got a plan B in the works. We're supposed to meet him at the track tomorrow."

"Another plan?" Austin asked.

Alana, who had been listening to the conversation over Austin's shoulder, slapped her hand over her forehead and covered her eyes. "I can't wait to hear this one."

"Yes, another plan," Jimmy mimicked on the other end of the phone. "Meet us back at Clockers' Corner in the morning. Same time, same place as last time."

"I'll be there, Jimmy." Austin pressed the button to hang up the cordless and turned to Alana. "The Bellvue thing is off. There's a new plan. I'm meeting Jimmy and the others in the morning. I promise this is the last time. Then we're out of here."

Just then, the sliding glass door opened again as Madam Tiffany emerged from the living room onto the deck. This time, Tiffany's Catwoman costume had been replaced by a bustier with a sharply pointed steel-tipped leather bra with black tassels swinging from the ends. She was carrying what appeared to be a plate of cookies.

"Who wants cookies? These are fresh from the oven. Who said I couldn't be like other moms?"

29

Bragg had seen a little bit of everything in his two-decade career as a detective on the New York police force. However, since Mayor Rudy Giuliani cleaned up Times Square, he was no longer accustomed to seeing the sheer magnitude of strip clubs, adult video—and bookstores, and streetwalkers that seemed to be everywhere he looked in Hollywood.

Bragg wasted no time getting out to California. He arrived in Los Angeles on Friday night, rented a car, and checked into a cheap motel on the Sunset Strip in Hollywood. Bragg chose a seedy location due more to its proximity to the area's numerous topless clubs than because of a desire for low hourly rates, around-the-clock adult movies, and free HBO. He immediately began to pursue his prime objective, which was finding Tony Martini and, in turn, Larry Lipwinkle. He had not yet thought of what he would do with Lipwinkle when he finally got him.

Bragg began by crisscrossing Hollywood and North Hollywood in his car for a brief orientation to the area's adult clubs. Right away, he could see this was going to be something akin to finding a needle in a haystack. Based on information Bragg had on Tony's bank card transactions, he felt Hollywood would be the best place to begin looking. If he had to broaden his search outside of that area, he would really have his work cut out for him, with countless more topless clubs located farther out in the LA area.

Bragg drove past a half dozen places on his preliminary search of Hollywood, starting with Cheetahs on Hollywood Boulevard and the Seventh Veil on Sunset. There was also the Star Garden on Lankershim and Crazy Girls on La Brea. Later he stumbled upon a couple more places called the Tropicana and the Love Tunnel. That wasn't even counting places up in North Hollywood like Deja-Vu, Hollywood A-Go-Go, the Industrial Strip, and Strippers over on Sherman Way.

Needing to start somewhere, Bragg chose to focus first on the specific places where Tony had used his ATM card. He'd start by questioning bouncers and circulating photos of Tony Martini at the Seventh Veil,

Cheetahs, and the Love Tunnel. Then he'd stake out each of the clubs and hope for a lucky glimpse of Martini either entering or exiting.

Bragg stopped at Cheetahs first. He flashed his badge and asked to see the manager. A bouncer led him through the newly remodeled club that looked pretty much like every other strip joint he'd even been in. The offices in these places were always down a corridor in the back, in a place the average customer would never think to look. He left a photo of Martini and asked the manager for permission to question the bouncer. The bouncer said he'd seen Martini and remembered him because of, as he put it, "the embarrassingly obvious boner he had when he left the club." Unfortunately for Bragg, however, the bouncer hadn't seen Martini around for a few nights and wasn't sure if he would be returning.

Bragg's next stop was the Seventh Veil on Sunset. He admired the dark ambiance of the club, with Roman columns and statues giving the place a unique vibe. This visit was similar to the one at Cheetahs, however, with the bouncer also remembering Martini due more to his tent than his face. That bouncer also remembered seeing Tony a few nights back, but not again more recently.

Bragg finally got a better lead at the third club he visited—a place on Hollywood Boulevard called the Love Tunnel. There, both the manager and a couple of bouncers remembered seeing Tony spending a lot of money on lap dances the weekend before and then again twice more during the week.

Knowing by that time that he was on the right track, Bragg went back to his motel and turned in for the night. He was reassured that he had solid leads on three promising places to stake out and wait for Martini to lead him to Larry Lipwinkle.

*   *   *

The Dude-Men were back at Clockers' Corner early on Saturday morning, no closer to hitting the jackpot than they were eight days earlier after their first meeting with Tommy Bahama Boy.

By the time Austin, Jimmy, Larry, and Tony spotted him at eight, Tommy Boy had already been to the Clockers' Corner concession stand to buy coffee and doughnuts. Tommy passed around hot coffees as the five men sat together on a long bench facing the racetrack.

Tommy was casually attired in a tropic blue Cozumel zip-front polo and tobacco-colored Palmetto linen drawstring pants, with Anchors Away thong sandals by Tommy Bahama.

"Guys, I don't want to waste any time here before I let you in on the new plan. It's much better than the Bellvue gig, believe me on that one," Tommy Boy said.

Four very short Hispanic men approached the bench where the gang was sitting—three of them had wavy black hair, the fourth was bald as a cue ball. Three of them stopped and nonchalantly seated themselves at an empty table nearby. The fourth short Hispanic man—the bald one—continued to walk toward the secret meeting on the bench.

"Psst," Austin whispered. "Don't look now, but there's a short Latino man over there who seems to making a beeline for us."

Tommy Boy looked up. "Oh, don't mind him. I invited him. He's the key part of the new plan."

"He is?" Austin asked.

"Hi, Tommy Boy," the short Hispanic man said with no detectable Spanish accent. As he reached the gang's bench, Tommy got up to shake his hand and offer him a seat alongside the group.

"Guys, this is Pat Lopez. Pat Lopez, these are the guys," Tommy introduced.

Austin now was able to get a better look at Lopez. He was short but strong, with heavily muscled arms. He was in great shape, but a leathery, weathered complexion gave away his age, which must have been in the midforties. He wore a white T-shirt, jeans, and boots.

"For those of you who don't know him, Pat Lopez here is a famous jockey, maybe one of the best there is," Tommy said.

"One of the best there *was*," Austin said. "He was great until nine drug suspensions over the course of the last decade kinda took a little of the luster off his career. It's funny—I didn't recognize him without his hair."

Lopez had been one of the most well-known and controversial figures around the sport of horseracing since coming to the States from Panama in the 1980s. He was an immensely talented jockey who had ridden for some of the top trainers in California and won two Kentucky Derbies during his heyday in the '90s. Lopez wasn't without his faults, however. In addition to being a great jockey, Lopez was also a loner and a manic-depressive who turned to drugs time and time again in an attempt to quiet his inner demons. Over the years, he'd become to horseracing what Darryl Strawberry was to baseball—testing positive for drugs, getting another chance, and then testing positive once again as the whole cycle repeated itself over and over.

Jimmy had heard of him too. "Wait a minute. You're Pat Lopez? *The* Pat Lopez, otherwise known as P. Lo?"

"You got that right, man," Lopez said.

"Yeah, they also call him Loco Lopez," Tommy said. "He's currently suspended for the ninth time for a positive drug test, just like Austin said. He's only riding right now because his current suspension is in the appeals process. His lawyers have the whole thing tied up in court. I have to say though, it doesn't look good. Loco is expecting a lifetime ban to come down any day now. It's a terrible shame actually."

"Stinking cock-sucking *maricons*," Lopez said as he spit on the ground. In addition to drug woes, Lopez also grappled with violent anger management problems from time to time. This was one of those times. "Why do they need to care about my personal life? It's none of their motherfucking business, if you ask me."

"You tell 'em, Loco," Tommy said. "It's none of their business what drugs you take or who sells them to you, man. They're a bunch of fascists, if you ask me."

"Maricons!" Lopez reiterated.

"Yeah, that too," Tommy added.

"Hold on a second here," Jimmy said. "Lopez got suspended using drugs that you sold to him?"

"Well, yeah, but not all nine times. Just the last couple two, three times."

Everyone was staring holes right through Tommy Boy. "Hey, what was I supposed to do? Everyone around the track's acting like Mother Theresa around this guy, trying to help him get straight. Nobody would sell to him. I saw an opportunity, and I jumped at it. After all, if the guy wants some toot, he should be able to get some, right?"

"You're a piece of work, man," Austin said, definitely not meaning it as a compliment.

"Thanks," Tommy said.

"Yo, Loco, what's up with the hair?" Jimmy asked.

"My attorney was trying to prove my last drug test was bullshit. The track said they'd compromise and do a new test—something called a hair follicle test where they check you for toxins in your hair. That wasn't gonna be good for me, so I shaved off all my hair as sort of like my personal 'fuck you' to those guys. I don't have one single hair left on my body. Not one."

"You shaved your entire body? Everywhere?" Jimmy asked.

"Everywhere, man. Gone."

"But we digress," Tommy said. "Let's get to the reason we're all here. All of us, including Loco. It's my next big plan, and Loco is the key."

"If you got a jockey in on it, that could only mean one thing," Austin said. "You plan on fixing a race, don't you?"

"Bingo, you hit it right on the nose!" Tommy said, pointing to the tip of his nose like in a game of charades.

"Here's the deal," Tommy continued. "Loco here owes me a lot of money for drugs, and I'll agree to let him slide on some or all of the debt if he cooperates. He doesn't care because he'll be banned for life any day now anyway. He just wants to help us out to pay off his drug debt. Then he'll try to go straight. He's thinking of becoming a jockey's agent!"

"So who are those three guys over there?" Jimmy asked pointing to the three Hispanics sitting at the table about twenty yards away.

Everyone looked over at the three men who had come in with Lopez.

"Those guys are Loco's friends. They're all jockeys. From left to right, that's Gonzalez, Martinez, and Rodriguez."

The three men smiled fake smiles.

Larry smiled back.

"The problem is, they don't speak any English—and between you and me—they all stink," Tommy said.

"Who says they stink? They don't stink!" Lopez protested.

"Are you kidding?" Tommy said. "Those guys couldn't even win if they were riding the only horse in a one-horse race. But regardless, the fact is they're all countrymen from the same town, they all love Lopez, and they will all basically do anything he says. I think it has something to do with Lopez getting them out of jail in their native country of Peru or some shit like that."

"Panama!" Lopez corrected.

"Panama, whatever. Sorry," Tommy apologized.

"In Panama, these men were once all very successful, but they each turned to lives of violent crime once their careers of choice didn't work out," Lopez said. "When I was back home in Panama City sitting out my eighth drug suspension, I found these guys, saved them from prison, rehabilitated them, taught them how to ride, and brought them to this country. It was part of my twelve-step program! The problem is they haven't been able to get a break here so far."

"They ride like they got loads in their pants, man. That's why they haven't gotten any breaks," Tommy Boy said.

Lopez ignored Tommy Boy and continued. "Gonzalez over there was a baseball player. He was a master batsman who hit .340 and played second base in the Panama league. They used to call him Gonzo. The problem was he was too small and never had any power. Despite his batting average, he had the lowest slugging percentage in the history of the league. Strictly a singles hitter. They ended up cutting him."

"No power—that could explain why he's not making much hay as a jockey," Austin explained.

"Whatever," Lopez said. "That's when he started hitting old ladies and tourists over the head with baseball bats and robbing them. I knew his parents, so I got him out of jail and changed his life by turning him into a jockey."

"Old ladies, huh?" Tommy said as he scratched his chin. "I like his style."

"Next to him, you have Martinez," Lopez continued. "He was a featherweight boxer who could really fight. He nearly made the Panama Olympic team until he suffered two detached retinas. Without much peripheral vision or depth perception, he couldn't fight anymore without really getting beat up bad."

"Poor vision. No wonder the guy is having trouble winning races," Austin surmised.

"Yeah, well he ended up beating the shit out of his manager and getting thrown in jail," Lopez added. "That's when I stepped in. Look at his size. I knew he'd make a good jockey prospect! I owed his brother Pablo a favor, so I got him released from jail and moved him in with me. He owes me his life."

"He owes you his life?" Tommy shouted. "Ha! Good luck getting repaid on that one. He still owes me twenty bucks I loaned him last Christmas."

"Last but not least, we have Rodriguez," Lopez said. "He was in the circus. He and his brother in Panama used to do a knife-throwing act. One day Rodriguez got nicked in the neck by one of his brother's knives. It was just a flesh wound, but it was enough to scare him out of the big top for good. Now his problem is he's too skittish aboard a horse. He refuses to take chances."

"You gotta have guts to be a good rider," Austin said. "By my count, that's three strikes against these guys from what I've heard so far."

"Rodriguez would be in jail if it weren't for me," Lopez said. "He got mad at his brother for almost killing him and got revenge by cutting off his knife-throwing hand. They put him away for ten years, but I owed him a favor from a drug deal he once helped me with. With his size, I figured he'd be a perfect jockey, so I pulled a few strings in the Panama court system and got his sentence commuted. The court released him into my custody, and the rest is history."

"Whether they're good people or not is irrelevant," Tommy cut in. "What matters is that they're bad jockeys. They never get any good mounts because they never win, and they never win because they never get any good mounts. It's a catch-22. The key is that bettors see what's happening, and therefore, nobody ever bets on them. People avoid them like the plague. They're hardly ever riding anything under 30-

1 odds! The best part is they're all willing to do almost anything for money at this point. They've all agreed to team up with Lopez for a cut of our action."

"So what's the plan?" Jimmy asked.

"The plan is to wait," Tommy said. "We wait until we find a race where Lopez, Gonzalez, Martinez, and Rodriguez all have mounts. It'll probably be a big fourteen-horse field or something, and Lopez's boys will no doubt all be riding longshots. Then the plan is to make all kinds of different bets on their horses. Once the race starts, Lopez is gonna swerve all over the track like a kamikaze pilot in order to wipe out the entire field. The entire field *except* for Gonzalez, Martinez, and Rodriguez, who should waltz home first, second, and third. It'll pay huge, and we'll bet a ton of money on it. We're talking exactas, trifectas, superfectas, all kinds of wagers. We'll spread our betting money all around and walk off with a shitload of cash!"

Austin, Jimmy, Larry, and Tony all looked at Tommy Boy, then at each other. Then they all smiled and nodded because the plan seemed to make some sense to each of them.

"And Lopez over here can pull this off?" Jimmy asked. "Are you sure?"

"He's one of the best riders ever to come down the pike," Tommy said. "He's a maestro in the saddle. He can do anything he wants."

"What do you guys say?" Jimmy asked the rest of the Dude-Men. "Are we in?"

Tony spoke up, "I'm in!"

Larry gave two thumbs up.

Austin waited to see everyone else's reactions, then weighed in. "This sounds great. Instead of fixing six, this time we only need to fix one. I'm in too. Let's do it."

"We're all in," Jimmy said to Lopez and Tommy Boy. "What do we do next?"

"Just leave it to me," Tommy said. "I'm going to watch the entries every day. As soon as I see a race where all four of these jockeys have mounts, I'll give them a call and then give you a call when we have the green light. It might take a while, maybe even a week until I find a race with all of these guys riding in it. But as soon as I find one, I'll inform Loco and let him and his guys take care of the rest."

"That sounds great," Austin said, looking over at Lopez. "By the way, how did you get the nickname Loco?"

"How did I get the name Loco? Just wait a few days. You're gonna find out."

30

The California Black Knights' Motorcycle Club had a membership of more than forty guys, and they were truly something to behold when they tore down the highway all together in cruising formation. Mostly though, they just hung around their home base, watching television, eating, napping, lifting weights, and repairing their rides.

As many as a dozen gang members might be living at the gang's headquarters in South Central Los Angeles at any given time, so the gang needed lots of room. The place they all called home was a grand old house with six bedrooms on Westmoreland Boulevard in the heart of South Central. Westmoreland was one of the area's most beautiful but forgotten treelined boulevards that harkened back to another age when South Central was more fashionable and affluent. Now Westmoreland and other streets like it are known more for being close to the corner of Florence and Normandy—the famous site where truck driver Reginald Denny was dragged to the street and beaten during the LA riots of 1992.

The Black Knights' home on Westmoreland was far from some run-down shack in a neighborhood where stray dogs roamed the streets, picking through garbage day and night. In addition to a plethora of bedrooms, the Black Knights' residence also had a long circular driveway and an enormous rebuilt garage. Both the driveway and garage were always filled with glistening Harley-Davidsons—in various states of repair—being primped and polished and then ridden off down the block in all their earsplitting wonder.

Matt and Mad Dog were back in town from Las Vegas. They were starting to get bored from hanging out at the Black Knights' headquarters with nothing to do.

Across town in Arcadia, the Dude-Men were back in the increasingly familiar position of having a few spare days to kill while waiting for their next plan to take shape. Austin went back to his mom's house to join Alana at the pool, but the rest of the group was not quite so sure what to do with their copious amounts of free time.

Having already visited all the prime tourist attractions in Los Angeles, Jimmy, Larry, and Tony took to a routine of excessive sleeping and sitting around their hotel room all day, waiting for the phone to ring. Nights were becoming a blur too. Jimmy got into the habit of driving out to Los Alamitos racetrack in Orange County for nighttime quarter horseracing. Tony and Larry stayed home and watched porno movies on their motel's SpectraVision system.

Tony and Larry both developed severe cases of cabin fever until Tony finally caved in to his urges and planned a triumphant return to the Love Tunnel. Tony got Jimmy and Larry to join him but figured he needed a couple more guys involved in the outing to turn the night into a true blowout party. After an invite to Austin was turned down, Larry suggested that Tony call the only other two guys they knew in Southern California—biker dudes Matt and Mad Dog.

Mad Dog's cell phone rang as he was passing the time out back in his garden. He was in charge of tending to the Black Knights' new crop of cannabis, which was tucked discreetly between the gang's heirloom tomatoes and a few rows of multicolored *Impatiens*. Mad Dog was not only an unemployed outlaw biker, he was also a gardener. It was a hobby he took quite seriously.

In addition to a fine knowledge of cannabis cultivation, he also knew that the *Impatiens wallerania* (otherwise known as sultanas, touch-me-nots, or busy lizzies) grew much better in his garden than the more temperamental *Impatiens hawkeri*. The latter species, otherwise known as New Guinea impatiens, required too much watering and would thrive best in eastern sun exposure, which wasn't available in Mad Dog's garden.

"Hello, is this Mad Dog? . . . Hi, Mad Dog, this is Tony Martini, your friend from the Pink Passage in Las Vegas, remember? . . . Yeah, yeah, Tony the Tent, that's me. Anyway, my friends and I are going out tonight to the Love Tunnel. It's my favorite titty bar in Hollywood. It's gonna be a big blowout. We'd like to know if you and Matt are in town and want to join us."

Mad Dog's face lit up. An invitation from Tony the Tent to join him at a strip club surely meant a night filled with the kind of wretched debauchery he loved to partake in. He ran inside to tell Matt the good news.

It took Mad Dog a little while to find Matt in the big house on Westmoreland. He looked in the garage and driveway but found Chopper and Snapperhead to be the only ones outside working on their Harleys. They both said they hadn't seen Matt in the last few hours.

Mad Dog went inside. In the living room, he saw Road Kill lying on the couch, watching NASCAR highlights along with Skull and Reaper, but there was still no sign of Matt.

Mad Dog took a futile peek into the kitchen, but the only guy there was Pin Dick, hard at work preparing the gang's feast of beans and franks for later that evening.

After looking nearly everywhere, Mad Dog finally located Matt sitting at a desk in the den. Just as Mad Dog moonlighted as a gardener, Matt was also a CPA. Mad Dog found him hard at work on the California Black Knights' Motorcycle Club's federal income tax returns as April 15 quickly approached.

"Matt, buddy, put down that adding machine and pick up your pecker!" Mad Dog gleefully yelled. "Tony the Tent just invited us out tonight! We're going to the Love Tunnel!"

* * *

Down in the basement of an empty industrial warehouse in Sylmar—a neighborhood on the northeast fringe of Los Angeles made up of industrial warehouses, two hospitals, low-income housing, and plenty of graffiti—Marcus Bellvue plotted his revenge against Tommy Boy and the others who were responsible for getting him kicked off the racetrack.

Bellvue had a lot of time to think about how he possibly could have gotten caught sawing off the horse's leg at the track. After all, he'd done that sort of thing before and was never detected. The fact he was busted this time had to mean that Tommy Boy and his friends ratted him out. It was the only answer. Getting caught days after being blackmailed just couldn't be a coincidence. That had to be it. Tommy Boy and his friends must have ratted him out. They were the ones who ruined his career, and now they were going to pay for it.

Bellvue's workshop looked like something out of a Frankenstein movie—with countertops filled with bubbling vials of assorted liquids hooked up to Bunsen burners and various other electric contraptions. The back wall of the cellar was lined with animal cages—big and small—that were home to animals of all sorts, ranging from cats and dogs to rodents such as mice, rats, and a furry raccoon. In the center of the room was a large metal slab attached to a small sink, and a rolling steel cart with scalpels, forceps, and an array of needles and syringes on top. The room's lighting came from assorted fluorescent desk lamps and few bulbs that swung down from the ceiling on electrical cords.

The only furniture in the room was a small desk and chair. Bellvue was sitting at the desk, hard at work preparing his "List of Death." These were the people Bellvue planned on killing in the coming days. The name at the top of the List of Death was Tommy Bahama Boy. Next to it was Bellvue's preferred method of execution in capital letters—LETHAL INJECTION.

Bellvue put down his pen and walked over to survey the animal cages in the back of the room. He wore a long black lab coat buttoned down to his knees. "Which one of you wants to help me perfect my latest serum?" Bellvue asked the wall of caged animals before opening the latch on a crate housing a plump guinea pig. The irony of using a guinea pig as his guinea pig was lost on Bellvue. He carried the creature over to the metal slab in the center of the room. Sensing danger, Bellvue's soon-to-be victim bit down hard on the veterinarian's index finger, drawing blood. Bellvue shouted an obscenity and dropped the guinea pig onto the slab, temporarily stunning the creature.

"Don't worry, little guy, you won't feel a thing," Bellvue said as he licked the blood from his hand. He rolled the cart containing his needles toward the slab for closer inspection. On the cart was the foot-long needle and syringe that Bellvue had shown Tommy Boy and the Dude-Men back at their motel the week before. Next to that was Bellvue's favorite weapon—a stainless-steel syringe in the shape of a long handgun with a thick needle protruding from the end. Bellvue picked up the needle gun and gripped the handle with his palm while wrapping his fingers around the elongated trigger mechanism. The trigger was attached to the plunger, which delivered the contents of the syringe through the needle and into the victim.

Bellvue lovingly placed the needle gun back on the cart and moved his hand over a trio of three smaller syringes that he had prepared earlier in the day. They contained three different serums that were all intended for the guinea pig. This was to be the final test of the poisons he had in mind for his former associates—especially for Tommy Boy. They were the same poisons used by most states in their lethal injections.

The first syringe was filled with sodium thiopental—a short-acting barbiturate intended to temporarily paralyze and render its victim unconscious when used humanely in the proper dosage. Bellvue, however, had in mind an intentionally inadequate dosage, which would leave its victim in a chemical tomb—wide awake but paralyzed, suffocating, and subject to extreme agony from Bellvue's second and third injections.

The second syringe contained pancuronium bromide—a veterinary drug used in animal euthanasia. This drug is designed to paralyze skeletal muscles while not affecting nerves or the brain. It also leaves a person conscious, but unable to speak or cry as it works its way quickly through the bloodstream.

Bellvue's final syringe was filled with potassium chloride, which was designed to deliver the final knockout blow to its recipient. This drug causes a massive cardiac arrest until the heart muscle finally ruptures and stops, resulting in instant death. Bellvue favored potassium chloride because it would cause excruciating pain while its victim was still alive.

It was that final syringe that Bellvue particularly liked. It took just a small dose of each drug to finish off the poor guinea pig. It would take much more to polish off Tommy Boy. Bellvue reached for his needle gun and filled its syringe to the brim from a large vial that contained the third lethal poison.

31

"So, Julia, what are you wearing, baby?"

"It's the middle of the night. I was asleep. Come on, John, you should know by now I don't wear anything to bed."

"Wow, that thought will get my blood flowing out here on stakeout. Listen, I'm sorry to call you so late. It's just that it's lonely out here all night, and I was thinking about you."

"Still no luck with finding Larry and my husband?"

"No, but I'm close. Real close. It could happen at any time. That's why I've gotta keep on this and keep from losing my patience," Bragg said as he spun open the lid on his coffee thermos with one hand and dipped into a box of Winchell's Donuts with the other.

Bragg was beginning to get frustrated after his first two nights of staking out the Hollywood strip clubs turned up no signs of Larry and Tony. He was sitting alone in his car in the parking lot of the Love Tunnel for the third straight night. Earlier stopovers at Cheetahs and the Seventh Veil had been unproductive, but Bragg knew that the Love Tunnel was his best bet. He couldn't let himself believe that the trail had gone cold, but he couldn't keep those thoughts from creeping into his head, considering his zero batting average so far.

Bragg's night-owl routine in Hollywood consisted of sleeping much of the day away and then waking up in time to make the rounds at his targeted titty bars. To pass the time at night, Bragg would eat, drink coffee, listen to CDs, and always keep his trusty cell phone close at hand. As the nights slowly drifted into the early morning hours, however, there would be no one still awake left to call. That was when Bragg decided he'd start calling Julia Martini with romantic late-night wake-up calls just to keep himself company and to keep her on her toes. The two would talk for hours.

Bragg's resolve to get Larry Lipwinkle hadn't wavered one bit, but every time he heard Julia Martini's sexy voice, it made him want to hurry the process along that much faster so he could get back to New York that much quicker.

For two nights running, Bragg had started the evening at the Love Tunnel before leaving to spend significant time at both Cheetahs and the Seventh Veil. With that strategy not working, however, Bragg decided to try a new approach on his third night and spend much more time at the Love Tunnel, which was the number one place on his list based on reports of Tony's recent cash card usage.

Redoubling his efforts at the Love Tunnel finally paid dividends for Bragg. He spotted Tony and Larry pulling into the club at just past midnight on his third night on the watch, the exact time he was on the phone with Julia Martini.

"Julia. It's them. I've spotted Tony. I see him, and holy shit, he's with Lipwinkle! I've got them, I can't believe I've got them," Bragg said into his cell phone as he dropped the doughnut out of his other hand and reached for his binoculars.

"Oh my god, you see Tony? He's there right now?"

"You bet your ass he's here, and so is Lipwinkle. I just saw them go into this joint. I've gotta go get in there and figure out what to do next."

"John, be careful."

"Careful? Of what? Lipwinkle and your husband? Think about what you're saying."

Julia laughed. "Yeah, I guess you're right. Those two couldn't hurt anybody. It's like Larry's the spaghetti and Tony's the meatball. They don't exactly scare people."

"That's right, and I'll tell you what else. I don't know what I'm going to do yet exactly, but I'll tell you one thing, now that I found them, I'm not gonna lose them. You can be sure of that."

"Go get 'em, baby. When you see Tony, kick him once in the balls for me too, would ya?"

"Anything you say, babe. I gotta run."

Bragg hung up the phone and rushed into the Love Tunnel through the front door. The club was dark and loud. Several dancers were gyrating on brightly illuminated stages, while others combed through the crowd, offering private dances and conversation. Bragg's first goal inside the club was to locate his two suspects. The first thing Bragg actually did was stop, momentarily, to admire the beautiful bare breasts of the lusciously seductive dancer, Exstasy, who was turned upside down and spinning around on a brass pole on the stage closest to the entrance. The second thing Bragg did, however, once he pried his eyes off Exstasy, was to recognize the faces of not one, but both of his prime targets—Tony Martini and Larry Lipwinkle.

Bragg was elated. He'd finally found his men. This was the moment he'd been waiting for for so long.

Tony was noisy and obnoxious and easy to pick out in the crowd, but Bragg hardly even noticed him. Instead, Bragg's eyes simply glazed over with rage at the very sight of Larry Lipwinkle.

As Bragg stared at Larry, fantasies began flooding into his head. In his daydreams, Bragg always envisioned himself cracking the side of Lipwinkle's head with a meat cleaver and then cutting his heart out of his chest while it was still beating. At this particular time, however, Bragg was caught off guard, with no meat cleaver anywhere in sight. He'd need to improvise. The only weapon he had on him was a .22 caliber Saturday night special, which he kept with him at all times in a small holster around his right calf. It wasn't going to be big enough to splatter Lipwinkle's brains all over three counties, but was better than nothing. A .22 could still kill a man if in the hands of an experienced shooter.

Bragg's gaze fixed on Lipwinkle. Tunnel vision set in. He reached down underneath his pants leg and drew his pistol. He gripped the gun tightly in the palm of his right hand and began to approach the table where Tony and Larry were sitting.

Pounding music drowned out all other sounds. Every eyeball in the club was glued to Exstasy's spring-loaded titties. Strobe lights cut through the darkness and lit up the stages. Bragg took a look around and noticed that he couldn't possibly be more inconspicuous if he tried. He could be naked and standing on his head, and nobody would notice him. Bragg looked down at his .22. He thought about the pop such a gun made when it was fired. He considered that the sound probably wouldn't even be heard above the pulsating bass beat that rippled out of the Love Tunnel's state-of-the-art surround sound speaker system.

No sound and no eyewitnesses. It dawned on Bragg that this was a perfect opportunity to take down Lipwinkle.

Bragg moved closer and sneaked up behind Larry's booth. Everyone in the room was mesmerized by Exstasy's gyrating bulbous ass. Bragg cocked the gun and pointed it at the back of Larry's head for a point-blank shot. His heart beat faster as he prepared to pull the trigger.

Suddenly, Larry began to move. He was standing up. Startled, Bragg looked around and quickly stuffed the .22 into his pocket. He watched Larry and Tony rise from their table. Bragg wondered for a second what was happening, and then he saw his prey welcoming a pair of guests with hugs and very elaborate handshakes. The new men were black and very dangerous looking—one short and bald, and the other big and hairy. Confused by this turn of events, Bragg backed away. He watched at a distance as the leather—and denim-clad black guys joined Larry and Tony and then disappeared into the VIP champagne room at the back of the club.

The whole episode lasted less than a minute, but in that instant, Bragg had missed his chance.

Exstasy's song ended.

"Shit!" Bragg shouted at the top of his lungs, just at the moment the club fell silent enough for it to be heard. Everyone turned around to look at Bragg and saw him standing at the back of the room with his fists clenched at his side as veins popped out of his neck. The music quickly resumed with the start of the next song, and everybody turned back around to see the next dancer, but Bragg's cover was blown.

Bragg stormed out the front door, infuriated as all hell about blowing perhaps the best and most unexpected chance he'd ever have to waste Lipwinkle and get away with it.

32

Another sunny day dawned in Southern California, and Alana was out at the pool early in the morning, putting herself through her daily morning yoga practice.

After warming up with three sets of sun breaths, Alana glided gracefully from pose to pose. She started in mountain pose and then stepped back with one foot and extended her arms in front and behind into Warrior II pose. She then proceeded to drop her right hand to the ground and lift her left arm toward the sky into extended side angle pose before rising and bending the other way into and extended triangle pose. She then cartwheeled down to the mat for plank pose, moving through a *vinyasa* of *shata ranga*, upward dog and downward facing dog, before repeating the whole sequence of poses on the other side.

Halfway through Alana's routine, a recently awakened Austin emerged onto the deck, wearing pajamas and carrying a Bloody Mary in a large glass with an even larger celery stalk protruding from the top.

"Stop it, Alana, you're making me look bad," Austin said as he put his drink down and sat at a table underneath an umbrella and out of the sun.

"Good morning to you too," Alana said. "I'll be just a few more minutes. Then I'll join you for a dip in the pool."

Alana continued her yoga practice down on her mat with lizard pose and then an extended stay in pigeon pose on her left side. She then repeated on the right.

Austin sipped his alcohol and, sensing that Alana was almost finished, tossed his robe aside and dove into the pool.

After a series of forward bends, Alana was back on her feet again in mountain pose, standing with her feet together and her hands in front of her heart in prayer position. She stood there with her eyes closed in deep meditation for a few minutes until ending her practice with the phrase "*Ohm shanti,* peace to you, *ohm shanti,* peace to others, *ohm shanti,* peace to the universe. *Namaste.*"

Alana opened her eyes to see Austin wading in the pool. She tossed her yoga clothes aside and then dove in to join him. The cool water felt good in the sun, and Alana was clearly uplifted from her yoga session. She was in a good mood, so Austin thought this would be the perfect time to let Alana in on the Dude-Men's new plan.

Austin told Alana all about P. Lo and all about Gonzalez, Martinez, and Rodriguez—the three struggling ex-con jockeys who were supposed to come in first, second, and third to produce a life-changing set of exacta, trifecta, and superfecta payoffs. The Dude-Men planned to bet heavily into those three pools.

"The exacta bet involves picking the first two finishers in a race, the trifecta involves picking the first three finishers, and the superfecta involves picking the first four finishers in order," Austin explained to Alana in a lesson of horseracing 101. "Each bet becomes increasingly more difficult to hit, but therefore, the rewards for cashing these so-called exotic wagers keep increasing exponentially every time another horse is selected in the correct order. Trifectas pay more than exactas, for example, and superfectas pay more than trifectas. All exotic bets can pay off hundreds, thousands, or even tens of thousands of dollars for each two-dollar bet on a single race, providing that the horses who finish on top are all longshots."

"Austin, I have to tell you that this sounds like a good plan, but remember that the Fix Six sounded like a good plan too until it all went to hell. All I'm saying is that I'll believe it when I see it," Alana said.

"Yeah, I admit the thing with Bellvue was a bad idea. I knew that from the start. But the Fix Six really *was* a good idea. We should have made a fortune on that, and we would have if it weren't for really bad luck."

"But the point is that you *did* have bad luck. Doesn't that tell you something? What it boils down to is that these guys—your college buddies—they're all a bunch of losers. I know that somewhere deep down you must realize that."

"I know that all Jimmy has done for me so far is get me in way over my head, but I also know I can't turn back now."

"It's not too late to back out, Austin. I've become quite good friends with your mom. I'm sure she'd give us a loan and help us buy our place down in Baja. Don't you see? You don't need to do this anymore."

"I know, but it's just that I've come so far with those guys. I think I can finally see the light at the end of the tunnel. If I back out, I know we'll be fine, but what about the rest of them? Tony's looking at jail time when the cops finally catch up to him, and I just can't leave the rest of them high and dry, either."

"You can't leave them high and dry? Listen to yourself. In another week or so, we're leaving for Mexico, and you'll probably never see them again. Who the hell cares what they think?"

Alana got out of the pool and toweled off before putting on a pair of sunglasses and lying down on her favorite lounge chair next to the pool. Austin climbed out of the pool after her and headed straight for his Bloody Mary.

"Alana, I know you're right. The guys have been nothing but bad news, but the fact is that I need to see this through to the end so I can say good-bye to the gang on good terms. I want to make sure everyone's cool before we leave. It's the only way I'll have a clear conscience. And as far as my mother goes, asking her for money is still a last resort."

"Committing another knuckleheaded crime should be your last resort, not asking your own mother for money, but hey, suit yourself, Austin," Alana said.

"I just don't want you to worry. I promise this is the final plan," Austin said. "Now can we please change the subject and spend a nice day together here at the pool?"

"I hope everything works out. I'm just trying to look out for you. Anyway, as much as I'd love to spend the day at the pool with you, I've actually gotta get going. Your mom and I have a shopping date. We're going to Rodeo Drive!"

Alana never considered herself a material girl. She wore nice clothes and always looked good but never spent a lot of money shopping for things like expensive clothes or jewelry. Through her years of yoga practice, she had annexed some of the teachings of Eastern religion into her own beliefs and shunned the importance of material wealth and possessions. She always had what she needed, and she never coveted the things she didn't have.

For the first time in Alana's life, however, that all started to change after her first week with Madam Tiffany in her luxurious home in the Hollywood Hills. Madam Tiffany's extravagance opened Alana's eyes to a whole new ritzy lifestyle. Alana took a long look at the things Tiffany had, and she had to admit that she liked what she saw.

Tiffany had the best of everything, and Alana was starting to believe that first class truly was the way to fly. Therefore, when Tiffany extended the offer of a Beverly Hills shopping spree for a new wardrobe, Alana jumped at the chance.

"You're going to Rodeo Drive?" Austin asked. "You don't even like the mall. The only store I've ever seen you shop in is Victoria's Secret. Since when are you into shopping?"

"Since I got here and met your mom," Alana responded. "She's great. She offered to buy me some new clothes and new shoes and a new handbag. We're going to all the best stores, she says! You don't expect me to turn down an offer like that, do you?"

Just then, Madam Tiffany came out to the pool through the sliding glass door. She was wearing a black and white Chanel outfit with a wide-brimmed black hat and dark oversized Jackie O sunglasses. "Alana honey, it's time to get dressed. We don't want to be late."

"Give me five minutes. I'll meet you in the car, Tiffany," Alana called out as she hurried inside to get dressed.

Austin looked at his mother. "Mom, I think this is the first time I've seen you fully clothed since I've been here," he said with a chuckle. "You should try to wear clothes more often. You look good."

Tiffany was unsure whether he meant it as a compliment. She thanked him anyway before changing the subject.

"You know you've got a great girl there, Austin. I must confess to hearing part of your conversation while I was in the other room, waiting for Alana. I'd hate to see you lose her because you insist on being a boneheaded stubborn mule," said Tiffany, definitely not meaning it as a compliment.

"I know, I know. All right already." Austin was starting to lose patience. "This is it. This is the last time. I'm gonna go through with just this one last project with my friends, then I'm done for good. Would that make you guys happy?"

As Austin rambled on, Tiffany noticed Alana had come downstairs and was on her way out to the driveway to wait in the car.

"Win or lose, this is the last time. I promise!" Austin went on. "I'm saying good-bye to those guys once and for all! You'll see!"

"That's nice, dear," Tiffany said before making her way to the driveway. Alana got into Tiffany's Rolls-Royce and rolled down the window. She could see Austin standing at the top of the stairs that led from the deck down to the driveway.

"You don't understand," Austin went on. "None of this was ever supposed to happen. This started as a little plan with Larry and his computer. It's just that everything kept going wrong. The whole thing just spiraled out of control. One thing led to another! It's not my fault!"

Madam Tiffany waved good-bye to Austin and got into her car. "Sorry, but we can't be late, dear. We'll see you later this afternoon. Ta-ta!"

Austin continued to call after Alana and Tiffany in vain. "This is the last time I'll ever get involved with something like this in my life. I promise! After this, I'm done with crime, and I'm done with my loser friends. I swear! This time I really mean it!"

Alana waved at Austin and rolled up her window. Austin kept yelling and pleading until Tiffany started the car, pulled out of the driveway, and drove off down the street.

*   *   *

Tony and Larry were sitting around their hotel suite as Jimmy paced back and forth, trying to figure out what to do with another day of waiting for some news from Tommy Boy. Jimmy was considering getting himself a little culture with an excursion to the Getty Center Museum on the west side of town when the phone in the motel room finally rang. Tony, Larry, and Jimmy all glanced at each other and then stared wishfully at the phone until Jimmy finally picked it up on the third ring.

An excited voice came through the receiver. "Jimmy, this is *it*, man! It's go time!"

"What's up, Tommy? You sound excited."

"That's because I am excited, man. This is *it!*"

Tony and Larry had been sitting around their hotel suite, watching Jimmy pace the floor all day while waiting for some news from Tommy Boy. This was the call they'd been waiting for.

"It's go time? You're saying it's go time? That's great news, Tommy!" Jimmy said as Tony and Larry ran over and tried to listen in on the conversation. "Now slow down and start from the beginning, man. I'm dying to hear this."

"Okay, here's the deal. I was over at Clockers' Corner this morning and decided to stick around until after noon to get a look at Thursday's entries when they came out, just to see if there would be a race on the card suitable for our plans. Sure enough, the entries came out, and there was a race that had our plan written all over it. It's a twelve-horse field for maidens, and all four of our jockeys—Gonzalez, Martinez, Rodriguez, and Lopez—have mounts in the race. Just like I suspected all along, Gonzalez, Martinez, and Rodriguez are riding longshots!"

"That's not only great, Tommy, that's awesome!" Jimmy said before turning to relay the news to Tony and Larry. "Tommy found a perfect race for us on Thursday. Gonzalez, Martinez, Rodriguez, and Lopez are all in the field!"

Tony and Larry exchanged high fives. Tony hit Larry's hand a little too hard, and Larry grabbed his hand and shook it. "Ow, that really hurt, you big lummox."

Tommy Boy wasn't finished. "And, Jimmy, I haven't even told you the best part yet."

"There's more? What could possibly be better than this?"

"Jimmy, man, I didn't just find us a race with all four of our jockeys in it. I found the *perfect* race with all our jockeys in it. Gonzalez, Martinez, and Rodriguez ended up with the three inside post positions, and Loco drew post five!"

"I don't understand, Tommy. What does that mean?"

"Don't you see, man? Our jockeys are all on the inside, close to the rail, and Loco is nearly right beside them. That makes his job easier. All Loco needs to do is break alertly out of the gate and then take a sharp right turn in order to set off a chain reaction and wipe out the entire outside part of the field. Horses six through twelve can all be wiped out at the start. That's killing seven birds with one stone. After that, all Loco has to worry about is finding a way to interfere with the number four horse. Once he's done that, Gonzalez's, Martinez's, and Rodriguez's horses will all be home free."

Jimmy's blood pressure went up about fifty points during the phone conversation, and he could no longer contain his excitement. "Ha, ha, Tommy! It's absolutely perfect! Wooo-hooo! We're gonna do this. We're actually going to be able to pull this off. Good-bye, Fix Six. Hello, Fix One!"

Jimmy was jumping up and down, and soon both Tony and Larry were jumping up and down too.

"Jimmy, let me finish," Tommy yelled into the phone. "So when I saw the entries and the way that this particular race was drawn so perfectly, I went ahead and called Loco to tell him the good news and ask him if we had the green light. He heard what I had to say and immediately gave me the go-ahead. He guaranteed me that Gonzalez, Martinez, and Rodriguez would all give the go-ahead too. That was the final piece of the puzzle. It's officially go time!"

"We got the green light," Jimmy yelled over to Tony and Larry, who were still dancing after hearing the previous news. "Did you hear me? We got the green light. It's officially go time!"

"That's it, man," Tommy said. "It's Thursday's third race. Post time will be at about two o'clock. Will you guys be ready to go?"

"You can count on us, Tommy. I'm gonna call Austin right away. We'll be ready on Thursday."

33

Austin spent all day Wednesday in Arcadia, strategizing along with the Dude-Men for the planned Thursday caper involving Loco Lopez and the three hapless Hispanic jockeys. As usual, each of the college buddies was given his own job to do.

The plan was to have Tony bankroll the bets and then lay as low as possible, just in case the Southern California fuzz was secretly on the lookout for him.

Austin would mastermind the gang's bets. Since only win bets affect the odds in a horse race, Austin planned on hiding all the Dude-Men bets from the public view by wagering exclusively into the exotics pools on exactas, trifectas, and superfectas.

Jimmy would place the bets only after getting the final okay from Tommy Boy, whose job it was to go down to the paddock before the race and wait to be given a predetermined signal by all four jockeys who were in on the fix. Once Tommy Boy had been winked at by each of the four jockeys, he would then relay the information to the Dude-Men and then leave the premises immediately to avoid being linked to the winning bettors by any witnesses.

Larry's job was creating a fake ID and phony social security number for Jimmy, since Jimmy was going to be the one making all of the gang's bets. Any two-dollar bet returning more than six hundred dollars required an IRS withholding tax. Jimmy would need to sign IRS forms and take a photo in order to collect the kind of money the Dude-Men were expecting to earn on the race. With a fake ID and social security card, the winnings couldn't be traced back to Jimmy in the likely event of an investigation, and he wouldn't have to pay taxes on the gambling income he was going to collect.

Austin calculated the Dude-Men would bet five hundred dollars on each exacta combination, two hundred on each trifecta combination, and twenty bucks on each superfecta combination, covering the whole field in fourth. Betting this much would ensure that they would end up pocketing nearly the entire betting pool on each wager.

The betting scheme wasn't going to be easy. Horse race wagering is pari-mutuel—meaning that horse bettors are essentially betting against each other and not against the house. Therefore, the more money that's bet on a winning combination, the lower that combination pays off because there's only so much money in each betting pool to go around.

Gonzalez's, Martinez's, and Rodriguez's horses were all going to be around 30-1 odds. Austin figured a two-dollar exacta on two of the three horses was going to pay around six hundred dollars even after all of the gang's bets were factored in. He also figured that because of all of his gang's bets, a winning trifecta with Gonzalez's, Martinez's, and Rodriguez's horses that would normally pay around six thousand dollars would only pay in the neighborhood of two grand for every two-dollar bet. Similarly, a superfecta involving Gonzalez's, Martinez's, and Rodriguez's horses plus a fourth horse, which should pay twenty-five thousand dollars for each two-dollar bet, would actually pay much less in this case.

Using that conservative math, a $500 exacta box would cost the gang $3,000 and would return around $150,000. Their $200 trifecta boxes would cost them $1,200 and pay off around $200,000. Finally, their $20 bets on all 216 different superfecta combinations would cost them $4,320 and pay off around $100,000, which would comprise nearly the entire superfecta betting pool for that race.

The total investment required on Tony's part to cover each and every combination involving Gonzalez's, Martinez's, and Rodriguez's horses in all the bets would be $8,520. That sum included betting every possible combination of Gonzalez's, Martinez's, and Rodriguez's horses in exactas and trifectas and then covering every possible combination of those three horses plus any fourth horse in the superfectas. Adding in $5,000 down payments to Gonzalez, Martinez, and Rodriguez to the $8,520 betting stake, Tony would need to lay out over $20,000, in advance, just to get the ball rolling on the race-fix plan. That figure was no problem for Tony, who had ten times that amount in cash with him inside his two attaché cases.

Adding the exactas, trifectas, and superfectas together, the gang's target payoff figure for the fixed race was nearly a half million dollars. If they put a few bucks here and there on each of the three horses to win, they might end up clearing something in the vicinity of $460,000 to $475,000 on the race if they played their cards right. That would translate to around $80,000 for each of the five gang members after they got done reimbursing Tony his original $23,520 investment and paying an extra $10,000 to each of the jockeys.

Lastly, Tommy Boy would cooperate with Lopez by giving him amnesty from his drug debts.

According to Austin's calculations, everyone involved was taken care of, and everyone would make out like bandits. He and Alana would have $80,000 in cash in their pockets to start their new lives in Mexico. With that kind of money floating around, he planned to make a clean break from his friends and leave them on good terms and with a clear conscience. Everything was falling into place.

*   *   *

Bragg took a couple of days off to lick his wounds from that missed opportunity to take care of Larry Lipwinkle once and for all at the Love Tunnel. He wasn't giving up, and didn't plan on making the same mistake again.

Bragg observed that Tony and Larry looked awfully comfortable at the Love Tunnel and awfully familiar with the Love Tunnel staff. Once and for all, he knew he could narrow down his efforts to that one club and concentrate on catching them on a subsequent Love Tunnel visit.

The one thing that still bothered Bragg was Tony and Larry's rough-looking companions from the other night. Bragg thought the men looked like bodyguards, and he wondered if that meant Tony and Larry were somehow wise to his presence in Southern California. Why else would the two losers have hired personal protection? What else could it be?

Bragg believed the only way Tony and Larry could have been onto him was if the Love Tunnel's manager or one of the bouncers had tipped them off. Either way, Bragg knew he couldn't touch Lipwinkle with the two biker bodyguards hanging around. He also knew he couldn't continue to loiter in his car in the parking lot any longer. He needed access to the inside of the club. He needed to be closer to the action to ensure nobody could tip off Tony and Larry and scare them off before he could get his hands on them.

Bragg gathered up his badge, nightstick, and sidearm. It was time to pay the Love Tunnel's manager a little visit.

34

The sign on the office door read Vinny Francone-Manager. Bragg had made his way to the doorway after snaking through a maze of bars, tables, and Skank Shift afternoon dancers en route to a narrow corridor tucked discreetly in the back of the Love Tunnel's main stage.

Instead of knocking, Bragg took the liberty of opening the door and letting himself into the manager's office, where he found Francone in the act of fondling a bikini-clad dancer who was sitting on his lap.

"Am I interrupting?" Bragg called out.

"Whoa, doesn't anybody fucking knock anymore?" asked Francone, who was caught off guard. "Damn right you're interrupting!"

"This is official police business, Francone. Lose the girl," Bragg demanded.

"You heard the man," Francone told the stripper. "Scram while daddy does some business, all right, baby?"

The girl readjusted her top and scampered away into the club.

"To what do I owe this visit from the police?" Francone asked.

"You've seen me coming around here for the past week, and you know I've been lying low and trying to find a wanted criminal named Tony Martini," Bragg said. "But now it appears you've been less than forthcoming with me. It appears you ratted me out, so I think the time for lying low is now over."

"I don't know what you're talking about," Francone said. "I've never seen Tony Martini in my life. If I had, I would have called you."

"It's too late for that now, Francone," Bragg said. "You're no good to me anymore. I'm going to have to start doing things my way around here. I'm going to need to use your office the next few nights until my guy makes another appearance."

Bragg looked around the manager's office. The room was not big, but it did have enough room for Francone's desk and big leather chair, plus a couple other chairs for visitors and a full-length black vinyl sofa. The walls were covered with naked photos of the strippers. Francone even had his own small bathroom with a toilet, small sink, and tiny stand-up shower stall. "This place will suit me nicely."

"Wait a minute, Bragg," Francone piped up. "You can't just waltz in here and set up shop in my office. I've got business to do. I've got rights."

"You have the right to shut the fuck up, Francone. You want to talk about business? Okay, let's talk about that business," Bragg threatened. "I've seen some interesting things going on around here while on stakeout. Drug deals. Drug use. Prostitution. Would you like me to keep going?"

"Hold it! Hold on a second. I already got a deal with the cops on that one. I do what I do, and they look the other way. Are you telling me the cops are reneging on their protection deal with me?"

Bragg had already figured the Love Tunnel had something worked out with the local cops. Most places like it did. He was ready to use that knowledge to his advantage.

"I'm not . . . I mean, we're not reneging on anything. But we could. We could do a lot of things to make life difficult on a club manager such as yourself. But I'm sure it won't come to that if you're simply willing to cooperate for a few days on this matter."

"Cooperate! Cooperate? What's in it for me?" Francone asked.

Bragg stood up and grabbed for his nightstick. He came around the desk and backed Francone into a corner. All the while, he was carefully watching the manager's hands to make sure he wasn't reaching for a hidden weapon in a drawer or behind his desk.

Bragg raised the nightstick in his right hand while pushing his left hand into Francone's chest. "What's in it for you? You get to keep your skull in one piece. That's what's in it for you. Do we understand each other?"

"Loud and clear," quivered Francone.

Bragg let go of the manager. "I need you out of this office by tonight. The police will only be requiring use of these premises for a few days. Then we can all go back to business as usual and forget this whole incident ever happened. *Capisce?*"

Francone could see he had no choice but to vacate his office.

*   *   *

The Dude-Men ate lunch in the Santa Anita Turf Club and waited for the day's third race to arrive. They were about to bet a lot of money on a single race, so they chose the Turf Club in order to blend in with other big bettors and maybe even be confused as the owners of one of the horses in the race. Tommy Boy's face was known all around the racetrack, so he opted to stay downstairs near the paddock, keeping his distance from the rest of the gang in order to avoid causing suspicion.

After the completion of the day's second race, Tommy Boy moved into position down at the saddling ring, where he would wait for winks from all four jockeys to indicate the fix was on.

Tony inhaled a slice of cheesecake he ordered for dessert and reached into his inside jacket pocket for an envelope of hundreds to give to Jimmy so he could make the bets. "You can count it. It's all there. Six thousand one hundred and twenty dollars."

Jimmy took the money. "Austin, what are our odds?"

"All three of Gonzalez's, Martinez's, and Rodriguez's horses were listed at 30-1 odds in the morning line. Gonzalez's one-horse—named Tricky Diva—is currently at 40-1. Martinez's two-horse—Lovely Lady—is 20-1, and Rodriguez's three-horse—Runaround—is right at 30-1 odds, just as expected," Austin said. "Lopez is on the five-horse—Fast and Foxy."

"Good, the horses we need to be longshots are all longshots, just like we'd hoped," Jimmy said as he pulled out his wallet and inspected the new social security card and California driver's license Larry had made for him. "And, Larry, you're sure these are good? Exact copies?"

"Fake IDs have been amongst my specialties ever since college. Don't you remember? I used to make them for all the coeds at CNJSU back in the old days. I'd give them the IDs, and they'd pretend they liked me. It was a pretty sweet deal. Anyway, I guarantee you those IDs are good. A policeman who moonlights as a bartender couldn't tell those apart from the real thing. I guarantee it. For today, you are officially Mr. Mike Hunt."

Austin burst out laughing. Seeing Austin cracking up, Larry finally lost his poker face and also busted out laughing.

"What's so funny, you guys? What the hell are you laughing at?"

"Oh, nothing. Nothing at all, Mr. Hunt. Mr. Mike Hunt," Austin said, holding his side from laughing so hard.

Jimmy looked down at the IDs and then back up at Larry. "You sonofabitch! You named me Mike Hunt? I can't believe you!"

Just then, a woman's voice came over the speaker system in the Turf Club. "Paging Mr. Hunt. Mr. Mike Hunt. Has anybody seen Mike Hunt?"

All four of the Dude-Men were in hysterics, banging on the table and doubling over with laughter.

"Who put her up to that?" Jimmy asked while wiping tears from his eyes.

"I did," Larry confessed. "I just wanted to lighten to the mood around here while we were waiting for this race. I figured we'd all be on edge."

"Good idea, Larry," Jimmy said. "Mike Hunt, I like that one. You're one sick fuck, Lipwinkle."

Just then, Jimmy's cell phone rang. It was Tommy Boy calling from downstairs in the paddock.

"Jimmy, I just got winks from all four jockeys. The fix is on," Tommy whispered into the phone.

"That's great, Tommy Boy. We'll take it from here."

"Perfect," Tommy said. "I'm gonna stop at the bathroom and then watch the race from the monitor closest to the exit. Once the race is over, I'm gonna get out to my car and get out of here. I'll call you tonight so we can divide the cash. Then we can all go out and celebrate."

"Keep your fingers crossed. We'll see what happens," Jimmy said.

"Oh, I'll keep my fingers crossed, but I can guarantee you one thing. You ain't never seen a race like the one we're about to see."

35

The twelve horses lined up in the starting gate for Thursday's third race at Santa Anita. Track announcer Troy Henman assumed the microphone for the call of the race.

"The field of twelve is all in line and waiting for the start, aaaaaand they're off! It's an alert break! There goes the number one, Tricky Diva, to the front. Wait a minute. What's this? Fast and Foxy appears to have taken a bad step. She's made a right turn directly into the paths of the horses to her outside! She's completely wiped out the number six horse! Jockey Pat Lopez appears to be steering Fast and Foxy even farther outside in an effort to gain control. He's now bothering several other horses! It's a domino effect! Lopez can't get control of his mount! It's total chaos out there, folks!"

Henman sounded as if he were about to hyperventilate as he continued to describe the carnage taking place in front of him.

"The seven-horse has clipped heels and has fallen. He's down on the track!

"The eight-horse has been pulled up to avoid tripping over the seven-horse. She's out of it!

"The nine has been pulled far back behind the traffic!

"The number ten horse has lost its rider!

"The eleven was knocked sideways and is now running the wrong way!

"The twelve has veered sharply toward the outside fence! She's jumping the railing! Now she's in front of the grandstand! She's running around through the stunned crowd! I can't believe my eyes!"

Tony loved every detail of what he was seeing. Lopez was backing up his promise to wipe out the field. "Oh, boy is this great!" Tony said as he stared out at the track.

"What's left of the field is now heading into the turn. It's the one, Tricky Diva, in front followed closely by the two, Lovely Lady; the four, Hollywood Vixen; and the three, Runaround! It appears Pat Lopez has straightened out Fast and Foxy and is now rushing her up to make a run at the leaders! He'll surely be disqualified, but he continues to ride the race anyway!"

The crowd gasped as Lopez hustled up Fast and Foxy and approached the leaders.

"Runaround has used a burst of speed to pass the number four, Hollywood Vixen. After the early mishap, here comes Fast and Foxy! She can't possibly keep up this pace! She's now coming up alongside Hollywood Vixen, who appears to taking dead aim on the leaders and is starting to make her move!"

The crowd rose to its feet.

"The jockey says 'go' aboard Hollywood Vixen, but wait! Hollywood Vixen is being bothered by Fast and Foxy to her outside! Fast and Foxy has bumped Hollywood Vixen! She's bumped her again! Pat Lopez has lost his mind! Fast and Foxy slams into Hollywood Vixen one more time! Oh no! Hollywood Vixen has crashed into the inside rail! She's broken through! She's in the infield! She's out of the race! I can't believe what I just saw!"

Austin, Jimmy, Tony, and Larry all sat in stunned silence in the Turf Club as they watched the events that they had choreographed unfold exactly as planned. Gonzalez, Martinez, and Rodriguez were out in front, and nobody was going to catch them.

"Oh, the humanity!" Henman screamed. "Including the sure-to-be DQ'd Fast and Foxy, there's only five horses left in the race as the horses come down the homestretch! The leaders are all tiring, but it's not going to matter. Fast and Foxy is being reined in by Pat Lopez! She won't finish! The only other horse left on her feet is the number nine, but she's far behind!

"Coming down to the wire, it's number one, Tricky Diva, in front! The two, Lovely Lady, has held second, and Runaround completes the order of finish in third. It's far back to the nine-horse who finishes fourth. Tricky Diva has won it, and she's 30-1! It's the first win of the year for jockey Manuel Gonzalez—the first win of his career! I need a drink! Where's my Scotch?"

The Turf Club crowd collectively moaned and groaned as they tossed out their losing tickets. Some in the room were taken aback somewhat, however, by the sight of four men wildly celebrating and dancing at the front of the room. All four men were gleefully yelling and congratulating each other. The heaviest of the four men had removed his blazer and was twirling it around in the air above his head. The tallest and skinniest of the four had taken the flower centerpiece off the table and was wearing it as a hat a la trainer Bob Baffert.

Downstairs, Tommy Boy had watched the race from the monitor closest to the exit. He jumped up and down and patted himself on the back as Gonzalez, Martinez, and Rodriguez crossed the line first, second, and third. "Daddy's got a six-figure payday, Daddy's got a six-figure payday," he sang to himself as he headed out through the turnstiles toward his car in the racetrack parking lot.

Tommy whistled as he combed through the aisles of cars in the immense lot until he spotted his fluorescent yellow convertible a few rows away. As he got closer to his car, he noticed his parking spot was being blocked by a large black conversion van parked horizontally behind him.

Tommy approached the van and tapped on the darkly tinted driver's side window. "Hey, anyone in there? You're blocking me in, dude!" Tommy called out.

He got no response.

Up in the Turf Club, the Dude-Men polished off a round of celebratory drinks. Austin ordered a bottle of the house's finest champagne as Jimmy calculated the gang's returns for the race at just short of half a million dollars. Austin and the guys embraced in one big group hug and started jumping up and down all together like a women's gymnastics team that had just won Olympic gold.

In the parking lot, Tommy Boy still could not locate the driver of the big black van and, therefore, could not pull his car out of its space. He was about to walk off in search of a security guard when he was suddenly bumped into hard from behind. He felt a sharp stinging sensation in his shoulder as he fell to the ground.

"What the hell! Bellvue, is that you? You dick! Why don't you watch where you're going?"

No answer from Bellvue.

"Well don't just stand there, you tool, help me up!"

Bellvue slid his syringe into the pocket of his black lab coat and extended his hand to help Tommy Boy back to his feet.

"Is this your van, Bellvue? Get it the hell out of here so I can move my car!" Tommy Boy said as he dusted off his Tommy Bahama pineapple-colored Island Outpost camp shirt, which was the perfect match for his pair of sand-dollar-brown Tarpon Bay shorts.

"Oh, I'm afraid that won't be happening, Mr. Bahama."

"What the fuck do you mean that won't be happening?" Tommy began rubbing his shoulder, which was starting to swell up like a balloon. He noticed a trickle of blood had stained his pristine pineapple-colored camp shirt "What the hell did you do to me?"

"What I have done to you, Mr. Bahama, is administer you a large dose of a drug that will paralyze you and leave you completely motionless in less than a minute. Then when you're sitting there like a helpless ball of jelly, I'm going to take you into my van and kill you in the most agonizing way possible."

Tommy Boy's reaction was predictably violent.

"Like hell you are," Tommy said as he lunged for Bellvue and grabbed him around the neck. He started to squeeze. "I'm bigger than you and stronger than you, and I could squash you like a bug, you douche bag."

Tommy Boy was strangling Bellvue, who had to fight to gasp for breath. His face started to turn red, but Tommy Boy's grip suddenly loosened around his neck. Bellvue was finally able to remove Tommy's hand from his throat. He noticed Tommy's legs were starting to buckle beneath him.

Tommy began to grab at his head and mumble as he sunk to his knees. "What do you want? Is it money? Just name it."

"What I'd like more than anything is for you to die, Mr. Bahama, and that's exactly what's going to happen in just a few minutes."

"Why? Why? Please! Please don't," Tommy pleaded as he slumped down to the gravel. "Noooooo!"

Back inside the track, the judges had just completed their review of the race and found that all trouble had been caused by Loco Lopez and his inability to control his horse, Fast and Foxy. Therefore, there would be no change to the order of finish, and the results of the race would stand.

At that moment, a second bottle of champagne arrived at the Dude-Men's table. This time, before opening it, Jimmy shook up the bottle and popped the cork to send a foamy stream of bubbly right into Tony and Larry's faces. Tony wiped the alcohol from his eyes and vowed to come up with some sort of revenge against Jimmy later that night at the Love Tunnel.

"Guys, let's cash out and continue this celebration later tonight at the Love Tunnel. It's my treat. Anything goes!" Tony said. "Wooo-hooo!"

Jimmy cashed the Dude-Men's winning bets as the rest of the gang ran downstairs to get their car out of valet so it would be waiting for Jimmy when he arrived. Jimmy was offered a choice to accept his windfall either via certified check or in cash. Jimmy chose cash and had to wait as a pair of uniformed guards brought up the loot from the track's money room on the main floor. The cash arrived bundled inside two canvas money bags and was handed over by the guards, who wore big shiny nametags, which read Stan and Earl.

The guards escorted Jimmy down to his car. Jimmy tossed the bags of cash into the back of his green SUV and peeled out of the parking lot as fast as he could with nearly a half million dollars lying in a heap in the back of his SUV.

Jimmy's SUV was just a few minutes behind another vehicle that had also left the track early that day—a big black van with darkly tinted windows. Inside the van, an assortment of needles and spent syringes rattled around on the floor alongside the pool of sweat that had formed a puddle under Tommy Boy's rigid lifeless body.

36

Despite the fact that he and his friends had just won nearly a half a million dollars at the track a few hours before, Tony was disappointed. The celebration plans he'd made for later that evening were not quite shaping up as he had hoped. Tony's idea involved a nice dinner and then a no-holds-barred night of hedonism at the Love Tunnel, sponsored by him. However, those plans quickly began to unravel as soon as the gang made its way back to the Arcadia Motor Lodge where they were staying.

First, the Dude-Men couldn't get in touch with Tommy Boy. This was strange because they pegged Tommy as the kind of guy who would be standing in the motel parking lot waiting for his cut of the loot as soon as the Dude-Men returned from the racetrack. Tony's second problem was Austin, who was in a hurry to get out of the doghouse with both Alana and Madam Tiffany and opted to return to his mother's house in the Hollywood Hills instead of going out with the guys. The third crimp in Tony's party plans was Larry, who apparently had drank a little too much champagne at the track and was now flat on his back, experiencing bed spins and turning two shades of purple. Jimmy offered to forsake a night of lust at the Love Tunnel in favor of staying in with Larry and holding his hair back when he puked. Besides, Jimmy thought, there'd be plenty of other chances to celebrate once he returned home to New York with all his cold hard cash.

Tony resorted to his usual fallback plan and dialed Matt and Mad Dog at the California Black Knights' headquarters in South Central. Matt answered the phone on the fourth ring.

"Matt! It's Tony the Tent calling, and, man, are you guys in luck! I'm sponsoring a party tonight at the Love Tunnel, and you guys are invited. Today is your lucky day!"

Matt didn't respond with the giddy enthusiasm that Tony had expected. "No can do, amigo," Matt said. "It's tax season, and I'm buried up to my beard under a pile of W-2s and 1099s over here. I'm not only a biker, you know. I'm also an accountant. Half the guys in the club had to file for extensions this year, and I've just got too much to do, bro."

Tony couldn't believe his ears. "Taxes? Shit, I forgot all about that!"

"Yeah, it's April 15! Have you been under a rock or something?"

"Something like that," Tony answered, thinking that he could now add income tax evasion to his growing list of crimes. "What about Mad Dog, what's he up to? Maybe we can still make a night of it, just the two of us?"

"I'm sure he'd love to, man, but your timing's off on that one too," Matt said. "Mad Dog's up in San Jose at the BBOA convention. He won't be back until tomorrow."

"BBOA?" Tony said. "What's that stand for, Bad-ass Bikers on Acid?"

"No, man, it's the Biker Botanists of America. Mad Dog's delivering the keynote speech on new hydroponic gardening techniques for growing fresh vegetables in nutrient-enriched water instead of soil. With all the emphasis on organic and pesticide-free produce these days, Mad Dog's intimate knowledge of hydroponics is in high demand."

Tony's mouth hung open, but no words came out. He didn't quite know what to say. His image of the two outlaw bikers had been shattered by the reality that one was a gardener and the other an accountant. "Well," he finally said. "If you change your mind, let me know."

Tony hung up the phone and hung his head in disbelief. His plans for the night had completely fallen apart.

"What's the matter, Tony, no luck?" Jimmy asked.

"That's all right, Jimmy, you stay here and take care of Larry," Tony said. "I have no choice but to go it alone. It's okay. I can take care of myself."

*　　*　　*

Tony was determined to have a good time at the Love Tunnel with or without his friends. He called a car service and went out alone. Once he arrived at the Love Tunnel, he figured he'd have all the company he needed. Tony walked in and reserved a corner table, where he kept himself entertained with the help of a bevy of beauties, who paraded past him every few minutes for twenty-dollar lap dances and a good laugh at the expense of Tony and his ever-expanding tent.

First up was Divine, a bleached and tanned surfer girl with a flat chest but legs that went all the way up. She danced for Tony to "Welcome to the Jungle" by Guns N' Roses. "Now I know why they call you Divine," Tony said as he paid the dancer and sent her on her way.

Next was Cherie, a voluptuous brunette with pigtails and a red lollipop, who rode Tony like a Harley-Davidson Dyna Glide roadster for the duration of the Motley Crue hit "Girls, Girls, Girls." When the song ended, Tony slapped Cherie on the ass and waved "Au revoir, my Cherie amour."

Next in line was Dee Dee, a top-heavy blonde who was named for her cup size—double D. Dee Dee stuck Tony's head deep into her cleavage and battered him senseless by jiggling her enormous breasts back and forth to the sweet sounds of "Love Rollercoaster" by the Ohio Players. The repeated bashing of breasts against the sides of his head left Tony dizzy and disoriented but also happy and satisfied at the same time.

Next up were Maxxxie, Trixxxie, and Phoenixxx, who danced for Tony simultaneously with a pseudo-lesbian show of enthusiasm. Tony contemplated how many strippers there were who had found ways to incorporate a triple X into their names as he invited the girls to join him for a couple of overpriced bottles of strip club champagne at a hundred bucks a pop. By the time the girls left, Tony noticed he was starting to feel the effects of all the champagne he'd had. That was in addition to the five tequila shots he'd done at the bar and the six Scotches he'd had earlier that afternoon at the racetrack.

He figured he was already well on his way to being drunk, so he decided to go for broke and call the waitress over for some more drinks. "Yo, waittail cocktress! Over here!"

The waittail cocktress Tony was addressing was a college student who worked at the club to earn her tuition. She responded by bringing Tony a six-pack of tequila shots and overcharging him.

The shots were down Tony's hatch in an instant. Tony pinched the girl's butt, winked, and said, "Thanks for the drinks, honey."

As the warm cactus juice worked its way to Tony's head, he decided it was time to heat things up a little with Coco—the Love Tunnel's most popular African American dancer. Coco's ass was a cross between Jennifer Lopez's and Florence Griffith Joyner's, and she could shake it with the best of 'em. Just one dance to "Baby Got Back" by Sir Mix-A-Lot, and Tony was mesmerized.

Tony left his table to sit at the stage for a few songs in order to see Bambii and Barbie's two-girl shower show. Tony watched as the two blondes bathed each other in an inflatable kiddie pool on the main stage before being showered with money by their adoring fans. Tony sat poolside in the splash zone to ensure he wouldn't miss a minute of the action.

After a quick trip to the men's room to towel off, Tony was back at his table just in time to spot his favorite dancer—the lusciously seductive Exstasy—heading in his direction. After back-to-back dances to "Brick House" by the Commodores and "Pour Some Sugar on Me" by Def

Leppard, Tony was hooked. He quickly forgot that all other girls in the club even existed and prepared for a long night of the beautiful Exstasy's pretend affections.

Meanwhile, back in the Love Tunnel's manager's office, located behind the main stage, Bragg was sitting at Vinny Francone's desk, waiting for the right moment to make his move. He had been alerted to Tony Martini's presence by one of the club's bouncers more than an hour ago, but he decided to wait and see if Larry Lipwinkle would make an appearance at some time during the evening. With no trace of Larry in sight, however, Bragg was starting to lose patience.

There was a knock on the office door. It was the college student waittail cocktress who had served Tony his tequilas. "Hey, you're not Vinny! Where's Vinny?"

"Vinny's not here tonight. Go away," Bragg snapped.

"Well listen, mister. I don't know where Vinny's at or who the hell you're supposed to be, but the sign on the door says manager, and that's who I want to talk to."

"What's going on?" Bragg asked.

"Listen," the waittail cocktress said, "I'm working here, serving drinks to pay my tuition. I can put up with being called 'honey' and 'sweetie' and every other godforsaken name in the book, and I can even deal with being propositioned thirty times a night because those things are part of the job. But nowhere in my job description does it say I have to put up with having my ass grabbed!"

"You had your ass grabbed?"

"Damn right I had my ass grabbed. I told the bouncers about it too, but they said they couldn't do anything because the guy's a harmless big spender, and they've already got their hands full looking after the dancers. That's why I'm here. I want you to kick the fat greasy drunk bastard out of here."

Bragg's ears pricked. "Did you say fat bastard? Are you talking about the guy in the corner booth getting all the lap dances?"

"Yeah," the girl said. "He also called me a waittail cocktress."

Bragg chuckled. Even he hadn't heard that one before.

"It's not funny!"

Bragg decided he couldn't wait for Larry to show up a minute longer. He had to make his move now. "Tell you what I'm going to do. I'm going to bring the guy back here and have a little talk with him. Will that make you feel better?"

Back at the corner booth, Exstasy was cuddling up next to Tony and fondling his love handles as twenty-dollar bills continued to flow out of his wallet and in her general direction. It was not surprising, therefore, that Exstasy was not thrilled when two big bouncers showed up at the table, asking Tony to follow them to the manager's office.

"That's okay, baby," Tony said. "They probably just want to give me the customer of the month award!"

Tony followed the bouncers around to the office in back of the stage. The bouncers pushed him inside, sat him down in a chair, and closed the door behind them as they left.

"Hey, so you must be the manager. What'd I do, win the prize for customer of the year?"

"Not quite," Bragg said as he circled around back of Tony's chair and turned the dead bolt lock on the office door. He turned back to face Tony, but was momentarily distracted by Tony's bulging tent.

Tony noticed Bragg's gaze. "Oh, don't mind that. The thing's got a mind of its own." Tony blushed. "Number one sign of a happy customer in your business, right, Mr. Francone?"

Bragg was not amused. "I'm sorry to have to tell you this, Mr. Martini, but I'm not Mr. Francone. I'm not even the manager here."

"Not the manager? Well, then who the hell are you?" Tony was starting to worry that this visit involved something more serious than the customer of the month award.

"Who am I? Well that's up to you, Mr. Martini. I could be your best friend or your worst enemy. It all depends on how much you feel like talking."

Tony suddenly went from worrying to pissing in his pants. "Hey, how did you know my name was Martini? Talk about what? Why did you lock the door? What do you mean my worst enemy?"

Tony got up from his chair and tried to unbolt the door before Bragg caught him by the arm and threw him back down on the couch. "Where do you think you're going? You're not going anywhere."

Tony was starting to sweat like a Baptist minister on Sunday morning. "What's this all about?"

"You'll find out soon enough, but I suggest you settle down, Mr. Martini," Bragg said. "It's going to be a long night."

Bragg tied Tony's wrists and ankles to a wooden chair, gagged him, and stripped him down to his boxer shorts while he interrogated him for over an hour. The gist of most of Bragg's questions centered around Larry Lipwinkle's present whereabouts.

Tony was not cooperative.

Bragg had done almost everything he could think of to break a man. He'd detained Tony, tied him up, and beaten him, not only with his fists but also with his nightstick. He'd stripped him down with hopes of humiliating him, and he'd even pulled out his gun and threatened to shoot Tony if he didn't come up with some information leading to Bragg's capture of Larry Lipwinkle. Thus far, Tony had been able to stay loyal to his friend. It meant a lot to him to remain loyal after his friends had stuck by him and brought him to California, but now he was scared out of his mind and didn't know how long his resolve would last.

Bragg's first tactic was to get Tony to call Larry and lure him to the Love Tunnel to join the party. When Tony refused, Bragg brained him with the butt of his pistol until Tony picked up the phone. Fortunately, Larry was passed out and therefore could not be convinced to join Tony at the Love Tunnel. With no chance of getting Larry to the club that night, Bragg went to plan B and pressed Tony to cough up Larry's present location. If Larry wouldn't come to him, he'd go to Larry, he thought. The problem was Tony wouldn't budge, and Bragg was running low on ideas of how to get Tony to talk. Besides beating him, there wasn't much else he could do short of killing him, and then he'd never get the information he wanted.

Bragg had one more idea up his sleeve. He'd use his uncanny ability to push someone's buttons.

"You're a married man, aren't you, Mr. Martini?"

"Mrrrrdddd. Whaaa yrrr whannnna knnnwww bhhh daat?" Tony mumbled through his gag.

"Your wife's name is Julia. She lives in Staten Island. She's actually quite an attractive girl, if I do say so myself."

Tony squirmed in his chair, trying to free his hands from the ropes that bound him.

"You wouldn't want anything to happen to your wife, would you, Tony?"

Tony was wildly shaking his head no from side to side. *Who in the hell is this guy?* Tony thought as he struggled against the ropes.

"I wouldn't want to hurt your wife, Tony, believe me, but I'd do it. All you'd need to do to prevent anything from happening to her is just tell me where Larry is. That's all, just that one little thing."

There was just one thing left for Bragg to do, and that was to play his hole card. It was time to tell Tony about his burgeoning relationship with Julia. He figured this would drive home the point that he knew all about Tony's wife and had the power to back up his threats.

"Your wife is really something," Bragg continued. "I paid her a visit, you know, after you left town. She came to the door with one of those 'Hairdressers do it with style' coffee mugs."

Uh-oh, Tony thought. *Julia really does have a coffee mug that says "Hairdressers do it with style" on it.*

"She gave me a vibe, your wife. Yessiree, she did. So you know what I did Tony? I called her and asked her out. You know what she did? She said yes."

Tony's blood was starting to boil. He was no closer to telling this lunatic where he could find Larry, but Bragg's story was successful in bringing him to his breaking point. Tony's face turned bright red as he began to wiggle spastically in his chair.

"So your old lady and I went out, and you know what, she's a pretty frisky girl, that wife of yours. After dinner, I took her back to my apartment, and she showed me her tattoo. You must know the one I'm talking about, it's right smack-dab on her ass. The one that says 'Fuhgedaboutit'!"

Tony was twitching and squirming around wildly in an effort to break free. He couldn't believe what he was hearing.

"Do you know what I'm trying to tell you, Tony?" Bragg bent down and stared his captive in the eye. "I'm trying to tell you I screwed your wife. Four times!"

Tony began to go berserk, just as Bragg had anticipated, but his reaction was not entirely the one Bragg had expected. Instead of bringing Tony to his breaking point, he appeared to push him over it.

Tony had completely lost it. In a fit of rage, he mustered all his might and lifted himself up off his chair like a battering ram, uppercutting Bragg's jaw with the top of his head.

Bragg fell to the floor, temporarily dazed from the head-butt.

Tony thrashed up and down while still attached to his seat. Finally, he slammed himself down on the chair hard enough to break it into a hundred wooden splinters that shot all over the office.

Tony yanked his arms free from the wreckage and clubbed Bragg in the side of the head with a broken armrest hard enough to immobilize him. Tony's arms and legs were free from the chair but still tied to each other, which made fumbling with the deadbolt lock on the office door a major challenge.

Bragg was flat on the floor but beginning to regain his composure just as Tony finally flipped the lock and turned the knob to force the office door open. Bragg reached for Tony's feet but was a split second too late. Tony had hopped out the door toward freedom.

The first thing that crossed Tony's mind was finding help. After all, he was still gagged, half-naked, and tied up around his wrists and ankles. Not able to cry for help and unable to run, Tony spotted a bunch of bright lights peeking through a curtain just up ahead at the end of a corridor. Tony heard music and voices from beyond the curtain. Fearing Bragg might still be on his tail, Tony propelled himself headfirst through the curtain toward the lights on the other side.

37

Mack Peters had been dating his girlfriend, Marjorie Flanders, for eight years and could have gone on dating her for another eight more if Marjorie hadn't finally given him the shit-or-get-off-the-pot ultimatum speech before a live studio audience during a trip to *The Jerry Springer Show* last fall. Marjorie said her biological clock was ticking, and she was no longer willing to waste another day of her life with Mack Peters until Mack produced a diamond ring and a wedding date.

Mack's response of "Why should I buy the cow when I'm getting the milk for free?" touched off a smattering of applause and round of "Woo-Woo-Woos" from the men in *The Jerry Springer Show* audience. They all seemed to agree that Mack should lose the broad, find someone younger and prettier than Marjorie, and move on. Mack neglected to mention to the audience that in Southern California, even more than elsewhere, gorgeous young movie starlets weren't exactly falling from the sky and moving in with forty-year-old shoe salesmen with receding hairlines and expanding belt lines.

The problem for Mack was he really wasn't getting any better offers than Marjorie's. The prospects of a better offer coming along were about the same as the chances of him growing back his lost hair and losing thirty pounds on his current diet of french fries, bagels, and Milky Way bars. Looking at a very long plane ride home from *The Jerry Springer Show* back to Los Angeles, Mack finally gave in and proposed marriage to Marjorie somewhere over Iowa. She accepted, and a wedding date was set for the following April.

With the wedding fast approaching, Mack's friends planned on giving his single life the send-off it deserved with an all-night bachelor party at the Love Tunnel Gentlemen's Club in Hollywood. Mack and his friends were ordering beer by the pitcher and having a ball. The celebration was going off without a hitch, leading up to the party's climax when Mack was brought up onstage and surrounded by a dozen of the club's best strippers, whose job it was to spend ten minutes disrobing him, kissing him, and sticking their tits in his face.

Mack was having a great time at his bachelor party until a madman suddenly came from out of nowhere and burst onto the stage. A man with a gag in his mouth and a boner in his boxer shorts dove out onto the stage and crashed into Mack's strippers, knocking them over like bowling pins. Mack looked around in bewilderment. Thinking that this was a part of the show, the crowd roared with laughter and applause.

Tony was flat on the ground in the middle of the Love Tunnel's main stage. He tried to get up but was having a load of trouble getting to his feet because his wrists and ankles, while free of the chair, were still roped together.

Amidst the chaos, the strippers began to get up and dust themselves off. Unlike the crowd, they knew this wasn't part of the show.

"What the hell is going on here!" screeched Divine.

"Who the hell's the pervert?" yelled Cherie.

"It's the fat fucker who's been hanging around here with all the money! He seemed perfectly harmless before, but now he's getting fresh. Look, he just made me chip a nail!" screamed Trixxxie.

The group of angry topless dancers descended on Tony. He tried to move, but could do nothing more than flop around the floor like a fish out of water.

"Ewww look, he's got a hard-on!" screamed Barbie. "He must be some sicko rapist or something!"

Widespread panic washed over the half-naked dancers, who believed they were being assaulted by some psycho who had undressed, slipped past the bouncers, and began fondling himself onstage. The girls surrounded Tony and started kicking him as he sprawled on the ground in a state of shock. Tony took a half dozen shots to the chest, each time hearing the snapping sound of a few more ribs giving way to the punishment. He would have considered the whole thing pretty darn cool if it didn't hurt so damn much.

As Tony struggled to his knees, Dee Dee jumped him from behind. She dug her long painted nails into Tony's back and ripped ten bloody trails into his skin before working his balls like a speed bag and dropping him like a ton of bricks.

Tony slumped to the ground clutching his groin, but the reflex left Tony's head unprotected and wide open to the oncoming onslaught of the angry Coco, who grabbed Tony by the hair and began ferociously slamming his head into the stage face-first.

Tony was lying under a pile of ten angry naked strippers, being beaten senseless. He had laid awake at night fantasizing of this scene for as long as he could remember, but now that it was really happening, it seemed less like a dream to Tony and more like his worst nightmare.

In reality, the savage beating Tony was receiving wasn't all it was cracked up to be in his fantasies.

That's when a bad situation started to get even worse. Phoenixxx and Maxxxie grabbed Tony by the legs and began pulling in opposite directions until Tony's legs dislocated from his pelvis, snapping him like a wishbone.

Bragg was far behind Tony, but he finally made his way to the stage to witness the carnage. He enjoyed watching Tony get his comeuppance, but Tony's misfortune was actually hurting his cause. He would now need to duck out of sight and think of another way to get to Larry Lipwinkle because after the beating he was taking was over, it was clear that Tony wasn't going to be much use to him anymore.

Tony was rolling around on the ground in pain when a pair of girls grabbed him and turned him over onto his back to give Divine a clear target on Tony's chest. Divine seized her chance and stomped him with the bottoms of her four-inch stiletto heels. Divine's shoes proved to be an effective weapon for cracking Tony's breastbone and puncturing a lung.

Cherie was standing next to Divine and taking notes on her stomping technique. She was wearing platform heels. They were not quite the lethal weapons that Divine's stilettos were, but they still proved capable of performing magic when it came to stepping on Tony's hands and squashing his fingers.

Mack Peters was in shock. It started to dawn on him that maybe the massacre wasn't part of the show. Mack tried to run but was frozen in place by fear. Plus, he was kinda getting turned on by the whole thing, so he decided to stay put and keep watching.

Witnessing the fracas onstage from across the room and sensing her girlfriends might be in trouble, Niko—the Love Tunnel's Asian martial arts expert stripper—decided to spring into action. Niko flipped onto the stage like Jackie Chan as the rhinestones from her bra scattered across the floor. Her karate chops landed with precision atop Tony's shoulders, breaking his collarbones like twigs.

Before blacking out, one of the last things Tony saw was the waittail cocktress college student, climbing onstage and beginning to whale on him with her serving tray. "This will teach you to feel my ass, you shit bag!" she yelled as her tray connected squarely with Tony's mouth. The blast sent a half dozen cracked teeth shooting across the room like rocket-propelled Chiclets. The force of the blow also dislodged the waittail cocktress's earrings and sent them whizzing past Mack's head one by one. Mack continued to just sit there in stunned silence with a silly grin on his face just a few feet from where Tony was getting the beating of a lifetime.

Exstasy approached the stage to see what the brouhaha was all about. Through all the commotion, she could see that the bloody pulp at the bottom of the vengeful pile of strippers was none other than Tony—the same man who had been so generous a customer of hers recently. She couldn't just stand aside and do nothing while her cash cow got slaughtered. Seeing that he was obviously hurt badly and unable to defend himself, Exstasy was finally able to round up a few of the club's bouncers and put an end to the bloodshed. By the time the final stripper was pulled from his limp body, however, Tony was a twisted, battered mess who was barely alive.

Unable to believe his eyes, Mack jumped off the stage to avoid the melee. He joined his friends at stage side to watch the macabre aftermath from a safer distance.

"What did you cheap fuckers do, buy me the discount special?" Mack hollered at his friends in frustration as he watched Bambii connect with one last blow to Tony's groin before the bouncers pulled her away.

"Look at that lucky bastard! His friends must've bought him the bonus plan!"

38

The morning after Mr. Lopez's wild ride aboard Tricky Diva was the longest morning of his entire life. Upon his arrival at the track at five-thirty in the morning, Lopez was immediately hauled into the stewards' office at Santa Anita to be given his inevitable punishment for reckless race riding.

Lopez was not surprised to be called in front of the racetrack's judges for what he expected to be a brief hearing to inform him that he was banned from riding effective immediately. What actually happened, however, was something much more shocking and disturbing, which he never prepared for. The stewards sat Lopez down and informed him that his original appeal of the drug suspension had been upheld. He would have been free and clear from his drug charges (assuming no future offenses), but instead he was now being banned for life on the basis of reckless endangerment during the running of the previous day's third race. Lopez couldn't believe it. If he'd waited just one more day, he would have been reinstated, but now his career was permanently over. It was all because he listened to Tommy Boy and his degenerate friends. It was all their fault.

Just when Lopez thought things couldn't get any worse, they did. On his way out of the stewards' office, Lopez ran into Gonzalez, Martinez, and Rodriguez, who arrived for work wearing brand-new snakeskin boots, new diamond earrings, and enough gold necklaces and pendants to choke Mr. T.

The stewards were aware of betting irregularities in the third race from the day before, which involved an inordinate number of winning exactas, trifectas, and superfectas on the unlikely winning combination. The judges, who had launched an investigation into the results, were aware that the first three finishers of the race in question were Gonzalez, Martinez, and Rodriguez. After seeing the three jockeys arrive at the track wearing new clothes and a load of bling-bling, Lopez knew the stewards would no longer have any doubts that the three jockeys were involved.

Sure enough, Gonzalez, Martinez, and Rodriguez were all immediately suspended as part of an investigation into race fixing. They'd become the focus of a criminal investigation and were each urged to seek legal assistance immediately.

The four jockeys were devastated. Lopez's career was over, and he was possibly facing jail time pending the results of the investigation. Gonzalez, Martinez, and Rodriguez were kings for a day, but had gone from the penthouse back to the outhouse in a matter of minutes. Lopez met the jockeys as they left the stewards' office. They told him the details of their tale of woe.

Misery loves company, and under the circumstances, the four men did what anyone in their shoes would have done. They ran out of the racetrack as fast as they could and ducked into the nearest bar they could find open at seven o'clock in the morning.

Lopez, Gonzalez, Martinez, and Rodriguez spent the rest of the morning drowning their sorrows as the reality of what had happened began to sink in. With each passing drink, the jockeys became more and more enraged at being led down the wrong path by Tommy Boy and his friends. The alcohol flowed and Latin tempers started to flare. The jockeys all vowed revenge against Tommy Boy and his gang. Lopez promised to track them down, find them, and make them pay for what they had done.

*   *   *

Austin and Alana woke up that morning sporting major-league hangovers. They'd spent the night before celebrating Austin's Santa Anita success story at an impromptu party thrown in his honor by Madam Tiffany at her place. Dinner was served, and then the locks came off the liquor cabinets, allowing Tiffany's top-shelf spirits to flow like water for the rest of the evening. Tiffany opted for a bottle of Johnny Walker's top-of-the-line Blue Label while Austin and Alana made a beeline for Tiffany's tequila collection that included unopened bottles of Patron Añejo and Jose Cuervo's Reserva de la Familia Millennium blend. The party quickly degenerated into a shot-drinking contest, which proved to be a losing proposition for Austin and Alana, who were both under the table before Madam Tiffany had even begun to break a sweat.

After grabbing large quantities of much-needed coffee and aspirin, Austin and Alana began planning to leave California for Mexico as soon as Austin could track down the rest of the Dude-Men in order to divide the money. Austin's share of the loot was going to be a little more than eighty grand. It wasn't nearly as much as he'd hoped to win in his original Fix Six scam, but it would be more than enough to get him and Alana started with a significant down payment on the property they'd been eyeing in Todos Santos.

Austin waited nearly half the day to hear from Jimmy and the Dude-Men, but when the phone finally rang, the news wasn't the news Austin had been waiting to hear.

"Austin, it's Jimmy. Sorry I waited so long to call, man, it's just that we're having a few problems over here, and we're not really sure what to do."

"Problems? What kind of problems? You've got our money, right?"

"Yeah, I've got our money," Jimmy said. "The problem is I haven't heard from Tommy Boy since he left the racetrack yesterday, and even worse, we seem to have lost Tony too. He went out to his strip club last night and never came back. I'm here at the motel in Arcadia with Larry, and we want to wrap this up as fast as possible, but we can't make a move until we find Tony and Tommy Boy."

"I'm sure it's nothing to worry about, man," Austin said. "You've got eighty thousand dollars of Tommy Boy's money. You know you'll be hearing from him soon. As for Tony, he probably partied a little too hard last night and decided to sleep it off at a motel somewhere in Hollywood. Maybe he even got lucky."

"I hear what you're saying, man, but it still doesn't add up. We've got Tommy Boy's cut of the money, and we haven't seen him yet? This is Tommy Boy we're talking about. I know him better than that. He wouldn't let eighty thousand dollars out of his sight for much more than a couple hours. That goes for Tony too. Sure he wanted to party, but he knows damn well how much money we're sitting on over here. Don't you think he'd have found a way to get back here? He wasn't even driving last night. He took a limo over to Hollywood, and he would have taken the limo home rather than spending the night in Hollywood at a cheap motel."

"I guess you're right, Jimmy. This really doesn't make any sense. What should we do?"

"I don't think there's much we *can* do except wait. I'll tell you what though, Austin, I sure would feel a lot better if you were over here with us while we wait to hear something."

"Say no more, Jimmy. I'll be there as soon as I can."

39

The better part of the day passed, and the Dude-Men still hadn't heard from Tony or Tommy Boy. They figured Tommy Boy would eventually show up at their motel, but they couldn't think of a single good scenario that would have led to Tony going AWOL on the heels of the gang's first successful racetrack score.

Austin drove to Arcadia to join Jimmy and Larry at the motel to wait for word from Tony or Tommy Boy.

"Maybe he decided it was a good time for him to get out of Dodge and decided to run away. Remember, even with the money we made yesterday, it doesn't change the fact that Tony's still wanted by the police. Maybe he just ran away," Austin suggested.

"I've thought of that, but it doesn't hold water," Jimmy said. "He would have collected his money if he was going to go somewhere. Not only did he not take his split of yesterday's loot, but he also didn't even take his own two attaché cases filled with cash. Look, they're still here." Jimmy pointed to the metal cases sitting on the floor in the corner of the closet.

"Yeah, I think there's almost a couple hundred thousand bucks there, plus his cut. Even Tony's not stupid enough to leave without that much money," Larry said.

Austin thought about it another minute. "Maybe he freaked out and flew home to Julia? Maybe he went home to try to patch things up? Maybe he wants her to come with him wherever it is he ends up going?"

"That would make a lot of sense if we weren't talking about Tony. Do you think he's the kind of guy who'd fly home to share a quarter-million dollars with his wife? If he's on the run—take my word for it—he's heading in the other direction," Jimmy said.

The whole situation was starting to make Austin anxious. Sure, he wanted his friend Tony to be okay, but he also had his own concerns to worry about. The sooner Tony and Tommy Boy showed up, the sooner they could divide the money. The sooner they divided the money, the sooner he'd get his cut, and the sooner he could leave for Mexico with Alana.

Austin's final theory about Tony involved Tommy Boy. "Has anyone ever thought about the possibility that Tony's and Tommy Boy's disappearances are linked to each other? Maybe Tommy Boy freaked out and did something to Tony. The guy is pretty slimy after all, you've gotta admit, Jimmy."

"I've thought about that, Austin. And I'm telling you that it's not a possibility. I've known Tommy Boy too long. He's a bullshit artist and into some messed-up stuff, but he's cool with me, and he's sure as shit not capable of something as big as kidnapping Tony. No, man, I don't know what the answer is, but that's not it."

"Well how do you explain how we can't find Tommy Boy, either?" Austin asked. "Don't you think he'd be wanting his money right about now?"

"I can't explain it, Austin. I don't know. All I know is that all we can do right now is sit here and wait for Tony or Tommy Boy to either call or show up," Jimmy said as he walked over the minifridge and grabbed a cold beer. "Just sit tight and wait. Once one of the guys finally shows, he may be able to tell us what happened to the other. In the meantime, I say we try to relax and get comfortable. Flip me the remote control, Larry, I think the evening news is about to come on."

*　　*　　*

After witnessing Tony's savage beating at the Love Tunnel, Bragg returned to his Sunset Strip motel room and weighed the options for his next move. Bragg was unable to edge past the army of EMTs that showed up in the aftermath of Tony's attack and, therefore, couldn't follow them as they rushed him to the hospital. He wasn't worried too much, though, because he knew it didn't matter. He could easily locate Tony by doing a quick check of all the local hospitals. Once he found him, he knew he could wait around Tony's hospital room until Larry showed up to visit. Bragg considered it a good plan. The hospital visit would be his next move. In the meantime, he knew he'd temporarily have some time to spare. The news of Tony's mishap might not reach Lipwinkle until Tony stabilized. Bragg didn't need to rush because he knew Tony wasn't going anywhere and might not be in good enough shape to see visitors.

With time to take a breather, Bragg enjoyed a day at the pool in the courtyard outside his motel. He considered calling Julia Martini to tell her what had happened to Tony but decided against it until he could find out more information about Tony's condition.

Bragg spent the day in the sun and returned to his room in late afternoon for a quick shower before dinner.

After eating, Bragg got back to the motel at eleven. He had a seat on his room's cloth sofa with a stain on it, put his feet up on the Formica coffee table, and prepared to watch the *Action 5 Evening News* with anchorman Brock McClean.

*   *   *

Mad Dog returned to Los Angeles from his BBOA convention and was kicking back with a beer and rapping to Pin Dick and Snapperhead at the Black Knights' home base in South Central. Mad Dog couldn't stop talking about his scenic ride on Highway 1 through Monterey and Big Sur on his way down from San Francisco. The drive was easily the highlight of his botany trip. Matt took a break from his tax records long enough to join the rest of the guys in the living room.

"That scenery down Highway 1 must've been bitchin', bro, but I'll bet it sho 'nuff can't compare with the titties we both missed seeing last night at the Love Tunnel. Tony the Tent called, but you were gone, and I was buried with work, so he had to go it alone. It sounds like we missed out on one hell of a night."

"Well shi-yit," Mad Dog growled. "The timing of those BBOA conventions always sucks. Oh well, we'll catch my man Tony next time."

"Yup, I guess you're right," Matt said. "Maybe he'll call back tonight. In the meantime, toss me another brew and turn on the TV. It's after eleven, and we already missed the start of the Action 5 News. I'm dying to see what that cracker Brock McClean has got to say tonight."

*   *   *

It had been a long day of hard drinking for the Hispanic jockeys, and with Loco Lopez leading the way, the jockeys were ready to get violent. They vowed to hunt down the men who were responsible for ruining their careers. While they were at it, they also planned to help themselves to any money they were owed in the process, plus maybe even a little something extra for their trouble. If they were the ones doing the suffering, they should be the ones reaping the rewards, they reasoned.

Lopez made one last tequila toast to the death of the gringo gamblers, with Gonzalez, Martinez, and Rodriguez each echoing his sentiments.

Lopez spoke up. "Come out to my car, amigos, I've got something I want to show you guys."

Lopez drove a tricked-out late-model Cadillac Eldorado that had been customized in a chop shop in East LA with the help of some old friends of his from the barrio. Lopez's Cadillac rode extremely low to the ground but had a set of hydraulic lifts installed behind each wheel, which could raise or lower the car considerably. It was the kind of car that had a furry steering wheel, shiny metallic rims, and could lean from side to side, front to back, and even bounce up and down at stoplights.

Gonzalez, Martinez, and Rodriguez stumbled out the front door of the bar and stood in the parking lot, waiting for Loco to pop the trunk. Lopez put the key in and opened it up. The trunk contained a wide array of potentially deadly weapons. "They don't call me Loco for nothing," Lopez said as Gonzalez, Martinez, and Rodriguez reached inside one by one to choose their preferred weapons.

Gonzalez, the former baseball player, found a baseball bat stashed in Lopez's trunk. "Ah, *muy bien*," he said as he twirled the Louisville Slugger around in his hands like a sword-wielding samurai in a kung fu movie. He spotted a random Honda in the parking lot that happened to be parked in the wrong place at the wrong time and targeted it for batting practice. Gonzalez swung the bat straight through the rear window of the car. The blow sent shattered glass all over the parking lot and put a big smile on Gonzalez's face. "Muy bien!"

"That's strike one, amigo." Lopez laughed.

Martinez, the former Panamanian boxer, didn't need the help of a baseball bat in order to turn a guy's face into cottage cheese, but after fishing around Lopez's trunk, he did find a weapon that was much more to his liking. Martinez tried on a pair of brass knuckles that Lopez had stashed away in the event that a minor traffic altercation might someday get out of control. Martinez's fists moved through the air like lightning as he shadowboxed with the brass knuckles on both hands. He bobbed and weaved his way over toward the poor unfortunate smashed Honda and delivered a devastating lightning-quick one-two punch into the car's quarter panel. His fists put two holes clean through the metal car body.

"I like it! That's strike two," Lopez said.

Finally, it was Rodriguez's turn. He peeked inside Lopez's trunk and found exactly what he'd been looking for. The former knife-throwing circus performer buried his head into the back of the trunk and came back out with a handful of knives of assorted shapes and sizes.

"Ahh, I see you found my knives, Rodriguez! I had those lying around in there from the time I took that cooking class down at the community college. I saved them for a rainy day," Lopez said.

Rodriguez started juggling the knives in order to get a feel of them. He took dead aim on the unfortunate Honda and threw the knives, one by one, into the car's tires, instantly flattening them.

"Whoa, I guess that's strikes three, four, five, and six," Lopez said as he began poking around in his trunk to see what weapons might be left for him.

Lopez pushed his spare tire to one side and grabbed the only two other items left in the trunk—a tire iron and a chain. "These will do nicely," Lopez said before he strolled over to the Honda and smashed out its windows with the tire iron and then wrapped the chain around the rear bumper and yanked it off.

Heavily armed with the former contents of Lopez's trunk, the jockeys hurried back to the bar to order another pitcher of beer and catch the evening news. Lopez put his tire iron down on the bar and asked the bartender to turn the channel to Brock McClean and the Action 5 news team at eleven.

*   *   *

Marcus Bellvue worked all day on a new all-in-one lethal injection at his east side workshop and then sat down at his desk for a little R & R before relaunching his revenge plans against the remaining Dude-Men.

Bellvue took off his shoes, cranked up his hi-fi stereo, and put a record of Liberace's "I'll Be Seeing You" on the turntable. As Liberace's golden tones filled the air, Bellvue went over to his top-secret wet bar across the room. He had a craving for one of his trademark concoctions—a bourbon and bong water cocktail.

Bellvue poured himself a highball of the B and B cocktail, which he invented. He swished the drink around his mouth in order to savor every drop, swallowed, and then slid into his cozy desk chair and waited for the buzz to kick in. He pulled out his notebook to check on the progress of his List of Death.

~~Tommy~~	~~IBoy LETHAL INJECTION~~
Jimmy	LETHAL INJECTION
Austin	LETHAL INJECTION
Tony	LETHAL INJECTION
Larry	LETHAL INJECTION

Bellvue was satisfied with the work he'd done in the lab. He'd replaced his three-step injection with a quicker yet equally effective single shot.

Bellvue's choice for the all-in-one poison was a phenol injection. Bellvue had a soft spot for the phenol because it was the poison favored in lethal injections used by the Nazis in the early phases of institutional genocide at Auschwitz.

An injection of 10 to 15 milliliters of phenol into a vein or directly into the heart was enough to kill a person within fifteen seconds. Bellvue filled his needle gun with ten times the necessary amount.

Bellvue looked at four names left on his List of Death. *That's four times the fun,* he thought as he relaxed in his chair, leaned back, flicked on the TV, and turned the channel to the Action 5 Evening News with anchorman Brock McClean.

40

Brock McClean was the king of the evening news ratings in Los Angeles for the fifth straight year, thanks to huge advantages over the competition in key demographic areas—such as women from 18-34, women from 35-49, and gay men of all ages. He delivered the news with an authority born out of his deep voice, strong square chin, and a wind tunnel-tested hairdo that made housewives everywhere dampen their drawers and dream of dumping their husbands.

As usual, all the day's important national and international news was delivered in the Action 5 Evening News's first ten minutes. After the first commercial break, however, McClean and the Action 5 news team had to dig deep for second-tier stories to deliver, especially on slow news days.

"Locally tonight, an investigation has begun at Santa Anita racetrack where allegations of race fixing have been swirling ever since yesterday when three longshots waltzed home following a hair-raising ride by troubled jockey Pat 'Loco' Lopez. Video of the incident appears to show Lopez crashing into his rivals on other horses on purpose. Officials at the racetrack declined comment, except to say that the investigation is centering around unusual betting patterns that took place on the race. Lopez and the jockeys of the longshots have all been suspended pending the results of the investigation."

Lopez was watching the news and translating the story for the three Hispanics. Gonzalez and Martinez had to physically restrain Rodriguez in order to prevent him from throwing his knives through the television set in the bar. In Spanish, Lopez told Rodriguez to settle down and save it for when they got their hands on the stinking gringo race fixers. He also asked Gonzalez and Martinez to quiet down so he could hear the rest of the newscast.

Bellvue was quite interested in the race-fixing story as well. He knew in his gut that Tommy Boy's friends had to be involved in it, and that just made him want to cross out the four remaining names on his list even faster than before. He wanted them dead so much that his hands began to shake. Thankfully, he had another tumbler of one of his patented bourbon and bong water cocktails at his side to calm him down.

The story also caught Bragg's eye as he followed along with the news from his Sunset Strip motel room. This couldn't be a coincidence, he thought. This had to have something to do with Lipwinkle and his friends.

In Arcadia, Austin, Jimmy, and Larry all sat up straight and watched the report intently once they heard Brock McClean say the Hispanic jockeys had all been suspended. They started to shit bricks once they heard there was an ongoing investigation that could lead the cops to their doorstep.

"Did you guys hear that? The track is wise to our scam. I'd like nothing more than to get the hell out of this town," Jimmy said. "Goddammit, where are you, Tony?"

Jimmy's question was about to be answered.

"In other news tonight, Action 5 News has word out of Hollywood of one of the strangest stories we've reported in a long time, and trust me, that's saying a lot." McClean paused for effect and to give his listeners a moment to absorb his witty humor. "We go now to Holy Family Hospital in Hollywood where field reporter Dottie Chang is standing by with this report. And I'll warn our male viewers that what they are about to see is extremely disturbing. The squeamish might want to leave the room."

"Hey, Larry, you better get up and leave the room," Austin kidded.

"Fuck off, Jackman," Larry retorted.

Bellvue sat up straight in his easy chair. He couldn't wait to hear the squeamish news.

The Hispanic jockeys yelled at the television screen as if the people on TV could hear them. They demanded McClean to come back on and give them more information on the racetrack story.

Bragg sighed and rolled his eyes. "A strange freak story in this town? What a fucking surprise."

Dottie Chang stood holding a microphone beside the sliding glass door outside the Holy Family Hospital emergency room. The words *Emergency Room* were prominent in the camera shot above her left shoulder. She wore a navy blue pants suit, a Hermes scarf, and a very concerned look on her face.

"Thanks, Brock. I'm standing here tonight outside the emergency room of Holy Family Hospital where inside, a man is fighting for his life after one of the most bizarre beatings in recent memory. It all started last night when things got out of hand in the early morning hours at an adult club in Hollywood called the Love Tunnel."

"Holy shit, guys, listen up! She just said something happened over at the Love Tunnel last night!" Jimmy said. Every eyeball in the Arcadia motel suite was fixed upon the TV screen. You could hear a pin drop.

At California Black Knights' headquarters in South Central, Matt threw down his beer and turned up the volume on the remote as soon as he heard mention of the Love Tunnel. "Holy shit, boys, it's a news story about the Love Tunnel. Shhhh!"

"The victim—identified by hospital personnel as a Tony Martini of Staten Island, New York—was admitted at around 2 a.m. when EMTs rushed him in with multiple injuries including a punctured lung, several broken bones, and severe head trauma. I'm also hearing rumblings that Martini may need reproductive reconstructive surgery."

"Oh my god, guys, it's Tony! We found Tony!" Austin yelled, not knowing if that was good news or not.

"Reproductive reconstructive surgery? Bet you can't say that one ten times real fast! I'm crossing my legs just thinking about it, Dottie!"

Bellvue giggled. His bong water and bourbon cocktail was starting to go to his head. The bourbon burned his throat and soothed his nerves. The bong water was refreshing and gave him a nice head rush, not to mention the munchies. "It looks like I'll be paying our fat friend a visit very soon. He'll be victim number 2," Bellvue said as he tapped on his List of Death with the eraser end of his pencil.

Over in South Central: "Oh shit! Did you hear that, Mad Dog? It's Tony! Tony got his dick kicked in over at the Love Tunnel last night!"

"Witnesses say the victim was involved in an altercation with several female dancers at the seedy club, who claimed he sexually assaulted them onstage during a bachelor party. Further details about the fight are unavailable, but doctors have informed us at Action 5 News that Martini is listed in stable but guarded condition and is currently being fitted with a body cast."

"Holy shit, I can't believe this. We've gotta get down there!" Larry cried out, unable to believe the news.

"Adding insult to injury for the alleged assailant, police are also looking into filing charges against him for his behavior in the sex club which led to the attack. Police sources tell us that possible charges include assault, lewd public behavior, and indecent exposure."

Matt and Mad Dog slapped hands. "Yeaaaaah boyyyyyy! Right on, brother!" they said simultaneously.

Bragg grabbed a motel notepad and pen off his nightstand and quickly scribbled down the name of the hospital where Tony was being treated. "Thank you, Dottie, for saving me a heckuva lot of legwork," he said to his TV.

"Thanks for the report, Dottie. Beaten up by a bunch of girls? Ouch, that's gotta hurt! We can only speculate what really happened at that club last night. It must have been quite a scene," McClean said with a chuckle. "I guess that'll teach him to keep it in his pants from now on."

The news about Tony brought much rejoicing in the bar where Lopez and the jockeys were getting sloshed. Loco translated the news of Tony's whereabouts to Gonzalez, Martinez, and Rodriguez, who were practically drooling at the prospect of finishing the job the strippers had started. Lopez told the jockeys to get their weapons ready for a trip to see Tony at the hospital the next morning.

"Finally, in other news, police say the body of a man they found dead in the foyer of a Pasadena home last night has been identified as that of Murray Garfinkel, an Arcadia entrepreneur who was also known under the alias of Tommy Bahama Boy. The body was discovered lying on the floor of the home by a family member and a female friend. Sources close to the investigation say the victim was pronounced dead at the scene with a severe blunt force trauma to the back of the head. Police are ruling the death a suicide. That doesn't make any sense."

Bellvue gave himself a pat on the back and proudly congratulated himself for a job well done. The drug-masking agents and postmortem head cracking he'd decided to give Tommy Boy had served their purpose by keeping the cops from suspecting his lethal injection.

"Next, stay tuned for weather with Claudia Skies, and sports with Lou Swinstien. How about those Lakers!"

Bragg, Bellvue, Lopez, and Mad Dog all flicked off their respective televisions and ran to phones to dial Holy Family Hospital to inquire about the earliest possible time they could see Tony. Too stunned to move, the Dude-Men sat in silent disbelief, not only about Tony's news, but also about Tommy Bahama Boy.

"What the hell is going on here?" Austin asked rhetorically.

"I can't believe what I just heard," Jimmy said, his voice cracking.

"I can't believe it, either," Larry added. "Did you know Tommy's real name was Murray Garfinkel?"

"That's not what I'm in disbelief over, Larry, you tool," Jimmy said. "I'm in disbelief that Tommy's dead."

"You mean you're in disbelief that Murray is dead."

"What the fuck are you talking about, Lipwinkle? Tommy, Murray, whatever. Either way, he's fucking dead."

Austin was thinking about the news report. "What they said just doesn't make any sense to me. Tommy Boy had more than eighty thousand dollars in cash here waiting for him. He wasn't suicidal. As a matter of fact, he was pretty fucking far from it."

"They also said they found him with the back of his head bludgeoned. I'm no coroner, but that doesn't sound like a suicide to me. No way, man. Tommy was definitely killed. The only question is by whom?" Jimmy pondered.

"Well, it could have been that creep Bellvue," Austin said. "He could have blamed Tommy Boy for ruining his career. Frankly, I wouldn't put anything past that guy. He looked like a real honest-to-goodness psycho, from what I saw of him."

"Or it could have had something to do with Lopez and the jockeys," Larry said. "You heard the news report—they all got suspended. Who's to say they didn't go out looking for revenge against Tommy Boy? Maybe the two stories are related?"

"That's a possibility, but we can't worry about that stuff right now," Jimmy said. "We need to focus on Tony. We've got to get ourselves to that hospital as soon as he's stabilized. I don't know if there's anything we can do for him, but we all should be there for him to show our support."

41

Alana spent the night packing her new Louis Vuitton bags and waiting for Austin to return to Madam Tiffany's with the money. She was expecting to leave for Mexico in the next couple of days and wanted to be ready to hit the road as early as possible.

When Alana informed Tiffany they would be leaving, Tiffany responded with surprisingly motherly compassion. The madam said, "Alana, honey, it just breaks my heart to see you go. I've really grown to love having you as my houseguest. I hope you're not leaving so soon on my account."

"Oh dear, no," Alana said. "I've loved being here and getting to know you. You've shown me a whole new world I never knew existed before."

"What, you mean the sex?"

"No, Madam Tiffany, the shopping!"

"Oh, don't even mention it, Alana. That was my pleasure."

"Mine too. It's just that I've been waiting to go to Mexico for so long, and now we finally have the money to do it. Plus, I really want to get Austin out of here as soon as possible before he gets into another harebrained scheme with his friends."

"I agree, but you have to admit that this particular harebrained scheme seems to have paid off. It's given you enough money to get you to Mexico, and miraculously, Austin didn't get caught. I guess he has a little of his mother's business sense in him after all."

"You're right, Tiffany, but this whole fiasco has brought out a side in Austin I never saw before. He was always a gambler, but he was never dishonest. I thought he had his stuff together enough to avoid getting involved with psychopathic veterinarians and drug-addicted jockeys. This whole experience has soured me, and I really just want to distance myself from it."

"Well, where you're going, you'll be far, far away from any of this madness."

"It will be tough to leave though, Tiffany. After all, you've spoiled me so much these last couple of weeks. I don't know if I can go back to living in poverty again."

"Alana honey, having money isn't everything, it's the only thing. Just make sure you have enough money to live well down there in Mexico."

"It's funny. I never thought about money until the last couple weeks, but living the good life here has opened my eyes. I still want to go to Todos Santos, but now I'm thinking much bigger. The problem is that we won't have as much money as we originally planned on having. The money's being split up too many different ways. When this whole thing started back in New York, Austin was talking about something like a quarter-million dollars. Now we only have about eighty thousand. It's enough money to get started, but it's not enough to afford the lap of luxury. I sincerely hope what we have is enough."

"That's what I've been trying to teach you all along. Don't just be satisfied with reaching your destination. Think about reaching your destination in style."

"I know, Tiffany, and believe me, I've learned. I'm still anxious to get going, though. I'm tired of being frustrated by the waiting and frustrated by the money situation. Now I just want to get the show on the road already."

Just then, the phone rang downstairs. The codpiece-wearing house servant was up at Alana's door in a flash to deliver the cordless phone. "Phone call for you, Mistress Alana. It's Master Austin."

Alana took the phone. "Austin, what's up?"

"It's bad news, Alana. Tony got beat up pretty bad. He's in the hospital. There's also even worse news about Tommy Boy that I don't want to get into right now. The point is, we may have to put off leaving for a day or two until we know that Tony's gonna be all right. We called the hospital, and they're not going to let us in to see him until tomorrow morning. We'll know more then."

"What happened, Austin? Are you okay?"

"Yeah, I'm fine, Alana. I don't want you to worry. What happened to Tony was totally unrelated to the rest of us. I just need to know he's okay before we leave."

"What about the money, Austin?"

"The money's safe. Like I said, this has nothing to do with that. He just got beat up by a bunch of strippers. It's a long story. I'll tell it to you in the car on the way to Todos Santos."

"Strippers! How serious is it?"

"It's bad. I'm going to stay the night with Jimmy and Larry at their motel and then go to the hospital in the morning. It's Holy Family Hospital in Hollywood. We called, and the earliest they'll let us near Tony is tomorrow morning. I'll call you in the morning and then swing by and pick you up on the way to the hospital. In the meantime, I need you to call Tony's wife, Julia, and tell her about this. I think she deserves to know, and besides, Tony might need her. And I think it's better she hear it from you than of the Dude-Men."

Austin gave Alana Julia Martini's number and said good night. Alana turned to Tiffany, who had been in the room listening to the conversation. "That was Austin on the phone. There's another delay," Alana said in a saddened voice. "His sleazy friend Tony is in the hospital. He got beat up in a strip joint or something. Now I've gotta call his poor wife in New York and tell her the news. Shit. I hope I don't turn into a poor sap like her. In the meantime, it looks like I'm stuck waiting again. I'm beginning to wonder if we're ever gonna make it to Mexico."

42

Early the next morning, a deranged veterinarian, four violent jockeys, a vigilante New York cop, two motorcycle gang members from South Central, and three friends of a man nearly beaten to death by a bloodthirsty mob of strippers were all on their way to Holy Family Hospital in Hollywood.

The Dude-Men were anxious to see Tony and had no idea they were on a collision course with Bellvue, Bragg, and the heavily armed jockeys—who all had the same idea after catching the Action 5 Evening News with Brock McClean the night before.

Austin, Jimmy, and Larry piled into Jimmy's green SUV and got an early start out of Arcadia in order to swing by Madam Tiffany's house to pick up Alana. Larry called shotgun, so Austin sat in the back with Alana, who gave him the cold treatment on the ride over to the hospital. The mood in the SUV was pretty solemn anyway, so nobody really noticed. All the guys could think about was Tony's condition. All Alana could think about was how she was on her way to Hollywood to visit Austin's fat-ass loser friend instead of on her way to Mexico.

Bellvue had been up most of the night at his Sylmar lab, putting the finishing touches on his three-in-one serum meant as a lethal injection for Tony and his remaining friends. Bellvue planned to pose as a doctor to gain access to Tony's room. He exchanged his usual black lab coat for a white one, loaded his poison syringe into his needle gun, got in his black van, and pointed it down the freeway toward Hollywood.

Bragg was up early too, but he had only a short drive to the hospital from his motel in the heart of Hollywood. Before leaving his room, he had time to call Julia Martini. He was going to tell her about what happened to Tony but was surprised to hear that someone had already called her to tell her the news. When Bragg reached her, she was on her way to the airport to catch a flight from New York to Los Angeles.

Julia loved the irony of Tony getting beaten up by strippers but decided she'd better make an appearance at Tony's bedside anyway to attempt to get back all the money he'd taken out of the bank.

Lopez and the three Hispanic jockeys had passed out at the bar across the street from Santa Anita. Out of force of habit, they were all up at the crack of dawn. The first thing they thought about when they woke up was killing Tony Martini. They drank some coffee, grabbed their weapons, and rushed out to Lopez's low-riding Caddy on their way to Holy Family Hospital in Hollywood.

At the Black Knights' headquarters in South Central, both Matt and Mad Dog were sick with worry and unable to sleep well all night. They planned to get an early start but were delayed somewhat when unable to drag the badly hungover Pin Dick out of bed in order to fix them breakfast. Pin Dick was the Black Knights' resident cook, and neither Matt nor Mad Dog could work any appliances in the kitchen except for the George Foreman Grill, which wouldn't do them any good at breakfast. Thinking with their stomachs first and their hearts second, Matt and Mad Dog fired up their hogs and drove off to get some breakfast before continuing on to Hollywood to visit Tony.

Bragg arrived at the hospital first, pulling his rental car up close in the hospital's large parking lot. His plan was to play it cool. He'd flash his badge and pose as a local policeman. The badge would give him full access to Tony's room and make him impervious to hospital restrictions on visiting hours and the like. Once he found where Tony was, he'd pay him a little visit, make some chitchat, disengage Tony's doctor call button, and sit and wait for Lipwinkle to make his appearance.

Judging by the injuries described on the evening news, Bragg figured Tony would have been admitted to the emergency room the night before and then transferred to intensive care or a private room that morning. He stopped by the front desk and was told Tony had just been moved to a private room up on the second floor.

Tony was in room 213, and Bragg found it with little trouble. Bragg peeked inside. The room was designed for two patients, but the bed across the room from Tony was empty, and Tony was the only one there. Bragg was satisfied he'd have the privacy he was going to need.

Bragg entered the room quietly and saw Tony wearing a full-body cast. He was propped up in bed but appeared to be asleep. His right arm and left leg were suspended in traction, hanging from an overhead contraption designed to elevate broken limbs and keep them suspended. The body cast covered Tony's neck, head, and chin. A large strap wrapped around Tony's head, holding in place a ghastly metal mouth guard that wired his broken jaw in place. He was missing his front teeth, thanks to the waittail cocktress's vicious assault with her cocktail serving tray.

Bragg actually felt bad for Tony for a few seconds until he remembered the reason he was there. He started to envision Larry lying in the hospital bed in the place of Tony. He daydreamed that he'd be the one who put him there. He pictured Larry lying there helpless, just like Tony. He fantasized about walking up to Larry's bedside and putting a gun between his eyes and pulling the trigger. He smiled as he pictured Larry's brains splattered all over the mattress.

Bragg didn't want to allow Tony to sleep through such an important moment. Knowing that Tony couldn't talk or call for help, Bragg awakened him by knocking on the cast on his head.

"Knock, knock, anybody home?" Bragg said as he continued to hit Tony's head harder and harder.

Tony's eyes opened. He slowly took in the room and noticed a man standing along his bedside. He was hooked up to a feeding tube and several IVs that administered an assortment of pain medications intended to keep him feeling good. Bragg wasn't surprised to find Tony's response to be one of indifference.

"You don't mind a little company, do ya, meatball?" Bragg asked. "I'm just gonna have a seat here in your room and wait for visiting hours to begin. I want to have a word with one of your friends. Is that okay with you?"

Tony looked at him but couldn't say anything with his jaw wired shut.

"What's the matter, cat got your tongue?" Bragg joked. "Blink once for yes and twice for no."

With a hint of recognition beginning to form in his eyes, Tony blinked twice.

"Is that a no?" Bragg said. "Well too bad, shitbag, because I'm staying here and waiting for your friend Larry whether you like it or not. I'll make you a deal: if you can stay awake, I'll even let you watch as I kill the bastard right in front of your eyes with my bare hands."

Tony tried flailing around, but the pain was too great. He reached for his call button but couldn't find it.

"You looking for this, scumbag?" Bragg grinned. "It's disconnected. There's nothing you can do, and nobody can help you. It's going to be a long morning. I suggest you just relax and wait for your friend and then enjoy the show."

*   *   *

Not surprisingly, Austin, Jimmy, and Larry hit traffic en route from Arcadia to Hollywood. After the detour up into the Hollywood Hills to pick up Alana, Jimmy's green SUV pulled into the hospital about a half hour after Bragg.

Bellvue and the jockeys were close behind, followed by the bikers, who'd gone out and scarfed down jumbo breakfast platters with extra bacon at the closest IHOP.

Jimmy, Austin, and Alana figured Tony would still be in the emergency ward. They headed straight for the entrance where Dottie Chang had taped her report the night before. Larry thought Tony would have already been admitted, so he split up from the rest of the group and went around the building to the hospital's main entrance.

It turned out that Larry was on the right track. While the receptionist in the emergency ward mistakenly directed Jimmy, Austin, and Alana to the intensive care unit, Larry was able to quickly find out Tony's correct room number from the people at the front desk. He caught an elevator straight up to the second floor to find room 213.

The door to Tony's room was closed. Larry knocked, not imagining that his worst enemy was waiting on the other side. "Hello, Tony? Anybody in there?"

Bragg's ears pricked. He slid his midnight special from his shoulder holster and moved toward the door. Faking a woman's voice, Bragg answered, "Who is it?"

"My name's Larry—Larry Lipwinkle. I'm here to see Tony Martini."

Bragg had waited for this moment. He was milking it for all it was worth. Still in his woman's voice he replied, "I'm afraid I can't help you. Only immediate family is allowed to visit."

"Tony doesn't have any family here, but I'm his close friend, and I'd like to see him. Why won't you open the door and let me in? Who the heck are you anyway?"

Bragg waited until he could feel Larry's weight leaning against the door and then swung it open as fast as he could. Larry lost his balance and fell forward into the room, landing flat on his back.

Larry looked up from the floor straight into the barrel of Bragg's .22. "Who am I?" Bragg said. "I'm your worst fucking nightmare, that's who."

Larry recognized Bragg right away but was coldcocked in the side of the head by the butt of Bragg's pistol before he could call for help. Bragg closed the door again but didn't have time to lock it before lifting Larry up by his collar and throwing him onto the bed alongside Tony. Larry landed on Tony's stationary leg, causing him to let out a muffled yelp as the pain shot through his body. Bragg picked up Tony's bedpan and smashed it upside Larry's head. The blow wasn't hard enough to knock Larry out, but it was more than enough to immobilize him on the bed and ensure he stayed quiet for a few minutes while Bragg prepared to finish him off.

*   *   *

After a wild-goose chase to the ICU ward, Jimmy, Austin, and Alana were finally on their way up to Tony's room.

So were Bellvue and the jockeys.

Bellvue had arrived in his black van and obtained Tony's room number at the first-floor nurse's station before donning his doctor guise. The jockeys arrived in their lowrider and opted for the ICU ward where Jimmy, Austin, and Alana had been minutes before. They too were directed up to Tony's room on the second floor.

Breakfast had slowed the bikers down, but they were now back on their choppers and rumbling toward the hospital as fast as they could.

Jimmy, Austin, Alana, Bellvue, and the disgraced jockeys were all on their way to Tony's room at virtually the same time. None of them knew the others were there. Bellvue was taking the elevator closest to the nurse's station while Jimmy, Austin, and Alana were on their way up the elevator located nearest the ICU unit. The jockeys were trailing close behind, going the same way. The elevator nearest the ICU was just a few doors down from Tony's room on the second floor. Bellvue's elevator was on the other side of the building.

The ICU elevator clanked its way up to the second level. The doors slid open, and Jimmy, Austin, and Alana walked out onto Tony's floor. The doors clanked shut behind them as the elevator returned to the ground floor to pick up its next load of passengers. At the same time, Bellvue's elevator let him off up on the second floor at the other end of the building.

"What number is Tony's room—213?" Alana asked as she, Jimmy, and Austin walked down the corridor from the elevator. "Let's see. Hey, guys, here's room 211. He must be right down here . . . 212 . . . 213. Here it is."

The gang arrived in front of a closed door. "Why's the door closed?" Austin asked. "Do you think it's all right for us to go in?"

"Check if it's locked," Jimmy said. "If it's unlocked, just walk on in. I'll be right behind you."

On the other side of the door, Bragg was already working over Larry. He was forcing Tony to watch as he pummeled Larry with his fists, elbows, knees, and the butt of his pistol. He positioned Larry in front of Tony's bed, so that every time he punched him, he would fall backward onto Tony's body cast. Tony was unable to help Larry or protect himself from the weight of Larry's body as he repeatedly crashed down from one of Bragg's swinging blows.

Austin tried the door handle and it gave way. "It's unlocked," Austin said as he opened the door. "Hello. Anyone home?"

Austin's entrance startled Bragg, who thought he'd relocked the door when Larry came in. Austin saw Tony lying on the bed and instantly glimpsed two more figures in the room out of the corner of his eye. It was Larry and a man he'd never seen before. Larry's face was swollen and bloody, but he was lucid enough to see his friends coming.

Larry cried out, "Austin, Jimmy, help!"

Jimmy's eyes bulged out of his head when he realized what was happening. He and Austin instinctively moved to their friend's aid. When they saw Bragg's gun pointed in their direction, however, they immediately backed off and started to make other plans.

Bragg had momentarily taken his eyes off Larry. Spotting his opening, Larry ducked down and bolted for the door. He wasn't quick enough though and was caught from behind and thrown back onto the bed by Bragg.

"Run, guys, he's a cop!" Larry screamed. "Get yourselves the hell out of here, and get someone to help me!"

Bragg swatted at Larry with his pistol hand and connected across Larry's jaw. Jimmy, Austin, and Alana momentarily froze in shock, then bolted for the door as soon as Bragg's gun swung back in their direction. They leaped out of the room before the detective had a chance to get off a shot.

"Which way?" Alana screeched.

"Right! Go right!" Austin responded as he took Alana's hand and tore off down the hall, with Jimmy at his side.

Alana spotted a tall rail-thin dark doctor in the hallway up ahead. "There's a doctor. We can ask him for help!"

Austin looked down the hall and saw the man up ahead. He stopped running dead in his tracks. "Oh, shit. That's no doctor. That's Bellvue!"

Jimmy saw him too. "Bellvue? What the fuck's he doing here?"

Bellvue recognized Austin and Jimmy. "Bingo," he said as he reached into his lab coat with his right hand and pulled out his giant stainless steel needle gun.

Jimmy, Austin, and Alana took one look at the needle, turned around, and ran the other way. They went for the elevator they had come in on. Up ahead, they could see the light blink on, indicating the elevator had just arrived on the second floor. "We're in luck. The elevator's here," Jimmy yelled as they made a break for it.

The elevator doors opened, but the elevator wasn't empty. Four small angry men slithered out. One carried a baseball bat. Another reached into his jacket and pulled out a tire iron.

Jimmy, Austin, and Alana stopped cold in their tracks. "Do you see what I see?" Austin called out. "It's Loco and the jockeys. They see us. They're coming right for us!"

Bellvue and the bloodthirsty jockey mob had the gang surrounded. They were closing in on them from both directions. Bragg peeked out of Tony's room and saw that Tony's visitors were up to their asses in trouble. They would no longer be any concern to him anyway. He had everything he wanted right there in room 213. He shut the door behind him and turned his attention back to Larry.

Bellvue was getting closer to the gang now. So were the jockeys, who were coming from the other direction. "You screwed us over, man," Loco said. "Now you're going to pay."

Alana looked back at Bellvue. She screamed when she saw the shiny foot-long needle in his raised hand.

The gang was cornered. There was no longer a minute to waste. Austin looked up and spotted a stairwell door just a few yards away. It was the last chance for escape, and he went for it. He pulled Alana with him. Jimmy stayed close behind.

Bellvue and the crazed jockey mob converged, but the gang reached the door in the nick of time. They sprinted down the stairs ahead of Bellvue and the jockeys, who were there an instant too late. The jockeys collided with Bellvue at the doorway and fell over each other, costing them valuable time.

Jimmy, Austin, and Alana had a crucial head start but no longer had the time to go find Larry some help. They ran downstairs and out of the hospital to Jimmy's green SUV in the parking lot.

Bellvue and the jockeys were back on their feet and trailing close behind.

43

Matt and Mad Dog arrived at the hospital and were on their way up to room 213. They made a brief detour to the gift shop. The clerk behind the counter shuddered in fear as Matt and Mad Dog made their purchases. Matt bought Tony a cute brown teddy he named Reggie. Mad Dog complained about the small selection, high prices, and lack of freshness in the gift shop's flower department before settling on some multicolored tulips accompanied by just the right amount of baby's breath. "Damn, I wish I'd remembered to bring something from my own garden. Their selection here sucks, dude!"

The elevator made its familiar clanking sound as it stopped on the second floor. The bikers stepped out—gifts in hand—and quickly found room 213. The door was locked.

"Door's locked, homey. What do we do?" Matt asked.

"I don't know," Mad Dog said. "Knock and see if anyone's home."

As Matt prepared to knock, he heard the sound of a ruckus emanating from inside the room. "Hey, check this out, Mad Dog. What's all that noise?"

"Something here ain't right," Mad Dog said. "The heck with knocking." Mad Dog shouldered his way through the door. As he stumbled inside, he couldn't believe what he saw. The bikers had unwittingly arrived in Tony's room in the nick of time.

Bragg was done pummeling Larry, and he was now preparing to finish him off. Larry was lying facedown on the bed on top of poor, helpless Tony. Bragg's .22 was aimed at the back of Larry's head.

Bragg looked up from Larry to see two mean-ass biker dudes coming into the room. They had very angry looks on their faces. "Hey, who are you? I don't want no trouble here," Bragg said as the moment he'd waited for began to slip through his fingers yet again because of these same two bikers.

"You don't want no trouble?" Mad Dog mimicked. "Well I'd say you got some anyway."

The Black Knights sprung into action. They rushed at Bragg, who could not react quickly enough.

"What the—" Bragg started to say before getting punched in the mouth with a right cross from Matt's teddy bear-carrying hand.

"Look out, Matt. Don't take your eyes off that gun," Mad Dog warned as he leapt through the air—boots first—aiming for Bragg's .22. Mad Dog's dropkick connected solidly with Bragg's right forearm, knocking the gun free and sending it flying across the room and out of reach.

Still holding his giant flower bouquet, Mad Dog swung powerfully at Bragg's head. He hit pay dirt with a huge sweeping haymaker to Bragg's temple, sending flower buds scattering into the air in all directions.

The stunned vigilante cop hit the floor with a bang. Matt was on him immediately.

"Mad Dog, check on Larry and Tony and make sure they're okay. It's time I teach this guy a lesson," Matt said.

Matt then picked up Bragg by the armpits, swung him around horizontally, and sent him flying through the hospital room's window headfirst. The sound of glass shattering was followed closely by a loud thud on the pavement below.

"I guess he won't be bothering Larry again any time soon," Matt said as he looked down to see Bragg's twisted, glass-covered body lying still on the sidewalk outside.

"Wooo-hooo! Way to go, Matt!" Mad Dog hollered. "Wait till the Black Knights hear about this. That move ought to earn you a cool biker name, for sure!"

Matt brushed shards of glass off the shoulders of his leather vest. "Thanks, Mad Dog. How are Tony and Larry doing? How bad is it?"

"Larry's beat up pretty bad, but I think he'll be okay. As for Tony, he's all fucked up in that body cast. I can't even tell how he's doing. I say we stick around just long enough to make sure the two of them get some help. Then we better get out of here before people start figuring out where the guy on the sidewalk came from."

44

"What the heck have you guys gotten me into? Who the hell were those guys?" Alana yelled from the backseat of Jimmy's green SUV as they motored down Sunset toward the Hollywood Freeway.

"I don't know who the guy in Tony's room was, but Larry said he was a cop. Somehow, they must've traced the racetrack fix back to us. He must've been there to arrest us. He got Larry and Tony, but he's sure as shit not gonna get us," Jimmy said as he took the freeway ramp at fifty miles per hour heading south.

"I'm not talking about the cop, you idiot, I'm talking about the *other* guys! You know, the ones with the weapons who chased us down the hall of the hospital. The same guys who are still right the fuck behind us in their cars. What about them?"

"Oh yeah, them. That's Bellvue, the psycho veterinarian, and the four jockeys who helped us fix the race the other day."

"And why the hell are they after us? They looked like they wanted to kill us," Alana said as she looked back and saw Gonzalez hanging out of Lopez's car window waving his baseball bat in the air.

"Actually, they really just want to kill Jimmy and me," Austin said. "You were only in the wrong place at the wrong time."

"In the wrong place at the wrong time? What the fuck does that mean? Since when is visiting someone in the hospital the wrong place at the wrong time?"

"I swear I didn't know anything about this, Alana," Austin said. "Evidently they're not the most stable people we've ever dealt with."

"Not stable? I was able to figure that out as soon as they started chasing us with switchblades and needles as big as my forearm. What I want to know is what are we going to do now? Where are we going?"

Austin hadn't considered that yet. "Uhh, I dunno. Where are we going, Jimmy?"

"We can't go to the cops, that's for sure. Not with half a million dollars of dirty money back at our hotel room," Jimmy said as he swerved through traffic on the Hollywood Freeway. "No, we've got to get our money and then get out of town as soon as possible."

"Maybe you could have considered that idea *before* all the racetrack rejects with weapons started chasing us," Alana said sarcastically. "If we can't go to the cops, then where the hell are we gonna go? You can't just keep speeding around until the news choppers spot us and interrupt regularly scheduled programming to televise our chase."

Jimmy's eyes lit up. "Wait a minute, Alana, I think you just hit on something. You said these guys were racetrack rejects, and that gives me an idea. Bellvue and the jockeys are all barred from the racetrack, right? Why don't we make a break for Santa Anita? They can chase us all they want, but they won't be able to follow us onto the grounds of the track. Security will stop them! The track is right down the street from my motel. We can duck into the track long enough to shake these guys and then get back into the SUV and haul ass to the motel to pick up the money."

"My car is parked over there too," Austin said as he turned to Alana in the backseat. "We can pick up the money *and* my car and split for Mexico right away. We'd just need to make a quick stop at my mom's to get our stuff."

"That sounds like a great idea, guys. But Santa Anita must be twenty miles from here, and there's traffic," Alana said. "Those guys are right on our tail. What if we can't make it?"

*   *   *

Jimmy changed course and headed for Santa Anita. He was speeding south on the Hollywood Freeway, with Bellvue's black van and the jockeys' Cadillac Eldorado lowrider chasing close behind. Traffic was moving, but Jimmy spotted nothing but brake lights up ahead as the flow of cars toward downtown Los Angeles grinded to a halt. Jimmy needed to find the best way to the Foothill Freeway east to Arcadia and Santa Anita. He calculated the best route in his head and angled over to the right lane before swerving off the Hollywood Freeway at the Alvarado Street exit. He glanced into the rearview mirror and saw that both Bellvue and the jockeys had made the turnoff onto Alvarado right behind them. He quickly turned again onto Glendale Boulevard, toward the Glendale Freeway North but still couldn't shake the pursuers. Increasingly desperate, Jimmy made his run for Santa Anita.

For five miles, Jimmy stayed one step ahead of Bellvue and the bloodthirsty jockey mob by weaving between cars, passing on the shoulder, and flooring the gas pedal. Every time Jimmy pulled another high-speed Mario Andretti driving maneuver, Austin and Alana would glance back and see—to their dismay—that the psychos were still close behind, following at speeds upward of eighty miles per hour.

"Look, up ahead," Jimmy said. "It's the exit for the Foothill Freeway. That'll take us right to Arcadia and Santa Anita. From there, we'll have about another five miles to try and lose these bozos."

The green SUV sped up the ramp to the Foothill Freeway toward Pasadena, with Bellvue and the jockeys just a few cars behind.

Suddenly, red brake lights were everywhere. Jimmy skidded to a halt as traffic swarmed all around him. Cars from the Glendale Freeway were merging onto the Foothill Freeway at a snail's pace as traffic moved at speeds under five miles per hour for as far as the eye could see.

The high-speed chase had come to a virtual standstill.

"Shit!" said Jimmy.

"Shit!" said Bellvue.

"Mierda!" said Lopez.

"Look at this. We're gonna be stuck in traffic for miles," Austin said. "What the hell are we going to do?"

"The traffic doesn't matter. We're stuck. Bellvue is stuck. The jockeys are stuck. I don't think they'd run out of their cars and come after us on foot. There's a road full of witnesses, and we should be okay as long as we keep the doors shut tight just in case. Besides, traffic is moving just enough. Just as long as we stay ahead of them—on the road—and in the car, we'll still be all right. If anything, maybe we can use this traffic to our advantage. Maybe they'll lose sight of us in this mess."

Jimmy merged the green SUV into the right lane and ground to a halt. He started moving and then stopped again. Started moving and then stopped. Moved and stopped, moved and stopped, moved and stopped.

Welcome to Los Angeles.

Not far behind, Bellvue and the jockeys were caught in the same traffic quagmire. Bellvue had the benefit of being at the wheel of a full-sized van. He could see the whole freeway from his perch in the van's cockpit. He couldn't move fast, but at least there was no chance of losing the gang's green SUV amongst the other cars, thanks to his prime view of the roadway.

The same, however, could not be said for the jockeys, who were driving in the lowest-riding car on the freeway and having trouble seeing beyond Lopez's own solid-gold hood ornament. They were stuck behind a wall of full-sized SUVs, including a Lincoln Navigator, a GMC Yukon, a Ford Excursion, a Range Rover, and a Hummer.

Gonzalez, Martinez, and Rodriguez spoke only a few words of English between them, but they were all adept at communicating in the universal language of American curse words.

"Move your ass-scratching, ball hair sack-of-shit Navigator!" moaned Rodriguez.

"Motherfucking, cocksucking son-of-bitch Hummer!" yelled Gonzalez.

"Stinking shit-wad bastard Excursion!" grumbled Martinez.

"I know, I can't see a motherfucking thing behind all these tanks," Lopez said in Spanish as he laid on his horn and leaned his head out the window to try to see up ahead and spot the green SUV.

Lopez had the idea of engaging the hydraulic lifts he had installed behind all four wheels of his Cadillac. The hydraulics were what made his car bounce up and down at stoplights, and he figured if he lifted all four wheels at the same time, he could raise his car up a foot or two, giving himself enough ground clearance to be able to see up ahead. Lopez hit the button, making his car bounce and lift in an impressive display of East LA automobile gymnastics. Even at the car's new height, however, the lowrider was still a few feet shorter than the Hummer up ahead blocking its view.

Lopez finally came up with a solution that worked. He had Gonzalez remove the sunroof and stand straight up through the top of the car like a periscope. With Gonzalez looking out from above, Lopez was finally able to keep abreast of the movements of Jimmy's car.

Bellvue was making slightly better progress through traffic than the jockeys were. He had managed to move to within two car lengths of Jimmy, Austin, and Alana and would be able to ram them off the road if he could only gain one more car length. Just then, Bellvue noticed the carpool lane begin to open up on the left side of the road. It dawned on him that he might be in trouble alone in his van if the others figured out they could get into the carpool lane and leave him in their dust.

Simultaneously, in Jimmy's SUV, Alana smacked Jimmy on the back of the head, "Jimmy, get in the carpool lane. It's opening up. Go for it!"

"Al izquerda, al izquerda!" Gonzalez yelled from his perch atop the jockeys' low-riding Caddy, telling Lopez to go "to the left, to the left" into the carpool lane.

"Gracias, amigo," Lopez said as he got over into the left lane and whizzed past Bellvue, who was still stuck in regular traffic.

"Dammit!" Bellvue cursed as he watched the SUV angle into the carpool lane and increase its speed from four miles per hour to a whopping seven.

"Yesss, we're losing them, we're losing them!" Austin shouted, exchanging a high five with Jimmy and a hug with Alana.

"I'm screwed!" Bellvue said, pounding his dashboard as he watched Jimmy and the jockeys roll on ahead. "Come on, Daddy needs an accident up ahead," Bellvue pleaded. "Oh please, won't somebody crash for Daddy?"

At that exact moment, a mile down the freeway on the other side of the road, a maroon Honda Civic sideswiped a red Toyota Camry. The Camry skidded sideways and careened into the median where it crashed to a standstill and burst into flames.

Jimmy and the other cars in the eastbound carpool lane had a front-row seat for the accident, and every one of them slowed to a crawl to get their best view of the action. The carpool lane ground to a halt in the midst of a world-class rubbernecking delay. Jimmy's green SUV and the jockeys' lowrider were suddenly forced to a complete standstill.

"What the hell is this?" Jimmy said. "I thought we were home free."

Up ahead, a woman sprinted from the smashed Honda Civic with her clothes on fire. She started rolling around on the shoulder in an attempt to douse the flames. Bellvue's mood improved considerably as he watched. "Daddy needed a crash, and that's what Daddy got. They'll never get away from me now," he said.

As Bellvue's black van continued to creep past the cars in the stalled carpool lane, he decided it was time to ease his seat back and relax and try to settle in for what might be the longest, slowest car chase in recorded history. Bellvue rolled down the windows of his van and fished through his CD collection in the center console of his front seat to dig out his favorite disc—*Liberace's 16 Greatest Hits*. He popped it into the CD player and went straight for track 16—Liberace's theme song.

Bellvue cranked the volume knob all the way up.

"I'll be seeing you . . . In all the old familiar places . . . That this heart of mine embraces . . . All day through . . ."

Bellvue was more than a little high. He was swaying to the music and singing along now.

"In that small café . . . The park across the way . . . The children's carousel . . . The chestnut tree, the wishing well . . ."

Bellvue's van ambled past Lopez's low-riding Caddy, which was still stuck in the carpool lane's rubbernecking nightmare. The wind from an open window breezed into the van, caught Bellvue's hair, and started unraveling his spiral comb-over one strand at a time.

"I'll be seeing you . . . In every lovely summer's day . . . In everything that's light and gay . . . I'll always think of you that way . . ."

The mad veterinarian was now coming up on Jimmy's immobilized SUV, which had its right-turn signal blinking but couldn't get out of the stalled traffic. Bellvue was flying so high from the song that he forgot to try to swerve his van into Jimmy's SUV as he rolled right past. Bellvue just smiled and winked at Jimmy's car as his comb-over continued flapping around in the breeze.

"I'll find you in the morning sun, and when the night is new . . . I'll be looking at the moon, but I'll be seeing youuuu!"

Oh yes. As always, Liberace's sweet crooning had cast its spell on Bellvue. It wasn't until the song wound down that he fully realized he'd blown past Jimmy's green SUV and was no longer following him. This was a problem since Bellvue had no idea where Jimmy was going.

Bellvue had no choice but to fake car trouble, pull over to the shoulder, click on his blinkers, and wait for Jimmy to catch up to him.

Traffic finally started moving slowly again in all lanes. Jimmy passed Bellvue, and the five-mile-per-hour chase was on once again.

Lopez was riding along in the right lane, with Gonzalez poking out of the sunroof. The cars ahead of him were stopped for no apparent reason.

Welcome to Los Angeles.

Traffic in the center lane began moving a little faster, so Lopez put his left blinker on and angled over one lane. He moved one car length ahead before traffic in his new lane completely stopped. Lopez watched as the flow of cars in his original lane hit a groove and started moving along at a good clip. Lopez put his right blinker on and moved back over to the right lane. Lopez moved up one car length, stopped, and then watched as the middle lane started moving again. Lopez banged on the steering wheel in frustration.

Lopez turned his left blinker back on and swerved to the middle lane directly behind a giant Cadillac Escalade. The middle lane then came to a complete halt. Now Lopez was not only stopped again, but he was also blinded behind another oversized SUV. As he continued to sit still, Lopez saw the traffic in the lanes on both sides of him begin to move freely. He banged on his steering wheel three more times. The process repeated itself for another mile.

Lopez finally lost his patience. "Which one of you *maricons* brought the weed, man?" Lopez asked as he popped his glove box open to reveal a fifth of Jose Cuervo tequila. "We're going nowhere fast, and I need something to calm my nerves."

Rodriguez reached into his pocket and unrolled a baggie filled with pot. Lopez took a huge swig of the Cuervo and passed it along to Gonzalez and Martinez as Rodriguez proceeded to roll a fat Cheech-and-Chong-sized joint. Rodriguez lit it up.

"Hey, who wants some music?" Lopez asked before popping an old Santana tape into the tape deck.

"Oye como va!" blared over the speakers as a cloud of smoke bellowed out of the lowrider's sunroof.

"Oye como va! Mi ritmo, bueno pa gozar, mu-la-ta!" Gonzalez sang before blowing a huge puff of smoke out the window.

An Orange County soccer mom in a Dodge minivan in the next lane gasped when she looked over and saw Lopez holding his steering wheel with one hand and the bottle of Cuervo with the other.

When the monster joint was smoked down to nothing more than the tiniest of doobies, Martinez took out a vial of cocaine and poured its contents across the surface of a small mirror he kept in his shirt pocket. Yet another Santana guitar riff played on the stereo, and the Hispanic jockeys settled in for what would be a long, slow go east on the Foothill Freeway.

A half hour later, Jimmy finally came up to the exit for Santa Anita racetrack. It was a dark day at the track, so there was no traffic on the off-ramp. Jimmy got over onto the exit lane and hit the accelerator for the first time in an hour.

"We're finally here," Jimmy said as he sped down the exit ramp and took the right turn onto Baldwin Avenue on two wheels. Jimmy zipped toward Santa Anita.

Bellvue and the jockeys followed close behind.

"Aha! I get it now—they're making a run for the track," Bellvue muttered to himself as he turned down the volume on his Liberace disc and readied his lethal needle gun at his side.

"I should have known. They're going for Santa Anita. *Arriba!*" Lopez called out as a rallying cry to his troops.

Gonzalez responded by putting down the Jose Cuervo and picking up his Louisville Slugger. Martinez joined in by slipping on his brass knuckles. Rodriguez followed suit by flipping the latch on his switchblade knife.

Jimmy doubled the posted speed limit of thirty miles per hour on Baldwin as he went straight for the track.

"What do I do?" Jimmy called to Austin. "Where do I go?"

"Head for the stable gate!" Austin responded. "It's not only the closest entrance to here, but it's also sure to be manned by guards. We can blast right through the gate and be through to the stable area before anyone even knows what hit them. After we bust in, every guard in sight will run out to the gate just in time to be there to stop Bellvue and the jockeys. They won't be able to follow us. They'll never be able to get through. It should work. We're bound to cause a huge commotion, but in the confusion, we should be able to drive from the gate right up to Clockers' Corner and then right out the other side of the racetrack before anyone even has time to think about us."

45

"Stan the Man" Simon was relaxing with a cup of coffee and enjoying a nice quiet morning at the stable gate security checkpoint adjacent to the Santa Anita backstretch. It was late morning, and training hours had long since ended. Stan's partner in the guard shack was off taking a crap and in no hurry to return to his boring job. That was all right with Stan the Man because late morning on a dark day was always the slowest time of the week at Santa Anita. Stan the Man flipped on his portable five-inch TV and turned the channel to *The Price Is Right*. He fiddled around with the rabbit ears for better reception.

Stan and his partner had very little action in the guard shack. They would usually just sit and watch TV or stare off into space at the San Gabriel mountain range in the distance. Occasionally, they'd take a look at the photos hanging from the walls of the guard shack—portraits of all the people banned from the racetrack grounds. At this particular time, those photos included four Hispanic jockeys suspected of fixing a race and a veterinarian who'd been barred for sawing off the leg of a dead horse. The photos had been up on the wall since yesterday, and being a very observant sort, Stan the Man had had more than enough time to commit all the names and faces to memory.

Stan the Man noticed that he was having trouble hearing the TV when the announcer said, "Come on down! You're the next contestant on *The Price Is Right*!" He turned up the volume, but it was being drowned out by the revving of a car's engine not more than a hundred yards away. Stan looked up and nearly fell out of his chair when he saw a green SUV moving fast in his direction.

Seventy-five yards: "What the hell's this guy doing? He's coming right this way."

Fifty yards: "Hey, he's not slowing down!"

Twenty-five yards: "Oh my god, he's gonna crash right through the damn gate!"

The green SUV smashed through the security checkpoint at sixty miles per hour, reducing the guardhouse gate to a million matchstick-sized splinters. Stan the Man didn't have nearly enough time to react, but now he was up on his feet and screaming into his walkie-talkie.

"Goddamit, where the hell are you, Earl?" Stan the Man yelled. "Pinch off that loaf and get your ass back to the guard shack! Someone just drove through the friggin' gate!"

No sooner did Jimmy's SUV crash through when Stan the Man spotted two more cars heading right for him. "What in the hell?" Stan the Man wondered as he positioned himself in the middle of the road as a human guard gate. This time, the vehicles were a big black van and a low-riding Cadillac.

Bravely, Stan extended his hand into halt position, swallowed hard, and dug his heels into the ground in a high-stakes game of chicken as the two vehicles got closer and closer.

Bellvue saw the guard standing in the middle of the road. He hit the brakes and swerved to a stop at the last possible second. Lopez was following too close behind Bellvue. He was speeding and didn't have enough time or motor skills to react. The lowrider fishtailed and crashed into Bellvue's van.

Too stunned to draw his weapon, Stan the Man rushed over to the wreck to see who was inside. Bellvue and the jockeys got out of their smoldering cars. Stan the Man was confronted simultaneously by all five of the faces from the mug shots hanging on the guard shack's wall.

"Hey, I know you guys," said Stan the Man. "You're the guys who are barred from the track!"

Stan the Man reached for his holster, but Rodriguez was faster. He went for his knife and threw a bulls-eye right at Stan the Man's gun. The knife's blade grazed Stan's hand and caused his revolver to fall to the dusty gravel at his feet.

Stan the Man clutched his hand in pain. Then Bellvue approached, giant needle in hand.

"You're not letting us onto the grounds, huh? Well, you just try and stop us," Bellvue smirked as he and the jockeys rushed through the checkpoint into the track's backstretch stable area.

Not too far ahead, Jimmy's SUV was stopped in its tracks. The stable area's roads were all dirt roads, and Austin hadn't anticipated that navigating the narrow passages between barns in a large vehicle would not only be difficult but also dangerous to both humans and horses alike.

Jimmy, Austin, and Alana got out of the SUV. Alana turned around to see Bellvue and the jockeys rushing past Stan the Man on their way through the stable gate.

"They got in. They're past the guards. We've got to hurry."

Jimmy, Austin, and Alana began to pick up their pace. They ran toward the safety of the heavily populated Clockers' Corner on foot.

*   *   *

The only other times Jimmy had been to Clockers' Corner were early in the morning on race days when the place was bustling with activity. It was a much different scene there at noon on a dark day. Jimmy and Austin had not anticipated Clockers' Corner being deserted when they got there. They also hadn't anticipated having only a small head start on Bellvue and the jockey mob, who were only a minute behind them on the dirt road.

Back at the guard shack, Earl returned from the bathroom to find the stable gate in shambles as Stan the Man wrapped a towel around his injured hand and screamed into his walkie-talkie for backup.

"This is Officer Simon at Gate 6, and we've got a major situation here! Three vehicles just came crashing through the guard gate! We've got three—count 'em, three—trespassers, plus five—count 'em, five—banned individuals who've gained access to the premises including four suspended jockeys and that nutcase veterinarian. It looks like they're running toward Clockers' Corner. I need all officers to respond! Immediately!"

All around Santa Anita, security guards grumpily tossed aside coffee cups, snuffed out cigarettes, and awakened from catnaps to join Stan the Man and Earl in pursuit of the trespassers.

"What the hell is this place?" Alana huffed as she ran alongside Austin and Jimmy, heading toward Clockers' Corner at the end of the immense Santa Anita grandstand.

"It's Clockers' Corner," Austin responded. "It's a place we're familiar with. We figure we can lose those guys and then double back to the car and get out of here."

Jimmy, Austin, and Alana sprinted through Clockers' Corner and came face-to-face with a locked gate that led to Santa Anita's track-front apron level. Jimmy tried the gate, but it wouldn't budge. "What the hell—this gate was never locked before."

"That's because we've never been here when the track was closed before," Austin said. "Those guys must be right behind us. We need to get out of sight. Let's try to hide inside the grandstand."

The threesome bolted for the nearest portal into the building—a pair of double doors that provided the only grandstand access directly from Clockers' Corner. The doors, however, were locked.

"Now what do we do?" Alana yelled. "Our only way out is back the way we came, and that's where those psychos are coming from. We're trapped."

"We're still not trapped," Jimmy said. "There's a second way out of here, through the stable area. It's a back way around. We can double back that way and still lose those chumps. It will lead us right back to my car. It should work."

Unfortunately for Jimmy, Bellvue and the jockeys were even more familiar with the racetrack grounds than he was. Bellvue knew that when the track was closed, there would be no open access to the grandstand from Clockers' Corner. There were only two ways leading in and out of Clockers' Corner, and both of them led back through the barn area toward the stable gate where they were coming from.

Bellvue knew he'd have Jimmy, Austin, and Alana cornered if he and the jockeys could block both access routes. He called over to Lopez, who was struggling to run fast while carrying both a long metal chain and a tire iron.

"Hey, Lopez, we've got them cornered," Bellvue yelled. "We need to split up to block both of their possible exits. I need two of your compadres to come with me. That will leave two of you to go around the other way and block their only other way out."

The five men stopped running as Lopez turned to get a look at Bellvue. "First of all, who the fuck are you? And second, why the hell are you here? What are you, some kinda freak?" Lopez asked. "Can't you see I'm busy?"

Bellvue was huffing and puffing hard from running and could only get a few words out at a time. "My name is Marcus Bellvue . . . I'm a track veterinarian . . . I'm here to kill those two scumbags who cost me my job . . . I wouldn't mind killing their little girlfriend too . . . From the looks of your weapons and from what I've heard on the evening news, I'm assuming you guys are here for the same reason."

"That's right," Lopez said. "Those fuckers had us fix a race and said we wouldn't get caught, but they lied to us. Now we're gonna make them pay. We're gonna cut them up and slice and dice their shit real bad."

"So work with me," Bellvue implored. "Five on three is better odds than four on three, wouldn't you agree?"

"Work with you? What the hell can you do? My man Gonzalez over here swings a mean bat. He's gonna brain those bastards when he finds 'em. Martinez here used to be a fighter. He punches pretty damn hard even without those brass knuckles he's wearing. And then I have Rodriguez. He's a knife expert who's gonna tear them to shreds. What the hell can you do?"

Bellvue reached into the pocket of his lab coat. He pulled out his giant steel needle gun and affixed a foot-long needle to the end. "What can I do? After you have your fun, I'm going to finish them off with this."

"Holy shit, man," Lopez said in wide-eyed astonishment as he gazed at the needle. "Put that thing away before you take somebody's eye out. I think we can work something out. Why don't you take Martinez and Rodriguez with you? Gonzo and I will head them off around back the other way. *Vamos*, Gonzalez, *ahora!*"

Jimmy, Austin, and Alana were still running. They turned around and rushed back out of Clockers' Corner and made a quick left-hand turn away from the main road where Bellvue was approaching. "This way out!" Jimmy yelled as he led the way. He was running about ten yards out in front of Austin and Alana. "Follow me. We should be home free!"

Suddenly, Loco Lopez appeared around the next bend, just feet ahead of Jimmy. "Not so fast," Lopez said. "You're not going anywhere."

Jimmy saw Lopez and tried to stop, but the gravel beneath his feet gave way, and he slipped down on the dirt road at Gonzalez's feet. Acting as Gonzalez's third-base coach, Lopez gave his cohort the sign for "swing away." Gonzalez swung and connected with a solid shot right in the small of Jimmy's back.

"Jimmy!" Austin yelled, taking a few steps toward the aid of his fallen friend before needing to change course and duck out of the way to avoid a swing from Lopez's long chain.

Lopez stood firm and twirled the chain like a gaucho swinging his bolas overhead, the deadly weapon slicing through the air. He was able to keep Austin at bay while Gonzalez delivered another solid shot to Jimmy's ribs.

Jimmy took the blow. "Arghhhh," and then spat out the only command that came to his mind at that moment. "Austin, get out of here! Go! Find some help!"

Austin felt Alana tugging at his arm as Lopez edged closer and closer with his chain.

Jimmy was able to get to his feet. When Jimmy started running, Lopez and Gonzalez turned to follow him.

Austin took advantage of the moment and grabbed Alana's hand and ran in the opposite direction, toward Clockers' Corner.

Austin and Alana rounded the corner and started to run. They had to go back through Clockers' Corner in order to get back up the main road to Jimmy's car, but they never made it as far as the main road. When they reached Clockers' Corner, Bellvue, Martinez, and Rodriguez were already there waiting for them.

Before he realized what hit him, Austin felt a jolt of pain in his left temple. Martinez had decked him with a right cross.

Austin dropped to the ground. He looked up to see Martinez standing above him, brass knuckles and all.

With Austin on the ground, Bellvue focused his attentions on Alana. "Well, what do we have here? You must be the damsel in distress."

Terrified, Alana wanted to run, but her back was straight up against a wall leaving her nowhere to turn. Alana stopped thinking about her escape, however, when Rodriguez's switchblade found its way to within inches of her throat.

Austin was still lying dazed on the ground. Martinez and Rodriguez went over to Alana and grabbed her hands, each holding one behind her back. This left her exposed to Bellvue, who was coming at her with his horrific needle.

"There's always room for one more on my List of Death," Bellvue said as his evil eyes fixed on Alana.

Bellvue closed in sneering menacingly. "What do you say I take care of this cute little thing first while her boyfriend sleeps it off?"

46

Larry was hiding in the stairwell adjacent to Tony's room and trying to lie and stay out of sight, along with his saviors, Matt and Mad Dog.

From Tony's room, Larry and the bikers had watched a team of medics scrape up Bragg's twisted body from the pavement below room 213. From the stairwell, they were able to eavesdrop on a group of doctors who were conversing in the hallway. They heard that Bragg was alive but banged up pretty badly, with more than a few broken bones.

A team of doctors finally found its way into Tony's room and made sure everything was back in order. The doctors were followed by a slew of maintenance workers, who were on the scene to scrape up shards of shattered glass from around the room and install a new plate glass window to replace the one Bragg had been thrown through a short time before. The maintenance men were in a hurry. They were told that they needed to have the room ready for a second occupant, who was scheduled to arrive in the bed opposite Tony's later that afternoon.

Larry breathed a sigh of relief that Bragg looked like he was going to make it—not because he was suddenly compassionate about the man who had once sent him to jail, but because he didn't want Matt and Mad Dog to be facing a murder rap. Especially one involving a cop.

Bragg wasn't able to talk, but the hospital staff put two and two together and figured out that his plunge to the pavement came from room 213 and probably was not an accident. The LA police were on their way, and Larry and the bikers were not interested in sticking around a moment longer than they needed.

When the coast cleared momentarily for the first time all morning, Larry found a brief window of time to sneak out of the stairwell and into Tony's room long enough to say good-bye.

"Tony, it's me, Larry. I just wanted to make sure you were okay, buddy. I also wanted to let you know that I'm gonna be all right too. Matt and Mad Dog saved me. Can you believe it? Two guys we met at a strip joint just ended up saving our lives. Life is pretty weird sometimes, huh?"

Tony grunted. He still couldn't talk or move a muscle inside his body cast.

222

"Well anyway, dude, the heat's gonna come down on us any minute, so I've gotta get out of here. Austin, Jimmy, and Alana ran out of here this morning. They were being chased by Bellvue and the jockeys. I don't know if they made it, but I bet they can take care of themselves.

"As for me, I've decided I'm officially out of the Dude-Men after what just happened. By the looks of it, the cops are onto us, and I want nothing to do with going back to jail. The police probably followed the money trail right back to our motel, so I'm not going back there. But it's still all good. You know why? Because I'm thinking of joining a new gang until this whole thing blows over. The Black Knights invited me to live at their crib in South Central if I'm willing to become an outlaw biker just like them. I'm seriously thinking it over. At least I'd have Matt and Mad Dog to take care of me. I figure if I'm going to be an outlaw, I may as well be an outlaw biker, right?

"So I'm gonna say good-bye to you, Tony. I probably won't be able to visit you with all the fuzz that's gonna be hanging around here, but I'll be thinking about you every day. The good news is that you're not going to be alone. Alana called your wife! Julia is on her way out here right now, buddy. I know she'll take good care of you."

Tony's eyes widened, and a look of sheer terror came over his face. All he could do was whimper. Tony knew that Julia would take care of him all right, but just not in the way Larry thought she would. There'd be hell to pay when Julia found out he'd lost his life's savings.

Larry, Matt, and Mad Dog all said their final good-byes to Tony. Then they scurried out of Tony's room down a back staircase and got on Matt and Mad Dog's hogs in the parking lot.

Mad Dog found his spare helmet, tossed it at Larry, and directed him onto the back of his chopper. Mad Dog and Matt both fired up their engines at once.

Mad Dog yelled over to Matt, "I can't wait till we get back to our pad, man. I'm dying to tell the guys about how you threw that pig right out the damn window. They're gonna eat that shit up. You'll get your biker name now, for sure!"

Matt's smile was beaming. He couldn't wait. A real biker name was finally within his reach. Mad Dog popped his clutch, and Matt followed suit. Both bikes rumbled to life and rolled out of the hospital lot. Larry secured his helmet and held on tight as Matt and Mad Dog took him away to his new home in South Central LA.

As the bikers drove away, they passed a speeding yellow cab going in the opposite direction. The taxi cruised up the hospital's driveway and screeched to a halt directly in front of the main entrance.

Julia Martini's flight to LAX arrived in late morning. She had only carry-on luggage with her, along with a piece of paper with the name and address of the hospital where Tony was staying. She wasn't coming to Los Angeles as much for Tony as she was for Tony's money, which she hoped to salvage if she could. She had no idea she was already too late.

Julia hopped in a taxi at the airport and directed the driver straight to Holy Family Hospital. When she pulled up into the hospital's driveway, she saw two big African American biker dudes rumbling out of the parking lot. There was a white man on the back of one of the hogs. He bore a striking resemblance to Larry Lipwinkle.

"Nah, can't be," Julia said as her taxi stopped right in front of the hospital's main entrance. Julia paid the driver and rushed inside to give her cheating, stealing husband a piece of her mind.

Tony's problems weren't behind him. They were only just beginning.

47

Stan the Man and Earl were joined by three other guards as they rushed toward Clockers' Corner on foot. They'd almost reached their destination when Stan the Man noticed a group of men out of the corner of his eye. They were moving swiftly on a second footpath that trailed behind a nearby row of stables.

Stan the Man heard shouting from what appeared to be three different voices—first in English and then in Spanish. It was Lopez and Gonzalez. They had caught up with Jimmy and had him cornered down at the end of a stable shedrow.

Horses were peeking out from their stalls all in a row, but there were no other people in sight as Gonzalez took a few practice swings with his baseball bat and Lopez twirled his tire iron around in his hands.

Stan the Man and the rent-a-cops drew their weapons and ran in Jimmy's direction.

Earl had been on the job for nineteen years, and this was the first time he'd drawn his revolver. The gun felt cold and heavy in his hand—much heavier than a doughnut and much colder than the hot coffee he usually carried. Earl felt shaky all over as he and his backups entered the barn where all the commotion had come from a few seconds before.

In one swift motion, Stan the Man whirled around the corner stall at the end of the barn and raised his pistol arm's length in front of him. He stared down the barrel of his gun.

At the other end of the shedrow, Stan the Man saw two familiar-looking jockey-sized men waving deadly weapons at a man who was already injured and cowering in the corner. Stan the Man waved a hand signal, giving Earl and the other guards the okay to leap around the corner and draw their weapons.

"Freeze, scumbags!" Stan the Man ordered authoritatively. He had always wanted to say that.

Jimmy was never so happy to see a rent-a-cop in his entire life. He started to yell for help but was silenced by a blow to the solar plexus with the butt-end of Gonzalez's bat.

Gonzalez and Lopez turned to see the officers facing them with their guns drawn. The guards blocked their only exit.

Lopez thought fast. He had two choices: He could either surrender or go down in a blaze of glory. He chose the latter.

Lopez tried to grab hold of Jimmy to use him as a human shield. The jockey was quick as a cat, but Earl's trigger finger was even quicker.

Shots rang out down the shedrow. Jimmy dove flat on the ground and looked up to see Lopez get hit in the arms and legs. Blood spattered everywhere.

Earl let out a primal scream, "Aaaaaargghhhhhhhh," that continued until he spent his entire fifteen-round clip. Like a man possessed, Earl continued to point his gun at Lopez and click off empty rounds. *CLICK, CLICK, CLICK, CLICK, CLICK.*

Gonzalez threw down his bat, raised his hands in the air, surrendered, and prayed out loud, "Jesus es el mejor, Jesus es el mejor."

Earl had a crazed look in his eyes. Stan the Man reached over and pulled the gun out of his trembling hands. "It's all right, buddy. Take it easy, man," he said.

The three other guards rushed down to the end of the shedrow to apprehend Gonzalez and tend to Jimmy and Lopez.

Jimmy was injured, and Lopez was shot up like swiss cheese. Luckily for Lopez, however, all his bullet holes were flesh wounds to his extremities. He was going to make it.

"Hey, Earl!" yelled one of the guards. "Where'd you learn to shoot like that, cowboy? All your shots were perfectly placed to disable the perpetrator without putting his life in danger. That's just like they teach you at the academy. You missed all his vital organs. Nice shooting, man!"

"Thanks, I appreciate that," said Earl, who had been aiming at Lopez's heart. Stan the Man hurried to the scene to tend to Jimmy, who was sprawled in the dirt at the end of the barn where he'd been cornered. "It's going to be okay," Stan the Man said. "Where are you hurt?"

"It'th okay, man, I'm gonna be fine," Jimmy lisped out of the corner of his swollen mouth as he put a hand to the mess of blood and dirt which coated his entire body.

Lopez was bleeding from copious flesh wounds and being escorted off in handcuffs. He turned toward Stan the Man and yelled as he was being led away. "That's the guy who fixed the race! That's him! You know what I'm talking about, right? The fixed race from the other day! It was him! You want him, not me! He did it! He fixed the race!"

Stan the Man looked back at Jimmy. He considered that Lopez and Gonzalez had just been ruled off the track for race fixing, and now they were back at the track and involved in an armed altercation with this mystery man. Lopez may have been onto something.

Stan the Man got a good look at Jimmy's face. Then it came to him.

"Now, wait just a minute here. I remember you now. You're the guy who won all that money the other day. I carried the money bags out to the car for you. He's right, isn't he? You're the one who fixed the race," Stan the Man accused.

Jimmy hesitated, his smooth-talking veneer for once deserting him. "No, I'm not. It was some other guy who looked like me."

Stan the Man knew he was lying. "You can't fool me that easy, pretty boy. Hey, Earl, we can't let this guy go. He's trespassing on track grounds, and now that I think of it, I remember him from the track on the day of the fixed race. Cuff him and stuff him, Earl!"

"Ha!" Lopez yelled. He raised his middle finger to Jimmy as the guard led him away. "If I'm going down, then you're going down with me, *pendejo*!"

Stan the Man puffed out his chest. He could practically see tomorrow's newspaper headlines in his head:

> "Guard Breaks Up Race-fixing Ring!"
> "Simon Says, You're Busted!"
> "Hero Guard Dating Angelina Jolie!"

Stan the Man could smell a raise and a promotion. He smiled as he watched Earl slap his handcuffs around Jimmy's wrists.

Jimmy could see that he was screwed.

*   *   *

Alana could see that she was screwed.

She was being held on either side by a pair of enraged five-foot-tall Hispanic jockeys, each one grasping one of her arms with one hand and a deadly weapon with the other. Her boyfriend, Austin, who'd gotten her into this mess, was lying on the ground in a daze, and there was a strange psychopathic veterinarian with a spiral comb-over holding a foot-long needle and standing right in front of her.

"You're dead meat, missy," Bellvue said as he squeezed his steel needle gun in his hand. "Don't worry. If it's any consolation, you shouldn't feel a thing. In a moment, you'll be dead."

All eyes were on Alana as Bellvue closed in.

Austin was able to sit up, and the cobwebs began to clear from his blow to the head. He was behind Bellvue and realized that no one was paying any attention to him.

Austin started to come to his feet, but he was moving slowly and was too far away from Bellvue to be any help to his girlfriend.

Bellvue's needle was just inches away from Alana. There wasn't a second to spare. Alana was on her own. She knew it was time to make her move.

Alana called upon all her years of yoga training and quickly sent her body into motion.

In an amazing display of nimble flexibility, Alana dropped down into the splits and simultaneously slid her hands up and out of the grasp of both Martinez and Rodriguez.

Bellvue's needle cut through thin air where Alana's torso had been just an instant before.

The jab missed Alana but connected squarely with Martinez's right shoulder. The needle plunged deep and found a vein. Before Bellvue had a chance to stop, he'd already pulled the trigger on his needle gun, compressing the plunger and driving his poison into Martinez.

Martinez couldn't believe it as he watched Bellvue withdraw the needle.

Stunned, Martinez fell to the ground. Soon he began to foam at the mouth and convulse wildly.

A few seconds later, Martinez's agony stopped. He stopped breathing and slumped over onto the ground with his still eyes wide open.

Austin was finally on his feet. He dove forward toward Rodriguez and was able to wrap both hands around the other man's knife hand. Austin struggled with the much shorter man for control of the switchblade.

Alana was on the ground, doing the splits. Bellvue did not know how she had evaded his needle. He hadn't counted on her yoga quickness and flexibility.

Bellvue was still trying to regroup from what he'd done to Martinez when Alana bounced back up to her feet.

Alana was pissed off and ready to strike. Bellvue realized he was about to get beat up by a girl at right around the same time that Alana delivered a swift knee solidly into his groin.

Bellvue crumpled like a rag doll. The force of Alana's blow was so hard that it knocked the needle gun loose from Bellvue's grip and sent it flying high into the air.

Alana kept her eyes glued to the deadly poison-filled needle and watched—seemingly in slow motion—as it ascended high into the air to its summit, and then started tumbling end over end back down to earth.

From above, Bellvue's spiral comb-over must have looked like a giant bulls-eye as the business end of the needle gun pointed straight for the top of his head.

Then, like a dart from the heavens that had sailed barely wide of its target, the needle missed Bellvue's head and landed with a thud in the side of his neck.

The needle dug deep, and the sharp sting of the huge weapon sent Bellvue down to the dirt on his hands and knees.

The needle gun stood straight up from Bellvue's neck. He knew his only chance was to remove the needle before the trigger could be pulled and the poison released.

Austin was still struggling with Rodriguez for control of his switchblade knife. Alana gasped as the knife suddenly disappeared between to the two men. Then Alana heard the sickening sound of the knife hitting pay dirt.

A loud grunt came from one of the two men.

Alana screamed, "Austin!"

For an instant, nobody moved or drew a breath. Then suddenly, Rodriguez's knees started to wobble beneath him. He took his hands off Austin and grasped the handle of his own switchblade as it protruded out from the center of his stomach.

Bellvue was on the ground just a few feet behind Martinez, still looking for a way to gingerly remove his needle from his neck. Rodriguez was oblivious. He took two unsure steps backward, stumbled, and fell flat onto Bellvue's back.

Rodriguez's weight came crashing down onto the needle gun in Bellvue's neck. His body depressed the gun's trigger and sent the remaining contents of the poison syringe straight into Bellvue's neck.

Bellvue and Martinez twitched and struggled on the ground for a few moments until finally all was quiet. They were both dead in seconds.

Austin and Alana put their arms around each other and hugged. Each cried on the other's shoulder, but the embrace didn't last long. They realized they were standing in the middle of Clockers' Corner in broad daylight with three dead bodies at their feet.

"Austin, we've got to get out of here. Let's get back to the car and go," Alana said as she started running back up the road toward the stable gate.

"What about Jimmy?" Austin called after her.

"Forget Jimmy," Alana called back. "If Lopez didn't get him, the guards would have. We've got to worry about ourselves."

Austin was running after her now. "Okay, but where are we going?"

"There's a half million dollars in Jimmy's motel room, remember? I'm going after that money."

Austin and Alana made it back to the stable gate and found the area deserted except for a few curious onlookers from the nearby stables.

"Where are all the guards?" Austin asked.

"They must be back there looking for us, or for Jimmy, or for the jockeys. Who the hell cares? They're not here, and that's all I care about."

Austin ran to the driver's side of Jimmy's SUV and was relieved to find the keys still in the ignition.

"Get us the hell out of here, Austin," Alana ordered as Austin turned over the engine and spun the tires.

"We're nearly home free once we're out of here," Austin said. "I'm sure the guards have the license number of Jimmy's SUV, but if we can only make it to Jimmy's motel, we can dump the SUV and pick up my car and the money. We'll be gone before they have time to find us."

Dirt and dust kicked up from the road as Austin floored the accelerator and pointed Jimmy's SUV away of the track and straight toward the motel and the money.

48

Austin and Alana drove to Jimmy's motel as fast as they could. They knew it would be just a matter of time before the bodies of Bellvue and the jockeys were discovered at Clockers' Corner, which would spur an all-points bulletin in search of Jimmy's SUV. Austin had left his Maxima parked in the motel lot when he'd ridden with Jimmy to the hospital that morning. Now Austin could go back to collect the Dude-Men's money and switch cars.

"Those people are dead, Austin, and I think I'm going to be sick," Alana cried. "I can't believe you got me involved in this. Those people were trying to kill me, and I didn't even have anything to do with all this. Seeing what I saw today, Austin, I'm never going to be able to forget it. No amount of therapy could ever erase this. I feel like I'm scarred for life, and it's all your fault."

"I know, Alana, I know. I'm so sorry, but I never could have predicted this. I didn't mean to get you into this mess, I promise. I guess I just wasn't thinking about the consequences of my actions."

Alana was still crying. "That's just it, Austin, you weren't thinking. And neither was I, until now."

"But it's going to be okay. We got away from those nuts, and now we have half a million dollars waiting for us. Jimmy, Larry, and Tony all got caught. The money's all ours. Once we switch cars, we'll be untraceable. We can drive down to Mexico with no muss, no fuss, and no one on our tail."

Austin pulled into the motel lot and parked in front of Jimmy's suite. Austin had his own keys to the motel room. He hurried from the SUV, unlocked the door, and stepped inside the room with Alana right behind him. He shut the door tight.

Austin walked to the closet, slid the door open, and reached down behind the other luggage into the bottom back corner to where Jimmy hid the gang's money. Austin felt two canvas satchels containing the money from the racetrack. He picked them up and poured out their contents on the bed nearest the closet. Austin also noticed Tony's twin metal attaché cases, which contained the remnants of his life's savings.

He pulled out the attaché cases and placed them on the bed next to the canvas satchels.

Alana sat on the bed opposite Austin and watched as he rearranged the gang's stacks of twenty and hundred dollar bills. Austin pooled the racetrack loot together with Tony's money. "Wow, Tony sure went through a lot of his cash in this short amount of time," Austin said. "I guess strippers have gotten quite expensive these days."

Alana didn't laugh at the joke. She was watching Austin handle the money and thinking about what she should do next. She thought she didn't want to stay with Austin anymore. She couldn't stay with him after what had just happened to her. Not after seeing those men die. Alana couldn't take her eyes off the money though—all that money. It was right in front of her now. More money than she'd ever seen in her life. She wanted it. Hell, she deserved it after what she'd just been through. It was enough to pay for her dream life in Mexico. It was the kind of money that could go toward buying her all the material comforts she'd experienced at Madam Tiffany's. She looked back at Austin, but all she could see now was the money.

"Think of all that's happened since we got this money," Austin said as he looked at the piles of cash he'd laid out on the bed. He arranged the money in front of him in six different stacks.

"It started out with me, Jimmy, Tony, and Larry," Austin said as he pointed to four piles of money representing the four of them. "Then there was Tommy Boy and the cut we were giving to Lopez and his jockeys," Austin continued as he pointed at the final two stacks of cash.

"Then we found out Tommy Boy was dead," Austin said as he picked up the stack of money representing Tommy Boy and placed it on top of his own stack. "The jockeys are no longer part of the equation, either." Austin picked up another stack and put it onto his own.

Alana's eyes were widening as she watched Austin's pile of money getting bigger and bigger.

"Then at the hospital this morning, that crazy cop caught up with Tony and Larry. We didn't stick around long enough to find out, but my guess is that those guys won't be seeing the light of day again for quite some time. This money's not going to be doing them any good now." Austin picked up two more stacks of money and placed them atop his pile.

"And finally there's Jimmy. The last time we saw him, he was running away from Lopez, but he never made it back to his car. I pray the guards got to him before Lopez did, but even so, he'll be going down for the race-fixing scam, for sure."

Austin picked up the final pile of money and combined it into his own stack.

"That's it, Alana. We're the only ones who made it. This money's all ours."

Alana's mind was racing now. There was a half million dollars in cash right in front of her. It was right there, right in front of Austin. So close that she could touch it, smell it, taste it. She wanted that money bad, but she knew it came with a price. She wanted the money but no longer wanted Austin.

The only reason Alana had stayed with Austin this long was she admired his loyalty to his friends. Sure she'd complained about it and even nagged, but it really meant something to her because it said something about the kind of person Austin was. It was the last strand of hope she was holding on to, but now all hope was gone.

Austin left the remainder of Tony's original money in the first attaché case—which still had somewhere between a hundred and two hundred thousand dollars left in it. He then opened up the second case, which was empty. He placed the gang's racetrack money inside—all five hundred thousand of it.

Austin picked up both attaché cases and went for the door. "We don't want to stay here any longer than we need to. Alana, honey, get the door will you? My hands are full."

Alana didn't move. She was still sitting on the bed, mulling over her options.

"Alana, honey, come on. Get the door, and let's go."

Alana asked, "Austin, where are we gonna go?"

"Come on, Alana, these are heavy. We'll talk about it once we get to the car."

"I'm not going anywhere until you tell me where we're going."

Austin put the cases down at his feet and looked up at Alana. "What do mean where are we going? We're going to Mexico, just like we've always planned. We'll be at the border in a few hours, and we'll be in Todos Santos in a couple days. What are we waiting for? Our time has finally come."

"I know, Austin, I know, but what's the rush? We've got all that money and all the time in the world," Alana said as she tried to think fast.

"You know what I want to do? I want to go back to Rocky Point with you," Alana said. "I loved it there. Will you take me back for a couple days before we continue on to Todos Santos?"

"Rocky Point?" Austin said with a perplexed look on his face. "Why do you want to go back to Rocky Point when we can go to Todos Santos instead?"

"We had fun at Rocky Point, Austin. Let's go back, just for a couple days. Can we, please? I need some time to decompress from everything that's happened here before I face the thought of starting our new lives."

Austin wanted to be anywhere on earth besides standing at the threshold of that motel suite a moment longer. "Okay, listen, Alana— fine, I'll make you a deal: If you help me with this door and get out of here right this second, we can go anywhere you want. We'll go to Rocky Point. Will that make you happy?"

"Yes."

"Good. Now can we please move it? Please?"

Alana had successfully bought herself some time. She got up off the bed and helped Austin with the door as he carried their money out of the motel room.

Austin popped the trunk of his Nissan Maxima and put the money inside. He got in the driver's seat and turned over the engine. Alana got in beside him and clicked her seat belt. He took one last look around to make sure the coast was clear and pulled out of the parking lot bound for the freeway that would take them south to the border and beyond.

"This is it. We're on our way. We're finally going, and we're never looking back. Yeee-haaa!" Austin screamed.

Alana looked at Austin and smiled an empty smile. All she could think about was the money in the back of the car.

"I'm never gonna look back, either," Alana said as she looked away. "In my mind, I'm already gone."

49

Bright sunlight peeked through the blinds into the Rocky Point hotel room as Austin slept off a raucous night of celebrating their arrival in Mexico.

After leaving Jimmy's motel in Arcadia, Austin and Alana had stopped to say good-bye to Madam Tiffany and get their things. Then they drove straight south for the border, crossing at Tijuana, and stopped at a hotel there for the night before continuing the 350 miles to Rocky Point—or Puerto Peñasco—the following day.

Unlike their last trip into town, Alana made Austin splurge for a hotel room instead of a tent on the beach. She had two suitcases filled with money and was no longer a woman who would settle for a tent on the beach.

Austin tossed and turned in bed, half-awake and half-asleep under a bright multicolored bedspread in a room on the top floor of the Bonita del Sol Beach Resort. His head was in a haze. He struggled to remember where he was, what he was doing there, and what he had done the night before.

Recollections of last night began drifting into Austin's consciousness. He remembered Alana being in a celebratory mood. She kept ordering him drinks—tequila shots and margaritas—all through dinner as the sun went down.

Austin's head began to ache, pounding as if someone or something was banging on it like a drum from the inside out. He was hungover bad. Real bad. Austin pulled the sheets over his head and squeezed his eyes tightly shut. His head kept pounding.

Austin remembered more about the night before. He remembered leaving the hotel and going into town to Micky's, home of world-famous titty-twisting hospitality and those lethal orange tequila punches.

Austin remembered sitting at Micky's for hours—or was it minutes—ordering one tequila punch after another. Alana was ordering them for him. Ordering one after the other, egging him on as he drank too much of the hell water too quickly.

Austin turned over in bed again. His mouth was parched. He needed to get up and get a drink of water. He also needed an aspirin, or two, or ten. He needed to ease the pounding in his head. He needed to get up out of bed, but he couldn't. He couldn't conjure enough energy to even lift his head up off his pillow.

Austin remembered throwing up at Micky's. He recalled it was the orange-colored projectile-type of vomiting reminiscent of Monty Python movies or Linda Blair in *The Exorcist.* Then he remembered Alana driving him back to the hotel and tucking him into bed after Micky had kicked him out.

Austin remembered where he was now. He was in his hotel room in Puerto Peñasco. He and Alana were supposed to spend the day at the beach and then leave for Todos Santos.

Austin's head was still pounding. He was awake, but he still kept his eyes shut to the morning light that was seeping into the room through the blinds. Austin reached across the bed, expecting to find Alana but did not feel her beside him.

Suddenly Austin started to remember something else about the night before. He remembered that Alana wasn't drinking at dinner. She kept ordering him drinks, but she didn't have any drinks for herself. Not a single one. Austin then thought about what happened at Micky's. He remembered Alana ordering him a slew of tequila punches, but buying none for herself. Not one.

Austin suddenly felt lucid and wide-awake. He yanked the covers off and sat up in bed. He looked around the room. There was no sign of Alana.

"Holy shit!" Austin said to himself in a hoarse voice as he looked around the room at nothing and nobody.

Then, across the room, Austin noticed his car keys on the nightstand on Alana's side of the bed, along with a handwritten note. Austin rolled over in the bed and grabbed the note.

"Holy shit."

Dear Austin,

By the time you wake up, I'll be gone. When you read this, I'll already be on my way to Todos Santos to pursue my dream. I absolutely can't wait to get there!

The first thing you'll probably notice is that I've taken all the money with me. Your worst fears are confirmed. Please understand I just cannot do this with you anymore. I would never be happy, and would always worry. I am sorry you made all of these plans. Please make other plans for something and someone else, not me. I just cannot get past what's happened.

My time with your mother taught me a lot. I will never forget her. Madam Tiffany taught me the value of money and that I should never in my life settle for anything less than the very best. She also taught me that men can be replaced a lot easier than money and the things it can buy.

I hope that someday you'll be able to forgive me for taking the money. The way I see things, it will make me a lot happier than it ever would have made you. If anything, I'm doing you a favor. You never would have found what you were looking for down in Mexico.

Take care of yourself, and good luck sleeping off last night's hangover. I'm sure it's a real doozy.

Adios,
Alana

"The money's gone? You gotta be kidding me!" Austin yelled as he crumpled up Alana's letter into a ball and threw it into the trash. He ran over to the closet where he'd stored the money, but sure enough, it wasn't there.

Austin picked up a lamp, pulled it out of the socket, and threw it across the room. It hit the wall and smashed into pieces. Austin sat on the edge of the bed and put his head into his hands.

"All that money. I can't believe she took all that money. Every damn dime!"

Austin mumbled some things about Alana that he definitely didn't mean as compliments, but when he actually took a minute to think about it and consider everything that had happened, he realized her actions made him respect her in some strange way.

"You got me, Alana. I'll have to admit, I never saw this coming."

Austin got up from the bed and tried to think about what he should do next. He started to ask himself which was more painful—losing Alana or losing the money. When he couldn't decide between the two, he decided that Alana probably had done the right thing.

"All that work and all that planning, for nothing. I came out of the deal with absolutely nothing," Austin said into the mirror. "Now I have to start all over again."

Austin thought about what Alana said in the note. She was right. It wasn't the money itself that thrilled Austin, but rather, it was getting the money. It was the thrill of the bet, the thrill of the chase, the thrill of action. The thrill of stealing. The thrill of winning.

"What the hell was I gonna do down in Todos Santos, anyway? Run a motel?" Austin asked his reflection. "There's no racetrack down there, no action. What was I gonna do? Settle down? Get married? Quit betting? Who was I kidding?"

Austin pulled himself together and got dressed. He checked out of the hotel and found he had just enough money on him to fill up his gas tank once or twice.

Austin started his car and drove off toward the main highway. He stopped right before the on-ramp to the highway. He considered his two options. He could take a left and head south to chase after Alana and the money, or else he could turn right and head back to Los Angeles.

Both directions led to the unknown. In Mexico, he wasn't optimistic he would be able to get back Alana or his money. In Los Angeles, at least he knew he could borrow some money from his mother. Maybe he'd even be able to find Jimmy or Larry or Tony. He could start over again—come up with a new plan or an even better scam. At the very least, he could go back to betting the horses.

Austin made his decision and sped off through the desert. He turned right and pointed his car back toward Los Angeles. If he hurried, he could be back at his mom's place by that night. Santa Anita was ready to close for the season, but that meant Hollywood Park was about to open across town the next day. It would be a brand-new start. He could be there in time for the daily double. The possibilities were endless.

EPILOGUE

Julia Martini discovered Tony in a sad state upon her arrival at his bedside at Holy Family Hospital. He was unable to talk or answer any of her questions regarding the whereabouts of the couple's nest egg.

The vacant hospital bed in Tony's room ended up being taken by a second body cast-wearing occupant. It was Detective John Bragg. After falling two stories out the window, Bragg was patched up and brought to Tony's second-floor room where he could recuperate next to another patient with similar injuries.

Julia was horrified when she found out what happened to Bragg. She visited room 213 every day for a month, splitting time between her husband's bed on one side of the room and her boyfriend's bed on the other. She wanted to leave Tony for Bragg but first wanted to find out where Tony's money was before breaking the news to him.

Julia sat in the room every day for weeks as Tony and Bragg slowly healed. The day finally came when Tony's jaw was ready to be unwired, allowing him to speak for the first time. When Tony came out of surgery, Julia was the first one at his side. She had lots of questions.

Tony told Julia he'd lost all his money, all two hundred thousand dollars of it.

After that day, Julia spent all her time over in Bragg's half of the room. Once Tony could talk, he and Bragg argued so much that the hospital staff finally separated the two patients into different rooms on different floors. Julia followed Bragg to his new room. Tony never saw her again. The last he heard, Julia had moved with Bragg to Hawaii to be closer to his daughter.

Tony's reproductive reconstructive surgery was a rousing success. Since he wasn't very good looking in the first place, his looks hadn't suffered much from having his face rearranged. When he was finally released from the hospital, he was brought back to New York and sentenced to six months in jail for the National Tote rip-off.

Upon his release, Tony returned to California where he had gained some notoriety for being the man nearly killed by strippers in what became known as the infamous "Love Tunnel Massacre." He eventually opened up his own brand-new strip club, which he named the Beaver Tent. His business is currently booming.

Larry's trial run with the California Black Knights' Motorcycle Club was a complete success. Larry moved into the house in South Central and, by summer's end, had learned how to ride a Harley-Davidson.

The Black Knights officially made Larry their first Caucasian member in a formal gang initiation ceremony. Afterward, another formal ceremony was held to award brand-new names to the gang's two newest members.

Larry graciously accepted his new gang moniker—Cracker.

Then Matt's dream finally came true. He was to be known for all eternity by his hard-earned new biker moniker—T-Rex.

Stan the Man became a legend around the backstretch at Santa Anita. He was hailed as a hero and given a big raise and a promotion. Everyone around the racetrack began calling him sir and saluting him whenever he passed by.

Angelina Jolie never called.

Earl posed for the cover of the August issue of *Guns & Ammo* magazine. A month later, Charlton Heston presented him with a plaque and made him an honorary deputy in the National Rifle Association's Los Angeles chapter.

Loco Lopez was sentenced to two years in jail after being found guilty of race fixing and attempted murder. Upon his release from the California State penitentiary at Lompoc, Lopez plans to become a jockey's agent at Santa Anita.

Alana Moore was never linked to the race-fixing scandal at Santa Anita racetrack. She took the money she got from Austin and started her own yoga studio and vacation retreat in the town of Todos Santos, Mexico. She spent everything she had left over on shoes, handbags, and jewelry from the Neiman Marcus mail-order catalog.

Alana is currently dating the goalie for the Mexican national soccer team. Her yoga business is booming, and she is generally regarded as the best-dressed woman in all of Todos Santos.

Madam Tiffany welcomed Austin back to her home in the Hollywood Hills with open arms. She gave him enough money to get him back on his feet and fixed him up with one of her most eligible dominatrices.

Madam Tiffany then turned her attention to her own love life. She fell in love with Police Chief Brown from the LAPD and married in a lavish ceremony in front of five hundred friends, police officers, and paying customers.

Tiffany said I do while wearing a black leather wedding dress and a 10-karat diamond tiara.

Nobody was ever able to figure out if all the policemen at the wedding were there on behalf of Madam Tiffany or Police Chief Brown.

Madam Tiffany has still been known to give Chief Brown freebies on occasion, but not quite as often as before they were married.

Jimmy pleaded guilty to all charges against him involving the race-fixing scam at Santa Anita. He served one year in prison and was released on probation.

He is now working at the racetrack—bribing, extorting, blackmailing, and generally doing everything he can to fill the void left by Tommy Boy's demise.

With the help of his mother, Austin was able to get back onto his feet when he returned to California from Mexico. He had a profitable meet betting at Hollywood Park and eventually earned enough money to move out of his mom's house and into a small ranch house in the LA suburb of Whittier.

Austin was reunited with Jimmy at Clockers' Corner. He made up a story about how the police seized the gang's half million dollars. He never told Jimmy the truth about Alana stealing the money. The way he looked at it, you couldn't steal what was already stolen.

Austin and Jimmy are currently working on ideas for their next racetrack caper.

THE END

Printed in the United States
200873BV00002B/295-351/A